YUGO'S WAY

G. T. PIERCE

AMAZING TREES PUBLISHING, AUSTIN

Library of Congress Control Number: Pending
ISBN: 979-8-9924283-0-8 (Paperback)
ISBN: 979-8-9924283-1-5 (eBook)

Printed in the United States of America.

For information about special discounts for bulk purchases or group activities, please contact the publisher at info@YugosWay.com.

Website: YugosWay.com

Sketches by Kat Sherby

You'll notice fairly soon this book has a *soundtrack*, so we put together a playlist on the main streaming services in case you want to listen along. If you'd like to add music to your journey with Yugo, go to YugosWay.com and you'll find links that make listening to the songs easy. Enjoy the tunes, the lyrics, and support the artists!

   – GTP

Words are just sounds vibrating in the silence, echoing briefly and vanishing away—impermanent, open to different interpretation. There are many words that can be used to say the same truth, but in the end there's only one truth. And that truth can be said with just one word. And that word is Love.

— MARION FREEMAN

WALDEN I

My name is Walden Harrison. I don't like reading books that start off going on and on for pages without giving you a clue who's doing the talking, so now you know that upfront. I probably shouldn't be writing this at all – my sister should. She's the writer in the family, but she says I have "first person experience" so I'm the one who should tell the story. At least I was smart enough to record the most important parts, the Yugo parts, so typing out our recorded conversations from my phone will hopefully make writing this a little easier. I sure wouldn't want to leave Yugo's words to my memory since it seems sometimes I remember things differently than other people (my sister, for instance).

Pieces of this story might be found online through blogs and social media that I figure are still out there, but the world wide web is so fluid it could all be gone tomorrow. Sis says if I don't try to write this all down so it's permanent, we'll lose the wisdom of a contemporary sage "like smoke from a vape." See, she's way better with words than me. She's convinced this story needs to be a book and I know she's right. Tangible, unchangeable, documented so it can be passed down…passed around. And now that I have more time on my hands, maybe this helps keep me busy. There's also a backstory that should be told that you won't find online that adds meaning to the happenings of the last few years, so I listened to my sister and my conscience and started writing things down.

I know doing this will open up old scars, and I figure it'll make me look bad in spots. Truth is I wouldn't have met Yugo if my life wasn't in a tailspin – mostly self-induced. I was spiraling out of control, stressed out by life, numbed out by alcohol, denying I was in any kind of trouble while everyone around me watched as I cratered. But in the end, all the mounting pressures, the self-deception, and the inability to keep my shit together led me to encounter an incredible teacher whose wisdom saved my life. And Sis is right. Yugo's amazing story, his aura, his love and message must be shared, no matter how it makes me look.

I've read books where the writers use *italics* to stress certain words they think are more important than the others, and I liked that. It helped me better understand what they were trying to say, so I'm going to try that too. Sometimes life is funny, and then sometimes it's not funny at all. I don't have a clue why good things happen to bad people or bad things happen to good people, but I am starting to think stuff happens for a reason – that there's some *Presence* directing what's playing out on this planet. Too many things that seem totally random and unrelated keep happening that over time eventually fall into place for this *all* to be just coincidence. But at the same time crazy shit happens, people die, natural disasters strike, relationships implode, and I'm back to wondering, *WTF?* Maybe I'll live long enough to understand more of the universal thread Yugo showed me, but I've learned it's more about changing my way of thinking than anything else. Maybe this book will change your way of thinking too.

I'm the owner of an ecommerce company called WaldensPets.com. We sell everything you can imagine for pets like food, toys, beds, cages, even clothes, jewelry and shoes. That's right – jewelry and shoes, *for pets*. While most of our sales come from people with dogs or cats, we have a loyal following of owners of obscure pets like flying squirrels, lizards, snakes, rats, tarantulas. Hard to find pet supplies is a niche because we're online only and don't have to worry about having tons of inventory in a bunch of retail stores.

How'd I get here? Once college was over, I had no clue what to do next. I blindly went to school from kindergarten to college, just like everybody told me to do, and I wasn't ready after school stopped to make *life deci-sions*. I mean, where'd the time go? It wasn't that I really loved school, but at least there was comfort being told where to go and what to do next. How was I supposed to all the sudden decide on a "career"? After searching for a job for months, realizing there were thousands of people with marketing degrees just like me who didn't have a clue what they wanted to do, I decided to go to grad school and get my masters. But, little deterrents kept coming up like the need for food and shelter and money and stuff.

During my college years I lived with friends who were on the "seven-year plan." I was the only one remotely close to graduating in four years. They too had money problems, but were still comfortably under the illusion that college life would go on forever and life was one big party. Eventually to fund those parties we started selling a little weed and hash on the side, at first just to pay for our stash, and then it grew a bit to where it became a modest income stream. This income stream led to streams of people coming over to buy "supplies" at our place – a duplex up on a hill outside campus our girlfriends called *Freak Mountain* after an old SNL skit they saw on reruns. Hoping to get out of college relatively unscathed (one arrest for being drunk in public – *really* drunk) and with a combination of limited funds to live on and a growing fear of getting busted at Freak Mountain, I decided against hanging around and going the grad school route. I also stopped being picky, took one of the first decent jobs offered, and moved out.

Fate delivered me to Purina Pet Care as a salesperson calling on area discount and pet supply stores selling Purina dog chow and all their other products. Purina was one of the biggest pet food companies in the country, and while the money wasn't great and it was far from the prestigious advertising agency job I went to college for, I got to drive all over Texas selling pet food and supplies. It was easy since my customers already knew all the Purina brands, and most customers were cool. We'd go out sometimes after sales calls, throw down some beers, hang out. Another good thing about the job – I love animals and this kept me connected with them. I worked as a vet assistant for two years going to college and loved every minute of it, so being in an industry with dogs and cats as the ultimate users of my products was awesome in my mind. It's sad I know, but sometimes I feel closer to pets than people – and I know I'm not alone in that. So, by pure chance, I went from college grad with no clue to pet supply sales guy with no clue. I couldn't think of anything better to do, and it kept me sheltered and fed.

I did a good job and stayed out of trouble, worked hard and played hard as they say. Eventually I was promoted to regional manager, then national sales manager. A pet supply industry veteran may not be the most glamorous career, but it is what it is and I was going with the flow. As my job titles grew, I became responsible for the big guys – the Walmarts,

Targets, and the new "big box" pet supply chains. What a pain in the ass they were. Short paying, fining us for phantom reasons, demanding crazy low prices and "slotting fees" to keep our products on the shelf. Borderline unethical. I liked the travel, and partying with customers and fellow reps was fun, but these big demanding customers made going with the flow impossible. And then, Nestle, a huge company that made Purina look tiny, bought us. And it didn't take long for me to realize I was going to have a *culture problem.* Meaning the corporate politics, ridiculous paperwork, and countless layers of approvals were not good for my long-term future.

Around this time, a friend of mine, Bryan, was building a marketing company with dreams of getting in on the ground floor of digital marketing – the internet, ecommerce, and such. He's one of life's stereotypes, always buzzing around the "right place at the right time." Although relatively young, Bryan was already rich from stock options he got at his first company out of college (oh to be so lucky to have a big job at Dell when they went public). Between that and some family money, he was financially set. But Bryan's brain is like mine. He has to stay busy doing something or he goes off the rails, and he knows it. To launch his new company, he planned to build a small portfolio of killer well designed websites first, then use those examples to attract big clients. He knew most large companies don't take chances on a new thing, so he needed guinea pigs.

I knew my days at Nestle/Purina were numbered – that I wasn't a good *fit.* And every time a big box store would blindside me with another crazy deal making me look bad I'd think, *screw this.* In a rare forward-thinking moment, after seeing where some customers were projecting big growth, I realized sooner than most that online stores were the wave of the future. They were much cheaper to run than brick and mortar stores, and way easier too. When I mentioned my crazy idea of starting a pet supply website of my own over many beers with Bryan, he jumped on it, saying his team could build me a site free that he'd use as a showcase for other potential clients. He was so excited it caught me off guard, so I went with it and never looked back.

Because Bryan is ridiculously good at everything he does, he and his team built an incredible website, one I could have never afforded – cutting edge for back then. We were one of the first to have customer product reviews, and ways to share favorites with friends which pet owners love to do (we did it even before Sahara – truly ahead of our time). Obviously, there's more to the story about the birth of our company, but this isn't meant to be a book on starting a business, so I'll leave it at that. Basically, I went from soon to be fired unhappy corporate executive to an ecommerce entrepreneur leading a new company – WaldensPets.com.

Here I must say owning a business and working as an employee for a company are *very* different – some ways good and some ways bad. There's comfort being told what to do working for someone else. You don't have to think too much, don't second guess yourself nearly as much, and you always have someone else to point your finger at and say they fucked things up. Not to mention it's far less stressful. The opposite is true owning your own business – especially in the beginning. You put every idea and decision under a microscope, many of them fail, and there's only you to blame. It wears on you, chips away at your confidence, makes you wonder if even the carnitas tacos you ordered for lunch was the wrong move.

But there's good parts to owning your own business too. When you have a good idea that brings in new customers, your ego and bottom line get the boost, not your bosses. When you want to sleep in, you sleep in. When you wake up after a few too many tequila shots the night before, you don't have to call in sick. When you feel strongly about a long-term strategy, even if it may hurt the company in the short term, you can stick to your principles and take a stand. (*Example*: Not selling cheap dog food made in China because the ingredients are insanely bad for your dog, even if everyone else has ultra-low-quality dog food for people who care only about price.)

Yugo helped me understand the importance of focusing on the good things in life, on staying away from negative thinking. It's something I've struggled with going back to my childhood, which for me was different than most. I knew from an early age my parents weren't *normal*, that they saw the world differently than other parents. There wasn't the usual family structure, always lots of people around who weren't part of our family – lots of drama, it seemed to me, which added stress.

While I consider myself laid back and love having a good time, I also like some structure, some consistency – being able to count on things. My folks were what most people would call hippies. Not "hippy wannabees" but all out peace, love, utopia, and commune type hippies. Homelife was about as *abnormal* as you could get. Chickens, goats, and all sorts of animals running around, people all living together, family or not. Moms taking care of everyone else's kids – yes, breastfeeding them too. Weed, free love, everything is everybody's, indifference about nudity. Things happened you couldn't control and it knocked me off balance sometimes.

Sis sure turned out differently, more self-confident, outgoing and accepting, so it's probably not just the environment but the way I'm wired – who knows?

From an early age I sensed the "real world" was different than where I was growing up, and that was confirmed when I went over to friends' houses outside the commune – friends I'd meet exploring in the woods or playing kids sports with in town. There was privacy from the neighbors and closed doors, family meals, clean homes, washing machines, real furniture, microwaves, pizza. Dads in business clothes with briefcases, garages with nice cars, TVs. I had a shrink friend I talked to off the record, and he told me my childhood explains why I sometimes think the glass is half empty. Sis says shrinks tell everybody the same shit about their childhood – that their childhood explains all their problems no matter what happened. I should say that Frazier is a constant in my life and my biggest supporter, although we are *very* different. And now I realize writing is exhausting – I must take a break.

Before agreeing with Frazier to do this project, I got her to agree to be my editor and helper since this writing gig is new to me – even add her insight and memories if she wants. Every author needs someone to read their writing and keep them on the right track, plus Frazier will make sure I don't leave out any important details. After all, she's a big part of this story too.

FRAZIER I

My brother is a special person. I know I'm biased. But growing up together over the years; watching him evolve, flourish. It's beautiful. The catalyst for his growth is Yugo. Talk about special people! Walden was blessed to spend a lot of one-on-one time with Yugo. To listen, learn, and grow. I've encouraged Walden for some time now to write about his experiences. To share the amazing teachings he heard. To help others who aren't so lucky to hear Yugo's wisdom firsthand. Finally, he's started!

Walden's an accomplished businessman and marketer, but writing a book is new to him. It's not in his comfort zone, at least not yet. He's an experienced writer of ad copy, website content, promotions. He'll work into this just fine. He wasn't sure the best way to start. That's the hardest part of writing any book. I suggested he begin with his background, then what led him to find Yugo. He asked me to be his editor. To offer suggestions and track his progress. I told him sure. I'd love to help any way I can. Plus, I'll add some details and nuance to the story. But, only if he lets me say what I want with no edits. No surprise, he was okay with that. Walden knows my heart is in the right place.

I won't change his writing style or content. Just proofread and offer ideas about the flow. It's his story; it should be in his voice. He's under the false impression I'm a real writer. That I have the experience to author a book. But that's not true. Yes, writing is a primary tool of my trade. But I usually write in 280 characters or less. Social media is my domain. That's very different from writing a book. But hey, experience is relative, right? And honestly, I'm thrilled he asked me to help. I know Walden. He won't spend a lot of time describing people. Won't elaborate on emotions or relationships. He'll stay focused on what happened. And that's probably good for our purposes; to get Yugo's words out to people. I'll try to add some context, background, flavor.

First a little more about our family. You may be wondering about my name, Frazier. I know. I've never met a girl named Frazier either. Its origin is a good snapshot of our family and our childhood. Walden and I have amazing parents who love nature, love people, love life! They've always worked to make the world a better place. In college, Father read the utopian novel *Walden Two* by B. F. Skinner. It changed his life as you will see. Among other things, it led Father to meet Mary, our mom. And it helped him discover his life's purpose, which was a big part of our lives growing up.

I was supposed to be a boy. Where we lived, there were no sonograms to tell parents a baby's sex. Father just knew. Cherishing the Skinner book like he did, he picked out the name Walden well before I entered this world. But surprise! On my birthday my parents were greeted by a bouncing baby girl. Undeterred, Father quickly improvised, and I was bequeathed the name Frazier. And when my brother was born three years later? His name was in waiting.

Our parents treated me and Walden to a wondrously unique experience growing up. We lived in a hopeful, Walden-like community all our own. Our backdrop was the majestic, incredibly lush forests of far northwest Washington. Right in between the town of Forks and Olympic National Park. There's no more beautiful playground on Earth. If you've never been to that part of the country, I promise, the beauty cannot be explained in words. It can't be expressed in pictures really. The incredible green is all encompassing. The massive, moss-covered trees. The moisture, the silence. It's so perfect it feels clean. There are no bugs, no stickers. It's like I picture heaven. Breathtaking environments like the Hoh Rain Forest were literally our backyard! We lived in a burgeoning social experiment called Nueva Tierra. While ultimately it couldn't measure up to B. F. Skinner's utopian dream of *Walden Two*, it was an amazing place to be a kid.

Nueva Tierra was a self-sustaining organic farm long before most people knew what that meant. We were surrounded by spectacular forests, waterfalls, mountains, and streams. Fruit trees were everywhere. Lush gardens of not only vegetables, but amazing flowers of every color. Raspberries, grapes, apples, cherries all grew wild for us to pick and eat whenever we wanted. Kids were encouraged to explore. To be one with nature. All the adults in our community helped nurture the children. Openness, love, sharing, and compassion replaced the norms of city life. Norms like competitiveness, materialism, greed. We raised our own chickens for eggs. Had goats for milk (and lawnmowers). There were more dogs and cats to play with than you could count. For me and my friends, Nueva was utopia. It spawned some of the happiest days of my life.

Our community school was very much like in the book *Walden Two*. You were encouraged to pursue what you enjoyed. What you were good at. This is quite different from most public schools. There students are forced to focus on subjects where they struggle. I don't mean to give the wrong impression. Our education at Nueva was well rounded. The teaching for basics like English, the sciences, math, history were all better than we could get in town. But if it was obvious math wasn't your strong suit, that was accepted. You weren't forced to spend all your time learning algebra and geometry. You were encouraged to excel at what you did best! The arts were stressed. Music, poetry, painting, writing, acting, pottery. I loved that.

Our communal entertainment was also like Skinner's book. Nueva was blessed with incredible talent, especially musically. The impromptu concerts on the rolling hills were amazing. Mary was one of Nueva's most beloved singers. Such a beautiful voice! Well-known bands of the time knew of our enclave. They would come hang out for a few days to get off the road. They'd play for us just for fun. In exchange, we let them stay free as long as they wanted. Nueva would feed them, house them. Take care of them. They loved the healthy food. The freedom to get away from the masses. For them it was a few days of detox from the world. And yes, one of those bands was "you know who." Jerry loved it there. He sometimes came alone. Sometimes with his love Carolyn, who was from Eugene. Sometimes with the guys from the band.

The community was first established by Father and four friends from college. They were all influenced by books like Huxley's *Brave New World*, the original Henry David Thoreau *Walden* book, Skinner's *Science and Human Behavior*. They read dystopian books too, like *1984* and Bradbury's *Fahrenheit 451*. But it was *Walden Two* they fixated on; it was the inspiration for Nueva. In my mind the results were amazing. I see Walden wrote about the need for cleaner homes and family meals like "normal people." Our society was based on love for all. Caring for all. Sharing with all. We strived to be one with nature. Whatever we took out, we tried to put back in. Walden was more enamored then, I think, with outward appearances. More with external comfort than inward happiness and peace. Reading over this now, I realize that's judgmental. I know we are all different. Who am I to judge?

Nueva Tierra was always adjusting, always changing. We tested new techniques to improve our community farms. We tried new ways to improve our education, improve our relationships. Personal growth, happiness, and peace were the primary goals. But Father says over time, the energy and focus required to continue evolving was lost. The founders dreamed of manipulating human behavior toward the betterment and greater happiness of the community (à la the character Frazier in *Walden Two*). But some of the new arrivals to the community dreamed more of peace, love, freedom, and weed (à la the hippy stereotype). The dual mind-sets worked together okay for a while. But Father says the latter diminished the mission. It blurred the intensity required to hold such an outlandish utopian dream together.

Father advocated and stayed true to the founders' vision throughout. Mary gradually softened somewhat to the peace, love, "live and let live" crowd. She was enamored with the music. She loved the community get-togethers. It did create some tension in their relationship. But rarely did they show it to me and Walden. My thoughts? We were all simply human beings doing our best. *Walden Two* was a book about a utopian dream. It was fiction, not true reality. At Nueva Tierra, human nature and Mother Nature both won. It was a grand experiment that produced a grand childhood!

Walden and I have some differing perspectives and memories of Nueva. There were times he didn't like the permissiveness. The openness of our home. The constant togetherness of the community. That may explain why at times he's uncomfortable around other people. His need for personal privacy. Who knows? I'm a people person who's surrounded by many friends. I relish being open and friendly with everyone. Walden keeps more to himself. He's not the open book I am. Never more than two or three close friends. He's been that way all his life, which works for him. Speaking of friends. It was one of Walden's closest but craziest friends who introduced him to Yugo. Now who would believe that could happen? That a wild fusion of energy and endless stories like Cody Barringer would give Walden a roadmap for finding inner peace. Such is the mystery of our magical little world...

WALDEN II

Building WaldensPets.com was fun but highly stressful. Bryan and his team of wizards taught me a ton about stuff I really needed to know to run a successful ecommerce business, but had no clue. Not only did they build me an incredible website, they gave me crash courses in digital marketing like how to buy search ads on Google and Bing, SEO techniques to bring traffic to the site, email marketing, affiliate marketing, etc. They spent a couple weeks training me in each area and said I could always check with them with questions – which I did all the time. Bryan's an incredible guy I'm deeply indebted to. There's no doubt without his generosity, smarts, and connections, Walden's Pets would not exist. And if Walden's Pets didn't exist, it's likely I wouldn't have felt the need to go talk to Yugo. Stress from running the business wasn't the only issue I was struggling with, but it was a big source of my worries. It's crazy shit that happens *outside* of my control that I struggle with the most – and feeling like I wasn't in control was a place I always tried to avoid at that time.

An example: This friend Frazier mentioned, Cody Barringer, helped us design a cool new dog toy that sold like crazy. It was one of the first *big things* to happen at Walden's Pets that helped us get through the early start-up days (I'm gonna start calling it WP for short). Cody has the most *awesome dog* on the planet, a black Lab named Max, who's the greatest frisbee catching dog I've ever seen. Max has boundless energy and never stops playing – coming back over and over to get you to throw the frisbee to him. It's crazy something as cool as throwing a frisbee and watching a dog make *spectacular* catches at the park would get boring, but after doing something a few thousand times, anything gets old. So when we'd lose interest, we'd look for people nearby us to throw the frisbee to so they would play with Max – and he'd go on and on.

We'd look over later and notice they'd grown tired of Max too and had thrown the frisbee on to the next group of people. Max would make basically a circle around the whole park, spending time with everyone who wanted to play with him – eventually coming back to us panting and exhausted. But there was one problem with Max and this game that drove Cody crazy. He spent a fortune on frisbees. It was rare for a frisbee to last more than two or three visits to the park. So one day, after smoking a little and having multiple beverages, Cody decided to do some heavy thinking and create a solution to his chewed up frisbee problem.

To my surprise, what came out was shear genius. Instead of coming up with just a short-term solution for his problem, Cody created a commercially viable product we could sell at WP that most all dogs love (and of course Cody gets a cut of the profits). His genius was realizing there's not that many superstar frisbee catching dogs out there, but there's a countless number of dogs that love to chase after stuff and bring it back. So, he combined the aerodynamics and feel of a frisbee (in an extremely durable plastic) with a lightweight chewable rope coming out each end and circling the disc for added durability. You could throw it like a fetching toy, which all dogs love, or like a frisbee (granted, the rope makes the disc fly less distance). But the tradeoff in added durability was huge. A great flying disc for dogs it isn't, but a fun toy that lasts a long time that's easy to throw and catch it is.

Max *loved* it – he was our test market – but truth is Max loves chasing rocks. The rest is history. We did our best to patent it, I used my pet supply contacts to connect with a dog toy manufacturer, and we churned out thousands of the new "Barringer 3500 Flying Dog Disc." I didn't have much money for marketing our new idea, so we put the item on Sahara, bought some display ads, hit it up with the right keywords, and it sold like crazy. I don't mean to brag, and after all it was Cody's idea, but the Barringer 3500 quickly became the #4 best-selling dog toy on Sahara, making us a nice amount of cash for over a year and a half.

And then...it didn't. Our "friends" at Sahara eventually took notice of WP's new wonder toy, and unknown to us, they went to work knocking off our little nest egg, carefully working around the patent. Within eighteen months of our launch, a flying dog toy strangely similar to the Barringer 3500 started coming up first on Sahara when you searched "frisbees for dogs" or "dog fetching toys." Our product could hardly be found. Oh, you could find it if you searched for it by the exact name, but if you searched for things like "flying discs for dogs" you'd see the Sahara knock-off first – and $2.00 cheaper than ours. What was *many thousands* of dollars in sales a week (and what helped us cover our overhead) suddenly fell to a couple a hundred dollars a week because of *nothing* we did – something totally out of our control. Such is the life of a seller on Sahara. Things like that happen all the time, where you think you're well positioned and have a good product or strategy in place, and change hits totally outside of your control. Yugo says change is the only thing in our universe that remains constant – *Change doesn't change because it's always changing so embrace it.* Easy to say...

I should tell you more about my friend Cody Barringer. He's who introduced me to Yugo so he's a very important part of this story. An interesting fact of life I discovered I'll mention now before I forget. Always be cautious when you meet somebody named Cody. I haven't known many Codys in my life, but all the Codys I do know are *crazy as shit.* I don't know if there's any truth that people with the same name often act in similar ways, like people named Albert being smart, but in my experience with the name Cody, it's true. Come to think of it, it's the same way with the name Rusty – I knew two growing up. One is already dead after jumping off a 55-foot cliff drunk and drowning. Onlookers say his last words were, "Dude, check this out." The other lives somewhere off the coast of Costa Rica in the jungle with the howler monkeys.

Anyway, Cody is one of my best friends but borderline insane, and we try to get together at least a couple times a month to talk about life and stuff. In general, most guys don't talk all that much about the important things in life. Guys talk more about sports, music, partying – reliving stories of our past. At least with Cody we can both open up a little and share more than maybe most guys. I think it's important everyone has that kind of outlet. Barringer is hilarious, but there's one thing about Cody that's a problem. When it comes to the news or some story he's heard that he's telling you about, you can never be sure what he says is 100% accurate. I've grown to believe it's not because he's purposely lying in a bad way – I did think that at first – but after being friends for a long time I realized sometimes he just gets the facts mixed up, or hears what he wants to hear instead of what's really true. And sometimes I think his memory just stores things in a different reality than everyone else's. Whatever it is, his sketchy memory is more pronounced than most, but it's not like he's lying or being manipulative in a mean-spirited way – bottom line, you just have to keep your guard up.

Cody's looseness with the truth has made me look bad in the past – look stupid. I'd repeat things he told me and others would quickly say I was full of shit. This happened with my boss back at Purina a few times, like when I told him Snoop Dogg died in a river rafting accident (a dog named Snoopy did die tragically when his family's raft flipped over on the Guadalupe). Or that popstar Alanis Morissette, who my boss loved for unknown reasons, left the music industry forever for a life of religious seclusion (how can anyone confuse Alanis Morissette with Cat Stevens?).

After sharing a few Cody stories with Frazier that she picked apart immediately, she suggested before I repeat anything Cody tells me, I should at least consult Wikipedia or do a Google search first to see if there's any truth to the story. (BTW I *love* Wikipedia. As a kid the old encyclopedia set in our community library was a mecca of truth for me.) I know you can't trust Wikipedia 100%, but how many "facts" did we learn from the textbooks of our day that are now considered wrong? Pluto is a planet, what started the Vietnam war, red meat is good for you, what causes ulcers – it goes on and on. I love Wikipedia because no matter the subject I almost always find something on what I'm searching for, and it's free. I'm amazed it's a nonprofit researched and written by people who aren't paid. It's cool that it's constantly in transition, being updated, corrected, *evolving* – and I hope improved upon. At minimum, it's the perfect research tool for checking out Cody stories. I send them a donation every year since I use it so much and they're a nonprofit. I don't want Wikipedia getting tainted by the never-ending search for profits.

Barringer has always been fascinated by my childhood, the fact I was raised by hippies in a commune in the Northwest – how me and my sister grew up in such an unorthodox environment. I think what interests him most are the stories with Frazier in them. I say that because when they're around each other, it looks to me like he's checking her out, always trying to say something to impress her or make her laugh. I know she's my sister and all, but Frazier is the type of girl that people notice when she walks by or comes into a room – males and females. It's partly her looks. She's got long, wavy light brown hair, dark brown expressive eyes, always has a nice tan that highlights her smile. But even more noticeable is the way she carries herself – always laughing, talking to everyone, making friends with total strangers, oozing confidence. She's the exception to that old adage to beware when people try to hook you up with someone with a "great personality." Many people would describe Frazier that way, but that doesn't mean she isn't good-looking too. I guess the way Cody reacts to Sis is how most people react. She's had that effect on the world around her, at least it seems to me, all her life.

Today we had lunch and I told Cody about the latest thing I'd done to piss off my girlfriend, the tension created, the wasted energy and wasted thought time that comes from a three-day long argument over nothing. Cody's a good listener, but his advice isn't the greatest, especially regarding relationships. I don't want to go into too much of the girlfriend stuff here because preparing to write this book, I read up on how to become an author, and one book that had some pointers on writing was a series of interviews with Kurt Vonnegut (I *love* Vonnegut too). He said he rarely puts the characters in his books in romantic relationships because the relationship takes over the whole story and the rest of the book becomes a side note. He says when people read, they always focus emotionally on the romantic relationship thread if there is one – that in the end, they won't care as much about the rest of the story lines in the book. That makes sense to me because it sure seems like it's that way in real life. Relationships often take over the whole story in your head, no matter what else is going on in your life. No matter if other things are more important to think about like your job, your health – even eating. So, my plan is to leave any unnecessary relationship stuff out of this book.

To get it out of the way, here's a Cliff Notes version of the relationships of the main people in the book – then we can move on. For me, I've had the same "on again / off again" girlfriend for over four years. She's great, way better than I deserve, but we're both independent and don't feel the need for anything more right now (although I think she's thinking otherwise post Yugo's help). The business and personal stuff I was dealing with back then – the stress and anxiety – put a strain on our relationship. She was actually the final voice that convinced me to go see Yugo.

Full disclosure, I was married years ago right after college but neither of us had a clue what love was – honestly, I have no idea why we got married so young. Unfortunately, one of her more pronounced character defects was dishonesty (and infidelity). To say my heart was broken isn't entirely true because I knew the morning I woke up after our wedding night I'd made a big mistake. But a person still feels like shit learning that someone you have feelings for is with other people. It wasn't the shortest marriage in history, but short enough that years later it's like it never happened – I mean, we didn't even get close to having one anniversary, which is almost funny really. When people ask if I've ever been married, my first answer without thinking is always no.

Cody's virtually always in a relationship, but they don't stay together for long – six to nine months is his sweet spot. I'm not sure if that's usually his choice or theirs, but he has what seems to be a magical way of never ending a relationship on a bad note, especially considering how many girl-friends he's had. Somehow after several months together, they mutually decide to move on with little to no fireworks, often remaining friends for years after. I don't know if that's because he's the world's greatest breakup artist, or if it's the nature of the girls he's attracted to – that they aren't looking for a long-term relationship either.

But Cody is usually in some type of relationship, his latest being an exotic looking singer/songwriter from Antigua who's great. Her name is Anastasia – I'm not kidding – and this time it's actually lasted longer than the usual six to nine months. Heck, it may even go long term. Cody seems *really* into her, much more than previous relationships, and like I said she's cool. Super talented, an incredible performer really – and very laid back for someone with her talent and beauty. That may come from growing up in a place like Antigua...Rasta-like and chill.

Bryan, the marketing genius, has a picture-perfect family life just like his career and work life. He's married to a beautiful lady, Ally, and they have two kids so cute they should both be in commercials. They have a labradoodle, a beautiful home in the hills west of town by the lake, and he coaches their kids' soccer and flag football teams. (I used to think Bryan's world was too perfect to be true. That he's a closet serial killer or that he had two secret wives with whole other families living somewhere in Oklahoma and Florida. That's how my mind works.) Frazier is my sister and her relationships are her personal business and not something I'll put in this story. I'll just say we were raised in a free-spirited open environ-ment as kids and that's one of the many things she's held on to from Nueva Tierra. I purposely don't ask questions, and when she's not asked, she doesn't share details with me. Let's just say Frazier is a free spirit, loves *all* people, seems far from ever being lonely, and I'll leave it at that.

FRAZIER II

AFTER READING Walden's latest prose I had to ask. What's the deal with all the dashes? He told me his head starts thinking too fast. The dashes let him keep writing without losing his thoughts. It may not be the easiest read. But I said, hey, if that helps you get everything out, roll with it. His "relationship round-up" was fascinating, huh? He covered the entire romantic lives of the main characters in this book in three paragraphs! Reading his brief entry for me made me wonder. Should I be flattered or offended? Frazier Harrison, outgoing friend to all? Or Frazier Harrison, free-spirited slut? It's a little hard for me to tell. Haha!

Walden's girlfriend, who I see he didn't mention by name, is amazing. Jessica is an angel. Such a blessing for Walden. She's helped him through many difficult times. Partly from her influence he's practicing some yoga, drinking less. He's eating healthier, living more in nature. Of course, Yugo has much to do with that too. Much more really. But it was Jessica who kept Walden on the ledge when he was really struggling. Before he met Yugo. Walden wasn't the easiest person to be around back then. Problems with the business, overthinking things, too much booze, stress. Life happening all around him.

Jessica told me it took work to grab Walden's attention when they first met. She would see him on the hike and bike trail walking George (his "Benji-like" rescue dog who's a charmer). Jessica has this adorable girl Bichon named Murphy, who would always stop and say hi to George.

Bichons are strong-willed. When they want to stop, they stop. Jessica was intrigued by Walden. He was oblivious. So she let her dog keep making the introduction. After a few random sniff sessions between the pups with little to no dialogue, Jessica asked Walden out for a drink. I love that about her. Confident, outgoing, go with your feelings. Walden said yes. The relationship grew from there. Two very different people, but with similar hearts. They seem right together. They make each other better.

We all knew Walden's first wife was a mistake. Now there's someone we won't mention by name! I think she was his first serious girlfriend. Walden and I don't talk much about relationships, but my guess? She was the first girl he went all the way with. At least that's what many of us thought. We figured that's what made it so hard for Walden to end it. To get out before he was in too deep. He may be the most loyal person I know. He didn't want to hurt someone who'd been that intimate with him. Walden figured it was best to let things be. To put up with the nonsense. To not create emotional turmoil by breaking things off.

She was one of those totally self-absorbed people. The kind who are hard to get along with. A narcissist, really. No matter the situation, the world always revolved around her. We all knew there was no chance the marriage would work. Even Cody knew. It took less than six months for it to fall apart. All in all, it wasn't too painful for Walden. He seemed more relieved than anything. A good learning experience, I say.

His comments about Cody are so true. I love him, but what a trip! One thing to make clear. Just because Cody and I flirt doesn't mean there's anything there. Although he's my younger brother, Walden is so protective. He jumps to conclusions, often wrong ones. This goes back to Nueva Tierra when he'd see me with friends and assume all sorts of things. I know it's because he loves me. That's just how Walden thinks. We view life differently. What's a big deal to him is often an afterthought for me. Like everything, so psychiatrists say, it's probably due to our childhood.

Somehow, even growing up in the love and openness of our home, Walden came out a little uptight. One experience he had that I did not was in the summer before his sixth grade. He always wondered about life outside Nueva. He was interested in what other kids were doing in nearby towns. He had a new friend named Jacob from soccer. Jacob's mom was big at the First Baptist Church of Forks. That summer Walden begged Mary to let him go to Vacation Bible School with Jacob. That's something I would never do. But the promise of snacks, games, and hanging around kids from town drew him in.

Both Father, and especially Mary, wanted nothing to do with it. Part of it was a concern over the curriculum. They weren't high on Baptist dogma. But they also wanted nothing to do with the drive. Forks was at least forty miles from Nueva. They weren't doing that trip back and forth every day for a week. This meant Walden would have to spend the night at Jacob's home that week. It wasn't my parents' way to say no to much of anything. So, Walden got five days of good Baptist teaching, and a week of guilt-laden parenting from Jacob's mom. My opinion? It scarred him. That's an impressionable age for any kid. All kinds of hormones and feelings are moving around. It's not a good time to lay guilt trips, judgments, and fear of retribution on a child. Just my theory. Thinking of it now still makes me angry. Because Walden was different after that summer. Tighter and more introverted.

Anyway, he's right about Cody Barringer and his stories. They are great, but you have to be careful. Consume them as entertainment and do not repeat! Walden's also right about the craziness going on around him. About things outside his control happening at Walden's Pets, and in his life too. Owning your own business is hard. Walden is a good business-man. He's intuitive. He hires smart people, works hard. Walden the busi-nessman's most important asset is persistence. When others throw in the towel, Walden puts his head down. Keeps plugging away.

That's why I decided to help where I can at Walden's Pets. It was hard watching my brother struggle through the early years at WP (I'll call it WP too!). The company would take two steps forward and a step and a half back. Big competitors are ruthless. Digital marketing is like herding cats. When Walden's SEO consultant said WP needed social media and a blog to help with organic search, he asked me for help. Of course I said yes. Social media and blogging are my forte. I was in the game long before the term "influencer" was around. But today I guess that's what you'd call me. It's so cool working with Walden toward common goals. Together we're an amazing team!

WALDEN III

I don't think of anybody other than myself

"Evergreen" by Bendigo Fletcher (from *Fits of Laughter*)

I SHOULD'VE NEVER AGREED to let Sis write anything she wants to with no edits. Frazier and her theories. Vacation Bible School did not jade me for life. Was Jacob's mom a little creepy? Yes. Were the teachers at First Baptist Church of Forks different than I expected? Yeah. Was I ready to come home after that week? I was ready after the first day, but I was young and missed my family and our dogs. Let's just say VBS and Baptist parenting wasn't for me – nothing like I'd pictured in my head. Frazier sometimes says I didn't like living in our commune, but that's not true either. I realize, especially now, it was a great place to grow up. We did things every day in the incredible forests around Olympic National Park other kids would die to do just once, and Father and Mary did a good job raising us. I just didn't embrace the free-for-all culture as much as Frazier and Mary did. The whole communal "everyone is always together" thing.

And, when I was almost twelve, I had what I'll call a predator I learned to always be on the lookout for – something that made life stressful on a kid. That's a personal experience I won't include here. I need to keep this story moving in the right direction. Let's just say Felicia Featherstone, a girl much older than me, probably messed me up a bit. Frazier's also wrong with her nonsense about the first person I went "all the way" with – I mean come on. Is this the place for that? Frazier *is* right about everything she said about my girlfriend Jessica – she's awesome, a true gift I don't deserve. And one more thing to clear up, I *did not* leave Jessica's name out on purpose.

As I said earlier, I read a few books before starting to educate myself on being an author, including some of the "classics." I noticed some of the better books had quotes at the beginning of chapters that were usually insightful. I'd read these quotes and think how smart the author was, sliding these intellectual lines into the story to add meaning (sometimes it seemed just for show). Anyway, I love music and especially songs with good lyrics, so I decided to throw in some lyrics before certain chapters where it makes sense. I'm doing this for somewhat selfish reasons because I've always wanted to be a music writer – to share great music with people. This sorta kills the two birds with the one stone. It helps me bring the story to life, and it gives readers music recs if you want to check out some really good tunes. All the artists are awesome, and these songs have lyrics that when I was writing the book hit me as *perfect*. Some align with the story so well it's eerie. I recommend you read the chapter first, then listen to the song. The Bendigo Fisher line above describes my mental state pretty well before meeting up with Yugo. In fact, writing this chapter helped me see clearly how consumed I was with myself – concerned about my own comfort and happiness and pretty much nothing else. You'll see.

Frazier is too modest about her influencer and blogging skills – as I expected. She didn't just "help" WP when we were struggling to get our footing, she was the *catalyst* to turn our fortunes around. The business started painfully slow as we worked to find new customers and build a brand. Cody's flying disc idea was a big boost to sales early on, and we were getting better at advertising on Google. But we struggled mightily to make payroll, to add employees, to pay our vendors and pay off the business loans. We certainly didn't make a profit. To say there was stress is an understatement. Sis got her start blogging in the early days of the internet, back when you could make a small fortune driving people from your website to click on other people's sites – back then it was called Google AdSense. She started doing it as a hobby, and got the idea from a friend who was making good money writing a blog about Furbys. Remember those creepy big eyed furry little toys that spoke "Furbish" and you taught them how to speak English? They looked like furry Chucky dolls to me, staring down at your bed, waiting to stab you in your sleep. Anyway, people went bonkers over them and this girlfriend of Frazier's was a Furby savant when it came to building their vocabulary – she was the Furby blogging queen.

Frazier was doing marketing stuff for a mid-size firm, but after seeing what her friend was doing, she started writing a blog for soccer moms, which was funny to me. Sis played soccer in high school, but she's never been a mom and had no clue what went on in that world. But she's got a knack for connecting with people and uncanny intuition. She saw how popular kids' soccer was, studied other soccer blogs, and created SoccerMomsUnite.com. She had all kinds of informative articles, funny videos of kids playing soccer, parents doing crazy shit on the sidelines. Frazier put links to cool stuff all over her site and people clicked and bought those products. Soon she was making more money blogging than she was at the marketing firm, so she quit her real job and became a full-time blogger, then a social media whiz. She branched out with blogs for other ridiculous fads like Pokémon cards, Pogs, Crazy Bones, Easy Bake Oven recipes – all kinds of crap really that were hot at the time. It was a true renaissance period for the internet and money was being made everywhere.

A marketing consultant told me to improve our SEO, we needed to get active on social media and have a blog, so I told Frazier about it and she asked if she could help. She even did it for free for a while – I pay her now. In fact, she's one of the highest paid people at WP now because without Frazier and the loyal followers she attracts, who knows where we'd be? I know it seems crazy, but Sis and her way of bringing people together may have saved our company. What I didn't know then that Frazier's known for years is people love looking at two things – little kids and pets. Especially when those kids and pets are *adorable*. Frazier launched a Walden's Pets blog, and then Facebook, Instagram, YouTube, and Twitter pages, and she flooded them with cute shit. She even gets our customers to send in content for us, doing contests giving away small prizes like $100 shopping sprees for the cutest pet videos. They send in endless streams of adorable things for us to post and it all comes to us basically free.

So, with Frazier's help, the business at WP finally took off. Our website traffic went up five-fold in less than a year and sales more than doubled. Her campaigns built loyal customers who'd recommend us to others, share our posts, send in cool new product ideas. It was a huge shot of adrenaline and it came at a time when we were close to letting employees go. I'm rambling about all this so it's clear to everyone that when Frazier says she "helps" me by doing some influencer work for WP, it's a *massive* understatement. Sis deserves credit for all she's done for me and the business – plus it's an important part of the Yugo story, which I'm getting to now.

Not long after Frazier came on full-time and during a *very* rough patch in my life, I met Cody Barringer for a late, long emergency "lunch" at Zilker Park downtown. *Crazy shit* was happening at WP and I needed a break to keep from exploding. It was a gorgeous day in Austin, buds bursting from the trees, spring's in the air – and it's a Thursday. One of Cody's favorite sayings is, "Thursday is Friday." He likes to kick his weekends off early so Thursday is the day of the week Cody looks forward to the most – it jumpstarts his weekend. I always wonder what Cody will be up to on those Thursday afternoons when we meet. Sometimes he's already drinking, sometimes he'll be coming from the Kava Bar, so mellow and slow talking I can hardly understand him. Sometimes he'll be smoking a doobie with total strangers.

This day he's focused big time on peeling an orange. Walking towards him, I shake my head at the sight of a big 6'4" bearded guy in a Widespread Panic t-shirt who looks like he'd kick your ass for looking at him the wrong way, peeling an orange so intently. Then I realize the reason for his focus. His goal is to peel this orange in one continuous string – to have the whole peel, once it's removed, be one long piece. He's about three quarters there when I walk up to the picnic table. I'm *extremely distraught* today, seeking out Cody for support, but seeing him alone operating on that orange softens my spirits – if only a little.

"Hey dude, what's up with peeling that orange? If only you could focus that intensely on your job."

Cody looks up quickly, then goes right back to peeling.

"I'm not peeling an orange, Walden. This here's a Minneola tangelo."

"A what?"

"A Minneola tangelo. Haven't you ever had one?"

"I've never even heard of them. What are they, some kind of new-fangled orange?"

"New-fangled orange, are you shitting me? This here's the best tasting fruit on the planet. Like a tangerine only better, juicier. Hardly any seeds, ever. Blows an orange away. And the coolest thing – the peel is *loose*. They have this sort of nipple on the tip you can grab easy and start peeling to create a work of art. Like this...wallahh!!!"

Cody successfully finishes the one-piece peel and wags it at me.

"You think I could do that with a regular orange? Huh? Not a chance man…wouldn't even try."

He breaks the tangelo apart and juice flies everywhere – he hands me a slice. "Here, try it."

He's right. It is like a tangerine only better. The juice is overwhelming, dripping down my chin. It's the best orange-like thing I've ever tasted. "Holy shit, this is incredible Cody."

"I can't believe you never heard of Minneola tangelos. One of the many things that makes Texas great. They grow 'em in Minneola down south by McAllen. It's how they got their name. Only problem is they're seasonal. I can only find them about four months out of the year."

Cody's been my sounding board for many months. I listen to his issues and problems as well, but lately there's been a barrage of things hitting me all at once and I hate to admit it, but much of our conversations are recently one-sided. It's getting harder for me to cope, and that's something I *really* hate to admit because I've always been one to "pull myself up by the bootstraps." I'm not supposed to have problems coping. That's for others who aren't strong like me, right? Truth is I'm drinking more than I should to stop the constant thinking, to stop the worrying, to help me get some sleep. I've always been one to enjoy multiple beverages with friends – drinking has long been a favorite pastime of mine – but more in a social sense I'd like to think, more of a *hobby* for me. Maybe there's a little denial there, but I never felt like I used alcohol as a crutch to get me by before. But at this time in my reality, there's no doubt it was a crutch. I was drinking sometimes alone, drinking not for enjoyment but to feel numb, taking shots of hard liquor because beer wasn't enough to get me there. Going to work hungover, feeling like crap at least two or three times a week, if not more. It was becoming my go-to numbing device from life, and quickly moving towards something even worse. Jessica noticed the consumption increase – Frazier too. Probably not Cody. This increase in drinking was not leading to a good place and I knew it, but damned if I knew what else to try.

"Cody, you're not gonna believe the *shit* that's going down at Walden's Pets."

"What's up now? Your offices on fire? Circuits blown and no power? Phone system meltdown?"

Cody was well aware of the *crazy shit* that happens at WP all the time. Stuff that comes out of left field, crushes our sales, kills a month. Everything he just guessed has already happened to us before, some more than once, although in truth it wasn't really a true *fire* fire – the kind that burns buildings down. Just a ton of smoke coming through the a/c ducts from frazzled wires and smoldering insulation after a fucking squirrel chewed through wiring in the attic. Of course, this led to the smoke alarms going off, blaring for over an hour before we got things calmed down, shutting down customer service calls. To add fuel to the flames you might say, the fire-retardant sprinklers kicked in from the smoke, soaking much of the office, paperwork destroyed, desks damaged. You know – just another day at the office.

"The power might as well be out. We're shut down…totally."

"Shut down? What do you mean, your website's crashed?"

"The website hasn't crashed, it's just down. We're being held for ransom really."

"Held for ransom? What the hell are you talking about?"

"Take a look at this. It's so absurd I didn't think you'd believe me, so I printed it."

I handed Cody an email I'd printed out, an email our customer service inbox received last night, whose effects we at WP started feeling early this morning. This is the exact email, word for word:

From: TheNegotiatorSamzo@protonmail.com
Sent: Wednesday, April 1, 2017 9:19 PM
To: CustomerService@WaldensPets.com
Subject: We have shutdown your website.

We have shutdown your website.

If you want us to stop our attacks; send 3 XMR (monero coins), which equates to about $300, to the following monero wallet address:
49tgJ9NbfWZK7688gvdse667vXnuxheKwAF1MoyNisL3uRpMn-B1Ah9bMcL9CTqF3CN

To verify it was you that made the payment to us. Send us a transaction id or screenshot so we can make sure we are no longer attacking your website. Use this website https://www.monero.co/how-to-buy-monero if you are not familiar with Monero and how

to send monero or you can use google. The sooner you pay the
sooner you get rid of us.

--The Negotiator Samzo

Cody looks up in disbelief, the same reaction I had this morning after I
read the email.

"You're shitting me. This thing's real? It came on April 1st you know.
April Fools?"

"April Fools I wish. They shut down our site. We've been down since
3:00 a.m. this morning."

"For what? They shut down your site for a lousy three hundred
bucks?"

"Yep. I guess it could be worse. They coulda asked for $30,000 or any
number really."

"Yeah, but three hundred bucks? It's not worth the time they took to
shut down your site and write the damn email."

"That's what I told them when I emailed back. I can't figure it out.
Apparently, these are hackers who just like creating pain for people. And
maybe the reason the ransom is so low is they figure no one will go to the
cops for three hundred bucks. They could be doing this to hundreds of
websites a day for all I know."

Cody is listening, but he's also finishing off the last slice of his beloved
tangelo.

"So what are you gonna do? If your site's down, you're losing thousands of dollars a day, not to mention pissing off customers who want to
order."

"I've got our tech guys on it, but whatever this Samzo outfit is doing,
they're good at what they do. We can't bring the site back up no matter
what we try – it's totally locked, in limbo."

"You gonna pay the ransom?"

"What would you do? It's only $300. But my fear is if I pay this off, they
may keep coming back for more. I know it sounds crazy, but I've started an
email dialogue with them trying to get them to ease up while our IT
people look for solutions."

"You look like shit Walden. You ok?"

"I don't know Cody. Life used to just flow. Wake up, go about my day,
everything for the most part worked out ok. I'm not saying things were
perfect, but everything wasn't such a fucking *struggle*. Between the tension

with Jessica, the continuous bullshit at WP, my worries about Father and Mary's health and how they both suddenly seem so *old*. I'm worried about paying our employees, who are counting on us to support their families, their homes, everything. I've stretched myself too thin. That nice place I dreamed of having in the hills is killing me. Leasing that damn luxury SUV when I have no need for a utility vehicle was so stupid. I'm taking money out of savings to pay bills just to get by each month. I'm supposed to be a successful entrepreneur, living the American Dream, finally making it. But things are starting to suck and have been for months now. I don't know, man. Something's missing..."

Cody pops a Shiner Bock tall boy and takes a massive drag while I'm in mid-whining. When I'm through he breaks into his full John Mayer, singing, "Something's missing, and I don't know how to fix it..."

He grins, looks at me, grabs another beer out of his cooler, and slides it over. I just look at it and keep on talking, shaking my head.

"Life these days, it's like I'm swimming upstream against the current – I'm a salmon struggling upriver every day, all day, with no relief in sight. Jumping blindly, madly swimming, just waiting for that bear to reach out, grab me in midair and swallow me whole."

I take the Shiner now, pop it, and match Cody, gulping down a quarter of the can. Cody looks at me and surprisingly says something that ultimately changes my life:

"Walden, I know things are tough and you're going through a rough stretch, but everybody's got it tough these days. True, you're getting hit from all sides – relationships, business, family, crazy shit like these Samzo people. But you're blessed, man. You've got a life most people would die for. You got a great girl who loves you, an awesome family, your health, your own business for Christ's sake. I'm not gonna go into that shit Mom used to say about the starving children in Africa and all, but it's true. You're stuck in a vacuum where you're fixating on the negative instead of being grateful for the positive – grateful for what you're blessed with. And you've been doing it for months now, man. Think about it, Walden. Most of what you just spewed out revolves around worries about money, material things. That's not what matters most. We're not on this planet for everything to always be roses. If life was always perfect, if everything worked out just like we think it should, it'd get boring as hell. Difficulties are to be embraced. Pain is actually good! Without pain there's no reason to grow, to learn, to change. Without pain, as they say, there's no gain."

He winks, gives me a little toast with his beer can, and takes a draw. "No offense, man, but you're starting to be a drag."

I take another monster gulp of my beer and stare at Cody. I know what he's saying is true, and it's not what I want to hear. But mainly I'm staring at him because that was the most profound, philosophical, coherent advice Cody's ever given me. Not even close.

"First of all, fuck you very much. That's not the kind of sympathy I came out here for, but second, what the hell have you been reading? Where did you run across wisdom like that? Even I can tell what you said is profound. While you were going on and on lecturing me I was thinking, hey that's *true*."

"Yeah, well fuck you too, Walden. I've just been talking some with Dylan." (Dylan's a musician friend of Cody's – a successful one at that. I think he's the one who introduced him to Anastasia). "I used to think Dylan was a fuckup, but the more I talk to him he's an ok dude. He's been going to a counselor now for a few months that he swears by – like a cross between a psychiatrist, a personal coach, and a mystic or something. You remember Dylan. Went through all that shit with his parents' accident, then their business went broke? Some guitarist from a band he sits in with, Bastards of Soul, was trying to help Dylan through some tough times. He'd been to hell and back – heroin addiction, all kinds of tragedy. The dude gave Dylan this supposed guru's name because he saw Dylan going down the same spiral he'd been on. Says he's changed his life. He's shared with me some of the stuff this dude says, and I gotta say, it's some *wise* shit. Maybe you should check him out. Honestly, I've been thinking about telling you about him for a while, even before your website got kidnapped."

"Guru, huh? Yeah, I remember Dylan but can't say I ever talked to him much. Remember he's a musician big shot that's squirrely – borderline out of control. I've never gone to a shrink before and don't plan on starting now. Things are a little rough, but it's nothing I can't get through on my own. Like you said, I just need to be more positive – look on the bright side."

My beer is drained. I ask Cody for another, and I take a very long drink, then another.

"This is no regular shrink, Walden. Dylan says this guy's like nobody he's ever met before – like a spiritual visionary. I think you should give him a try. That is, if he agrees to work with you."

"What do you mean if he agrees to work with me? Isn't he like any other counselor you just call up and schedule an appointment with?"

"Oh, he's far from typical from what I hear. Dude interviews you first to see if you're worth his time. Apparently if he doesn't like your vibe, he nicely sends you away. Dylan says he's the poster child for the saying "don't judge a book by its cover." I mean, Dylan's a decent guy and all but he's always been a screw-up. Now, I've seen a real change in him. His eyes even look different – clearer, more present."

"Well, I'm glad he's helped Dylan, but I don't like talking about myself to people – especially strangers. Just the thought of going to a therapist depresses me even more."

I chug the rest of my beer and notice Cody is watching me.

"Like I said, Walden – you look like shit, man. Here. Dylan gave me this guy's card in case I ever started feeling helpless or lost...or knew somebody else who was. Take it. Couldn't hurt to just check him out. Hell, he might not even take your sad ass anyway."

And Cody looks into his wallet, finds the card, and hands it over. It reads:

BJ I

Brett Jesak sits in his palatial office high atop Fountain Plaza overlooking the city of Portland, the hustle and bustle of downtown streaming below. With a magnificent view of Mount Hood in the distance as the perfect backdrop, his office is one of sophistication and excess, with a conservative opulence that exudes both professionalism and extreme wealth. The office is massive. The floor-to-ceiling windows facing east, accenting the spectacular views, encompass the building's entire top floor. His desk, as always, is clear of any unnecessary paperwork or clutter; everything in its proper place. Brett knows, has always known, that everything he does, every detail of his life down to his shoes or the writing instrument he uses, matters. He has learned through his business life that while in the end pure intelligence, intuition, and drive is what matters most, it's style, persona, and outward aura that separates the highly successful from the outrageously successful.

And outrageously successful is how the world describes Brett Jesak. As the founder and largest shareholder of Sahara, perhaps the world's most recognized and prolific company of the past century, Brett has built an empire that includes online retailing, entertainment enterprises, unparalleled cloud computing, logistics, defense contracting services, and more. Known for his energy, drive, and vision, Brett thrives on competition; being told he cannot do something, that it is impossible, then finding a way to do it. Presiding behind his expansive Bocote desk, sitting in his custom-made $250,000 office chair made to his exact specifications, attired in the uniform of a business executive that screams success and money, Brett is at the top of the financial food chain not only in America but in the entire world.

But it has not been easy for Brett, as you would expect. Journeys to the highest peak of a profession rarely are. Jimi Hendrix, Howard Hughes, Mike Tyson, Ernest Hemingway, Elvis Presley all are good examples of this truth. Brett tells himself almost daily that the sacrifices he makes in the areas of friendships, relaxation, hobbies, entertainment, and other vices most humans consider more enjoyable than work are worth the wealth, the fame, the worldwide acclaim and attention. Ironically, part of his nature comes from a lack of true inner confidence, driven by childhood teasing and trauma that is covered up by his incredible drive, immaculate attention to detail, and a competitive spirit to prove everyone wrong.

One of Brett's direct reports enters the room, quickly reviews a presentation on sales growth in Asian-Pacific markets, and leaves the data brief for his further review. Their interaction is polite and efficient. But there is no superfluous dialogue or the friendly chatter that often occurs with business associates who fight the daily battles of business together. Brett knows how his employees feel about him. He's overheard them talk; is well aware he's referred to as "BJ" behind his back. He knows the way they use it as an unflattering term, and feels a certain disappointment that they lack the energy or motivation to come up with a derogatory term more creative, less obvious. A man of his stature, one who treats underlings as he does, surely deserves a nickname more clever than simply his initials, which just happen to mean the act of fellatio. When he overheard his CFO railing to colleagues about Brett's relentless badgering to improve the quarterly P&L say, "That jizzmeister BJ, the son of a bitch," he actually felt heartened. He almost took the enhanced derision as a compliment.

A yellow-orange sun slowly vanishes over the horizon as Portland bids another day adieu. While the lights of the city start to burn in the darkening afterglow of the day, Brett glances over at one of his favorite new products. It's an innovation that works like a personal digital assistant, developed by the AI team he recently assembled at Sahara. Unlike the standard model the engineers are prototyping now to sell to the masses, his is custom-designed in the shape of an Egyptian pyramid, all black and surrounded by a mesh-like material you see on high-end audio speakers. Studying the overall design of his personal model, thinking about the implications and influence this new device will have on the general public,

dreaming about the absolute fortune Sahara will ultimately make from
this ingenious device, Brett says:

"Hey, Amanda."

"Yes, how may I help you?"

"Amanda, who is the richest man in the world?"

"Warren Buffett, chairman and CEO of Berkshire Hathaway, is the
world's wealthiest man."

Staring out the window at the minions streaming home on the criss-
crossing traffic arteries of the city, in their Civics, their Corollas, their
Dodge minivans, Brett clutches his gold-plated coffee mug and notices a
tightness in his chest, the inescapable feeling of not being good enough,
and an intense longing to be held.

WALDEN IV

I probably ought to quit my drinking
But I don't believe I will

"Rachel's Song" by James McMurtry (*Where'd You Hide the Body*)

AFTER CODY GIVES me the card I ask, "What kind a name is Yugo Free? That can't be his real name. Sounds like some kind of bit..."

Cody explains, saying that's the first question he had too. "Dylan told me he changed his name to Yugo several years ago, that his real name was Marion. Marion Freeman. Might be hard being a dude named Marion. Maybe took some shit over the years. Said he's a young guy, early thirties. Dylan also said Yugo told him he went through some kind of transformation a few years ago that made clear his purpose was to help people. Said the Universe told him to change his name. Who knows? Cutting his last name from Freeman to Free is obvious. It's a funky name – *awesome* really."

"Can't say I blame him for ditching Marion. Why Yugo? Where'd that come from?"

"You ever hear of Yugo the car?"

"Nope. There's a car named Yugo?"

"Not a car – *the* car. It was a brand of car sold back in the '80s made in

Yugoslavia. Dylan says Yugo feels our society is too commercialized, too materialistic, and it's getting worse. The Yugo was one of the worst cars ever made but they advertised it like crazy. And amazingly, people in the US ate it up, at least for a while. It sold like crazy until people finally realized it was truly a piece of shit. Then it flopped big time. Yugo the dude thought Yugo the car was the perfect example of unbridled consumption and the power of marketing to get us to buy almost anything, even when it sucks. Go look it up. There's videos of the old commercials on YouTube that're hilarious. It's his metaphor for the insanity of out-of-control consumption and the stupidity of following what's in. Pretty cool name for a spiritual teacher if you ask me. *You Go Free!*"

Cody using the words "unbridled" and "metaphor" is another shocker. I'm catching a little buzz now, almost done with tall boy #3, and I study Yugo's business card. There's no website, no phone number, no address. Just a card with a name and his odd title, printed on thick recycled paper that looks like tan papyrus. There's a logo in the upper left corner, printed in dark green, that's an informal drawing of a big circle with a triangle inside and an eye inside the triangle – not hard straight lines or a perfect circle, but loose, handwritten. The only contact info is an email address. I look at Cody. "This guy isn't trying too hard to reach new clients, huh? No phone number, no address, no website? I don't know about any '80s cars named Yugo, but I admit the name Yugo Free is pretty cool for a philosopher. Man, do I want to be free of all the shit flying around in my head these days."

Cody and I hang out another hour or so at the park while he gets into full "Thursday is Friday" mode. It's good being outside, good getting my mind off Walden's Pets, good not thinking about the money being pissed away every minute our website is down. It also feels good getting my head nice and numb with the Shiner Bocks. Our talk eventually drifts to more low stress topics – sports, the line-up for this year's ACL music festival, Cody pointing out cute college girls hanging out or exercising around the park. I notice a beautiful Collie chasing after a frisbee, his owner tossing a Barringer 3500 Flying Dog Disc, or at least it looks like ours, not a Sahara knockoff. It's a much-needed afternoon break, even if I am drinking in the middle of a workday. I'm grateful for Cody and his friendship – for his being an outlet to talk to. The sad truth is there aren't many other people I ever talk to who aren't either co-workers, my girlfriend Jessica, Cody, Bryan, or Frazier. Mary and Father are harder to talk to as they get older, especially Mary whose short-term memory started going downhill even before Father's health issues. When I try to hand Cody Yugo's card back, he says to keep it, that I need it more than he does. And again he says he's worried about me, to reach out to Yugo *now*.

I get back to the office still feeling a buzz. The last thing I want to do is write an email to "The Negotiator Samzo." I've emailed him, or them, three times today begging for mercy while my IT team tries in vain to get the site back up. Paying this bullshit ransom seems the only way to stop the kidnapping quickly, but why should I trust these guys? My last email to them stated my concern, and this is what came back while I was hanging out with Cody in the park. Their English could use a little work, but then again, so could mine:

From: TheNegotiatorSamzo@protonmail.com
Sent: Thursday, April 2, 2017 4:29 PM
To: CustomerService@WaldensPets.com
Subject: RE: We have shutdown your website.

We are aware of the damages we cause. We used to do demonstration but unfortunately it does not persuade enough. So now we do all out attack until we get a response or paid for a low ransom.

Fortunately for you it was us and not the other groups that exist. As they would of brought you down entirely and not stop their attack or respond to you even after payment of ransom.

With us, we may be criminals but we have honored our word to stop attacks.

And we now will offer to help you protect against any further attacks from the much worse groups. (for example of groups: RMX squad, Arvando Collective, BB4DC – you can look them up on google).

If one of these type of groups attack you; it will be much more ruthless than us.

When you are able to verify payment to us; we will tell you what steps to take to protect yourself and we promise to not bother you again.

--The Negotiator Samzo

Back then, I had no idea what Monero coins were or how to send them. I'm sure they demanded to be paid that way to avoid detection, to avoid being traced. I call my accounting manager and ask her to research this, to figure out what we need to do to make this ridiculous ransom payment – it's priority #1 and keep me posted. I pull out Yugo Free's card from my pocket and think about my talk with Cody. I Google the word "Yugo," and this is the first snippet that pops up from Wikipedia:

"The Yugo was a small car made in the former nation of Yugoslavia that survives in the American consciousness as the ultimate automotive failure. Poorly engineered, ugly, and cheap, it survived much longer as a punch line for comedians than it did as a vehicle on the roads. Many attributes of the Yugo led it to become known as the 'worst car ever.' The car was cheap and not constructed well. Most owners experienced break-downs, and the Yugo usually did not fare well in crashes. Also, the fuel efficiency was extremely poor for a car of its size."

Well I'll be damned – Cody was dead-on with this one. The Yugo sounds like one *shitty little car*. It's amazing he even got the country they made the car in right, but I guess Yugoslavia and Yugo aren't that hard. I slide Yugo's card in my desk drawer. I may be a little shaky today, and yes, I am already thinking about my next drink if I can ever get out of here tonight. But psychiatrists and spiritual gurus are not what I need right now. All things considered I'm doing alright – I'll leave that stuff for Dylan and his friends. I'll just do my best to work through things on my own, and try to follow Cody's surprisingly good advice to stop being so negative.

I look back at my computer screen, not wanting to check emails or get any work done. I go to Wikipedia and search "minneola tangelos." This is the first paragraph:

"The Minneola tangelo (also known as the Honeybell) is a cross between a Duncan grapefruit and a Dancy mandarin, and was released in 1931 by the USDA Horticultural Research Station in Orlando. It is named after Minneola, *Florida*."

Minneola, Texas my ass, but hey, he was close. Is there even a Minneola in Texas? I check and yes, it does exist – it sounded familiar. I see how Cody could get that mixed up, but it's out in East Texas not South Texas where they're famous for growing ruby reds. One thing's for sure, there's no citrus growing out in the piney woods of East Texas. Not bad for ol' Cody though, I think. One outta two ain't bad, and he was really close on the tangelos. More like one and a half out of two. Which reminds me, I've got to pick up some of those on my next trip to the grocery store – that and a twelve-pack of Shiner Bock.

That night on the way home from work I stop off at a bar close to the office – it's more a Mexican restaurant really. Their food is just average, but they make *killer* frozen swirl margaritas made with tequila and sangria, and they add Everclear for an extra kick. Two and you're feeling no pain. In fact they're so strong there's a two-drink limit, then they cut you off. My day's been so shitty, I know two's not gonna be enough to numb the *crazy* thoughts swirling around in my head, but the bartender knows me from popping in after work sometimes, so after two ritas he has no problem giving me a quick Patron double shooter and a couple Tecates to top it off. Four or five tall boys at the park with Cody, two Everclear laced margaritas, a double tequila shooter, and some beers with only chips and salsa since breakfast – I'm toasted.

Driving home I'm playing the "close one eye game." You know, the one where you're seeing double traffic lines on the road, so you have to close one eye to figure out where the real lanes are. The office is over thirty minutes from my house, and it's a winding, hilly road to get out there. I focus hard to stay in the lines – it's dusk, visibility is poor, and the frequent S-curves on the road don't make it easy. I feel relief when I finally get to my neighborhood, but as I make a left turn just two blocks from my house, a cat or something darts across the street, diverting my attention. By the time I look up I misjudge the turn, hop the curb, take out a mailbox, and smash into a big live oak tree. The tree doesn't fall – it's just bent a little at an odd angle now.

Shit! Panicked – it's not that late and people could be out walking the neighborhood – I don't get out to check the damage. I put my SUV in reverse, back off the curb, and drive straight home, pulling into the garage and closing the garage door behind me even before getting out of the truck. Talk about a close call – to some maybe even a wake-up call. I do *not* need a DUI right now. Holy shit, *what am I doing*? I glance at my damaged front end only briefly as I hurry into the house – it doesn't look good, but I don't want to deal with that now. Fixing an expensive SUV like this will cost thousands. And being it's a lease, I have no idea how that's all going to work. I walk into my place, grab a beer from the fridge, and take a deep, long drink – just need something to help me settle down and get some sleep. My dog George is there taking it all in, loyal and excited as always to see me. He greets me at the door, tail wagging, tongue hanging out, happy as hell I'm finally home. Man oh man, thank God for George.

FRAZIER III

READING Walden's last chapter brings back memories. What a difficult time. Reliving this part of his life is like remembering a different person. Walden is usually a great guy. An awesome brother. A good boss. A fun person to be around. But he was struggling even before the WaldensPets.com shutdown. Life had given him a lot to manage all at once. The Samzo kidnapping simply ignited all that was building around him for months. I'm reminded now just how much he's grown since finding Yugo.

Okay, Walden asked me to finish this part. Airing out his personal struggles is unfair to him really. But I will say this upfront in his defense. Today's Walden would have responded very differently. So, when WP.com went down, he became what's best described as *unhinged*. It was the end of a quarter when revenue numbers are critical. Walden was working with the bank for new financing. The funds were to invest in marketing and new people to drive growth. A strong sales quarter was critical to get loan approval. Walden closely watched WP sales numbers every day. Just one slow sales day dampened his mood. Imagine what a week with *ZERO* sales does to a month. Now imagine what it did to Walden.

Buying Monero at that time was an ordeal. An account had to be established. Approvals and authentication was required. It took over twenty-four hours for that. There were daily purchase limits for new accounts. Walden could only buy $75 per day. Then had to wait each day to buy $75 more to get to $300. Samzo was slow to respond to his emails saying the ransom was paid.

At first Walden attacked his IT team, demanding answers and action. There were threats about job security. Serious name-calling. Questions about competence. It was *ugly*. He emailed Samzo over and over. He pleaded for sympathy, begging them to release the site. He berated his staff. He blew up at his executive assistant Haley (his most important employee – she keeps the place running). She came to me in tears, saying she was quitting. He screamed at me when I suggested we use social media for damage control. BTW, we did, and it worked! Yes, sales were missed during the shutdown. But WP lost no loyal customers to speak of.

Jessica told me those days with Walden were hell. She cut off communication with him after Day 3 to keep her sanity. I didn't realize he was drinking with Cody at the park that first day. That explains the fireworks in the office later that night. He slept very little. He drank very much. He worried, researched, obsessed, and worried some more.

Eventually the ransom payment went through. The site went back live. But it didn't end right away. They hit Walden up for another $300. They said they'd hold off another shutdown for forty-eight hours to give him time to pay. Their rationale? For the second payment, they'd tell Walden how to protect WP from this happening again. The continued meltdown was painful to watch. During this time, our IT guys figured out what was happening. They took measures to install new security. And Walden paid the extra $300 just to be sure. In all, WaldensPets.com was down for seven full days.

Amazingly, Samzo did validate to Walden that what IT put in place was a good solution. WP.com would never hear from Samzo again. What nice guys, huh? What did they do to cause the shutdown? A *massive* DDoS attack by people who really know how to shut down a website. Hindsight shows WP.com simply needed better security. A "behind-the-firewall" firewall. C'est la vie.

Walden said writing about Samzo triggered intense negative emotions. He didn't like reliving how he'd acted. Or, overreacted. It's funny reading Walden's last chapter. He spent more time writing about hanging out with Cody in the park than his meltdown! A key tenant of Yugo's teaching is to be aware of negative thoughts and emotions. Walden now works consciously to avoid being attached to negativity. So, he asked me to finish this part of the story, saying: "Sis, you've been on my ass to write this book to get Yugo's ideas out there to help people, but writing this part isn't good for my spirit. You do it. You know what needs telling. I only ask two things: 1) don't make me look like a dick, and 2) your 'no edits policy' is bullshit."

Of course I said yes. Summarizing the website shutdown saga is only part of it. I knew succinctly recapping everything else going on would be hard for Walden. Oh, and being the loving sister I am? I agreed he could edit this chapter all he wants since it's all about him. Walden can change whatever he wants. He asked for brevity, so here goes:

Walden loves animals and so do I. It's probably from our days at Nueva Tierra. Pets and other animals were all around. He always has at least one dog and one cat. Usually more, but always one of each. He says he keeps them primarily for "research purposes" for his work at WP. That's somewhat true. Goodness knows the amount of food, toys, and treats he's tested on them. But we all know the real reason he has them. He loves them. He needs them. They're his best friends.

His cat Bob was *awesome*. A beautiful black Manx. Somebody left Bob at a vet friend of Walden's when he was only a few months old. They couldn't pay the bill, so they just left the cat there. A kitten really. Nice, huh? Walden was thrilled to take him home. Manx are known for having almost no tail. It's just a tiny nub, a "bob" tail as they say. Hence the name. Bob was the coolest cat ever. Dog-like in many ways, but still *cat cool*. A hunter. Bob was Walden's favorite and lived with him for many years. And then, just before the Samzo fiasco, Bob vanished. Poof, into thin air.

It's almost certain the coyotes got him. They're known in his area for picking off cats and small dogs. Walden knew of the danger. But he always thought Bob was safe. He had his claws, was super smart. A tree climber like no other. But Bob was a fighter when he had to be. That probably hurt him in the end. I'd seen him turn back much bigger dogs. Walden posted signs everywhere. He scoured the neighborhood after work for days. He called all the shelters. Nothing. No sightings, no trace, no body. A sure sign of coyotes. It hit Walden hard. He blamed himself for not being more careful with Bob. But it wasn't Walden's fault. Bob was always kept inside when Walden was away. And Walden made sure before bed he was inside at night. I consoled him, saying Bob was a prowler. It would have been wrong to keep him inside *all* the time. Walden was devastated. *RIP Bobby*. I loved you too.

Next. One of Walden's dearest friends from college, a good friend of Cody's too, has serious addiction problems. Drinking mainly, but also pills. A deadly double-whammy as Walden says. She lost her job from the drinking. Got arrested twice in a six-month period. All her family and personal relationships are shattered. Years of broken promises, lies, blow-ups, and disappointments will do that. Walden and Cody are the only humans left who care about this friend (who will remain nameless).

What Billy Crystal said about male/female relationships in *When Harry Met Sally* is often true. That "men and women can't be friends because the sex part always gets in the way." That wasn't the case with this girl. She had many platonic male friends. And she could party with the best of them. Before addiction she was an incredible athlete. Ultimate frisbee, biking, hiking, snow skiing, distance running. She had lots of female friends too. But she hung with the guys more than any girl I've ever known.

Two weeks before his cat Bob vanished, Walden got a distressing call at work. His friend was in the hospital on life support. In a coma. She was shopping at an HEB around noon. She'd bought her groceries and made it back to the car. But instead of making a simple right turn to exit the parking lot, she kept driving straight ahead. Plowed right through the storefront windows. Police thought she may have passed out. Or she was trying to kill herself. Apparently, she hit the accelerator rather than the brake. Possibly it was a mistake. The police said she was going fast on impact. She wasn't wearing a seat belt. Her head smashed into the windshield.

Several people in the store were hurt. Her blood alcohol was 0.32% *before noon on a Tuesday*. The legal limit in Texas is 0.08% so she was *four times over*. She also had significant levels of lorazepam and diazepam in her system. Although not totally surprised, Walden and Cody were really shaken up. They both feel responsible in a way. After all, it was partying together over the years that spawned her addictions. They'd done interventions. Got her to rehab twice before. Interventions that obviously didn't work. Remarkably, she pulled out of the coma and is still alive at this writing. And still drinking. *Insane.*

Yes, there's more. Walden will tell me if I left anything out. Father and Mary are getting older, and with that comes health problems. It's life. Mary is struggling with dementia. It's early onset because she's *not that old*. It started slowly a few years ago and is now getting worse. Anyone who's helped someone with Alzheimer's knows it's highly stressful. Highly frustrating. Father is a constant presence that's always there to help Mary. And then...

Father's always taken care of himself. Good diet, daily exercise. Walden and I always say he'll live to be a hundred. Around this other chaos in Walden's life, Father suddenly got chest pains. Out of the blue. He thought it was indigestion. They persisted and his left arm grew very heavy. Father being Father, he told no one. He put up with these symptoms for several days. Then he finally went to the ER. The doctors found multiple blockages in his heart. Two were total blockages. The doctors believe he had a small heart attack before going to the ER. Possibly a stroke. *Four stents* were inserted.

Thankfully Father eventually came out okay. His doctor said with that much blockage, it's a miracle he didn't drop dead. Father's exercise regimen had saved him. Apparently new arteries had grown *around* the totally blocked areas of the heart. *Amazing* what the human body can do. Father's always been one driven, determined man. All this family trauma was high stress. And all of it fell on Walden. Mary was obviously no help. Her dementia got much worse during the ordeal from fear of losing Father. She was just another helpless person for Walden to care for. Unfortunately, I was gone when all this happened. Unable to get back to help. In the Australian outback with a girlfriend. Out of the country and unreachable.

Which brings us to the kidnapping and shutdown at WP. Obviously, Walden's system was already on overload when the website went down. And (*Walden now adds, including adding all of the italics you see in this chapter for emphasis*) this leaves out the relationship issues going on with Jessica—caused by worries from all of the above. It leaves out the already stressful atmosphere at WP—from worrying about letting employees go, taking away their livelihoods, and from the shrinking cash flow. It also leaves out his ever-expanding reliance on alcohol, which *exacerbated everything,* and didn't stop after hopping that curb and running into a tree. In short, it was the perfect recipe for finding Yugo. My, how the Universe works...

YUGO I

*I can't grow up
'Cause I'm too old now*

"Peter Pan" by James McMurtry (from *It Had to Happen*)

THANKS TO FRAZIER for quickly moving through my rough patches. I knew if I wrote about them I'd ramble on about all kinds of stuff that isn't important. She's good at getting to the point instead of the long, drawn-out ramblings I sometimes write. I hate to admit it, and maybe it makes me a bad person, but I get almost as emotional reading about Bob as anything else that was going on back then. What a *bad ass cat* he was. Fact is, the craziness going on during the Samzo kidnapping and the emotional turmoil swirling around me was tugging at my sanity. I eventually pulled out Yugo's card and emailed him asking for my first appointment, but truthfully, it wasn't until a few months *after* that appointment that a last straw happened causing me to completely melt down – to finally surren-der. Frazier wasn't there, she didn't live through that *last straw*, so it's impossible for her to accurately describe what happened to me and Jessica that insane night. But I'll let that wait for another day. I haven't processed it well enough to write about it coherently yet, and I need to get to the heart of this story, which is Yugo and his teachings.

I know I used two James McMurtry quotes in a row, which I'm sure is a no-no in literary circles. Now that I think about it, the fact I used back-to-back McMurtry songs to parallel my life shows I was one sad puppy. That plus James describes the human condition so well you could use his lyrics to start most chapters of any book. Hopefully it's clear by now I needed to talk with someone to help me make sense of everything happening around me – the emotions and chaos overwhelming my life, the anxiety. I was truly at a place where nothing made sense. I saw no reason or meaning in life. And in these days of political divisiveness, worries about the economy, about climate change – or the debate if climate change even exists – racial tensions, global tensions, people on edge angry all the time, it all leads to unhealthy levels of anxiety in everybody. I don't care who you are. Life is hard, it's complex, it's stressful in this digital age. Maybe it's just me, but people seemed happier, friendlier, more at ease and at peace with each other when I was younger. Seems everyone smiled more back then, before we were all walking around staring at our phones, checking our feeds. But I guess that just makes me sound old – sound like my old man. I'm just saying, maybe not so well, that after Yugo's counseling and experiencing what his words of wisdom and support did for me, I'm certain we could all use a little guidance, some positive reinforcement, some *love* to see us through these tough times.

Which leads me to ask this question about us humans in general. What makes it so hard for us to surrender and ask for help? To go talk to a counselor or a shrink or a spiritual teacher? Reading over the last chapter made me wonder – why is it so important that I explain why I went for counseling? What's that voice inside me saying so loudly I have to justify it to other people? I think there's a mindset many of us have that says we're weak if we ask for help – we're failing when we seek counseling. I'm here to tell you that thinking is *bullshit*. It's all ego driven, worrying more about appearances than becoming a better person. How can we get better and grow without asking for help – without learning from others? We should all seek it without feeling ashamed, fearful, or "less than." Ok, so there's my speech. I heard basically the same thing for months and did *nothing* about it, so hopefully when life throws you curveballs, you'll be smarter than me.

Which gets us to Yugo. Once I remembered where I put his card, which took me longer than it should since I was buzzed when I slid it in my desk drawer that night, I sent him an email. Cody suggested I use Dylan as a reference to explain how I heard about Yugo. We'd run into Dylan a couple weeks after I got Yugo's card, and I must admit he was different than I remembered – not so flighty, not so primed to go start a party. He was more *grounded* it seemed, more comfortable in his own skin. It was a noticeable change, but I downplayed it. I asked him about Yugo, and he went on and on about what a great dude he was, that he was a mystic, that he was *"light, man"* – that was his catch phrase.

So, I finally emailed Yugo and said I was struggling through some personal issues, that he was highly recommended, and I wanted to talk about maybe getting some counseling. Yugo responded faster than I expected and we set a time to meet. The address he gave me was just south of downtown, right across the river on a busy stretch of older, almost landmark type buildings known for live music, cool independent shops and good restaurants – a somewhat touristy part of town, but popular with the locals too. Although the buildings on this street have been around for decades, I knew the lease for a place at this address would be sky high. Real estate in this area has soared to ridiculous levels – downtown is the place to be. Googling the address, the location showed up as a restaurant and coffee house I've known for years for their killer breakfasts and late hours. That seemed odd. The address also said second floor, which was strange too – I didn't remember that café having an accessible second floor.

Because of my nature and my already overexplained feelings that I felt like a failure, I was *nervous* contacting Yugo. Something Cody said about having to be "approved" by Yugo to be a patient got me thinking this guy wasn't going to have any interest in working with me. I'd never talked to a psychiatrist or counselor or anyone about psychological issues, so I had no clue what to expect or how I was supposed to act. I pictured a dark wood paneled office, a large couch with the doctor sitting behind an impressive desk – a cute receptionist who wants to listen in on our conversations. Then I remembered this guy's named Yugo Free – a *Philosopher, Guidepost and Light*. This wasn't gonna be like the typical shrink's office you see on TV or in the movies. I bet a couch wasn't in the cards. I made the appointment for a Thursday afternoon so I could leave the office a little early, then meet Cody after, who would probably be in his "Thursday is Friday" mode. My plan was to decompress with Cody after going to counseling to decompress.

Yugo's address was indeed the Omelettry Lane Café, a place I'd eaten many times, often late at night with the munchies if you know what I mean. It's not far from one of my favorite live music venues down the block and across the street. Their seven-grain pancakes and hashbrowns are perfect for soaking up excess alcohol after a long night of live tunes. I checked around outside the place looking for some stairs to take me up to the second floor, then walked to the back looking for any stairs – nothing. There's a second story on most of the shops and restaurants along the block, but I always thought they were apartments or storage rooms for the people who owned the places. I'd never seen any business activity on the second floor of any spots on this street.

I walk in the restaurant, hit by the comforting smells of fresh brewed coffee, bacon, and hot cinnamon rolls. Omelettry Lane is the prototypical organic, breakfast-centric, good vibes kind of restaurant – lots of wood, knickknacks everywhere, plenty of plants, the menu written on a chalkboard over an open kitchen. The place was packed as usual, and I looked around to see if there was a stairway hidden in the back or maybe in the small hallway where the bathrooms are – nothing there either. I went back to the front and waited to catch the eye of one of the waiters hustling around the tables. Finally, I got the attention of a girl heading to a table with coffee refills and asked if she knew where I could find someone named Yugo Free.

"Yugo? Sure, just a sec." She went and refilled the coffees, put the decanter back on its burner, and came back.

"So you're here to see Yugo, huh?" She smiles and sorta looks me up and down. I feel a twinge of insecurity.

"See that open door to the right of those shelves? His place is up through there. Just be sure before you go in his office you give a little knock so he knows you're there. I don't think anyone's with him now, but sometimes we miss people. His regulars just go up the stairs when they get here."

I look over at the door, which I've never noticed before – near a back corner, by some shelves holding condiments and potted plants. It looks like the door to a closet, or maybe the door to the restaurant's business office.

"Hey, thanks. Are you his receptionist?" I ask, trying to be clever.

"Sure," she said grinning. "We all do whatever we can for Yugo – he doesn't ask for much." She rushes off to help a table and I walk over to the door. As I get close, I see a piece of copy paper tacked to the wall with writing from what looks like a green Sharpie marker that reads *Yugo Free* with an arrow pointing up. I walk through the door and head up the stairs, leaving the smells and the sounds of the café behind.

The top of the stairs immediately open to a room I take for a waiting area. There's a few comfortable chairs – cloth covered loungers – some plants, a few pictures hanging on the wall of nature scenes, animals, some concert posters. Otherwise it's extremely sparse – more like the living room of a college apartment than a counselor's waiting room. There's an expensive looking hybrid style bike up against one wall – Yugo's transportation I assume. There's beige meditation pillows stacked against one wall. The windows are open, letting in a breeze, though it's already hot this time of year in Texas. A fan is running, oscillating back and forth. The smell of his office grabs my attention – fresh, like how it smells outside before it rains. There's also a lingering scent of sage and palo santo, fragrances I recognize from the candles we burned at Nueva for quiet times and meditation – candles Frazier still uses to this day. There's an open door straight ahead. I assume it's Yugo's office, and I walk over, lightly tapping on the door frame to let Yugo know I'm here. Nothing. I knock again, this time more loudly, but again no reply. One more much louder knock and I hear, "Hey man, hang on," coming from behind another door, this one closed and on the far-right wall. After a few seconds there's a loud flush and the sound of running water. The door opens and out comes Yugo, drying his hands on a small cloth hand towel.

"Hey, Walden Harrison? Awesome meeting you, dude. Come in, come in." He waves for me to follow him as he walks through his open office door, pointing back to where he came from.

"That's the restroom whenever you need it. These old pipes have seen better days, so remember to go very lightly on the TP. Three, four squares at a time at the most, and try to break them apart if you don't mind... unless it's an emergency."

I look down at the floor smiling. My initial meeting with a highly touted spiritual teacher and he's lecturing me on proper toilet paper etiquette. He walks into his office and I follow behind, checking out the surroundings. The office is so *casual.* Books line the walls on makeshift shelves. There's several piles of books on the floor as well, but the piles are neat, everything in its proper place. Facing the back wall is a small, worn, wooden desk and chair – certainly not an imposing psychiatrist's desk you sit in front of while the doctor scrutinizes you from behind. There's an open laptop on it, I assume the one Yugo emailed me from. The east wall has old wood framed windows facing the street, open to let in some air, with smaller shelves underneath holding plants, candles. An oscillating fan is running along with a ceiling fan keeping the air moving around the office. There's two chairs like from the waiting area in the center of the room with side tables next to each, and two more chairs are against the wall – I assume for sessions when there's more than one person. More meditation pillows are stacked in and around those chairs. The floors are old beat-up hardwood, but there's beautiful throw rugs on the floor, tans and greens with light powder blues in the patterns. The room is painted a soothing light brown – the trim is natural wood. It's an unassuming, comfortable room, peaceful, nothing like a stuffy, clinical office. I follow Yugo, who gets to his chair in the center, turns around, smiles, and offers his hand.

"Yugo Free, Walden. Welcome, have a seat…let's talk."

I shake his hand and say hello. The first thing I notice about Yugo is his smile – wide, bright, infectious. He's wearing a mint green plain t-shirt, comfortable looking but very worn khaki shorts, and old huarache style sandals that are woven cloth rather than leather. He's medium height and has an athletic build though not over the top – but he's obviously in very good shape. He has a dangling silver earring that looks like a thin curving ring of some kind, a couple of braided bracelets on his wrists and one ankle, and long camel-brown hair well past his shoulders down his back that looks sorta like natural dreads. His skin is chestnut brown, caramel, very "surfer dude" tanned – or possibly he's Black? Cody said nothing about his ethnicity. His dark green eyes grab my attention almost as quickly as his smile – sparkling, open, present. He has a tattoo on one forearm that's the same logo I saw on his business card, the circle and triangle with an eye inside. He has a four-day old beard working, one that grows in the goatee area but not so much on the sides. It's hard for me to tell how old he is – probably low thirties like Cody heard. Dylan was right, he sure doesn't look like your typical psychiatrist or counselor.

"So tell me," he says as he sits down, "why are you here?"

No small talk. No, did you have any problems finding the place? No, how do you know Dylan? Just, "Why are you here?" Here's our first conversation, as best I remember:

"Well, I'm feeling a lot of stress lately. At work mostly, but also with my girlfriend, with family."

"Uh-huh."

Long pause.

"I'm starting to feel more and more like life is really hard. It used to not feel that way. I mean, I used to just do what felt right in the moment and things would usually work out ok, but it seems now stuff is happening outside of my control that's hard to deal with."

"Right."

Another pause.

"You know how things are. The daily grind is getting to me. Every day is starting to feel the same. Work, go home, exercise, eat, hang out, repeat – sorta like the movie *Groundhog Day*."

"Yep. Pretty cool movie."

Another long pause. I'm beginning to be sorry I signed up for this.

"But at the same time, insane crap is happening all around me like never before that's way out of my control. And the world doesn't make sense so much anymore – people seem different. I can't relate to what everybody's into anymore. The stupid TV shows, the moronic movies recycling the same story lines over and over…I mean, *Fast and Furious 12*? The thousands of microbrew IPAs everybody's drinking, everyone binge streaming the same shows. This fixation on how you look on social media. I mean, what's the point? It seems like such a huge waste of time."

"I agree with that." Yugo calmly studies me and smiles.

I'm talked out already and we're less than three minutes in.

"And…I guess I'm drinking a little more than I should…."

"Walden. You know what all this means?"

"No, not really. That's why I'm here."

"All this means is you're growing up. That's it. Internally, mentally, spiritually you are growing up – *evolving* you might say."

My first thought is who the hell are you to tell me about growing up when I'm a responsible business owner? I've been a "grownup" since I left college – or at least pretended to be. But I keep that to myself.

"Growing up? I'm not sure I follow."

"You're finally starting to feel unsatisfied with life. You're realizing how you, and how most people in our culture, are wasting so much time. That the current fads are nonsense. You're beginning to see there has to be something more to living well on this planet than making money, entertaining yourself, and putting on a show for other people. That means you're growing up, Walden. Getting wiser. More conscious." Yugo's *presence*, his clarity, is somewhat startling. "It's different for everyone. Some people don't grow up until they're in their sixties or seventies. A few are more intuitive than others and grow up as early as eighteen, even younger. Most start growing up, at least a little, in their mid to late thirties or early forties. And, as you probably know, there are those who will never grow up at all. Life is but a blur."

Still a little pissed from being told I'm only now "growing up" I say somewhat sarcastically, "So, when did you start growing up?"

Yugo grins, scratches his chin while looking at me, and says, "Nine years ago, Walden, when life's events kicked me in the balls." Long pause...

"So, what you're telling me is all my issues are simply from "growing up," and maybe life kicking me in the nuts. And I just need to learn how to handle that better. Right?"

I'm looking for a quick and easy fix, and that seems like something I can do with a little help.

"I'm not telling you that at all. I'm just commenting on why you're feeling the way you're feeling now. It's nothing unique – it happens to most everyone at some point."

Then he smiles a big smile and says, "Now Walden, I'll ask you this question one more time. *Why are you here*? And maybe this helps. There is no right answer. In fact, it's possible this is a question you consciously don't know the answer to now without some digging. But let's try anyway."

What followed was an almost hour-long conversation focused around me and my struggles. Yugo asked questions to help me get under the surface of what I was really trying to say. He directed the conversation down the path he needed, I think, to get a read of my true motivations for being there. Mostly he listened and let me unburden myself, making a few notes along the way. As I talked, I thought to myself how everything kept coming back to me saying life no longer made sense – that everything happening around me was just so random.

When I finished, Yugo said it sounded like I was no longer getting satisfaction and joy out of life. That the daily routine, the responsibilities, the familiar relationships on one hand were too predictable and draining. But, on the other hand, I was starting to realize that trying to control the outcomes of life through hard work and planning is just an illusion – that *shit happens* (his words), and I don't have any control. That I'm beginning to see that the "routine" can be blown up in an instant.

"What this means," he said "is you're feeling the need to align yourself with a purpose, with a *reason for being*. You're seeing the impermanent nature of everything that's around you – your business, your loved ones, even your sanity. And that's scary. You're sensing the growing need to answer the questions, 'Why am I here? What is my purpose?' You need a better reason to get up in the morning than making money, impressing people, and entertaining yourself. You need fulfillment. You need internal, spiritual, personal growth!"

And I just sit there listening, trying to soak it in.

"Walden." By now Yugo's eyes are wide, beaming, and intense. "You're at a stage in life that's perfect for hearing my philosophy and ideas! If, and these are big ifs...if a) you believe what I just said *sounds true* in your heart from your experience. And b) if you are *willing to work.*"

Now, I believed what he said sounded true, but it also sounded a little like self-help mumbo-jumbo. What I knew I needed was change, was direction, was wisdom and a different perspective – and probably someone to talk to about my problems. But could this mellow looking surfer dude in shorts and sandals really make a difference? I thought about Dylan – he was a partying mess most of the times I'd been around him. I thought about how he was so much calmer now, more at ease and confident, not looking to get wasted all the time. Cody and Dylan both told me about others who raved about how Yugo turned their lives around – one girl called him a "miracle." But for me, commitment to something like this is hard.

So I say, "What do you mean by *willing to work,* and what would our working together look like? Is it once a week? How long does this type counseling usually take? Months? Years? And what are your charges? I figure it's by the hour?"

Yugo studies me for a while, then says, "Those are mostly logistical unimportant questions we can go over later. This is what's important. Listen, be *present,* and let me know how you feel when I'm done."

This first meeting with Yugo, our conversation is all by memory and I think it's accurate. It's hard to remember what was said exactly, and like I mentioned earlier, once the sessions started, I recorded them all on my phone, so I have audio for most of what Yugo shared. Here's what he said to the best of my memory:

"Walden, what I'll share with you are certain actions to do, certain ways of living, certain Steps if you will, that if you do them will help you find purpose, will give you more meaning in life and a reason to get up in the morning. It's nothing exotic, nothing over the top special and hard to grasp really. Just things I've learned through personal experience, moving through life, through research and reading, through talking with others, trial and error, that help the human soul return to its *Essence.* At the same time, and maybe just as important, the behaviors and steps you'll learn are good for the planet, good for Mother Earth, and good for the community and other beings. This helps others along the way. This is part of what I mean by saying it *adds meaning* to life. There's nothing religious about what we'll cover, but it is *spiritual*. Some people are cool with that from a counselor, others aren't. Do you consider yourself a religious person?"

"Religious? No, not really. I was raised in a commune actually, in the upper Northwest. There wasn't any what you'd call mainstream religion going on there. Jesus was a thing people talked about sometimes, but not the 'believe in me or you're going to hell' Jesus I hear about sometimes around here – the kind I heard about at a Baptist church as a kid." I sense a knowing smile from Yugo. "Where I grew up it was more of a compassionate, peace and love, hippy kind of Jesus. You know, give to the poor, blessed are the meek, share with others, love your neighbors – that sort of thing. None of that stuck really, although I do pray sometimes. More than usual lately, although I'm not sure who to. There were some influences at the commune you'd probably call Buddhist. We had quiet times, and in school they started teaching meditation when they thought you were old enough. My folks are still into that, my sister. I haven't meditated in years."

Yugo jumps in enthusiastically, "Ok, that's cool! It doesn't sound like it's a big deal in your case, but please understand this. If you are religious, Christian, Muslim, Jewish, Buddhist, Native, Islamic, Hindu, whatever, I don't want to change your core beliefs. I don't want to move you away from your religious traditions. Those are important to hold onto. I don't believe anything I say will go against your religious upbringing, and my hope is to strengthen that core, add light, compassion, a new perspective. What we'll be talking about is not like theological doctrine. And there is no judging or moral superiority here. Instead we'll be talking about spirituality, about presence, about your *internal being* – about a spiritual way of living that's better for you, and better for our planet. A way of living that's regenerative and transforms us!"

I soak this in as best I can, trying to stay present and really listen like he asked, then finally say the nagging thought that's been in the back of my head this whole time.

"Works for me, Yugo. Hey, I heard from a friend there might be some kind of test? Some kind of process I need to go through to get accepted? What's that look like?"

Yugo laughs. "There's no test, Walden, there's no formal process. Oh it's true I don't take in everyone who comes to me. In the beginning I just assumed the Universe was sending me people who would benefit from our relationship, people who would grow and in turn make our world a better place. But over time I learned that's not always true. So now, all I do is talk openly with each person to understand if their heart is ready – to try and understand why they are here. Then use my intuition to see if they're at a spot where they're willing to make life changes for personal growth."

"That's it? There's nothing more selective about it?"

"Well there's the one other requirement I already mentioned. There are people I meet with who haven't reached that point where they've hurt enough, or experienced enough, to feel the need to do this work. To honestly *show up*. Without real effort, there's no point going forward. So, I'll need your personal commitment you'll come to our sessions and truly work the lessons. If not, we're wasting our time, and our time on this Earth is very short. Let's not waste it. Of course, you don't know today what this work might be, so I'm aware it's an unfair request now. If you like what you've heard, you can come to two sessions and see what you think. Then, if it's not for you, we'll shake hands and say goodbye."

Yugo's kept a continual, almost uncomfortable eye contact with me this entire time, and then adds, "There is one other reason a person may not be invited on this journey, Walden. Some are so secure and 100% certain that they *know*, so sure that everything they believe is "The Truth," that trying to break through that shell and add new ideas and depth either takes years or is impossible. Usually ultra-religious people no matter the faith or denomination. As I said, my intention is not to change anyone's religious tradition, but there are some who aren't comfortable even considering new ideas outside their strict belief system. That's why I asked if you view yourself as religious. If a person feels they have the truth, that's awesome! They don't need to get frustrated listening to me. I've tried a few times and my average of success is well below the Mendoza line."

After that statement Yugo looks away and seems deep in thought, maybe thinking of those he couldn't reach.

So I joke and say, "Ha! Under .200, huh? I can see why you'd want to avoid that."

Yugo's either unimpressed I know Mario Mendoza's infamous batting average or he's still daydreaming. There's a pause, then he regains focus.

"As for you, Walden, I'm good on my end. You seem acceptably open. You answered the question 'Why are you here?' quite well actually – once you got rolling. So, what do you think?"

Now I feel a little cornered.

"Ummm, ok. Let me think about it for a couple days – it sounds great and all. I know I need some help, at least someone to talk to. How about my questions? The ones you said were logistical. How often do we meet? What's the cost? About how long does this usually take?"

Yugo stands up and starts walking me to the door, placing a hand on my shoulder. "We meet once every two to three weeks depending on how things are going. That way there's time for the information to sink in, to be processed. Plan on an hour and a half per session. I build in quiet time at the end to sit and just *be*. We can determine the best day and time for both of us if you think it over and want to continue."

"Ok, sounds good Yugo – thanks. Oh, and what about the cost?"

"That's totally up to you, Walden. I don't charge for our time together, but if you think your spiritual health is getting better and want to show appreciation, you can donate whatever you'd like. And to whoever you'd like as well."

Dumbfounded, I stop and look back at Yugo. He's already turned around after walking me to the door, going back to his small desk.

"And as for how long it may take," he says more loudly, over his shoulder as he's walking away, "it usually takes no more than fifteen visits to go over everything and cover questions, sometimes less. Some students like to come back and just talk…that's cool too."

"Ok," I say, thinking to myself, *WTF*? "Let me think about it and I'll get back to you…."

As I turn to head down the stairs, out of the corner of my eye, I think I see Yugo shaking his head.

WALDEN V

I can still feel the hole
Where the revelation nailed me to the wall
Now I can't recall
If there was any revelation there at all
Just some kids getting high about it all

"Hideous Glorious" by the Barr Brothers (*Queens of the Breakers*)

I'D ARRANGED to get together with Cody after my meeting with Yugo at a county park on the lake by the dam. It's beautiful and usually not crowded on weekdays – a great place to chill. I knew I'd need to talk to somebody after my first visit with Yugo, and no one was more clued into my visit than Cody. Yugo's meeting went longer than expected, so Cody's already there when I arrive. He's got a cooler and a couple of those small chairs without legs that have beach prints on them – the kind that fold up and have straps on the back so you can carry them like a backpack. He's also got a Bluetooth speaker with some tunes going and a bag full of snacks. I feel guilty – all I have is my sorry self and a bottle of water. I should have brought at least some munchies.

My plan was to not drink today, or at minimum not day drink before five o'clock. I walk up as Cody's exhaling from a joint in full "Thursday is Friday" mode. He's also drinking a bottle of Little Kings Cream Ale, a favorite of his when at the lake. Cody looks hilarious in his little beach chair – a massive guy sitting basically on the ground with his legs all splayed out. But because these chairs are so portable, he *loves* them – they even have a small cooler compartment on the back and of course cup holders.

I open my bottled water, take a swig, and sit in the chair next to him, saying, "Hey, what's up?"

"Not much, dude, welcome to paradise. How'd it go with Yugo?" But before I can answer, Cody's sitting straight up in his chair looking half-crazy and pointing. "What the fuck's that?"

"What do you mean what the fuck's that? It's a bottle of water, genius."

"I know what it is, Walden. I mean, what the fuck are you doing with that? Don't you know bottled water is outrageously bad for our planet?"

Surprised by how adamant he is about something so trivial I say, "Well I know it's plastic and all and that's not great, but I'll throw it in the car and recycle it at home. No big deal."

He pushes on. "No big deal? No big deal? That's what they said when they started killing off the buffalo. Walden, haven't you heard about the Great Pacific Garbage Patch?"

"No."

"It's a shitload of plastic and trash that's been building up in the Pacific Ocean for decades. It's full of all kinds of plastic garbage, but it's mostly water bottles…taking over our seas. Last I heard it's twice the size of Texas – horrible for marine life. So much shit they'll never clean it up. And I read every ten years it triples in size. Think about that!"

"Are you shitting me? I know there's issues with garbage floating in the ocean, but I've never heard of any floating patch of plastic twice the size of Texas. Cody, that's impossible."

"I'm not kidding, man – it's true. Todd Snider even wrote a song about it called "That Great Pacific Garbage Patch." You should check it out, man. All the facts are in there."

"You're getting your facts from a Todd Snider song?"

"Hell *yeah*." Cody emphatically rolls on. "And the people using all these plastic bottles and shopping bags think they're not hurting anything because they recycle them or throw their trash away. Well that doesn't matter. Much of our recycled trash gets shipped over to other countries, tons of it gets thrown into the sea or never reused. They say over one third of all used water bottles end up in the ocean. Shit man, use your head. We've got to start boycotting plastic before it's too late – especially *single use plastics* like bottled water. It all ends up in gutters on the street or the drainage ditch, which flows into creeks, which goes to streams and rivers and eventually it all ends up in the ocean. Anybody that litters these days is a clueless jerk, and anyone buying bottled water is just as bad in my book."

Not expecting to be blasted for simply drinking water, I mumble an apology and set my water bottle on the ground.

"Here, man, take a cream ale instead. These babies are ok cuz they're in glass. Everything I drink is in either glass or aluminum…natural stuff's reused way more than all that plastic shit. Plastic's bad news, man, indestructible for five hundred years."

And so, my plan of not drinking before 5:00 is shot without a struggle. Cody pops off the top and hands one over. He's right, Little Kings are perfect for the lake. Man, does it go down smooth.

"Sorry, dude, didn't mean to go off on you, but holy crap I'm worried about our oceans and what we're doing to them. So few people are paying *attention*. I mean, I just don't get bottled water. The shit's free right out of the tap."

He takes another drag on the doobie, exhales slowly, and finally sits back more relaxed. "Now back to my first question. How was Yugo?"

So I tell him about my meeting, that Yugo's really a different kind of dude, like no one else I've ever talked to. He's got a calmness about him – maybe a better word is *coolness* about him. I tell him he's right about not judging a book by its cover. He sure doesn't look like a counselor or spiritual teacher – more like a surfer dude or a reggae singer. That the most vivid thing I remember from our meeting is Yugo's *presence* – how he was so intently focused on our conversation, on my body language.

"Awesome, dude. Dylan says that about him too. That he's so *present*. I don't even know what that means. So, you get accepted? Did he agree to work with you?"

"Yeah, I think so. Yugo said he was open for me to come back and get started. But you were sorta wrong about that part. There wasn't really a test or anything. We just talked for a while, and he asked why I was there…"

A group of college kids walk by towards the water, loud hip hop music in tow – I think it's Lil Wayne but I'm no expert. Girls in ridiculous thong bikinis drinking White Claws, frat boys in their Ray-Bans. Cody's eyes follow them all the way down to the water.

"I didn't say there was any test, dude. You heard me wrong. All I said was I heard he doesn't always work with everybody that goes to see him. So, when do you start?"

He takes another toke off his joint, offers me a hit, which I decline, and uses condensation from his beer bottle to carefully put it out for later.

"I'm not sure. I told him I had to think about it."

"What? Think about it? Are you nuts? What the hell is there to think about? Did he tell you what his fees are? They're nothing! It's free! When Dylan told me that I almost crapped my pants. I didn't say anything about that because I figured you'd say something like 'I'm not going to anybody so lame he can't even charge a fee.' This dude's awesome, man, everybody says so. Think about it, Walden. Yugo's *free!*"

He smiles and winks, making sure I caught his little pun.

"Yeah, yeah, I know – that part threw me off big time. I was expecting a couple hundred an hour minimum. His office is low key, nothing super nice. But rent has to be crazy high where he's at. Did you know his office is on top of Omelettry Lane? How in the hell can he afford an office in that part of town and charge no fees?"

"Who knows, Walden, but that's not important. What's important is you're slipping, man, you're really squirrelly these days and I'm worried about you. You've got black circles under your eyes, you're anxious as hell. I promised your girl Jessica I wouldn't say anything, but she reached out to me the other day. Asked me to try and get you to counseling. Honestly, it's the second time she's done it. Frazier even called me, worried about how you're doing." Cody's eyes kind of stare off and I figure he's conjuring up a mental picture of my sister.

"What? They *both* called you?" I'm shaking my head. "Jeez…listen, man, I don't know. I like Yugo and he seems super smart and tuned into something. But you know me. It takes me a while to commit. Things don't add up and I've got questions. It's not like he's a doctor I can research or a counselor I can look up on Google and check out reviews. He doesn't even have a website for God's sake."

Cody is exasperated. He opens another bottle of cream ale, takes a long slow drink, and lets out a heavy sigh. "Ok, Walden, you say you got questions? What are they? Let me have 'em and I'll do some research."

"Research? What are you gonna do? I've tried finding any info I can about Yugo online and there's nothing."

"Remember that guitarist with the Bastards of Soul? The one that told Dylan about Yugo in the first place? He knows people who grew up with Yugo out in West Texas. I bet they know something about his background and can fill me in on his story. He's the one that told Dylan why he calls himself Yugo Free."

"Yugo grew up in West Texas? No way. He looks like he grew up in California or Jamaica or Maui. Anywhere but West Texas."

"That's what I heard, man. I'm serious, Walden. I can do some sleuth work and find out what you're looking for – anything to get you some peace of mind and get those ladies in your life off my back. You know the girl I'm seeing, Anastasia? She knows this guitarist dude from doing gigs around town. She'll give me an intro and I'll hit him up with any questions you got as long as they're reasonable. What's troubling you, my son?"

So I went over the questions swirling around in my head after meeting Yugo. Questions like:

How can he afford that office space? It's gotta be at least ten grand a month.

What are his credentials, and how long has he been a counselor?

Why doesn't he charge for his sessions and how does he make a living?

Where'd he really come from and how old is he? (I'm not buying this West Texas story.)

He said something about life kicking him in the balls. What happened?

There were a few others I threw at him I forget now. I was trying to make Cody's assignment as hard as possible to buy me more time. Cody put the questions in Notes on his phone – with his memory and current condition there's no doubt he wouldn't remember all I wanted to know.

"I'll do my best, Walden, but some of this is personal shit…the getting kicked in the nuts thing? Give me some time and let's see what I can dig up."

We had a good relaxing rest of the day at the lake. Knowing I was a few miles from my place and not that far removed from wiping out a neighbor's mailbox – which I'd left an anonymous envelope in saying *sorry,* with some cash to fix it – I had no interest in driving home blasted, so I tried to have just a few cream ales. Cody's the type that always seems a little buzzed but never appears all that fucked up no matter what he's into. We swam and just laid around in the water on Cody's noodles, the lake water so clear, still nice and cool this time of year.

We talked to the college kids for a while – it's interesting to hear what younger people are thinking these days. It's crazy how Cody can get total strangers to talk to him about anything, although in this case I think they were more interested in scamming some of his weed than anything. I went ahead and joined in a little too – it'd been such a stressful day. I don't partake very often so it hit me pretty good – made me damn thirsty too, so in truth I had a few more cream ales than I should have. Watching Cody talk to the girls, who got pretty trashed on their White Claws and his white widow, was hilarious. I loved just sitting back and listening, watching Cody work. He truly thought he had a chance.

Sunsets out there are always majestic and this evening was no different. My intention was to meet Cody after the Yugo appointment and figure out what to do next. I did enjoy my first meeting – I somehow felt better just being around Yugo, being able to let things out. I'd never been around anyone who made it so comfortable to talk about personal stuff without feeling self-conscious. But the truth is by the time I was leaving the lake for home, the Little Kings and a couple of hits had numbed me enough to where I'd successfully pushed most of those thoughts about Yugo into the background – it no longer seemed all that pressing.

As we're walking back to our cars from the lake Cody says to me, "Hey Walden, like I promised, I'll do everything I can to find out more about Yugo, but only if you promise me one thing."

"What's that?"

"No more bottled water, dude, or bottled anything for that matter. Deal?"

I promised and watched Cody slide into his truck.

I stopped off at the sandwich shop to grab something to take home and eat before bed. Less drinking and more consistent meals were the goal, and one out of two wasn't bad. George meets me at the door, barking and running in circles, excited to see me like I'd been gone for weeks. Man do I love that dog – my little brown ball of fur. After flopping on the floor while I gave him a good scratching, pulling on some of his favorite chew toys and playing fetch with his tennis ball, I checked emails while eating. Since I was out of the office most of the afternoon, I was relieved to see only routine stuff had come over – nothing to get excited about. Then I checked the *Chronicle* to see what was happening in the live music scene for the coming weekend.

After finishing off my last bite a thought hit me and I went to Wikipedia and searched "Great Pacific Garbage Patch." To my surprise, it came right up with a significant amount of information. *WTF?* What Cody told me today sounded crazy. So I read through it and yes, Cody was pretty accurate in his description of what some call the "GPGP." Some of his facts were a little off but for the most part, at least if you believe Wikipedia, it's true. Here's what I read at the top:

"Researchers from The Ocean Cleanup project claimed that the patch covers 1.6 million square kilometers *twice the size of Texas*, and three times the size of France. Some of the plastic in the patch is over 50 years old, and includes items such as 'water bottles, baby bottles, plastic lighters, toothbrushes, pens and plastic bags.' Research indicates that the patch is rapidly accumulating. The patch is believed to have *increased 10-fold each decade* since 1945."

Holy shit – increasing 10-fold every ten years? Cody *understated* that. How long before this mass of plastic overtakes the whole ocean? Wikipedia had a long write-up on it with what looked like solid facts from numerous sources. This line also caught my eye: "The U.N. estimates that *only nine percent* of all plastic has ever been recycled."

Why isn't this public knowledge to everybody? Why isn't this taught in schools to children so we can start changing our consumption habits *NOW*? I mean, we hear daily when a Kardashian breaks a fingernail, or Harry Styles is hanging out with somebody new. There's a floating mass of plastic garbage in our ocean *three times the size of France*, and somehow I don't know about it? Where's *60 Minutes*? Maybe this is an indictment on me. Maybe I'm one of the few uninformed people who've never heard about it. But the Great Pacific Garbage Patch needs to be seriously discussed now. Action to stop this "10-fold growth each decade" needs to start *now*. In retrospect, I see why Cody jumped down my throat. I'm actually impressed he's out there trying to make a difference, doing what he can to raise awareness and change people's behavior. It's getting pretty bad when Cody Barringer has become my trusted source for news and information.

FRAZIER IV

OUT TRAVELING HAVING fun the last few weeks. Catching up now on Walden's progress. I like Walden's writing style better than mine. How he lets it flow! I write like a social media nerd. Like a machine gun. Short bursts. I'm back from camping out near Big Bend. I was feeling cabin fever and had to get away. So I hooked up with a few friends, and we lived it up in the great outdoors. It's breathtakingly beautiful out there. Hard to believe that area is part of Texas. So mountainous with such dramatic landscapes. The best thing about being an influencer for a living? You can do it almost anywhere!

An interesting note on Walden's last post. I told him about the Great Pacific Garbage Patch years before his lake outing with Cody. I even did a piece about it on the WaldensPets.com blog. Most pet owners really care about the environment. So I did a series on plastics and recycling. Ideas on how to reuse plastic containers from pet products. Like the huge plastic tubs used for bulk kitty litter. The insanity of the GPGP was featured in my story. Pictures and facts about its unbelievable growth. Motivation to stop the madness.

Obviously, that was a different time for Walden. He wasn't listening then to anything that might hurt sales. I'd asked Walden for some time to stop selling products in plastic. Or at least make environmentally friendly items come up first in search. Today, WP.com always shows non-plastic items first. Almost all single-use plastic products are gone. Before Yugo,

Walden didn't always think about how his actions affected others. How they might affect our environment. Especially actions that seem trivial like drinking bottled water. But when you think about it, how many people actually do, including yours truly. Hey, you have to love Cody and his passion. Crazy dancing bear!

You know a very cool surprise with this project? I'm learning new things too. It means Walden's getting into it because he's never been a "sharer." Reading about things he never told me before means he's opening up. His night after work drinking Everclear margaritas? Crashing into a mailbox in the neighbor's yard? News to me. That explains the "fender bender" he casually mentioned at work. And the rental car he was driving for almost two weeks.

The story about his first meeting with Yugo? I wasn't aware that happened either. At least I didn't know the right timing. Cody told me late that summer Walden finally agreed to go see Yugo. But this first meeting was in late spring that year. I checked with Walden. He confirmed he first met Yugo in May. Then sheepishly admitted he never told me about it. Walden didn't start going to Yugo regularly until September.

Apparently, Walden didn't want Jessica or me on his back. He made Cody swear not to say a word to us about his first meeting. He knew if we knew he'd met Yugo, we'd be all over him to keep going. That was the "old Walden." Think about it. People raved to Walden about Yugo. His first meeting was awesome. His services are free. And he could quit after the first two meetings, no questions asked. What's not to love? And still, he waited almost four months to go back.

Walden blamed Cody for taking so long to get back with answers to his questions. Cody says it wasn't easy getting those answers. It was hard finding people who knew anything. Harder still to get them to talk. Cody also said it was tough to tell the BS from the truth. Lots of hearsay. Cody claims it only took about a month to get back to Walden. That leaves three months for what? But all that doesn't matter. What matters is Walden made it!

Another thing I realized rereading previous chapters. I forgot to chime in on his comment about Felicia. I haven't thought about her in years. Felicia's at least four years older than me, seven or eight years older than Walden. She was one of the older girls who showed me the ropes at Nueva Tierra. His predator reference raises my radar. Felicia was wild and a flirt. She knew she was pretty and used it to get her way. She teased the men and boys when she felt like it.

And I hate to admit this. She taught me early on how a girl can use her looks to get her way. How a glance or an action can create a stir. That many men think with the head in their pants, not the head on their shoulders. I've always been a tomboy. How can I not be growing up in a commune in the woods? But truth is, I used Felicia's tricks some to get my way. Sometimes still do now. I asked Walden what happened with Felicia. He's got me very curious. But he said he doesn't want to talk about it, so I won't pry.

Felicia's family was on what Father called the "other side of the fence" at Nueva. As I said before, Father was a leader in the community. A Founding Father. He and four others had the idea for starting Nueva Tierra, but in my mind he was the real leader. Studying *Walden Two* and other utopian books convinced them that a community based on applied behavior analysis could work. I haven't read *Walden Two* in years. But I do remember thinking after reading it that Father resembled the Frazier character in that book. Serious, more dedicated to making things happen than the others. Highly driven, super smart. He viewed our community as an important test case. A test to see if there was a better way for people to live together in harmony.

I saw Walden referencing Wikipedia. I use it a lot too for my blogging. This from Wikipedia states the philosophy Father and the other founders used:

"*Walden Two* embraces the proposition that the behavior of organisms, including humans, is determined by environmental variables, and that systematically altering environmental variables can generate a sociocultural system that very closely approximates utopia.... The community encourages its members 'to view every habit and custom with an eye to possible improvement' and to have 'a constantly experimental attitude toward everything.' The culture of *Walden Two* can be changed if experimental evidence favors proposed changes."

So, Father and his friends tested all kinds of things to see if they increased the happiness, productivity, and efficiency of Nueva. Then, they changed up processes and procedures based on those experiments. It was like living in a human petri dish. Everyone was encouraged to find their own special skills and talents. Then to excel at those talents. We all felt useful. Everyone worked toward the common good. We felt obligated to do our part. The betterment of the whole society was our goal. That and living in harmony with nature.

We all knew the importance of preserving our natural resources. To be healthy people we had to maintain a healthy environment. And the result of Father and his friends' experiment? People were happy and the community thrived. Many of the artificial stresses of the "real world" went away. Materialism was almost nonexistent. Everything was owned by the community. The land, the structures, the food sources, the animals. Most residents owned little more than the vehicle they arrived in, some clothes and a few furnishings. And the quality of life was amazing!

Father and his friends weren't the only ones with utopian dreams for a better world. There were other communities like Nueva Tierra that sprouted up around this time. Walden Seven in Michigan, Los Horcones in Mexico, Sunflower House in Kansas. Those are a few I remember. They were created, I'm sure, with a similar model to Nueva's. Founded on the principles laid out by Skinner in *Walden Two*. I know about them because Father invited people from there to visit. They sometimes stayed in our home. He and his friends visited the other places too. Always looking for new ideas. He loved Los Horcones, loves visiting Mexico.

Reading more about *Walden Two* on Wikipedia, I came across one aspect Walden didn't like about our little paradise:

"The community also dissolved the nuclear family through placing the responsibility of child-rearing in the hands of the larger community and not just the child's parents or immediate family."

Walden adored Father and Mary growing up, as did I. But he didn't think so highly of all the adults in Nueva. When another adult tried to discipline Walden or teach Walden, he didn't take to it well. Walden wanted his parents, not Nueva's community approach. Now Nueva wasn't hardcore like the book. Kids weren't raised from infants in a community learning center like in *Walden Two*. We lived with our parents. But the responsibility of parenting and teaching all children, not just your own, was engrained in our community. I love Mary and Father dearly. But for me, I understood the logic of spreading child rearing amongst the whole community. We were very fortunate. We had good parents. Some of the kids did not. This at least gave all children a better chance to grow up healthy. To be loved and well taken care of.

Which leads me to the "other side of the fence" as Father called it. Communes were still a big thing at this time. The hippy lifestyle had spread across the country for many years. And Nueva Tierra had many things going for it that attracted people. A beautiful location near the West Coast. Incredible resources. The land, the water, the wildlife. And a great infrastructure from the hard work of Father and the founders. Combine that with an open, loving, communal culture. A culture respectful of all people. Respectful of nature. It eventually became a people magnet. Once a few of what Father considered hippies caught wind of Nueva, word spread like wildfire. And the people came.

Now let me be clear. To most people, Father back then would be considered a hippy. Hippydom is in the eye of the beholder. But Father was all about creating The Great Society, not having a party. That was the difference. Over time Nueva attracted as many people interested in peace, love, and partying as in building a community based on applied behavior analysis. Music in the hills, festivals, and good weed became more important to some than social experiments and a scientific approach for the greater good.

And Felicia's parents were on "the other side of the fence." They were the peace, love, and party type. And Felicia? She was a wild child, truly raised by the community. Although her family all slept under the same roof, you couldn't tell who her parents were. They seemed more like older friends than parents. Felicia said her mom was seventeen when she was born. Walden called her two little brothers "wild animals." Let's just say she was a trip.

At first there were strict requirements to get into Nueva. That ensured Father and the founders' experiment had the right people to build this new society. But finding dedicated, like-minded people willing to work hard for a better world was always a challenge. It became harder as the culture in the country changed. Over time, to help Nueva grow, community votes were held. Some of Father's strict requirements to live at Nueva were overturned.

Father said when entry requirements and expectations were relaxed, a slow, inevitable decline began. And it ate him up. Ultimately, this division of purpose led to the demise of Nueva Tierra. Father saw it coming sooner than others. He realized without an intense and uncommon focus, maintaining a *Walden Two* model that worked was impossible.

So, when I was sixteen, we Harrisons packed our belongings in a trailer behind our van. We grabbed our two dogs and headed south to Central Texas. To the cypress lined rivers and clear spring-fed creeks around Wimberley. Far different than the rainforests of Washington, but truly beautiful too. I still keep in touch with some friends from my childhood home. Nueva Tierra lasted a few more years after we left. There's no doubt we could have lived there longer. I'm sure until I left for college. But things happen for a reason. I feel blessed I could experience my childhood there.

But I'm also glad we moved to Texas when we did. There's no doubt it was very hard for Father to walk away. But it was good for me, and it was even better for Walden.

Mary never said it out loud, but she was okay with the "other side of the fence." Father knew this too. As the peace and love people came to Nueva, Mary welcomed them. Father usually stayed with the founders. He wanted to change the world. But Mary loves music and the arts. She liked chilling on the hillside, playing songs, singing, talking to newcomers. While not significant, I could sense tension as the decision to move was made. You know. How a kid can feel it when your parents' relationship is strained.

Truth is, Mom worked as hard as anyone at Nueva. She was a focal point at the school. A head teacher and a community leader. But she also loved relaxing when the work was done. Father watched each new member from a distance first to size them up. Mary simply welcomed everyone with open arms.

One thing you can say about Father and Mary. They sure knew where to put roots down. I loved the great Northwest. Loved the Hoh Rainforest. The gardens, the waterfalls, the massive trees. Loved driving into Forks for burgers at Sully's. But I love so many things about the Texas hill country too. The huge cypress trees along the creeks are truly magical. What great places to grow up! So, there's a little more about our family.

Walden is relieved he's at the Yugo part now. But I warned him. Writing about the Way will be the hardest part. He seems to think it's as simple as transcribing his recordings. Maybe so, but I doubt it. The way people talk isn't always so easy to read. I'll help him of course, when he asks. Here's to a few more surprises!

YUGO II

"Randy Described Eternity" by Built to Spill (*Perfect from Now On*)

FIRST OFF, it wasn't four months before going back to see Yugo, it was just over three, and when you factor in it took Cody over a month to get back to me with answers, it's more like only two months. Also, a quick comment. Frazier's note on leaving Nueva shows how differently we remember things. Her quote about Mary's preference for the hippy element at Nueva was that she never said "anything out loud" about it – that Sis could sense tension between Father and Mary, but they never vocalized anything.

My memory is Father and Mary argued about who she hung out with all the time. And Mary sometimes chided Father about his "stick in the mud" friends who were too serious for their own good. Mary was open about her love for the songfests in the hills, open about her more laid-back approach to life than Father, loved welcoming newcomers to Nueva no matter who they were. The move to Texas was totally Father's idea – Mary was quite against it at first. She loved Nueva Tierra and didn't have a problem with how things were evolving there.

I can still feel the friction in the van that day we drove away from our home deep in the woods of Washington for the last time. What a crazy day that was for a kid. The thrill of adventure and something new, combined with the fear of change, the anxiety of moving to Texas which sounded so wild, so *country* – plus the worry that Father and Mary were fighting. Frazier, our mutts, and I just hung on for the ride, and what a ride it was getting down there – over 2,400 miles and more than five days driving through every kind of terrain and weather you can imagine.

Frazier is right though about the two different factions emerging at Nueva Tierra eating Father up. He believed that after years of hard work and determination, he and the founders had developed, then scientifically proven, a viable alternative to the "rat race" of normal society. Maybe not a utopia, but a system of living with more cooperation, more happiness, more joy and love than in the real world. And then, he felt it all slowly slipping away. He knew the legacy he hoped to build would not survive. It took a strong man to just up and drive away from creating something like Nueva Tierra from scratch. Something he built with years of service, perseverance, brains, and intuition. And Frazier is also right about the move to Texas being good for us in the end – all of us – Mary included. She grew to love it here.

I want to get to Yugo's part of the story now, even though there's some loose ends out there like the questions Cody was researching for me. I'll get into his findings soon, but to summarize, the answers he came back with did nothing to dissuade me from going to see Yugo again. It's true it took some time to get my ass in gear and surrender to the fact I needed help. And the events that crazy night with Jessica – I'll get to that part too eventually – finally gave me the push I needed to send Yugo another email. My message to Yugo apologized for the long delay getting back to him. It stretched the truth a bit, which I now realize I do all the time, and blamed my busy schedule – needing to watch after my folks, being swamped at WP, yada, yada, yada. I'll admit I was concerned Yugo might reply not to bother coming back since he made it clear he wanted dedicated "students" who promised to do the work. But it turns out he wasn't negative at all. He was encouraging and seemed happy to hear from me. He mentioned again we could meet together for two sessions with everything casual and open, and if I didn't feel comfortable where things were going, we'd shake hands and say goodbye.

It felt good going back to Omelettry Lane to see Yugo, like I was finally taking an important step moving my life's direction down a better path.

Walking into the bustling restaurant, I took in the scene, soaked in the wonderful smells of breakfast, and checked with a waitress to make sure it was cool for me to walk up to see Yugo. She smiled and waved it was all clear, and I headed up the stairs for my first *real* session. His office was unchanged since my first visit other than the windows were closed – it was September so too hot outside for that. His bike was leaning up against the wall in the front room, meditation pillows stacked, fans blowing to help the A/C cool things off. I tapped lightly on the frame of Yugo's open office door and heard a casual, "Hey, Walden. Come in. Come in, my friend."

Entering his office I was welcomed by his warm smile, his clear, calming eyes, the soothing vibe. He was in a Carolina blue plain t-shirt, but the khaki shorts and worn sandals looked like the same ones he was wearing months ago. He extended a hand, offered me a seat, and from there began powerful sessions for me that ultimately transformed my life. Being self-conscious about taking so long to come back, I sat down and explained why it took a while to reach back out – to sort of apologize for holding things up. But before getting too far, Yugo held up his hand and stopped me. "Walden, it doesn't matter what kept you from coming here then, or what brought you back here today. What matters is that you're here now, and that you're truly ready to *listen*."

I must put this out to you too. Frazier was also right about this part not being easy to write. I went back and listened to the first couple of sessions I recorded with Yugo. It wasn't the first time I've replayed our meetings, but it was the first time I did it with the intention of writing his wisdom down for others to read. I realized some of our conversations were geared to my personal situation. To questions I asked specifically to help me based on my problems at the time – my personal experience. The good news is the Way is all here, but the bad news – it's not as easy as me typing out the recordings and calling it a day.

Yugo has clear steps that are universal for everybody, although he didn't like calling them steps because he says that rips off AA. I'll obviously share all of these. Frazier's social media posts, which will come up later, also helped. But the main problem is people don't talk like they write. What's clear and understandable in a conversation sometimes reads like crap when you put it down on paper. My promise to you is I did the best I could to present the Way as it was spoken to me, and Frazier of course helped. I've added some notes from memory of the non-verbal communication going on, so you get a feel for how things were flowing. And Yugo sometimes used "air quotes" with his fingers, so when you see quotation marks in his dialogue, that's from me remembering those.

Yugo's email confirming our appointment said other than "occasional words of wisdom" he hands out, there's no published materials, guidebooks, or literature for our time together. He said he's ok with me recording our sessions "for future reference" if I want to. He said some people like having an audio record to go back and revisit. Some don't want any documentation of what was shared in such a personal and possibly "vulnerable environment." I took that to mean some people don't want hard audio proof of some of the shit they've done floating around. He added students are encouraged to bring a notebook to write down thoughts or feelings that resonate during sessions, to list questions they have about his philosophy so they aren't lost during the discussion.

Yugo always starts our meetings with a "counseling session," asking me how things are going in my life, getting me to open up about what's bothering me, my challenges and problems – learning where I need a push, some help or advice. For the most part, I've left out all the counseling sessions – you don't want to read that shit. Then he moves on to the steps, or *elements*, that are part of the Way. That's what is transcribed here. Usually he goes over one element in a session, sometimes two. Then, we always close with a twenty-minute sit together in silence.

Because many of my personal questions, rambling responses, and whining about life's challenges aren't relevant to getting Yugo's Way out, you won't see a whole lot of dialogue from me. This is as pure as I can get it. After a little small talk, this is how it all started on session one – there's a few ground rules he covers first:

YF: Ok, you recording now? It's on?

WH: Yep, it's on. All set.

YF: Ok, let me say this again about recording. You remember my email?

WH: Sure, the one that said you're cool with recording these sessions?

YF: Even if you think you won't say anything incriminating here, you never know. People take things differently. Something you say that seems harmless to you now could really hurt or piss off somebody close to you. I strongly suggest after each session you download the audio off your phone to a thumb drive you keep under lock and key – clean it off your phone asap. That way there's less chance you'll lose it too, that it gets erased or something.

WH: Good idea – got it. I don't think anyone cares what I'm saying here anyway.

YF: You never know. First, I want to be clear why we're meeting together. Why I do what I do. What I feel I am *called* to do. I'm here to evolve people's way of being. To change their actions and thoughts to be in love for other people, in love for our planet, and in love for all of creation. (*Wide smile – I mean, really wide smile.*)

WH: Ummm, ok.

YF: I've come to realize my primary purpose is to assist in the evolution of humanity toward consciously chosen love. That's where my life's experiences and events, and where the Grand Universe has brought me today.

WH: .....

YF: Walden, you ever been to an AA meeting?

WH: Uh, nope... (*I'm caught off guard by this.*) I mean, I know I said something about drinking too much and all when we first met, but I don't think it's really a *problem* – you know, like I'm an alcoholic that's drinking every day or...

YF: Yeah, sorry. I didn't mean it that way...like you had a problem and needed to go to AA. It was kind of a rhetorical question. Why I asked is to find out if you knew what kind of language flies around at those meetings?

WH: Language? What do you mean?

YF: I've heard some of the most spiritual, inspired, life changing shit in all my life at AA meetings. Incredible wisdom from people who've seen the very depths of darkness...literally at death's door. You want to hear wisdom? You want to hear truth, honesty, and a way out? Don't go to church, man. Go to an AA meeting. It's raw, it's real, and the shit works.

WH: Ok?

YF: But the reality is the language at AA meetings is blue as hell. F-bombs flying around the room, mother f'ing this and mother f'ing that. Sweet looking old ladies with mouths of sailors. That's what happens when people try to find the right words to describe real emotional *pain* – to somehow find words that convey how *low they felt*. Sometimes the only words that suffice, the only ones that even come close to describing the hell you've been through, are raw, filthy, hard. Sometimes that's all that will do.

WH: (*Surprised by this opening line of dialogue.*) Ummm, ok...

YF: So that's why my language is sometimes raw. It's influenced by the rooms of AA. It rubs off on you. That and growing up hard. And, some of what we talk about needs raw words to get across the most meaning, to get the ideas I share to *sink in*. Some people are surprised, even put off by that. They hear I'm a spiritual teacher or philosopher, and when I let an f-bomb fly they cringe and think, what the hell?

WH: (*I smile while he's saying this. It doesn't mean shit to me, but I wasn't expecting a foul-mouthed guru.*)

YF: I know, I know. I'm working on it. Sometimes there are better words to use than profanity. Sometimes I'm just lazy. I'm better now than when I started, and if you're turned off by it, I can consciously stop it. But my message loses a little juice...know what I mean? So, you cool with a few expletives every now and then, or should I focus and leave them all out?

WH: Cussing doesn't bother me none. My language isn't the best either. I mean, I try not to use the p-word or the c-word, things like that, but keep it real. Give me whatever the best words are that's gonna help me out the most.

YF: Cool. I like to get that out of the way first. I had a lady come see me in the early days. Unconsciously I swore right up front and she looked at me like I was Satan. Me saying what she considered bad words meant I was a *really* bad person. That's all it took for her to turn me off, to shut down. It was all my fault. Never saw her again, but it was a great lesson. Now I always ask first. I'll put my language settings on moderate (*laughs*).

WH: (*Laugh a little nervously.*)

YF: Some people say I don't sound much like a mystic or guru, and I like that better than being called a blowhard – one who uses flowery language trying to impress. As I said on your first visit, you won't hear a lot of theological dogma or religious high-brow shit from me. I try to keep it real. Understandable. Not too many parables or underlying meanings coming out of here. (*Points to his heart.*)

WH: (*Slight smile and nod.*)

YF: And that leads to my next point about *words*. One thing to remember as we talk. Words are only pointers that lead the mind to think in certain directions. Words are not hard reality. Why? Because they can hold such different meanings to different people. When you hear the word *police*, it probably means something different to you than to a Black dude living in south Chicago. When you hear the word *hungry*, it means something totally different to you than to a single mom of three living in the slums of Juarez. If you're a devout Muslim and you hear the word

Muhammad, it probably means something different to you than to a Christian living in Nebraska. Words are *pliable* because people's experiences with words can be so different. And it's not just the intellectual meaning of words. It's the *emotional* response you feel inside that certain words create. Hearing the word *rain* brings a very different feeling emotionally to a farmer in Iowa than to a businessman taking clients to a ballgame at Yankee Stadium. See what I mean? Yes, there's standard definitions for words in the dictionary, but they can have different meanings and emotional responses in people based on your culture, your upbringing, your environment.

WH: Yeah, I get that...makes sense. How you understand words depends on your experience with those words – like how you were raised, where you live.

YF: Right! And I'm telling you this now because what we're gonna be talking about are *ideas*. Possibly new ideas to you. And I don't want you to get too hung up on certain words. They're a starting place, they are necessary to get a point across, but they aren't *hard*. A good example, there's a word that's been a lightning rod for anyone talking about spirituality since the beginning of time, and that word is *God*. In a book by Anne Lamott, someone said, "God is the worst nickname ever," and I think that's true! Why do we focus on that one word to describe the Ultimate Being when there are so many cultural variations? Say the word *God* to people from different religions, and they each have different mental pictures in their head. Sometimes that image is a white male sitting on a throne with a stern look on his face. Oftentimes not. Bottom line, that one word, *God*, has many different meanings depending on your culture, worldview, or your faith. I say all this to you now so you know. When I say a term like *Higher Power* instead of saying *God*, insert in whatever word works for you for the Supreme Creator. Cool?

WH: Yeah, I see what you mean. I'm with you. *God* is a word most people define as their God *only* – the one they believe in. So when you say Higher Power, I should relate to whatever my conception is for God.

YF: Yes! So while I may say the word *God* from time to time, I don't like to use it often. There's too much baggage. Instead I'll use terms like Universal Creator, Ultimate Being, or Higher Power. The Great Spirit or Great Mystery is the English translation for Wakan Tanka – words some indigenous people use for God. Love that imagery. Or sometimes I'll use a personal favorite, The Divine Energy of the Universe. But the important thing to remember is they are all words pointing to the same thing, if you get my drift – to the same *Ultimate Being*, whatever your faith. I don't want to alter who or what you consider your Higher Power.

WH: Got it – works for me.

YF: Because when we're talking about *God*, unless you're an atheist who doesn't believe the definition of that word exists, we're all talking about the same *entity* although our names may be different. We're talking about the Creator of our Universe. The Absolute *Uncreated*, the Everlasting Divine Energy on this planet and beyond. The Supreme Being we look to for guidance, support, love, forgiveness, inspiration, healing.

WH: Absolute Uncreated, huh? That's an interesting one. Ok, I think I get it.

YF: Beautiful – that's important. And one other note on words. You'll find I use the word *consciousness* at times, but some students tell me that's a word that makes their eyes glaze over, like the word *cosmos*. If that's true for you, when I say *consciousness*, like we need to increase our consciousness, try substituting the word *awareness*. That word's more relatable to people for some reason and they're close enough in meaning to get the idea.

WH: Think I'm more an "awareness" kind of guy too…

YF: Ok, next. Please remember I'm here to help you, Walden. To listen to what's going on in your life, to be a sounding board for you to unload the shit that's keeping you stuck. A resource to open up to about relationships, fears, anxieties, addictions, obsessions, depression, questions, whatever. That's our main focus, right? Getting your head clear and feeling more in the flow of life.

WH: I mean, that's the reason I'm here, yeah. My expectation is to come in and talk about what's bothering me, things I'm struggling with – then hopefully you'll have some good advice to help me cope, to get better at life. Worrying about my business is taking up way too much time. I'm not treating my girlfriend Jessica right, and I know I'm drinking too much. And, I'm hoping like hell you're not just going to say go to AA. That ain't happening. I can get that advice from anybody.

YF: I got you…don't get all stressed out about the AA shit. That had nothing to do with you. So that's how we'll start each session – with a time for you to talk and me to listen and understand your personal situation. Then share insights, some advice, and hopefully some answers. After that, we'll switch gears and I'll talk about ideas, philosophies, and practices that if you do them, will lead to personal growth, more freedom, more happiness, and a stronger feeling of purpose. Eventually most people realize they're getting more out of that part than the counseling sessions. It's those ideas and actions, the actual work, that makes their lives more manageable and helps relieve the insanity.

WH: So, half the time we're together is like counseling with a shrink and the other half is more like school? Or church?

YF: Yeah, sorta. Except calling it school or church is such a drag. How about we call that part "Personal Transformation toward Light" (*huge smile*)? Or you can call it what I call it which is the Way. This is the *work* you will need to do. Some elements of the Way are philosophical, spiritual, even cosmic, and some are just practical ways to have a longer, healthier life.

WH: (*Keeping my options open.*) Ok. That's the part you said we'll go over some in our first couple of meetings, and if I'm not buying what you're saying I can call this all off, right?

YF: Right. Today we cover the basics, but we'll get to one element of the Way, so you get a feel. You said you meditated some back in your days as a kid growing up, right? You said you lived in a commune? I'm interested in hearing more about that sometime.

WH: Yeah, it was a place up in northwest Washington called Nueva Tierra, and commune is a good description. You could also call it a social experiment, but that's a longer story. We had what they called "Quiet Time" there that started when kids were about eight – when you were old enough to sit still for a little bit.

YF: So you grew up in the Northwest? Awesome country! I lived up there when I was little – less than two years but I remember all that green. All those trees. It's good you have some meditation experience. I'm surprised how few people have any experience with meditation. We'll close each session with a sit together in silence – usually twenty minutes if that's ok.

WH: I haven't really meditated in years, but I do remember the breathing exercises we'd do, slowing down the head, sitting in silence trying to quiet the mind – I never was very good at it.

YF: We won't put a "good" or "bad" label on our time in the great silence. It is what it is. Positive outcomes *always* come from this practice, whether you know it then or not.

(*Long pause while Yugo takes a drink of water.*)

YF: Before we jump into what's happening with you today, know this. Many of the ideas and philosophies we'll talk about were originally written or spoken by others. I'm just a conduit, taking that wisdom and putting it in today's terms. I'll share ideas and actions I've learned that work – that help people make sense of the human condition and our place in this world. I believe the Grand Energy of the Universe has raised my level of consciousness and raised my state of being so that I can help other people to do the same. But please know, I've been influenced and inspired by many far wiser than me.

WH: Sounds good, Yugo. I'm open to trying almost anything within reason.

YF: And one last thing. When I use life examples to add meaning, I don't like to say "you" do this or "you" do that because that makes people defensive. Like I'm talking about *you*. I also try and stay away from saying "I" do this, or "I" do that, although I do the same unconscious, mechanical shit that I'm stating others do. I try to use the collective word *we* when giving examples because for the most part *we* all act the same. Make sense? Ready to get rolling?

WH: (*A little apprehensive.*) Ok, I think I'm ready...let's do this.

YF: There's a water cooler in the bathroom if you want a drink before we dive in. Cups on the shelf are clean. Then let's hear what you've been up to these last four months...

NOTE: After getting a glass of water, I spend the next half hour talking while Yugo listens to what's bothering me today. WP.com things, Jessica relationship things, worries about Father's health and Mary losing her mind. I'll spare you the details. Just know Yugo listens intently, he takes in everything – and he asks the right questions to get me to realize that some of what I'm saying doesn't match what I'm truly *feeling* inside. That I'm creating a false picture of myself, putting forth an image, playing a role to Yugo even in therapy. He says awareness of this is *huge* and he helps me feel better. Then we go to his first step, or I should say first *element* of the Way.

YF: The first element is a core idea, a core understanding, that intertwines with all the other elements, and it is this: We are all primarily *spiritual* beings, first and foremost. That's easy to say, but hard to really believe because we live our lives so much in the physical realm – with our senses. We hear that we're spiritual beings and shake our head yes. But our actions don't show we *really believe* this. We see, we taste, we feel, we smell, we hear, we screw. It's all physical reality around us. This is what gets our attention because it's so obvious. Our physical well-being gets all the attention. But taking care of our *spiritual condition*, our consciousness, is the *most important thing* – nothing else comes close. Think about it,

Walden. We spend hours and hours every week, thousands of dollars a year, working out our physical bodies. Hitting the gym, going for a run, taking an exercise class, jumping on the bike. But rarely do we take even five minutes out of any day to work out our spiritual bodies. It's so out of balance. Do you work out, Walden?

WH: Well usually, yeah. I have a routine. I fall off and miss a few days, but I try to work out at least four or five times a week. I like to run with my dog, do some weights, bike. Sometimes I work out every day when I'm in that phase, you know, trying to get some weight off.

YF: Right. And how much time do you spend a day working out your spiritual body? Praying? Meditating? Journaling? Using the power of self-observation and self-awareness to consciously get to know your true self better?

WH: Not much really…to be honest hardly any time at all.

YF: Welcome to the party, dude. You're just like everyone else. We spend almost *zero* time on our spiritual condition, especially when compared to the time we spend on our physical condition. And this doesn't stop with working out. Look at how much time we spend on our *physical appearance*. Doing our hair, putting on makeup, trimming the beard, dressing the way we think other people will like, buying the right clothes. It takes a lot of time, man.

WH: I guess it is a little crazy when you compare the two – how much time we spend on physical looks and physical fitness versus our spiritual fitness.

YF: The difference, once you're conscious of it, is eye-opening. It takes very little introspection to see it's true. Now listen. Here's the reason why what I'm saying is so important. Our physical bodies are only temporary. We're physically on this Earth for a very short period of time. As the saying goes, our life on this planet goes by in the blink of an eye. But Walden, that's where we humans focus *all* our attention. Remember this…

YF: (*He pauses, clasps his hands, and stares into my eyes.*) We are primarily spiritual beings, so focusing on our spiritual wellness and our *spiritual evolution* is the most important thing. Why? Because our spirit is **eternal**. Stay with me here, Walden. We are, inside of our temporary phys-ical "shells," *eternal beings*. When you look at life in this way, what happens in our external world, our physical world, becomes not all that important. It's not something to get so wrapped up in. The external life that's happening around you is mostly irrelevant other than those events that happen to help you *evolve your Being*, to raise your consciousness, to develop your internal spirit.

WH: So you're saying there's no sense getting so worked up about the crazy shit going on around me, the things outside of my control, because they're so temporary that in the big picture it doesn't really matter?

YF: Exactly! Now, I'm not saying something like relationships are unimportant, because they are important. We are here on this planet as relational beings, to help others. I'm also not saying how we live our lives is unimportant. Doing life well is important to our spiritual evolution – it helps us learn, helps us grow, also helps others. But most people are focused on the wrong things, material things, the physical realm, and always have been. It's all about our *spiritual development*, not what happens in the little blip of our physical existence here on Earth. How does what happens during our seventy-five brief years on this floating blue ball compare with preparing for all *eternity*?

WH: I thought you weren't going to talk about religious dogma – things like eternal life and heaven and all.

YF: Ahh, good comment. I'm not talking about religion – about heaven per se here, Walden. I'm saying we are all spiritual beings, awareness or consciousness if you will. Energy at our core. You can sit in silence and *feel* it. That spark, that energy. We know through thermodynamics that energy cannot be created or destroyed. It simply changes states. There are many thousands of people who've had documented out of body experiences who've come back after death. And it's a reality these experiences are reported by people from *many* different religious faiths and backgrounds. When the physical body dies, its energy, its spirit, moves on.

WH: (*This piques my interest. What happens when we die has always intrigued me.*)

YF: But I'm not gonna tell you what happens long term after our physical death. I have no idea, and anybody that says they know for sure is lying to you. No one has, as they say, been there and done that long term (*wide grin*). But it's cool you pointed out I may be talking shit so soon. As we talk together, always take what you want and leave the rest. There may be things I say you simply can't agree with, and that's cool. The truth is there are two leaps of *faith* I ask my students to take for this Way to have the most meaning. One is that there is a Universal Presence, an Ultimate Creator out there who is far greater than us, and two, that human beings have a soul, a spirit. Most people I share with are ok with that, and surprisingly, some atheists are cool with what I present in the end too. It just might not have as much juice.

WF: Well, I've always thought there's some entity overseeing things, something that created this Earth, this universe. And I can tell you for certain I know there's a soul in this body – that I'm spirit. All that takes for me is being alive, feeling my emotions, knowing the real me is in here somewhere (*pointing to my heart*).

YF: Good, good. Now back to the primary idea. Back to why what I said about improving our spiritual health is so vitally important. Have you ever really thought about the concept of "eternity," Walden? About what the idea of eternity *really* means?

WH: No, not really. I can't say I've ever really thought about it. I guess when I think of the word *eternity*, I think it means "forever," but that's kinda vague, huh?

YF: Very few sit down and really *contemplate* the true meaning and implications of eternity. I know my head could never get around it other than thinking it's a *really* long time. Then I was turned on to this song by Built to Spill. Doug Martsch is the leader of the band, and supposedly, some dude he knew had a youth group teacher growing up who'd use a similar story to put fear in kids' hearts about spending eternity in hell. Now I don't want to do *that*! For our purposes, it's a cool tune that helps us visualize the concept of eternity better than any philosopher ever could. Makes me understand why getting worked up about all the petty shit that happens to us every day doesn't matter so much. Check this out.

Yugo picks up this beautiful, varnished wooden box that's on the floor under his chair, opens it, pulls out a small slip of paper, and hands it to me. This must be some of his "words of wisdom." I look at it and he says, "Read it, out loud."

A little caught off guard by this, self-conscious, I start slowly and read:

"Randy Describes Eternity" by Built to Spill (written by Doug Martsch)

Every thousand years
This metal sphere
Ten times the size of Jupiter
Floats just a few yards past the Earth
You climb on your roof
And take a swipe at it

With a single feather
Hit it once every thousand years
'Til you've worn it down
To the size of a pea
Yeah, I'd say that's a long time
But it's only half a blink in the place we're going to be.

WH: *(Somewhat mesmerized.)* Wow…that does help you visualize, maybe even quantify a little. Shit……kinda trippy.

YF: *(Smiling.)* Right? The human mind usually can't imagine that shit. We can't even comprehend thirty years from now. You should hear the tune too man, it's wild. Check it out before we get back together again.

WH: I've heard of the band, heard a few of their songs actually. I'll check it out.

YF: Beautiful! So, Walden. Here's the take-away idea, ok. Eternity is a long ass time if you buy into one of my leaps of faith and to what most religions teach. That our souls are *eternal*. But instead of focusing on growing our spirit, on increasing our consciousness, humanity worries about the external things that happen here on Earth. The pursuit of money, fame, power, popularity, sex, the rat race. The average lifespan on our planet, about eighty years, isn't one-tenth of the time it takes for that sphere to come by so you can get up on your roof with a feather and swipe at it just one time! We all have to *wake up*, man, to become more conscious of our spiritual, internal health and focus on what's really important. *If just five percent of people started doing that today, think of the positive impact we'd see on our planet, in our families and communities!* Less materialism, less worry and stress, more love, more consciousness of what really matters, more care for Mother Earth, more honesty and openness.

WH: I'm with you, Yugo. Makes all the sense in the world to me.

YF: I'm not saying the physical part doesn't matter at all, but I am saying we need to recalibrate the balance, and in a major way. You with me?

WH: I'm with you…

The Practice

YF: Ok, for your first practice, your first assignment over the next two weeks till we meet again. I call these *practices* because that's what we're doing. Practicing, like learning to play an instrument or getting better at a sport. I want you to spend at least thirty minutes a day doing something purely for your spirit – working out your spiritual body. Some suggestions: Take a walk by yourself in nature. Start the day by saying a prayer of thanks to your Higher Power, and ask for strength to treat others and yourself with love and compassion. Find a daily meditation book and do a reading each morning. Sit in silence and just *be*, quieting the mind and feeling the energy of your spirit inside of you. Thank your Creator at night before bed for keeping you alive today and blessing you. Maybe keep a gratitude notebook to help remember when something hits your consciousness that you are *truly grateful* for. It doesn't matter what you do, or when you do it. Just make sure to set aside the time to work out your spiritual body at least thirty minutes a day. Doesn't have to be all at one time. Break it up and do multiple small things if you want. And one more thing, Walden. Do your best – every damn day. Got it?

WH: Yep I got it. I'll probably do something in the morning before I hop out of bed, maybe close the day with a walk in nature, a little quiet time. Only thirty minutes though? I was expecting something more than that.

YF: The purpose of these practices is to change your being, change your thinking, but they have to be reasonable or you'll never stay with it. Trust me, if you're doing no spiritual work now, thirty minutes will seem hard at first. As we work together, hopefully that time grows on its own. Here's what works for me. I'm pretty good at working out my physical body every day. I've trained myself so every time I work out, the thought comes into my head, "Yugo, have you worked out your Spiritual body today?" I usually do a sit in the mornings right after getting out of bed, and again at night before going to sleep. Then try my best to stay conscious and present during the day. We'll talk more about that later. The key is, like I stressed before, you have to *do the work*! My suggestion is to track it, prioritize it. If you don't, your mind that's so stuck in the physical realm will put spirit work on the backburner. I guarantee you that.

Yugo gets up and grabs a couple of meditation pillows and throws them on the floor, I'm assuming for our closing twenty-minute sit in silence that he talked about. He looks over at me with a bright smile.

YF: Ok, Walden, you good? I don't want to hear any bullshit about you being too busy and not doing the work next session. Cool?
WH: Cool....

This is the 1st element of Yugo's Way:

We are primarily Spiritual Beings who live on for all eternity. Take time each day to work out your spiritual body, strengthening your eternal, internal Being.

BJ II

REMEMBERING the beautiful actress obviously flirting with him at lunch with the entertainment division, Brett Jezak smiles to himself. He has come a long way from that awkward, unathletic kid who was teased unmercifully on the playground. Growing up in Florida, sports was king, especially football. Brett realized early in life that his physical abilities would lead him nowhere. The futility of his game in the schoolyard, be it soccer, basketball or even kickball, was quickly recognized by all. As for football, Brett knew better than to even try.

This and his appearance, not necessarily offensive but simply different, made him a prime target for bullies and tough guys at school who, as usually happens, were athletes. Brett spent time most days thinking to himself that one day these idiot jocks would all be working for him, would be dreaming they could be like him, would be kissing his ass once he built his business empire. He'd heard other brainy, chess club type kids make similar statements. He knew most kids considered "nerdy" had this same dream. But in Brett's case, he believed without a doubt it would become true.

His lack of physical skills, coupled with his unorthodox looks, made Brett persona non grata among the girls at school. He was short for his age, had a head simply too large for his body, massive feet for his size, and a duck walk gait that was too much for any youngster to overcome. When he began losing his hair around the age of seventeen, Brett cursed the gods and threw himself even harder into academics; into his business ideas and dreams of starting a company that would one day make him amazingly rich.

While awkward and emotionally harmed by the cruelty of other children, Brett always had supreme confidence in his mental abilities, always knew he was smarter than everyone else in class, even the teacher. As he grew older in his professional life, like a chameleon, he also had the smarts to adapt to his environment. He was quick to give up on the whole hair thing and started shaving his head, way before it was in vogue, especially for white guys. He vigorously studied men's fashion. He focused on changing and upgrading those peripheral elements of his appearance where he had control. But the most important boost to Brett's self-image, by far, was the realization over time that to many members of the opposite sex, money really, really matters. More than hair, more than muscles, more even than Brad Pitt good looks.

Brett stares out at the spectacular views of Mount Hood in the far distance as he daydreams, the sun reflecting off its snowy uppermost peaks. Sahara is really starting to cook. Those long years of hard work, the naysayers biting at him constantly because of low profits, seem behind the company for good. Profits are rolling in. The new divisions, especially cloud computing and web services, are flourishing. The business press now adores him. Brett's thoughts quickly go back to the woman at lunch, the exceptional cleavage she taunted him with, tossing her hair back just so, then giving him that look. This is somewhat new territory for him, but it isn't the first time a girl he knows is way out of his league has come on to him out of the blue. To be honest, his vastly improved options with the ladies, who not long ago would have totally ignored him, is the most tantalizing and adrenalin-inducing perk of his business success thus far.

Suddenly, the thought of Nichole shakes him back to reality and he tries to erase the lustful images swirling in his head. Nichole, his angel from heaven, the first girl to give Brett any hope of a real relationship, his Nichole. They met by chance at the college library, searching for the same book for an economics class. He was attracted to her immediately; to him she was perfection, although it's true at the time most any girl captured his attention. Nichole found Brett different than the other guys around campus, the stereotypical frat boys and jerks looking only to party and get laid. The two chatted briefly in the library and walked out together by accident, bumping into each other again at the exit doors. She was interested in business and economics too, so there was something in common for them to talk about, which eased Brett's awkwardness. She was far more cerebral to Brett than other girls, and he could talk to her about business theory, economics, and investing ideas.

Nichole soon recognized he was highly intelligent and had potential; she didn't mind that he was unsure of himself socially. She could be herself around him, even have the upper hand. The day of that first meeting, walking back to their dorms, she realized this as he fumbled clumsily for the right words to say. Brett was so nervous his heart pounded like it would leap from his chest, but hearing her laugh at his little jokes helped him relax, if only a little. It took a few meetings, some more awkward than others, but Nichole eventually realized Brett's one-track mind, relentless determination, and obvious infatuation with her might lead to a fine husband who one day would become very wealthy.

To Brett, for that first year, he was in shock a girl as pretty as Nichole would even talk to him, much less have sex. In his late teens, the thought occurred to him more than once that it was highly likely he would die a virgin. Through a sheer force of will, he pushed that thought back into the far recesses of his mind, but still it popped up from time and time, greatly depressing him; even Brett couldn't control his thoughts entirely. But Nichole changed all that. The relief Brett felt from avoiding what he considered the terrible fate of unchosen celibacy was indescribable.

Not long after graduation, Nichole and Brett married and fell deeper in love while they chased Brett's vision of creating a company like no other. In the beginning, Nichole was a crucial reason Sahara made it through the bootstrapping phase, doing every task she could to keep the fledgling company from fading away like so many start-ups do. She worked just as hard as Brett; was just as determined to make Brett's dream a reality. While she did everything Brett and the company needed as they struggled to get by in those early days, Nichole eventually knew when it was time to step back; to exit Sahara and leave running the business to Brett.

Over the years, Brett became even more of a workaholic, striving to make money and prove to the world he was a success. And Nichole became the loving, faithful, nurturing wife, always there to support him, to help him on the journey any way she could. Only after many more years of sacrifice would Nichole start to think about pursuing her own dreams. *I really love her*, Brett thinks, knowing that without Nichole to lean on, to share with, to scream out his frustrations and fears with, he would not be where he is today.

But images of the stunning actress flirting with him at lunch come back. They are too strong, and Brett's mind surrenders. His lustful thoughts rage on relentlessly. *She wasn't even wearing a bra. That was obvious when she rubbed her breast against me shaking hands. And she purposely ran her hand down my leg under the table. That was no accident. And that shot she gave me up her dress when she pushed back from the table? That teasing way she glanced at me knowingly, almost winking as she spread her legs? I could almost see all the way up to her panties...if she was wearing any.*

Sweat begins to form on Brett's forehead and upper lip. He feels the heat, then finally realizes he has to clear his mind; has to get back to work. Suddenly he says,

"Hey, Amanda."

"Yes Brett, how may I help you today?"

"Who is the richest man in the world?"

"The richest man in the world is Carlos Slim Helu, the CEO of Telmex, América Móvil and Grupo Carso."

With a painful hard-on and a speeding heart rate, Brett winces, swivels his chair around to the three massive monitors on his desk, and proceeds to pound out a memo on cost-cutting measures in Sahara's Pan-European operations.

WALDEN VI

IT'S a few weeks *before* my first real session with Yugo, before going over that first element, and I'm finally meeting up with Cody after his research mission to find answers about the questions I threw at him – to shed some light on the story of Yugo Free. Sorry this is a little out of order, but I knew I had to get to Yugo's Way, then squeeze in the parts about what was going on in my life where I can. It took Cody over a month to get back to me, but he'd been traveling with work, and my mission required he go out to West Texas where Yugo supposedly grew up. We're meeting at one of our favorite Tex-Mex spots and I'm curious to hear what he's learned.

You might be interested to know that despite his disheveled lumberjack looks and seeming lack of any self-discipline whatsoever, Cody's actually a successful businessman. His Uncle Jack started a small home security installation company years ago, and Cody and his cousin Dwayne helped out doing installations around town. Cody had gone to college for a short time, but came back home when his brief collegiate football career ended *suddenly* (that story's hilarious). Working this security installation gig was supposed to be a temporary thing to bring Cody some cash while he figured out what to do next. But Uncle Jack wasn't a hard worker, and over time he fell into bad health or just got lazier, and he basically let Dwayne and Cody have the company as long as they'd pay him a decent salary while he sat at home and did nothing. It was his form of social security, assuming they didn't screw things up. Dwayne is not a "people person," he hardly says a word around strangers, so he was happy Cody got half the business so he could handle the human interaction parts. Dwayne knew he didn't have the personality or people skills to make much happen on his own. But home security installation and staying on top of the latest technology is his game – he's a master at that.

As you know, Cody loves meeting new people, and early on he made it a point to meet some of the largest custom home builders in the area. The real estate market was booming, and many of the homes they were building were these ridiculous mansions around the lake and out in the hills. These places need high-end state of the art security systems, so Cody positioned their company as the *premium* security systems solution – the one trusted by the truly wealthy. Through schmoozing and partying with them, Cody got the trust of custom builders who'd recommend him to their clients, and before long he and Dwayne were running crews all over Central Texas. It's perfect for Cody. He manages people and relationships, the builders, the clients, the salespeople. And Dwayne handles the technical and operations parts of the business – the installations, the hardware, the cutting-edge security tech, the crews (although Cody helps manage the crews – Dwayne's just not good with people). They're now thinking about expanding into the Dallas-Ft. Worth area, which explains the business travel.

I've ordered a top shelf Herradura and Cointreau margarita, munching on some chips and salsa, almost done with my drink when Cody shows up about fifteen minutes late, out of breath.

"Hey, man, sorry I'm late but Anastasia's leaving town for a few weeks doing some gigs around the state. I wanted to see her before she left."

"No big deal, Cody. I'm just mainlining some tequila and thinking about the intel you're gonna share. How is Anastasia by the way? I haven't seen her in a while."

"Oh, she's great, when I can see her. Playing in a band makes it tough though. Sometimes when I'm off and want to see her, like nights and weekends, she's off doing shows..."

"Well that's a first. You wanting to spend *more* time with a girlfriend. You're the one always bitching about not having any free time to do your own thing."

"Yeah, yeah, I know. It's unstable."

Cody's looking around frantically, searching for a waiter. The restaurant is packed and loud as always. "Anastasia's kind of turned the tables on me, dude, and it feels weird. One reason we're still together is she's so independent. We can each do our own thing. But sometimes I get a little jealous to spend more time with her. I'm starting to see how that feeling can suck."

He's made eye contact with our waiter, who's coming over to the table now. Alejandro has worked here as long as I can remember – well before I started coming around. He's a wise, old gray-haired Mexican that's a familiar fixture – one of the things I love about this place.

"Hola senor," he says to Cody. "Ha pasado un tiempo. Mexican martini and a Bob?"

"Yeah it's been too long Alejandro. Good to see you, man. That's a strong *Si mi amigo* on the drink. Walden, you want a Bob?"

A "Bob" is the crack cocaine of the food world. Think the best spicy queso you ever tasted topped with taco meat, guacamole, pico de gallo, and jalapenos. Their chips are extra thick so they hold up dipping into this crazy addictive goo. Once you start eating it, you can't stop.

"What the hell," I say. "It's a Bob kind a day. Let's have a large Bob, and I'll have another margarita too, Alejandro, while you're at it."

Cody grabs a chip, dips it in the salsa, and looks at me. "How you doing, Walden? Sorry it's taken so long to get back to you. Between the business travel and Anastasia, and trying to run down reputable people to get info on Yugo…it's been a bitch, man."

I tell Cody no big deal, thinking to myself after all, I purposely gave him a long list of questions to buy myself some time.

"How'd the business trip go?"

"Good and bad, Walden. I don't know. There's huge potential out around Dallas. Tons of big expensive new homes going up, and from what we can tell there's not another security system installer out there that comes close to what we can design. But setting up new operations that far away, the added travel, the headaches, hiring new crews? What the hell for? I don't need the money and Dwayne's already busy as hell."

"Yeah, sometimes I think this new 'Go Big or Go Home' mantra is full of shit. Sometimes all I want is for Walden's Pets to just go away so life would be simpler."

"Yeah, I'm thinking simpler is better too. Dwayne's still 60/40 on doing it. I was gung-ho at first until all the travel hit me and I realized how much work it'll take to find good people and get it set up right. Now I'm not so sure. It does make a lot of sense to keep growing, make a dent in the market, then maybe just sell the whole damn thing to one of the bigger security companies in Dallas. Sit on my ass like Uncle Jack. We'll see…"

Our drinks show up and Alejandro drops the Bob on our table with another basket of chips and more salsa – he's a pro. Cody grabs a chip and dives deep in the queso, shoving the whole thing in his mouth, cheese dripping off his beard, and says, "Enough about me and my petty bullshit. Let's talk about my research on your new friend Yugo."

"You dig up anything good? Gotta admit, I'm really curious about this dude."

Then Cody says something sobering, especially coming from him knowing he's already a bit challenged with the truth.

"Now let me throw this out there first, Walden. I did the best I could, man, but it wasn't easy tracking people down that knew or still remembered Yugo. Some folks I could tell were full of shit. If I didn't hear the same story twice, I may have blown it off unless I liked it. Parts are a little gray, there's holes. I hit up the leads from Dylan first and went from there. It was kinda cool though. Like playing detective."

Cody drains his glass in basically one large pull and pours himself another from his silver Mexican martini shaker while I go at the Bob like I haven't eaten in days, one chip after another. He pulls out his phone and opens up Notes. Here's the story from our late lunch that included two more rounds, the Bob, and gorging myself on a *Deluxe Dinner*, their signature combo:

"Yugo's dad was in the Air Force, a highly respected pilot, and the family moved around a lot. Yugo grew up like most military kids, moving from one base to another every three or four years. Because of his skills, his dad was in a Special Units group that did secret reconnaissance missions all over the globe, sometimes gone several weeks or even months at a time. Rumor has it he met Yugo's mom on one of those missions. His dad was stationed all over before moving to Texas." Cody looks down at his phone, squints, and reads, "At McChord Field near Tacoma, Washington, Edwards Air Force Base in California, and Hurlburt Field in the Florida panhandle. When Yugo was around thirteen, his dad got transferred to Dreyfus Air Force Base out in Adeline. One of my contacts was old Air Force and he knew all the bases and shit – worked with Yugo's dad on the base. I couldn't get him to shut up, but all he knew about was the Air Force stuff."

"So *that* explains how he ended up in West Texas. He sure didn't seem like a small-town country dude to me. He's more California surfer cool, you know?"

"Yep, from Washington to California to Florida and finally to Adeline,

Texas...yeehaw! I'm not sure where he was born. Just that he showed up in Adeline around middle school." Cody grabs another chip, smothers it in queso, and munches away.

"That kind of moving can't be easy on a kid. Moving just once was hard enough on me. Can't imagine doing it three or four times."

"No shit, and neither can this. The reason he stayed in Adeline and stopped moving around? His dad apparently died on a mission when Yugo was fifteen. A top-secret kind of thing so no details or explanations about what really happened are out there. My air base source tightened up on this – couldn't get nothing out of him."

"Oh man...to lose a dad that early in life? A father he probably idolized being a pilot and all. I can't imagine. Poor Yugo."

"Yeah, but hold on. I also heard another version. That his dad went sorta crazy from all the missions, from all the stress. That it's one reason he went from being stationed at high profile air bases in nice stops across the country to Dreyfus in the middle of nowhere. I only got this from one source, but he said Yugo told him his old man went nuts and he just bolted. Left everything with his mom, just kissed him goodbye one morning before going to work and never came back. I believed the first version more, maybe because I wanted to. And I did hear that story twice."

"Wow. Either way that's some heavy shit for a kid that age – losing your father, left to live alone in a new place with your mom?"

Cody's dressing up the taco on his salad plate, tossing the guac on top, adding salsa. He continues, "He and his mom weren't alone though. Yugo has a sister, a twin sister actually. MaryAnne is her name. Kind of funny, huh? Marion and MaryAnne. Bet with names like that and twins, those two were *really* close. Heard his sister was an awesome high school athlete, a track and basketball star. Yugo was a bad ass too, but after his dad died, or left, he stopped playing sports. All the coaches were on him to play, but he blew them off and just drifted. From there he kinda dropped out and just hung on through school until he could move away."

"His teenage years sound tragic. Did you find out what brought him here?"

"Apparently if you grow up in Adeline there's two types of people. Those who love it and stay there for life, maybe leave for college and go back to raise a family. And those who hate it – try to get out of there as fast as they can. I hear it's a very conservative, clicky, quirky kind of place. Families living there for generations who think their shit don't stink. You know, small towns and the upper crust who think they're royalty somehow because they've made it in a dump little town."

"So Yugo was one of the haters who wanted out, huh?"

"Exactly, and I don't blame him. Adeline felt like the birthplace of the moral majority to me, and you know my feelings on that shit. The moral majority is *neither*. Trust me, I got my share of *looks* hanging around that town."

"Ha! The thought of you stoned, pounding drinks in a restaurant, getting the little old church ladies antsy cracks me up. And I know your views on the moral majority. Can't say I disagree." I'm cleaning the Bob bowl with my finger now, getting every last drop.

"Walden, I swear, man, there ain't a church on every corner, there's two. And the place is nothing but mesquite trees, flat land, and dirt – some really shitty country. Word is Yugo hated it there. A far cry from California or the other cool places he'd lived. Supposedly on the last day of school his senior year, he left that very day. Story is he went out to New Mexico then Arizona for a while, hiked in the desert, the Arizona Trail. Then up to Colorado for a few years – worked there as a ski instructor and bartender. Not sure why he moved here. Maybe started missing his mom and sister, wanted to be closer to them, Adeline of course not being an option."

"Ok, Cody, tough childhood, lost a father, stuck in a desolate place he hates, leaves as soon as possible to hang out in the desert and then chill out skiing. So what does he do for a living now to make money? How come he doesn't charge for counseling, and how the hell can he afford that office space?"

Cody takes a bite of the enchiladas Alejandro has delivered with our next round of cocktails, wipes his beard with a napkin, and looks at me a little weird before answering.

"Well, the intel I got here seemed really squirrely at first, like it was some kind of movie script or happy horseshit made up story. But being I heard this story in Adeline and I heard virtually the same story from people who know Yugo in Austin, I'm about 84% sure it's true."

"84%, huh? That's a pretty low mark for you Cody. You really think it's true?"

"You listen and you be the judge. Seems possible to me. How else does someone with no apparent revenue stream afford an office at that spot and not charge his patients?"

So here's the story Cody laid out for me: When Yugo was fifteen, he was the star quarterback on the JV football team and led the basketball team in scoring. Cody says if you move in from out of town, you have to be a badass to get playing time in a place like Adeline, especially at QB. After Yugo's dad died (or left), he quit playing sports and started drinking and smoking weed, probably to numb the pain. Apparently, he started dabbling in selling the stuff as he got older. Not as a big-time dealer, but just to make some playing around cash – kind of like us in college. When he went to Arizona and spent time in the desert, things escalated to psychedelics, mushrooms, and such, natural plant-based mind alterers and no hard stuff, but still. Moving to Colorado, skiing and bartending, Yugo found the perfect clientele for his wares, where he led a wild life selling psychedelic contraband to the wealthy while playing on the slopes of Colorado's incredible Rocky Mountains – the life of a ski bum and nature lover some people dream of.

Yugo didn't intend to sell drugs to make big money. He just wanted to cover the cost of his supply, have some left over for the few friends he had, and pay for the exorbitant rents that Colorado ski towns are known for. As the story goes, when the money coming in got larger, Yugo was one of the first on the planet to move to bitcoin to handle some of his transactions so the money couldn't be traced. Many of the wealthy bigwigs coming to town looking for psychedelics were concerned about security, and demanded they be able to pay in "non-traceable currency." Then, something happened and Yugo went off the rails. Cody couldn't get all the details here, but supposedly he was in terrible shape, close to death, so messed up with alcohol he ended up in a rehab far away – like serious six-month type rehab.

So here's the happy horseshit part, but I must say after listening to Cody I might believe it too. When Yugo came out of rehab, he had no clue where his laptop was and he didn't really care. Bitcoin was in its infant stages in 2010 when he started making clandestine transactions with it, and $1 equaled 1300 bitcoins. I know that sounds insane now, but look it up – it's *true*. That means 30,000 bitcoins, which is what Cody heard Yugo had, was worth something like twenty-five bucks back then, so he didn't even think about his bitcoin account. It was meaningless, especially after coming out of rehab clean, sober, and vowing to stay away from using – and especially ever dealing again. Several years later, he found that old computer and while messing around with it discovered his old "worthless" bitcoins that were now worth something like $3,000 *each*. As karma and our fucked-up world would have it, that twenty-five bucks in bitcoin was now worth $90 million – *poof* out of nowhere.

Go figure, but if this *is* true I say bravo, Yugo! Finally, the world smiling on a dude who's had a rough go! Supposedly, once he found his lost laptop and learned the value of his bitcoin, he cashed out. And, an even crazier note I *still* can't get my head around. At the time I'm writing these words, one bitcoin is worth something like $30,000. Meaning, Yugo's wealth, if he had held onto his suddenly found bitcoin fortune, would be worth *$900 million* today. I mean, *WTF*? How can that even be?!?! It makes me wonder how many drug dealers are now multi-millionaires, maybe even billionaires, just because their illegal "industry" was using this untraceable currency way back when. Think about it. Yugo had something like 30,000 bitcoins which equaled under $100 back then. What about all those big-time dealers that had thousands of dollars in bitcoin when it was priced so low? That's worth billions now easy. Again – *WTF*?

"So that's why he doesn't charge for his services, Walden. The dude's loaded. That's how he can afford that office space."

"Well that's one of the craziest stories I ever heard, Cody. A dude getting big time rich out of the blue for *nothing*. Maybe with bitcoin that kind of crazy shit happened more than we know..."

Cody looks pleased with himself. "What can I tell you, Walden. That's the facts as I was told them. Took a helluva lot of work on my end to get this intel, you know."

"I know, Cody, and thank you. Your ace detective work explains most of my questions, but not all of them. Like, how'd he get into counseling – into spiritual work? What happened to send him to rehab? I bet that's what got him to start *growing up*, as he says. And how'd he go from this partying, drug dealing, depressed, traveling nomad dude to maybe the calmest, most put together, *present* person I've ever met?"

Cody is picking up the check this time, putting his credit card down on the tray as he talks. He's such a good dude. "I hear you, Walden, and to be honest, I'm curious to learn more about this dude myself. I'm gonna do more digging and let you know what I learn – also see what Dylan thinks of all this and if he knows anything more. Something brought Yugo back from what sounds like near death from alcoholism. Something happened to turn him into this spiritual guru. Dylan tells me some of the shit Yugo talks about...it blows my mind."

Then Cody gets a serious look on his face and bears down hard on me as Alejandro walks away with his credit card. "One thing you gotta promise me when you start going to see him Walden, and *you are going back to see him.* You gotta share some of his wisdom with me, even more than I get outta Dylan. I've done my part. I did what I promised. Now it's time for you to man up and do what you promised me. Get back in touch with Yugo now and get some help for your sad, sorry ass."

"I think you got a deal, Cody. You've done well, assuming your sources are good and your research is close to accurate. One thing I do know. Wikipedia won't have anything on this for me to do a quick fact check."

"Wikipedia? What's that got to do with any of this?"

"Nothing, Cody. Just thinking out loud…"

And by now you know the sad, sorry truth here. It still took me a couple of months before I went back to see Yugo, before I set off on my journey to elevate my way of thinking. I don't know exactly why or what I was looking for – I mean, what else did I need?

YUGO III

Your rebirth will begin when you can see
A way to elevate your way of thinking how it should be
A higher conscience is all you need to set you free

"A Simple Aspiration" by the Sadies (from *New Seasons*)

MY FIRST REAL meeting with Yugo had gone better than expected. I left feeling uplifted, a little lighter, like I'd left a load of garbage behind – and I had a clear assignment to work on. I also left that first session thinking the practice to "work out" my spiritual body thirty minutes a day wouldn't be hard. It made sense and I was fully dedicated to the cause. But I learned quickly it wasn't so easy – Yugo's warning was true. For some reason I had no trouble staying committed to my physical body workouts, which usually last about an hour. But when it comes to spending just thirty minutes of quiet time, reflection time, meditation time, it's hard to carve out the minutes. And, when I did force myself, my mind usually raced, fought back at the stillness, was *distracted*, thinking of things I needed to do. I also realized that feeling of well-being and love I felt walking down Yugo's stairs after our meditation time to close our session lasted only as long as seeing an idiot driver go over not one, not two, but three lanes of traffic to avoid missing an exit. The not so kind thoughts and words that erupted automatically jolted me out of my spiritual pink cloud. Just saying, whatever I got from Yugo and our sessions, I'd need to learn how to carry those positive feelings over for more than just fifteen minutes.

My next appointment with Yugo was mid-morning two weeks later, and I decided to go to Omelettry Lane a little early to have a late breakfast before we met. The food there is so good – I went for the seven grain whole wheat pancakes. They come out a little crunchy, kinda toasty on the edges with real butter and maple syrup, four strips of crispy bacon, and two fried eggs over medium – I'm in heaven. I'm sitting facing the door going up the stairs wondering if Yugo is meeting with another patient when about mid-meal a woman comes down the stairs, business dress, professional, maybe late thirties.

One of my character defects is looking at virtually every woman I see and checking them out. I don't know why, my guess is it's in my DNA, but I can't stop myself from looking at women without sizing them up, not sexually really, maybe some, but just seeing if they're attractive to me. I feel bad about it sometimes honestly, like I'm an old horndog looking around clandestinely checking out the ladies, but I can't help it and it's harmless – and nobody except me knows I'm doing it, at least I don't think so. I never act on any of it. It's just an internal mind thing that happens spontaneously (I've been this way since third grade when Jennie Stone, this beautiful teacher at Nueva, got me noticing such things). One thing's for sure, Cody is far worse at this than I am, but that's not saying much.

Anyway, this lady is attractive, sexy even, dressed a little too promiscuously for a counseling session in my opinion – her top few buttons undone, light brunette hair tied back in a ponytail, long, going halfway down her back. High heels, nice legs from what I can see, and glasses that top it all off nicely. I know...it's wrong.

She comes down the stairs smiling to herself, and I wonder what she and Yugo were talking about – what she was sharing. She's got a confident glow, maybe I'm making that up, but she seems ready to take on anything. As she walks out of the little opening, she spots a table with several people sitting around it, a table that's been pretty loud frankly while I've been eating breakfast. Someone sees her and yells hello, and she greets them all with a smile, hugs a couple of people, and sits down for a second to talk to them. I wonder if these are friends who just happen to be eating at the restaurant this morning, or if this group is somehow connected with Yugo. They're an eclectic bunch, meaning they seem from different walks of life. I'm now unconsciously staring at her while thinking all this when she catches me looking her way and sort of smiles – uncomfortably. Damn,

I'm caught. I quickly look down and eat my pancakes, trying to be as nonchalant as possible. A couple minutes pass, and I hear a chair push back on the floor. I glance up slowly and catch her backside as she walks out the door...nice. I know, I know. What can I say?

I finish my breakfast and head up the stairs, hoping for another good session. I've had a decent week at work – sales are good, Frazier's new digital marketing hire is working out. But things with Jessica aren't great, mainly because she says I'm still drinking more than I should, and also, as she puts it, I'm not *really there* when she needs me (and I guess she's right). My mom's dementia is getting worse, so much so even she notices it now. A new common phrase of hers is "my memory just isn't what it used to be." The understatement of the year.

My new cat Gato, a gray stray I'd call almost feral who slowly integrated herself into the family, has gone missing again. I thought my dog George might have trouble with her when I started leaving food outside trying to coax her to let me pet her – once I was sure she didn't have a home. But when she finally grew comfortable enough to hang around the yard some, and then after several weeks finally come into the house (a big step), it was shocking how well she and George got along. Now they nap together side by side. It's great having another cat around, but there is a downside to Gato. In her heart she's still a *wild* cat, and every so often she vanishes – sometimes for days. Up until now she's always returned, sometimes not in the greatest shape, but this time I'm worried she may have had a fate similar to Bob's. In other words, all I have today for Yugo is typical life bullshit – nothing major. After our beginning counseling session about "me," we move on to more important things – the next element of the Way:

YF: So before we begin, how was your time practicing? Spending thirty minutes a day working out your spiritual body?

WH: Oh, ok I guess. I thought it'd be easy. I was looking forward to getting a spiritual practice going, but it's harder than I expected. The first few days went ok, but then I forgot about it one morning so I had to squeeze in all the workout time at night and didn't feel like I had thirty minutes – it was rushed. Sorta went downhill from there.

YF: Sounds very normal, Walden. I'd be surprised if you came back here glowing about two weeks of spiritual bliss. Just like workouts to get your body in shape, spiritual work also takes time. You have to start slowly but keep a daily routine so your spirit gets into a rhythm, so you get to where you feel *off* if you don't do your usual practice. The important thing is that you push through and get to where you feel something's *missing* without some kind of daily meditation, prayer time, or time alone in nature.

WH: It's been years since I spent any time looking at things internally or spiritually, maybe all my life honestly. There's no doubt it'll take time to become a routine.

YF: The important thing is to keep it up – *don't stop.* And you must prioritize! Reality is, most people who don't stay on this path simply can't make time to do this first element, so it all fizzles away. And, you'll see as we meet further, there's more work to be done each day. Some of your worldly distractions will have to take a back seat, will need to fall away. Time wasters like TV, surfing your phone, social media if you're into that sorta thing, online shopping, maybe even cut back a little on the drinking (*smiles*).

WH: ......

YF: So, today I want to go over a new concept for you that will hopefully change the way you think. As I said earlier, some of the steps we go over will be practical common-sense work and some may be a little *out there.* Here's the first idea that may be like that, completely new to you, and it's this: We must always remember that our thoughts are *real,* and because they are real they have significant power.

WH: Our thoughts are real? Not sure I follow what you're getting at.

YF: (*Long pause while he studies me.*) What I mean by this is that our thoughts are not exclusive to us in our own little heads. They're not self-contained in our brain and sealed away from the world out there. Our brains, our minds, create thoughts which in the end are energy, brain-waves. And these thoughts, or this energy, is dispersed into the atmosphere just like the wireless data that's constantly sending content to your cell phone or Apple watch or the Wifi in your home.

WH: Uhhh, ok?

YF: Here's a good mental picture for you, Walden. We are all, each one of us, our own cell tower, walking around transmitting our data into the Universe. Almost no one realizes this, but our thoughts are continuously flying all around the atmosphere, like data being transmitted from a cell phone tower out into space. It's no different from all the invisible data streaming around this planet through the air – text messages, wireless networks, *The Office* streaming on your phone, radio waves, TV signals. In the same way all that data is *real,* even though we can't see any of it, our thoughts are real, even though we can't see any of them.

WH: Ok, that image helps a little...

YF: And, since our thoughts are real, they have real power, real conse-quences. Not only in our lives, but in the lives of others living on this planet. Negative thoughts can bring negative events. Positive thoughts bring about positive, beneficial things!

WH: You're talking about the power of positive thinking. Sure, I've heard of that.

YF: Now, I'll make a blanket statement I think you'll agree is true for many. Our world is full of people who feel they have no purpose in life, maybe even that they don't belong here. There are many who suffer from aimlessness and a feeling they can't make a difference. Agree?

WH: Yeah, I think that's true about some people. Hell, it's right about me sometimes.

YF: So here's the good part. If we want to start doing something that's tangible to make a difference, to change the world, something that gives us purpose, we can all start today by *changing our thoughts*. I call the stream of thoughts flying around our planet, this mass of human brain waves, the "know-osphere." Like the word atmosphere for the air, or biosphere for biological life on our planet. It's not a unique idea from me. I got it from Teilhard de Chardin, who wrote about the idea, but he called it the "noos-phere." I like *know-osphere* because we should *know* about our thoughts, be *aware* of what we're thinking inside. Then we can change them for the greater good.

WH: Know-osphere like the atmosphere, only it's our thoughts floating around up there. I like that – easy to remember. But you're right, Yugo, this is a bit out there...

YF: Really contemplate this, Walden, since it's a new idea for you. Every minute, every day you're churning out an almost endless stream of thoughts, sending data out into the know-osphere which is circling our Earth. Like the carbon dioxide being released into the atmosphere from burning fossil fuels, the shit being released into the atmosphere from mankind's collective thoughts is toxic. Bad intentions, resentments, hate, fear, jealousy, greed, selfishness – it's all real energy circulating around the planet like the pollution spewing from a coal plant filling our airspace. No wonder things can be so tough down here.

WH: (*Recalling my thoughts at breakfast...checking out that woman leaving Yugo's office.*) Yeah, I can get my head around this. Thoughts don't just stay in your head because they're an energy that has to go somewhere. I've never considered that. I think terrible thoughts all the time, but the one thing that saves my conscience is I think I'm the only one who knows about them. Holy crap to think all my thoughts could be out there floating around!

YF: Yes, but don't take the wrong lesson here, Walden. I'm not saying there's an entity always looking over your shoulder that knows your thoughts and is waiting to punish you for evil intentions and bad thoughts. I have no idea about that shit. What I am saying is you should be *actively conscious* of your thoughts, be aware of them. Know that negative, bad, self-centered thoughts are hurting our know-osphere, are ultimately harming other people, so you should consciously stop them. Be aware of them and don't let your mind wander around on cruise control. And taking it up another level, know that good, positive thoughts are sending out good vibes around our planet, positive energy you could say, and that helps other people! The motivation to stop being consumed by negative thinking isn't to avoid getting caught or punished by some omniscient being. We all should be thinking positively to help *nurture* the know-osphere and ultimately the direction of our entire planet – to improve the karma for all!

WH: So don't look at it like Santa Claus looking over my shoulder judging if I'm thinking bad or good thoughts, but instead remember that when I have bad thoughts, bad vibes are going out into our atmosphere, so stop it. You're talking about paying more attention to my thoughts – being more aware of what's going on inside my head.

YF: Exactly. You're getting this. I'm talking about *waking up*. About moving away from our mechanical way of be-ing! No one can know another person's thoughts or feelings through external senses. Oh, you may be able to sense someone's pissed off, or happy or afraid. But nobody can see what's really going on inside your head. But aren't your thoughts, your emotions, your feelings the most *real* thing about you? Isn't the activity going on in your head what makes you *you*? And yet, we all go through life with our minds on autopilot, chattering away, sometimes totally unaware what we're thinking. It's all about self-awareness, about *self-observation*! Consciously think good things, have positive thoughts, and that sends out positive energy, good karma. It's like life-changing waves crashing out into the Universe, into the know-osphere, which then responds by bringing back ripples of good for all. Treat negative thoughts like you'd treat poison coming into your body. Purge them as fast as you can! Turn instead to thoughts of compassion, hope, kindness, love, gratitude.

WH: Well I've had some pretty shitty thoughts lately. Not long ago I had some motherfuckers shut down our website for seven days for three hundred lousy bucks and I wanted to kill them.

YF: (*Nodding.*) And now you see, Walden, how *motherfucker* is probably the best word you can use to get that anger out, right? Nothing else gets to the heart of how pissed off you were – to your true feelings. Acknowledge it, purge it, then let it go! As we've all heard, Walden, *shit happens,* and it will continue to happen. And when it does, we must be conscious of our thought-life and do our best to let things go, to see the light. It's ok to have negative thoughts – everyone has them, they're a natural part of being human. Just don't dwell on them, don't *obsess* over them.

WH: Yeah, well I wish I woulda heard this idea sooner. I've held on to negative shit all my life...still holding on to it. When bad things come into my head, I need to remember it's not only taking me down, it's hurting other people too.

YF: Yes! But Walden, I can't stress this enough. You must *practice* this element of the Way. It's not something that will come easily – trust me! It takes much more conscious effort than working out your spiritual body every day. It's not natural. For some reason the human brain, the mind, sometimes *likes* negative thoughts and emotions. For example, we all like to dwell in self-pity.

WH: Yeah, I've heard that one from my girlfriend...

YF: We must approach spiritual growth *collectively*. We are all on this planet together as one whole living human organism. Our thoughts, our intentions, our actions affect not only ourselves but the whole of our planet. When higher thoughts, higher consciousness, higher love is emanating from many people, the whole world shines. All of creation benefits. And likewise, unconscious negative thinking, harmful emotions, and unhealthy unloving intentions bring down the collective whole of our Earth.

WH: (*Realizing what my thought-life has been like lately.*) There's a lot here, Yugo. I'm trying to soak in all the implications. Assuming what you say is true, I've got a ways to go...

YF: (*Huge glowing grin.*) Now here comes the best truth of it all, Walden, from knowledge handed down for centuries through esoteric teaching. Positive, conscious, loving thoughts and intentions are far stronger than negative ones. *A few hundred loving conscious souls can counteract the nega-*

tivity and harmful thoughts emanating from tens of thousands. Knowing this truth is an inspiration to get on the good path, to understand the reality that it's not only "me" I'm working on. This work helps all of humanity, all of our planet. And it doesn't just help human beings, but all creatures on this Earth. We're all in this together! This, Walden, adds purpose to the life of every living soul. We can all make a difference just by being conscious of our thoughts, and every little bit really does count! But it takes awareness of your internal thinking, and then the discipline to alter that thinking when you become aware it's running off in the wrong direction.

The Practice

YF: So here's the next practice until we meet again, but don't forget, keep up the thirty minutes of spiritual exercise each day too. Eventually in this Way, you'll see how all these work together. This sounds simple like the last one, but you'll find just because it's simple doesn't make it easy – *especially* at first.

WH: Ok, let me have it.

YF: (*Pauses and clasps his hands under his chin like praying.*) I want you to be conscious of your negative thoughts, Walden. Instead of letting your mind run mechanically on its own like we all do every day, I want you to try to be aware when you're thinking negatively. This takes practice and takes time to develop. You could even call it a skill, but the key is to get started.

WH: Ok, so you want me to be aware when I start thinking bad thoughts?

YF: Right. Sometimes you'll catch your negative thoughts right away. Like when someone cuts in front of you at the checkout line, you're instantly pissed. You turn on the news and some politician's doing something stupid and immediately you're screaming how they're fucking up the world. But most often, it takes time to realize your thoughts have gone negative. You'll suddenly realize you've been thinking bad thoughts for the last ten minutes. Like thinking about the business and how it's going well, but then this competitor pops in your head, they're making things hard and costing you money and stealing customers and what can you do to get back at them? Or your parents call to say they need something done around the house. You have to drop everything now and go check on them, and slowly you fall into a thirty-minute pity party driving over to their place. Get it?

WH: Yep.

YF: The key is awareness through *self-observation*. Being conscious of what your thoughts are, then stopping them when you notice they have bad intentions, when they're negative. And then eventually, and this is even harder, then replacing those bad thoughts with good ones. Thoughts of compassion, or gratitude, or empathy.

WH: And you expect me to try and do this all the time?

YF: I want you to do your best. I don't want you to have unrealistic expectations or get down on yourself. Let's set an aim of catching your negative thinking three times a day. If you're like me and every other human on this Earth, you'll have plenty of chances to catch just three. This gets you thinking *in a new way*, raising your consciousness of your thoughts. Just doing it once a day makes a difference, but let's shoot for three.

WH: Ok, I think I got it. Keep working out my spirit thirty minutes and day, and try to catch myself thinking bad shit at least three times a day.

YF: You got it. And here's some pointers. Some people ask for this, but you haven't. You might write this down. These are negative thoughts and emotions to look out for: anger, resentment, fear, self-pity, anxiety, jealousy, hate, greed. There's more of course but these are the easiest ones to catch. Self-pity probably takes longest to notice...we like it the most. And I was surprised studying emotions to learn that of all the negative emotions, shame is considered the lowest level, the most *dangerous* of emotions. It's different than guilt, which is more about moral questions – feeling guilty about doing something. Shame is more insidious, more soul crushing. It's about feeling inadequate, not good enough, unworthy or unlovable. When we feel deep shame, we question our right to be alive, to even exist. It minimizes our very sense of self, our very being, our feelings of worthiness or purpose. *Beware* of feeling shame. We are *all* worthy!

WH: Got it.

YF: And on the positive side, here's thoughts or emotions to turn toward instead: kindness, compassion, empathy, love, acceptance, forgiveness, gratitude, patience, joy. Of course there's more of these too, but these are good ones to let yourself fall into. The best part is to remember when you catch yourself, when you reverse your thinking, you're *helping the know-osphere* too! You're counteracting the bad shit circling around up there with your positivity. This practice isn't just about you. It's about all of us!

WH: (*Writing these in my notebook that's filling up after just two sessions.*) Sounds like a plan, Yugo. I'm with you.

YF: (*Gleaming smile.*) And one more thing, Walden, before we close with our twenty minutes of silence. Remember when we first met? We talked about you becoming a student and I said you could try two sessions and then decide if you wanted to keep coming?

WH: (*Smiling now too.*) Yeah, I remember (although I really hadn't thought about it since we got going).

YF: Well, what do you think? Your trial subscription has come to an end.

WH: Yugo, I think you're stuck with this poor, messed up bastard for the long haul.

This is the 2nd element of Yugo's Way:

Our thoughts transmit real energy into the know-osphere, impacting ourselves, other people, and our planet. Be aware of thoughts and emotions, stay positive, and counteract the negativity influencing our world.

FRAZIER V

Our thoughts are real and they feed the know-osphere? It took time
to open my heart to that. To let the idea sink in and settle. Now, I realize
I'm polluting the know-osphere every day. Judgmental, self-centered,
anxious thinking creeps in all the time. Thanks to the Way, my awareness
is improving. It feels good when I catch myself. When I become aware
what my mechanical mind is doing. It makes me think of Yugo and that
makes me smile.

Walden asked me to jump in and write this section too. He said it has
more to do with me than him. That may be true. After Walden's first few
visits with Yugo, he sat me down and played back parts of the sessions.
The Way parts. I was captivated by Yugo's teachings. They made me feel
hopeful. I could hear its essence was from love. He wasn't preachy. He
wasn't hard to understand. His ideas were clear with real application
behind them. Being a marketer, my marketing brain started churning. I
immediately asked Walden:

How widespread is Yugo's following?

How's he getting his message out?

Are these ideas shared on his website?

Is he doing social media and do you follow his posts?

Has he written any books?

First Walden laughed. Then he said he has no clue about the size of his
following. He doubts it's large. Yugo has no website; he does no social

media. Walden can't follow any of Yugo's posts. They don't exist. He doesn't even have a phone for his office. At least one Walden knows about. Any books? Walden laughs again; says he doesn't even have literature. Yugo hands out small pieces of paper for handouts during sessions.

Ok, I admit it. My upcoming actions were a smidge selfish, but done for positive reasons. Being an influencer selling products for a living was getting stale. I was a little bored, unfulfilled. And the occasional negativity can be hard to ignore. I've always dreamed of being a singer. Like Mary, who is incredible, but more than casual singing. I had dreams of leading a band, like Anastasia. A modern-day Stevie Nicks. What could be more awesome?

But all careers get old over time if you don't keep them fresh. I have many musician friends around town. I see them drag around their equipment. Set up and tear down, show after show. They say being a musician can get old. Even the very successful ones. Well, maybe not the performing part. The audience adulation part. How could that ever get old? But hey, if being a musician eventually gets old, so can being an influencer.

Anyway, I was looking for a way to add spice to my work life. To make a difference. Use my platforms to do more than sell dog food or soccer shoes. My audience all totaled is several million. There's the niche blogs for hobbies and such, selling products. The corporate social media and blogs for a variety of companies. The personal social media following for fun stuff. Truth is there's lots of eyeballs on my content.

Even before hearing of Yugo I'd been thinking. How can I use this influence to do good work? How can I find a higher purpose? When Walden said Yugo didn't do anything special to spread his teachings, I saw **opportunity**. I told Walden more people should hear this! Everyone I know could use his wisdom, me included.

At first, I asked Walden for his audio to share with others. Then realized sending Walden's counseling sessions into the world wasn't a great idea. So I poured a glass of wine, let my mind wander. Could I incorporate Yugo's Way into my blogs? Could I include snippets of his words on The 'gram, TikTok, and Twitter? Could I create a campaign around Yugo's Way that would spark curiosity? Build an audience? Grow interest where people looked forward to the next post? Even better, shared this content with friends and followers?

I had no reservations putting Yugo's teachings on my own blogs and social media. On SoccerMomsUnite.com and the others. I saw no backlash from that. But I wondered about doing company blogs and posts. That's where half my influence lies. I talked about it with Walden. WaldensPets.com was the safest and easiest place to try first. His concerns were understandable, and I quote:

"What if people think it's just religious shit and we piss customers off?"

"What if people take it as political? You know how divided our country is. You can't even eat vegetarian without someone making it political."

"What about Yugo? We'd need his permission first, and we can't publish his words if there's nothing in it for him."

"Yugo may not want the publicity. He's a mellow, low-key dude."

And finally, "Why take the risk, Sis? People love the dog and cat videos. It's working, so why screw with it?"

All valid questions and concerns. I suggested we think about it. I'd develop ideas on how to use it on the WP blog and social media. Walden would consider the plusses and minuses. See how his heart felt. Obviously we agreed to check with Yugo first. If he was against it, no need to spend any time on it. Walden would ask Yugo his thoughts at their next meeting. Then we'd go from there.

There was positive energy already working on Walden. By the time of my inspiration to spread the Way, he'd already had four sessions with Yugo. His internal being was already changing. Had I raised this idea with Walden pre-Yugo? Profits over purpose would have shut this down fast. Now he was actually considering it. I could tell he wanted to do it. After a week of reflection, I showed Walden my plan. Without hesitation, he said let's go for it!

Walden reported Yugo was overjoyed when asked if we could share the Way. His eyes lit up! Yugo told Walden his purpose is to teach the Way. To live the Way. But he doesn't have the expertise to spread it. It's his calling to teach others, then let the Way find its way to other people. Yugo said fate had already connected him with other students who were spreading the word. He said when he first met Walden, the Universe told him to "hold on." To stay connected with Walden. Now he knew why... maybe. He said you never know for sure why things are the way they are.

Funny anecdotes. I got these quotes straight from Walden's recordings. When asked how we could compensate him Yugo said, "These ideas are free. No one should pay for air." Walden pressed, saying what we sent out should be copyrighted. That Yugo should get credit and paid for its use. Yugo said, "You can't copyright the ideas and understandings from centuries of thought. The Divine Principle in the Universe, the source of what I and others share, isn't concerned about credit or payment. I could care less about that shit."

But Yugo did have some requirements. He did not want a focus on him. Using his name, Yugo Free, was okay. Nothing else. No pictures or likenesses of any kind. No contact info. No email addresses or other ways people could contact him. We were told to leave his identity a mystery. "Use an icon of some kind if you wish." Why? First, he didn't want a flood of new client requests. He had more people who wanted to meet with him now than he had time for. And, he preferred the Universe send people to him naturally.

Also, he didn't want the attention. Didn't want to clutter up his peaceful existence. Another quote: "Without simplicity, peace, and serenity in my being, the source will dry up."

Yugo's biggest demands:

1. This could not become a commercial enterprise for him, one where he made money from our sharing the Way.

2. And, quote, "I need to review the words we choose to express these ideas. Sometimes what I say in a session can be better said when given time to craft it in written form."

So, he wanted editorial privilege. He wanted his privacy. He wanted it to be free. And that is all.

Here's what got me amped up the most. After hearing Walden's audio sessions, Yugo's voice, his cadence, his confidence, his love, I was most excited to get to meet Yugo personally. You see, to other people my act may seem put together. I may look confident for the world to see. Walden always pictures me as this strong person. But inside I'm a screwed-up mess. There are times when I'm nothing but a bundle of insecurity. Truth is, I know I need Yugo's help too.

Regarding Walden's initial concerns? Here's our consensus:

"What if we piss off customers?" Those who get upset by Yugo's wisdom won't make great customers anyway. There will be Yugo agnostics. Those who say it isn't for them. But the number of people really angry should be small. Reward wins out versus risk.

"What if people take this as political?" So what? People with that bent make everything political. There's no escaping it. Besides, their hearts might be changed too. Let's change hearts!

"What about Yugo?" As you know, he's in!

"Why take the risk?" Simple. Because we have a platform to help others. We can spread waves and waves of positive vibes. And that will do more for our planet than selling pet supplies ever could. We're thinking, let's go and clean up that know-osphere!

So, we all agreed to share Yugo's Way. And as I said, the reach from my followers in all mediums is significant. The strategy for Walden's Pets? Introduce it first on social media to raise interest. Build anticipation. "Coming Soon! Secrets to Living a Happier Life." Get people used to the idea that inspirational ideas are coming. Then we'll create posts for each element of Yugo's Way. It's no different than sending out the Steps of AA one at a time. With a brief write-up to explain each one. Include inspirational photos and imagery. Videos whenever I can come up with good relevant ones. Of course using pets, children, happy people where it fits for WP.com. My blogs will be the main content hubs. Social media will be the arteries flowing out Yugo's teachings. The strategy is to engage all my followers and hope they take it viral.

Yugo has the idea to enlist a few former "Way students" to follow my blogs and social media. To have them answer questions people may have. To help facilitate a dialogue. To inspire comments and online discussion. Engagement as we say. On WP.com's properties, we'll keep doing other posts like we usually do. The tiny puppy sleeping in a huge dog food bowl. The cat drinking out of a dripping faucet. But an element of Yugo's Way will be interspersed every two weeks. We have four sessions already to kick this off!

When we send Yugo related messages, we'll use this beautiful picture of a Portuguese Sheepdog as an icon. They're such an incredible breed. Dignified, wise, devoted, joyful – they're amazing shepherds. Nothing will be said. But the inference is this wise, beautiful creature is somehow connected with sharing the Way. It speaks to our pet audience on WaldensPets.com and ties into the company. It also provides Yugo cover. He loves the idea.

The element you see at the end of Yugo chapters is how we began most posts. Followed by a quick summary. Nothing too long to bog down the reader. Attention spans are short! Of course Yugo helped us craft these. This took some time and effort, which was a blessing for me. Oh, Yugo had the Way down in his head. But the three of us worked in unison to get the wording just right. It was surprising to see Yugo had virtually nothing written down. He just opens up and the words start flowing.

The campaign rolled out slowly at first. But soon we noticed those viewing were sharing the Way much more than our usual posts. Comments and engagement were strong across multiple channels. It spread virally far beyond our regular audience. It went nuts on a Reddit thread. It was a huge success on WP.com. The message was shared. People were touched. Some hearts were changed. There was very little negative feedback. Almost zero.

It had even more legs on my specialty niche blogs. My personal social media posts. Here I could be more aggressive. More in your face with Yugo's message. And most (not all) people loved it. Lengthy dialogues sprung up. Connections were made. We heard of Yugo's Way chapters and clubs starting up. Little refuges for people to join together with other like-minded people. A resource to help one another get through life. Millions were exposed to the Way at least once. It spread hope and peace, and most importantly Love.

For the upcoming element of Yugo's Way, Walden wouldn't let me go so far as to name the company Sahara on WaldensPets' posts. But I did use the name Sahara on all of mine. And the outcome was **mind-blowing** (although WP.com was guilty by association). I'll let Walden share that very cool morsel. That alone made everything worth it. Walden and I sometimes do high-fives. Yugo says it only takes a hundred people thinking positive thoughts to counteract many thousands thinking negatively. That means we facilitated a huge positive karma boost for Mother Earth. Yes!!!

But like I told Walden while nagging him to write this book. Posts, blogs, digital dialogues, they are all fleeting. Our collective conscience moves on so quickly. Worldly distractions wipe away our focus. In no time, people forget what was important just days ago. That's why I'm so proud of Walden. He's doing what he can to ensure Yugo's ideas are permanent. Can be passed on, read, reread, and contemplated. And one other very cool result? I got to meet alone with Yugo several times. It brought me more understanding about myself. And more peace.

YUGO IV

"Our Planet's immune system is trying to get rid of us."

Kurt Vonnegut

INSTEAD OF SONG LYRICS, this quote from author Kurt Vonnegut says so much in so few words I had to go with it. Seems sorta true – and he made that quote years ago. On my next visit with Yugo he went through two elements, so this chapter is a two for one. As usual, Yugo started the session listening to my personal crap and helping me with my mental outlook on situations I'm struggling with. (On the positive side, my cat Gato came back! She's one tough little lady.)

Before digging into the Way, Yugo asked me how my practices were going, and I told him ok overall. The thirty minutes of spiritual exercise was becoming more routine – I even looked forward to it most days. But for the second practice, some days I'd totally forget to catch myself three times thinking negative thoughts. That's going to take some focus. The second element from today's session is the one that Frazier said had a *"mind blowing outcome"* in the last chapter. Honestly it gave me great personal satisfaction, although Yugo would probably say satisfaction isn't the *real* emotion I felt. I should also point out again, most of the quotation marks in Yugo's dialogue are his finger quotes, although I probably added some:

YF: So some days you caught yourself falling into negative thinking, but some days you lost focus of the practice and didn't catch yourself at all?

WH: Yeah, I hate to say it, but it's true. I'd set my aim in the morning and then life would get in the way. I'd get home from work and realize I went all day without really ever paying attention to my thoughts.

YF: *(Nodding.)* It's a lot like working out your spiritual body every day. The more you do it, the easier it gets, but only if you work at it. Keep making the aim to do it and keep consciously checking your progress. Maybe put a reminder on your desk. The ultimate goal is to recognize negative thinking whenever it happens, not just three times a day.

WH: Understood. Yeah, when I remember to look out for it, there's plenty of times I catch my negative thinking. Lots of opportunities like you said. I just have to get better at being conscious to stay conscious.

YF: *(Chuckling.)* Ha! Well said. Speaking of negative thinking, let's move on to this. Some words that I say might cause a negative reaction in your body. If that happens, be present and feel that constriction in your chest, that rush of blood to your head when you hear something and you mechanically recoil inside. Don't let that happen without learning about yourself. Don't just feel that negativity and move on. Ask yourself, what caused my body to react that way? Sometimes you'll realize your body's first mechanical reaction is *wrong*. That you aren't even really thinking about what was said. Your body and emotions are just responding mechanically as they always do to certain words, whether what you're feeling is true or not. And whenever you do recognize your immediate emotional reactions aren't *true*, when you can change your negative *mechanical* reactions to life, you are *changing your being*. That's evolution, Walden – personal evolution.

WH: Ok?

YF: So here's an example. I've had some rough shit happen in my life. People I love dying, tough situations, difficulty coping, problems with acceptance. This shit jaded me and my relationship with God, especially when it came to religion and church people where I grew up. I saw them judging other people, judging me, then watched their actions and saw they were hypocrites. They'd go on and on about Jesus and how only he could *save* me, and how special they were because *they were saved*. Their judge-mentalism created lots of anger, and it got to the point where someone would just say the word *Jesus*, and I'd tighten up inside and shut down. Why? Not because of Jesus the being, who he was and what he did on this

Earth, but because of the people who I couldn't stand. The people I wrongly associated with the *word* Jesus, the people I thought were so condescending and hypocritical who were throwing his name in my face. It took me years to realize I had nothing against Jesus, he is *Love* and *Light*. But man, did I need to work on my feelings about these other people. Now when I hear the word Jesus? I think of love and compassion, wisdom and peace. I don't get all defensive and knotted up inside. That's what I mean by evolving internally – changing your thinking, changing your *being*.

WH: I can relate to some of that. I had a friend in Washington whose mom was big in the Baptist Church. It got to where I tried to avoid her because she was always throwing her beliefs in my face – judging me and my family is what it felt like.

YF: Yes. But you may at times research these negative internal reactions that keep coming up and feel you're right to have these feelings. That's ok too as long as you don't dwell on them. Our instincts are sometimes justified. The point is to become aware of those mechanical negative reactions to people, to words, to things. Then to consciously look at them, take away their negative energy in your body and grow...evolve.

WH: Well I gotta admit, it's gotten to where I just hear the word *Sahara* and my blood pressure skyrockets. That company...all the breaks they've gotten from government subsidies, tax breaks, the free press, stealing product ideas from small businesses. The way they treat their sellers and employees.

YF: (*Nodding in what I think is agreement.*) I started with this dialogue because we're going to talk today about a subject that makes some people *recoil*. To close their minds right away when they hear certain *words*. Over time they've learned to do so, from the media, from conflicting information on both sides, from mechanical thinking. But it's too important an issue for humanity to gloss over. It's a crucial element to living in harmony. If you're one of those whose chest constricts or blood pressure rises when you hear these words, I beg you to please, open your heart and *listen*. Then decide for yourself. Don't let your political affiliation or news media buzzwords get in the way. So Walden, these words are climate change and environmentalism – the growing awareness that we must take better care of Mother Earth now before it's too late.

WH: Hey I agree. No worries about me getting all hot and bothered. I hear the words *climate change* and get worried about future generations, not angry and confrontational. It's so weird when you say you're concerned about pollution or the warming planet and people look at you like your talking about killing puppies or something. How can something as straightforward as taking care of the Earth be political? It's just common sense, right? I mean, I know there's always a struggle for power and you've got huge lobbies and such trying to keep things the status quo, but it seems so obvious with all the population growth, the industrial growth worldwide. We can't just keep doing things the same way without consequences down the line.

YF: Right. It's simply doing the right thing. Being good stewards of what our Divine Creator made for us, then instructed us to take care of. What ever happened to the Boy Scout mantra from the "good old days"? Back in the 1940s, the founder of the Boy Scouts famously said, "Try and leave this world a little better than you found it." That saying later morphed into, "Always leave the camp cleaner than you found it." So how can we be against using that same philosophy for our planet?

WH: I got no idea. Father used to say something just like that all the time – leave things better off than before you got there.

YF: Yes! But clearly we are *not* doing this. Look at our Earth today. The air quality is so bad in many US cities we have "air quality warnings" all the time in the summer. Actual warnings telling children and the elderly to stay inside. It happens all the time in Austin – too many days to count – and in all the big cities in Texas. Shouldn't this *alarm* everyone? Don't go outside because it's not safe to *breathe*? There's wildfires burning like never before, oil spills killing marine life, ruining our beaches, rising temperatures, melting glaciers, the rising sea levels. And all this can be *seen* by the naked eye. It's right in front of us. The increase in serious weather events like hurricanes and tornadoes. It's obvious we're not leaving this world better than we found it, and all it takes is looking around. This isn't a wild theory, it's what we're all *experiencing*.

WH: Preaching to the choir, man. Cody and I talk about this all the time. We can *feel* things are moving in the wrong direction. It's gotten so damn hot around here...

YF: No shit it has. It should be about our own experience, not what we hear on some "news" show or slanted social media. Let's look at three of God's amazing creations and see how they are doing. Nothing's more incredible than a butterfly, right? From caterpillar to cocoon to beautiful butterfly. California's monarch butterfly population is down over 90% and many butterfly species are in serious decline worldwide. When's the last time you saw a monarch butterfly?

WH: Can't remember the last time, and I'm outside all the time.

YF: How about frogs? Is there a more amazing animal than a frog? Amphibians, God's creatures living in water and on land – from tiny tadpoles to frogs. I used to see frogs and toads all the time when I was a kid. Frogs were always in the yard, in the creek. You ever see frogs much anymore, Walden?

WH: You're right. I used to see frogs all the time but I hardly ever see a frog anymore.

YF: Because their populations are dying worldwide. From manmade pollution, from industrialization and sprawl, from radiation possibly from the hole in the ozone layer, from rising temperatures. What about the coral reefs? Maybe our planet's most unique and beautiful biosphere. Divinely created beauty, diversity, amazing colors, sanctuaries for marine life. Scientists say <u>at least half</u> of the world's coral reefs have died since the 1950s. Some researchers say as much as two thirds has been lost. So some may argue, is it really 67% or is it closer to 50%? Does it really matter? Who cares when both numbers are so alarming? Rome is obviously burning here.

WH: Scary stuff. I agree it's alarming and you're right – it's visible. We can all *see* it.

YF: Yes, it's all around us, and I haven't even mentioned bat populations, turtles, honeybees. How will our crops and plants grow without sufficient numbers of bees to pollinate them? The reality is, Mother Earth's most amazing creatures are dying, and we as a culture don't seem to care. We cannot be bothered.

WH: I think a big issue is it's become a political hot potato and some people don't want to come across as liberal tree huggers...

YF: The changing climate is a *human issue*. A situation we've *all* been a part of creating that we *all* have to do our part to resolve. And those companies and entities and people who are throwing out misinformation, saying scientists and environmentalists and the green movement are only in it for the money? They're simply doing the old switcheroo. They are the ones spreading lies and bad data, denying that mankind is a serious contributor to climate change. They're the ones throwing half-truths and conflicting data into the public to create confusion and stall real change. And the motherfuckers are all doing it for two reasons. For money and for power. The health of this planet for our children be damned. It's all about money, Walden, and we are sitting by not pressing harder for change because these assholes are making this political when it's not! *It's about human beings doing what our Divine Creator asked us to do since the beginning of time.* Take care of this Earth and all of its creatures.

YF: (*Pauses, takes a drink, then a big breath in and out and smiles.*) So, if you haven't figured it out yet, Walden, this element is about living in harmony with creation. It's about the *absolute truth* that to live in harmony with ourselves and with other people, we must also live in harmony with nature. If we don't take care of our home for future generations, there will be no home.

WH: I hear you, Yugo. That was a core value growing up at Nueva Tierra. It was constantly stressed if our community was going to make it, we had to take care of our land, the gardens and trees, the animals, our water, take care of what we did with our trash. I just wish there was some clarity around what I could do now to make a difference. I mean, I recycle and all, but in my heart, I know that doesn't help much.

YF: There's three primary things we can all do now, Walden, before the situation gets irreversible. First, we must take better care of our air and accept the scientific fact that burning fossil fuels intensifies the "greenhouse effect" that warms our planet. The greenhouse effect is a long known process in the Earth's atmosphere that can't be disputed – and we're making things worse. So, we must thoughtfully transition from burning fossil fuels for energy, and embrace and invest in renewable energy sources like solar, water, and wind power. Fast track new technologies. Listen to this. The world's oil consumption is estimated at over *97 million* barrels of oil *per day*. How can anyone think we can keep burning through that much oil per day without eventually having a negative impact on our environment? In case you're wondering, a barrel of oil is 42 gallons. So that's *4 billion gallons* of oil consumed *every day*. And how much longer can this crazy consumption go on? The World Population Review estimates there's about fifty years of known oil reserves left. Only fifty years? This could happen in *our* lifetime, Walden. Even discounting the enormous environmental impacts from burning fossil fuels, we should embrace other renewable and regenerative forms of energy now because supplies are running out sooner than later. It's as if we are all asleep.

WH: Holy shit, Yugo (*writing these numbers down in my notebook*). Almost 4 billion gallons a day? I'm gonna look these numbers up to see if what you're saying is true. That has to take a toll...I can't even imagine where all that oil comes from.

YF: Or how much money is being made, *every day*. Imagine *that*. Now I'm not saying oil is inherently bad. The advancements and comforts fossil fuels have given humanity are enormous. But like with many things, we humans have overdone it, and they're almost gone. We've thrown nature out of balance. Only a fool would think everything can change overnight, but the time is *now* for significant action before we run out of time.

YF: (*Pauses again to settle – he's more intense than usual.*) Second, we must take better care of our waters, in particular less pollution, more conservation, and better access to those in need of clean drinking water. Not to mention we must do something about the overfishing taking place in our oceans, wreaking havoc on marine life across the globe. And particularly alarming to me is this floating plastic mass of garbage that's overtaking our oceans. I don't know if you've heard, many haven't, but there's a floating mass of plastic in the sea that's twice the size of Texas and growing. We must all stop consuming single use plastics, especially bottled water. I think personal consumption should be outlawed. I get it there's emergency situations when we need bottled water, but let's put it in cans, right?

WH: (*I chuckle at this.*) Oh, I've heard all about the Great Pacific Garbage Patch from a buddy of mine.

YF: (*Slight frown.*) I sense a lack of understanding here, Walden. Bottled water is one of the most harmful products ever made. Terrible for the environment, for people, for animals. And people are drinking the shit thinking they're being healthy, making a good life choice, while throwing away a piece of plastic that's never going away. It's totally unnecessary when we can drink tap water in a reusable container – filter it if that's important to you. The shit didn't even exist really until Coke and Pepsi realized people weren't drinking as much of their sugary drinks as they used to. They needed something to replace sales, and the marketing geniuses said screw making up new drinks. Let's just sell water. And how stupid are we? We love it, and they charge more for fucking *water* than for sodas! It's insane.

WH: Hey, I didn't mean to laugh, Yugo. I hear you. I've made it a point to stop buying plastics, especially bottled water. A friend of mine almost kicked my ass not long ago for drinking an Aquafina. Pretty sure he got that mindset indirectly from you.

YF: Well, I'm not promoting violence, but hallelujah to your bro! Ok, the third thing. We must take better care of our forests and jungle lands. They are vanishing at alarming rates. It's estimated the world loses *over fourteen million acres* of forest land every year. The Brazilian Amazon rain-forest, the very lungs of our planet, is being decimated. Large swaths of Southeast Asian forests are gone, converted to growing palm oil. Not to mention all the lost forestland here. Like all of this, there are debates over exact numbers, but the bottom line is with numbers *this large,* arguing about a few million acres here or there doesn't matter. It's believed the world has lost about one third of its forests so far, an area twice the size of the United States. So there's two realities going on that together are like pouring gasoline on a fire. On one hand, as the population grows and more countries are industrialized, we're pumping out more and more carbon dioxide, methane and other greenhouse gases. On the other hand, we're cutting down the very forests and jungle lands we need to clean our air.

WH: Scary stuff. That's a new one for me. I mean, I knew forests were gradually getting cut down, but I've never heard numbers. Fourteen million acres a year? You have to wonder how long that can go on without serious issues...

YF: There's an amazing documentary everyone should see called *A Life on Our Planet* by David Attenborough. I doubt anybody has seen the changes on our Earth up close over the years more than him. That's why it's so powerful. It's straight from his experience, his travels, what he's witnessed. Great cinematography. His passion and his optimism are inspirational.

WH: I haven't seen it but I love David Attenborough. Watched his nature shows all my life. I'll check it out.

YF: (*Smiling.*) You'll find it's required viewing on our next homework assignment. So those are the major problems, Walden. The question is, what can *we* do about it? How can *we* make a difference?

WH: Yeah, that is the question. I'm starting to feel we've waited too long on all this and our impending doom is unavoidable. There's lots of pessimism out there saying it's too late.

YF: Bingo! You just nailed the first one. As bad as things seem, *we mustn't lose hope.* It's imperative that people don't give up. That humanity doesn't just throw up our hands and say, "Fuck it." Technology is changing faster than ever before. Countries across the globe are finally having serious talks *together.* Renewable energy, especially wind and solar power, have made huge advancements in a short period of time. There's crazy science and engineering going on like Negative Emissions Technology around direct air capture that vacuums up carbon dioxide already released. There's new carbon neutral fuels being tested like "solar methanol." New technology may help pull back some of the mistakes we've already made that can help if we start making necessary changes *now*. Some of the world's best and brightest minds finally have some funding to really dig into finding solutions!

WH: Didn't know any of that stuff. Might have to Google those up too.

YF: *(Nodding yes.)* The power of the internet can bring good – educational websites, videos, even social media. Better information has more people engaged than ever before. We can't think it's too late to make a difference or let group negativity bring us all down. We must remain optimistic that our climate situation will improve, and most importantly, we must *all do our part*.

WH: So what does that mean – do our part?

YF: Let's first look at climate change. When you need a new car, go electric. EVs now have longer battery life, charging stations are more available, and EVs are priced about the same as regular gas cars with similar features. Going forward, *only* buy electric if you can, period.

WH: Well that sounds nice and all, Yugo, but EVs aren't cheap.

YF: You're right. I don't mean to be unrealistic or naïve here. Obviously there's many who can't afford an EV. But for the millions of people shopping for cars who can afford them, go electric now. Payments are reasonable if you go for entry level EV models. You'd be surprised what a Tesla 3 costs now versus new gas cars...very little difference. And with no need to buy gas and hardly any maintenance, they may be cheaper to own or lease overall. Making electric cars is much simpler than combustion engine cars...fewer parts. As more EVs are made, prices will drop. Eventually they'll be cheaper than gas cars. It's all about volume so let's grow that demand!

WH: I've been leasing this big SUV I don't really need for some dumbass reason. I should check when that lease is up. Maybe lease an electric?

YF: Do it *now*, Walden. There's no time to wait! And don't stop with cars. The same goes for lawnmowers, edgers, blowers. Gas lawn equipment spews out tons of carbon dioxide and monoxide – more pound for pound than cars. I'm not saying electrics are trouble free and perfect, but it's a helluva lot better on our atmosphere than gas engines.

WH: Hey, I do need a mower for the house. Hadn't even thought about an electric.

YF: Other ideas. Consider solar panels for your home. I can't believe solar panels aren't mandatory for all new home construction. Hopefully that comes soon. Set your thermostat way down in the winter and warmer in the summer – conserve energy wherever you can. As for our waters, also conserve! Try not to water your lawn more than once a week, and do it less if possible. Future generations will look back one day and say, "Are you kidding? They were spraying clean drinking water on grass?" And of course you know this one. Stop buying bottled water. And for your business, buy water dispensers that hold those five-gallon refillable water jugs and refill those over and over. Like the one in our bathroom. Works great. Get one for the home too. But don't stop with bottled water. Avoid other products packaged in plastic, especially those huge plastic laundry detergent bottles. Look for alternatives. Don't buy anything that's a *single use* plastic item. If you use it only once, it sure as hell don't need to be in plastic.

WH: You got me on the five-gallon water dispensers at work. Hadn't thought of that. Cody would go ape shit crazy if he opened the community fridge at Walden's Pets. We stock bottled water in there for employees and visitors. Forgot about that. Boy would he be pissed...

YF: Good, that's progress! And this involves thinking about what you eat too. Some foods are more harmful to our environment to produce than others. It's better for our Earth, and probably for yourself, to eat less meat. It's better for our Earth if you eat more locally grown produce – saves on transportation emissions. Better to avoid foods that generate a lot of waste, like fast food. I'm not saying to totally cut out any of these, they're personal choices, but be mindful about what you eat, about how and where food is produced or grown. That creates a healthier you and a healthier planet.

WH: (*A little overwhelmed.*) This all touches so much on how I live...on my daily decisions. There's so much to consider.

YF: (*Smiling.*) That's the best part, Walden. Because there's so much we all can do, *every day*. As far as providing clean water to impoverished areas, there are many nonprofits doing great work we should support. For overfishing, the same goes there. I can help you with names if you're interested. I'm amazed more politicians aren't talking about what's happening with the overfishing of our oceans. Watchdog groups say overfishing is a *top five problem* on our planet today. It's not about stopping fishing, or even cutting back that much. From what I read it's about better managing when, where, and how we fish. Like better managing our forests, which we've gotten much better at in the US over the last fifty years. There's progress, but more needs to be done. It's time we all slow down and let Mother Earth breathe.

WH: Cody talks about overfishing. He's got family who are fishermen down on the Texas coast. They're seeing smaller and smaller catches, have been for several years. Think it's partly because of that. Need to learn more there too.

YF: (*Finally slowing down, taking another sip of water.*) So Walden, let me summarize what you can do to make a difference, on top of what you're already doing like recycling at home and work. We must all take responsibility for what we buy, for what we drive, what we eat, what we use, what we throw away. Do what we can to conserve energy, to reduce our carbon footprint, to conserve and protect water, to not *over-consume*. It's time we realize Mother Earth can't be a never-ending provider of endless streams of goodies for our happiness. It's time to treat our planet like Boy Scouts again. It's time we all return to leaving this world better than we found it!

WH: Cool Yugo, and something I needed to hear. I can tell this one's a biggie for you. You're usually so calm and peaceful, but not so much with this one. I've noticed your language is a little cleaner in our sessions, so whenever you throw a *motherfucker* out there I figure you're passionate.

YF: Yeah, well I'm sorry about that. I'm consciously trying to get better. It does no good to call people names, I know that's true.

WH: Hey, no need to apologize to me...

YF: And one last thing I hesitate to bring up, but everything is made political these days, so here goes. We the people must take responsibility now for how we vote. The stakes are just too high for humankind. And I know me saying this brings politics into it, but it is what it is. When the science, the data, and just as importantly what we all *see and experience* is so consistent, I choose to support those candidates who at least acknowledge these problems exist. I'm not saying science is perfect because it's not. It's changing all the time, like everything else on this amazing planet. But *directionally* the science is clear. What we're all witnessing is undisputable. It's everyone's personal decision how to vote, there's so many different variables to consider, so I say vote your conscience. But for me, if a candidate denies these problems even exist? No thanks, man. And one thing I think we *all* can agree on. We need better candidates. More passionate, conscious, caring people running for office. Sometimes we're left with no *real* positive options at all. I also believe the younger generations, my generation, needs to wake up and make our votes count to overturn the apathy and misinformation around these issues.

WH: More like all generations...

YF: Amen, brother. Amen. Walden, we're covering two elements today because they're interconnected. Actually, you could say the next one is a subset of what we just talked about. Let's take a quick break, I've gotta hit the head, then we'll pick it back up...

YUGO GETS up to go to the bathroom and I watch him walk out of the room. He's wearing what looks like those same khaki shorts even though it's late October and getting cooler outside. All that ever changes with his "look" is the color of his t-shirt and his hair – if it's pulled back in one large tail or out in a loose dreads look. But his sandals never change, the ankle bracelets, the dangling odd shaped silver loop earring (which is really cool). He comes back smiling, holding out a cold can of something for me.

"Sorry I'm so amped up today, but I worry about our future generations, man. How tragic it would be to leave our children and grandchildren with a world unfit to live in. We mustn't do that, Walden! Here, this yerba mate will pick you up. We've got one more to go!"

"Yerba mate? What's that?"

"It's a plant native to South America that makes amazing tea. This Clean Cause is made in Austin and it's awesome. Lightly carbonated, natural. Brings me more clarity some afternoons. It's an organic caffeine that gives you a clean boost, doesn't give me a fake buzz like other energy drinks." He smiles. "It may be my only serious vice, but they donate 50% of their profits to addiction recovery, so it's for a good cause. You should check out their business model and do something like that at Walden's Pets."

Yugo pops open his can and takes a long drink – peach flavored I see. Mine's raspberry and it's just what I need. Talking about climate change and the environment going to hell isn't what I expected today, but it does make sense. To be in harmony with life we must be in harmony with nature. The two go together. It was drilled in me at Nueva Tierra and I know it's true. Yugo sits down and we dive back in:

WH: You know, Yugo, speaking of future generations, I'm holding off having kids. Worried about how things are going with climate change and all the other crazy shit happening around the world. But my parents are dying for some grandkids. My girl Jessica is starting to talk about it more, but man, I'm getting older. I've always wanted things to be at least as good for my kids as I had it, and I'm not sure that's possible anymore.

YF: Stay positive, Walden, stay positive. Life goes on and humanity must procreate. Now the first two elements of the Way we went over are spiritual, and most of the elements we go over are spiritual. But there's a few like these two that are in the physical realm, so I keep them together. This one is quick and connected. Let's look more closely at a word I used earlier, *over-consume*. Since the early 1900s, we've seen an out-of-control increase in consumption. It's been fueled by the rapid growth of the media, and in particular in the advertising that funds this media. Beginning with newspapers, then radio, then exploding with TV, humans were bombarded with ads saying if we'd just buy this product, everything will be ok. If we dress like this, or drink this beer, or drive this car, or wear this cologne, we will be *happy*. The industrial revolution turned into the century of trying to find happiness consuming shit we don't really need.

WH: I thought when you said "over-consume" you might be talking about my tequila consumption.

YF: *(Laughing and then winking.)* Ha! That one's for later, Walden, but it may not be what you think. In the early 2000s things got even worse with smartphones, social media, platforms like Twitter, Instagram, TikTok, podcasts where people use their fame to gain our trust to sell us all kinds of products we don't need. In the beginning, people saw a few ads in a newspaper, or would hear a block of ads on the radio. Now we're constantly bombarded by a never-ending stream of online ads, many of them targeted directly at us personally, all trying to get us to buy shit we don't need.

WH: *(Feeling a little guilty...this is kinda what Frazier does for us at WP.)* Yeah, I know it's crazy, Yugo. With people watching less regular TV, I thought advertisers would have it rough since there's not a large captive TV audience anymore. But now, advertisers can hit you anytime you're looking at your phone. And for most people, that's all the time, so there's an endless stream of ads thrown at us all day.

YF: Right, but the difference now is these ads aren't just thrown out there for the masses. They are targeted specifically for *you personally*. Through tracking, these advertisers know how you think, know what you like. They know what you've been searching for, or sometimes what you've been talking about. Then they hit you with the perfect ad to instantly fulfill your "need."

WH: It's nuts, I know.

YF: And this causes 1) unhappy people, always looking for the next thing to make them happy, and it never does, and 2) big time over-consumption as we buy more and more products we don't really need. Think about the waste of energy, the fossil fuels burned, the massive amount of plastic that packages all this shit. The landfills overflowing with useless discarded bullshit. And this is true for all kinds of products – with fast food, with drinks, with personal care, prescription drugs, cars, clothes, toys. It's *everything*.

WH: (*Again, a little guilty.*) Guess we gotta keep that GDP high so the market stays strong...

YF: (*Nodding.*) Yeah well, that may have been the mantra for the last hundred years, but it ain't sustainable forever, Walden. And through all this deluge of advertising constantly hitting people, there's a development that worries me almost as much as the endless stream of online personalized ads. That's your friends at Sahara...and others to be fair.

WH: Sahara? Now you got my interest up. What's the deal with them?

YF: Well I'm not talking about *only* them. They're just the most dominant so they're easiest to call out. What I'm talking about is the relatively new ability to satisfy a perceived need almost immediately. Today, not only are we bombarded with ads creating false needs, but we can instantly search a place like Sahara and order online without even thinking, "Do I really need this? Can I afford this?" We pay for it with imaginary money like Sahara Pay or Apple Pay or a credit card, then it's delivered to our door sometimes the same damn day. And don't think Sahara doesn't know the incredible *power* of getting you what you want *now*! It was their long-term strategy. *Instant gratification* through immediate ordering and insanely fast delivery.

WH: I know that's true. One of our biggest hurdles at Walden's Pets is getting products to customers fast enough. Now it has to be next day or it's not good enough. We're not Sahara so we can't always do that.

YF: But think about it. We don't need to get dog food next day. We don't need to get a book, or a toy or a video game, next day. But now, we *expect* it, and when we know we can get something almost immediately, good judgment goes out the window and out comes the credit card. Out of control online shopping is one of the newest addictions afflicting our world. It's numbing our souls, it's harming our planet, it's creating false hope as people try to find happiness in "things." And does society view this with caution and concern? Hell no! Instead, we view companies like Sahara as modern miracles. I've helped friends move, and you'd be amazed how much stuff I see never even opened. Unopened Sahara boxes everywhere. And you really think they needed that shit *next day*?

WH: You know I hate those bastards at Sahara, Yugo. Keep it coming!

YF: It's not just them, Walden. Maybe they're the biggest, but there are many others. Another thing is this new technology they recently launched called "Amanda." I mustn't let it dampen my spirit, but I'm amazed a company can create a listening device to hear what we're talking about, what we're interested in, and instead of being alarmed by this invasion of privacy, people actually *pay* for it. We buy it, then display it prominently in the house like a trophy. Like it's our own personal *servant* waiting to cater to our every need. Think about it. If the government gave us one of these things for free, we'd all be screaming about intrusion, like it's *1984* and Big Brother is watching us. But when Sahara designs it, then convinces us we really *need* it to make our lives easier, we gobble them up like bottled water. (*Yugo's looking away now with a pained expression*).

WH: Well you don't have to worry about me owning Amanda. I'd never let that bitch in my house...

YF: (*Yugo laughs and smiles.*) Always helps to add some humor with these two elements, Walden. Honestly, these are two I like talking about the least – these and one more coming later. My aim is to create positive vibes, loving emotions that evolve our thinking and our *be*-ing. Clearly these two topics dwell on negatives. But the reality of where we're heading *compels* me to talk about these elements early on. It's my prayer you're a little more hopeful about our environment now than before this talk. Just remember, these two elements are interrelated. Over-consumption is a growing problem, and that creates greater environmental strain on our Earth. And it's likely to get worse – because of new technology, new media sources, the instant gratification of online shopping, and yes, because of Amanda too.

The Practice

YF: Ok, this is a break from adding spiritual exercises to your plate, but keep practicing the spiritual work you've already started. First, begin to follow your heart when it comes to living in harmony with nature. If some of my suggestions ring true for you, do them. If you have your own ways of "leaving this world at least as good as you found it," follow your own ways. Individually, and then collectively, we *will* have a positive impact on our environment. Let this be your guide. Be conscious about what you are driving, what you are eating, the energy you're using, what you're consuming, what you're throwing away. Do your best to *change* behaviors you're doing that are harmful to our planet. Make sacrifices for Mother Earth where you can. We have all become too *comfortable.* Maybe the changes are in your personal life, maybe some are in your business life at Walden's Pets like getting water coolers for the office. As more people wake up and live in harmony with nature, even small stuff makes a difference. Second, become more *conscious* about what you're buying. Do your best to buy only those things you truly need. You'll find in our materialistic world this is sometimes difficult to do, but the *awareness* you cultivate to not over-consume will grow, become more habitual. It will bear fruit.

WH: Ok, Yugo – got it. These elements are sorta downers, but I'm already thinking about your ideas. Keep the thermostat down with winter coming, I'm thinking 68. Maybe lease a Tesla 3, eat smarter, stay away from plastics. Oh, definitely get the bottled water out of the company fridge. Remember to think, do I really need something before buying it? Lots of other opportunities I'm sure.

YF: Excellent thinking!

WH: You didn't come right out and say it, but what I heard in this last element is we should slow down or even stop impulse ordering from Sahara – maybe all impulse online shopping period. Not ordering from Sahara might be hard for most of your other students, but it'll be a breeze for me. I haven't ordered from them since I knew better.

YF: (*Big grin.*) Cool. Just two more exercises. First, before we meet again, watch that David Attenborough doc, *A Life on Our Planet*. It's less than an hour and a half, and it's awakening and inspiring. It'll worry you, but it also brings hope that it's not too late. Second, stay positive, Walden. I'm sorry if today was a downer, but it's meant to create positive change, to bring us back in harmony with nature. We can't give up or our Earth is lost. Now, enough about that. Let's jump on the pillows and have us a good sit!

This is the 3rd element of Yugo's Way:

Mother Earth is all-giving, but she needs our help now. We must restore her by taking responsibility for what we buy, what we drive, what we eat, what we throw away, what we support. Changing our way of be-ing does make a difference.

This is the 4th element of Yugo's Way:

Consume less and consciously make choices in harmony with

nature. Don't be seduced by the false promises of materialism or the allure of instant gratification.

Walden Note: Now to the cool part about Sahara that Frazier mentioned. Most of the elements Yugo summarized beautifully during our sessions – he recited them by heart. But when it came to element #4, he summarized it by saying, and I quote, *"Stop buying shit you don't need, especially online, because you can't buy happiness and the pursuit of instant gratification will get you."*

Obviously, Frazier had some work to do to create a good, eye-grabbing headline for her blogs and posts, so the three of us got together and talked about the best wording. Frazier was quick to jump on the Sahara angle since she thought it would raise clicks and engagement for our campaigns. Having their name in the headline would increase visibility. I quickly said, *"Hell no."* The thought of getting Walden's Pets tangled up in some sort of legal pissing match with Sahara scared the crap out of me. But Frazier kept pushing the idea, saying our campaign was still in the "awareness phase" and needed an extra jolt to send it to the next level.

Surprisingly Yugo wasn't against including Sahara by name. He was all about getting the elements in front of as many people as possible as fast as possible to create the most change. So we compromised because I wasn't backing down (and it was the right decision for Walden's Pets). We agreed as long as Yugo got final sign-off on the wording, Frazier would call out Sahara in her headlines and content on the business, social, and personal outlets she controls. Walden's Pets, on the other hand, would publish the 4th element as it's written above. The summary on our blog and social media posts would decry materialism and the allure of instant gratification, how it creates unnecessary impulse purchases, but there would be no mention of Sahara by name. After all, we're an online company too – there's a fine line here.

Frazier being Frazier, she tapped into the most high-profile shopping event of the year, the upcoming Thanksgiving holiday with all the insane holiday shopping shit that centers around Black Friday. And Frazier hit it *hard.* She even did some funky TikTok videos to kick things off. Remember, since we released these elements one at a time to build anticipation, the fourth element came out right after the third. We'd just inspired our audience to protect Mother Earth and conserve. Our readers and followers were greased to do what they could to make a difference.

Here's Frazier's headline, which got the most views, shares, and comments of any posts she did…by a mile:

Don't be seduced by the false promises of materialism or the allure of Sahara's instant gratification trap. Boycott Sahara on Black Friday and Cyber Monday, and send a donation to your favorite charity instead. Make yourself heard!

See what I mean? The reaction wildly exceeded expectations. To explain, the posts came during a time when the public was primed to use their mass influence to affect large, seemingly untouchable corporations. This was at a time when Reddit groups were hugely impacting company stock values – GameStop and AMC Theatre stocks exploding, weed stocks like Tilray going through the roof, etc. So when readers saw how thousands, then a few million were taking the pledge to say no to unbridled materialism and over-consumption, we had a real movement going on. Not nearly as publicized as Reddit's stock manipulations – what happened to GameStop was crazy…you can look it up. But hey, we still had a hell of an impact. Market pundits and investors got wind it could be a rough Holiday Season and thus bad Q4 for Sahara – Black Friday was gonna be a bloodbath. Sahara's stock, which had been on a meteoric rise for years, started falling – about 15% total after all the damage was done. Unthinkable at the time.

Now I've never met the man, so my prejudice comes from what I read about the company in the press, how they treat us as sellers on their marketplace, how they ripped off our best products, and how they treat their workers. But hearing the impact this had on Brett Jezak, the founder of Sahara, was both *mind-blowing* and exhilarating. As the largest Sahara shareholder by far, the press estimated he lost *over $11 billion* in the stock drop. Unbelievable. Who said *We the People* can't make a difference!

It was also gratifying to learn that *Giving Tuesday*, an event that happens every year to encourage charitable giving, saw more donations given that year than ever before. Their mantra is instead of buying stuff on Black Friday and Cyber Monday, donate to your favorite charity on *Giving Tuesday*. You know, more like the true spirit of Thanks*giving*. Frazier put information about *Giving Tuesday* in all her posts and it really built awareness and momentum. Why send more money to Sahara over Thanksgiving when you can help worthy causes and people in need instead? Another two birds with one stone event!

Now, in the spirit of transparency: Because as a culture we're addicted to shopping, our attention spans are incredibly short, and the company is a behemoth that just keeps on growing, Sahara and all of its shareholders, including Brett Jezak, came out fine in the end. I can't remember what the stock price fell to after Yugo's element hit the scene, causing the 15% drop, but looking at the market at this writing I see Sahara is very close to an all-time high even with all the shit that's going on in the world right now. In fact, if memory serves, I think it only took a couple of quarters before Sahara was making record profits and rolling again. So while it was very nice to feel we had a huge impact at the time, it was only, as they say, "on paper" for Mr. Jezak. Even so, I bet he was sweating bullets and really worried, at least for a while. And I'm certain because of the social media fanfare and the connection WaldensPets.com had with Yugo's Way, Sahara punished WP by dropping our products lower in their search results or out of the "buy box" entirely. But hey, there's absolutely no question it was worth it. To quote one of Frazier's favorite lines, "C'est la vie."

WALDEN VII

My sisters and my brothers see 'em like no other
All my favorite colors

"Colors" by Black Pumas (from *Black Pumas*)

IT'S a Friday night and Jessica and I are going out with friends to check out Anastasia and her band. We've seen her perform before – on the patio of a coffee house/brewpub and at a couple of street festivals around town – but it's been a while. Her career has really taken off since then, and this is a big night for Anastasia. She's playing a local live music mecca that's been around since the 1950s. One that legends like Stevie Ray Vaughn, Buddy Guy, Robert Plant, Alejandro Escovedo, and tons of other famous musicians have graced the stage. While world renowned in music circles, it's a small venue and that makes it even more awesome – an intimate place to catch live shows (and ironically, only three blocks down the street from Yugo's office). One of my favorite songwriters, James McMurtry, has had a "residency" here most Wednesday nights for the last year – he's a great guitarist too, electric and twelve-string acoustic. Only problem is James and the band don't start playing until midnight, so being a weeknight, it really hurts the next morning.

Anastasia isn't the headliner, she goes on second around 10:00, but she and the band are amped about the chance to play such an iconic building.

Of course Cody is psyched as well, so several of us are going out to see how the band's progressing, and show our support for Anastasia – and Cody. My entrepreneur whiz friend Bryan and his wife Ally are coming, Frazier and a friend are supposed to show up, Cody said Dylan and some of his running buddies are coming, his cousin Dwayne too.

Cody's been out of town lately traveling to the Dallas area scoping out business options, so between that and my work, Yugo's sessions, and taking care of my aging parents, we've hardly talked – I haven't seen him since his initial "Yugo rundown" at the Mexican food joint. WP's office isn't far from the club, so rather than go home and drive back into town, I'm going over early after work to have some brews with Cody and learn what else his investigative work has uncovered about Yugo.

Cody told me Dylan introduced him to a fellow "student" who knew a lot about Yugo, that he'd also made good progress on the phone with his Adeline contacts out west, and he talked to a couple of people who've worked at the Omelettry over the years – said he has some solid info. Truth is, after going back to see Yugo, feeling his presence, I'm not concerned about making sure Yugo is qualified enough to help me. After only a few sessions, I already know Yugo's heart – he's already helping me. I'm completely comfortable with him as a teacher and counselor. But his story, where he came from, how he got here, how all this wisdom and perspective was packed into such a unique and unlikely package still had me extremely curious. I looked forward to hearing more intel on Yugo and what brought him to this place in life.

Cody told me there's a spot for bands and their crew at the back of the club behind the stage where we can hang out, a mini-VIP area, and to get there early around 7:00 to talk. We could grab some free beers and munchies and catch up before the music starts.

When I get there Cody's more subdued than expected. With free beer, Friday night live music, and hanging out with friends, I expected a fully lubricated, high energy Cody. But you can tell he's nervous about Anastasia's big night, nervous for her, and he's doing his best to stay under the radar while she does her thing. I remember too, he's a pro at this – he may already be a six-pack in.

I walk to the backstage area of the club and see Cody grazing the spread. Cody says to grab a beer and some snacks if I'm hungry, and to meet him outside the back door – there's a small, secluded patio out back for the acts to smoke and hang out. I grab a Shiner, some chips, a few veggies with ranch, and head out. When I walk up, Cody's pulling folded sheets of paper out of his back pocket, spreading them out on the patio table. I put my plate and beer down, sit, and say, "Hey, dude – long time, man. We can't wait to see Anastasia tonight. Can't believe she's playing *here*! I mean, how many unreal shows have you and I caught at this place? Super cool, huh?"

Cody looks up from his papers, "Yeah it's cool. Unbelievably cool. You know, she was playing for free at any place that would have her just six months ago."

"Yeah, it's amazing! How is she feeling about tonight? Nervous or just excited?"

"That girl don't get nervous, Walden. It's crazy but maybe that's what makes some people great. She knows she's good and just loves to perform. She's stoked."

"How about you? You seem a little, oh I don't know, *tighter* than usual."

"Yeah, it's weird, Walden. This chick, man...I've fallen for her bad. I just hope so much that all goes well tonight. But hey, why should I worry? This crowd could heckle the shit out of her and she wouldn't care. Just fling her hair back, smile that big, beautiful smile of hers, and break into another tune."

"Well, she's come a long way in a short time. Here's to a kickass night, dude!"

We click bottles, each take long drinks, and I glance down at Cody's papers on the table.

"What you got there? Looks like a homework assignment you crammed in your pocket."

Cody looks down and smiles. "This here is my intel, dude. I made sure to write it all down so I wouldn't screw up any of the details. I didn't find answers to all the questions you threw at me, but most of them. Pretty proud of myself. But before we dive in, we haven't talked in so long – I don't even know how it's going with you and Yugo. He helping you out? You don't look quite as *shitty* as you did last time I saw you. That's progress, right?"

"Yeah, Cody, he really is helping. I've never had someone I can open up to about all my fears, my faults, all the fucked up shit going around in my head. Yugo makes it easy to get the garbage out, then he stays calm and helps me see things in a new light."

"Very cool! You learning any of those profound *elements* Dylan tells me about?"

Now I'm the one pulling something out of my pocket. "Yeah, I am. After I talk about my screwed up life, Yugo goes over an element or two. Some are practical, some are kind of wild ideas. Check this out."

I hand over the first slip of paper Yugo gave me – the lyrics from Built to Spill about eternity. "Read it."

Cody looks at it strangely, then says, "Chile Verde Veggie Omelet – Hatch green chiles, three organic farm fresh eggs..."

"No, no, turn it over. Yugo's a strange dude, man. The rare times he gives me anything to take home, he hands me a small slip of paper out of this box. I realized he takes the old daily specials menus from down in the restaurant and uses the blank sides to make his copies. Cuts up the sayings into strips. Crazy."

Cody shakes his head and flips it over and reads, "Randy Describes Eternity..."

He finishes and says, "That's some wild shit, Walden...a little mind expansion! This Yugo dude...I told you. Ok, you had more questions... check this out."

And Cody starts in, referring to his notes when he needs to for details. "You didn't ask about this, but it's relevant about his parents. I learned when his dad was in the Air Force early on, he got stationed at a place called Camp Lemonnier in the African country of Djibouti. Dude said this was a US naval base in East Africa, but there was an Air Force unit assigned there too called the 449th Air Expeditionary Group. Yugo's pop's name is Michael, Mike Freeman, and he went on various missions across Africa. Who knows exactly where or how, but he met Yugo's mom while over there. She and her family are from South Africa, which is a long way from Djibouti. Maybe she was going to the University in Djibouti City and they met there somehow? Her name's Faith, so after getting married she became Faith Freeman."

I'm smiling as he's reading off the base names and African city. Impressive work for Cody.

"His mom is from South Africa, huh? So Yugo's Black? I wondered about that..."

Cody's draining his beer, gives me a side look smirk, and gets up to grab another brew. When he comes back, he hands me another Shiner but he's clearly ticked off about something.

"You wanna explain to me why when a person is multi-racial with even a small *fraction* of Black lineage, they're always referred to as Black? Seth Curry, Tiger Woods, Lisa Bonet, Meghan Markle, Bob Marley. Hell, even Barack Obama for that matter. His mom was White. They all have a parent who looks Black and another parent who's obviously not. So why does society label them all as Black just like you did with Yugo?"

Not expecting this line of questioning, I stammer and say I'm not sure. Cody continues.

"All I can figure, it's one of two reasons. Either the Black race is so superior to all the others it's the dominant race, so it trumps everything else. Or historically, our society is so fundamentally racist, even a person who's a quarter or an eighth Black is labeled as Black. I think it's pretty easy to guess where the majority of people around here fall under those two scenarios. Think about it, Walden. You got any other explanation?"

"Well I never really thought about it. I assume that's how people want it – that's how they prefer to be identified. I mean, they've always called Tiger the first truly great Black golfer, so I assumed that was cool by him even though his mom is clearly Asian. Maybe because his dad Earl was the dominant parent and he's Black? Seems to me Obama always embraced being called the first Black president. Honestly, I had no idea his mom was White. You sure about that?"

Cody's taking a swig now, thinking deeply, "Interesting, Walden. You're right. I guess there's three possible reasons. Maybe that's how people want it. It's how they want to be viewed and how they view themselves. I'd be curious to know how others of mixed race feel about it. I know it's sometimes a negative for Anastasia to be labeled a "Black artist." There's places around Texas after seeing their press photos tell her and the band they don't book acts like hers, automatically assuming they're hip hop, rap, or R&B."

Now I understand why Cody's going down this path. Anastasia grew up in Antigua. Her dad's West African and her mom's Irish. Apparently being labeled a "Black artist" is costing Anastasia some gigs.

"Really? In this day and age? That kinda surprises me. Sounds downright racist."

"Oh, they don't come out and say it in a racial way. They say something like, 'No thanks, we're a country and western club,' or 'we only book Americana acts,' something like that. I read an interesting article on this the other day. Not sure if I agree with it, but it makes some sense to me. Think about how the Black race has been treated in this country over the years. Since Africans were shipped over here on slave ships, our society did everything in their power to keep people with any Black heritage labeled Black no matter how much White blood was in their bloodline. A slave woman had a White man's child and that kid was almost always raised a Black slave. Why? Because they needed them to do all the hard work, to stay in the free labor pool – to pick the cotton. They didn't want to lose their slave labor. For a long time in this country, people of mixed heritage were subjected to what was called the 'one drop rule,' meaning even one drop of African blood in a person meant they were Black."

"One drop rule? Are you shitting me? That sounds ridiculous."

"I shit you not, Walden. Go look it up."

Cody's on a roll now. No doubt the "tightness" is going away with each beverage.

"Now in contrast, think about how this country treated Native peoples. The US government and communities everywhere did their damnedest to get rid of any sign of Native Americans as fast as they could. Either kill them, assimilate them in with Whites, or move them off to a reservation somewhere out of sight. Why? Well this article said it was to keep consciences clear. That the fewer true Natives that were around, the less we were reminded how the White man wiped out their culture, entire civilizations. It didn't take long before people who had some Native blood were looked on as White. There's people all over this country with some Native blood, but they aren't called 'Indians' by the White man. They've been considered 'White' for generations. It's because they didn't start out in the free labor pool. This was their land, so they were seen as a barrier to be wiped away and forgotten."

"Hmmm...interesting theory. Does make some sense, but since we're both White, how in the hell can we relate? Maybe I'll ask Yugo what he thinks about it, how he identifies. I wondered about his ethnicity...it's very hard to tell. Why can't we all just be called human beings? Why does there always have to be a label? But we need to get on with it, Cody. Jessica will be here any minute. How about more info and a little less lecturing, huh?"

"Ok sorry...sorry. Got off on a rant. Anyway, Yugo's mom was a small Black woman from South Africa, and his dad Mike was a tall, very white military dude with a buzz cut. I bet back then in a town like Adeline it was a little uncomfortable for them as a couple, and the kids."

Cody studies his papers and moves on.

"Ok, as far as having any credentials to be a psychologist, I have no idea. Nobody I spoke to has any knowledge of Yugo going off to school or getting degrees. Seems he just started counseling people one day and the people came. I'm sure the fact he doesn't charge a dime helped him get going. He's befriended many in the homeless community from what I hear. Maybe he started with them."

"He talked about *growing up* after life kicked him in the balls. Any info on what happened? He talks sometimes about AA and rehab. Any idea what got him there?"

"Well, you know about his life in Colorado and his supposed drug dealing. There's no doubt he was in a party scene drinking, weed, doing some psychedelics. But more than one person said Yugo liked to have a good time but he wasn't a hardcore druggie or drinker when he was younger. More of a mellow party dude selling the stuff for some income who'd test his wares every now and then."

Cody surveys his notes, seems uneasy, shakes his head, then takes a big, long drink off his longneck. He asks me to run grab a couple more beers and more snacks. When I get back, he gets to the heart of the matter. "Ok, here's what I heard set Yugo off, what eventually landed him in rehab. You already know about his pop dying or leaving when he was young. I'm starting to think the guy just bolted on them by the way. So, Yugo leaves Adeline right after graduation, hikes around New Mexico and Arizona, then settles in Colorado, all going pretty well. But leaving the two people in the world he loves most behind, his mom and twin sister MaryAnne, bothers him. That's one reason I think his dad just left. It made Yugo feel like he was no better than his old man since he sort of abandoned the family too...just my theory. Yugo supposedly talked to them almost daily, sent money home as his "business" grew. MaryAnne was an incredible athlete and went to a junior college nearby and ran track, then later went somewhere in North Carolina on a track scholarship. AT&T or something?"

"You mean North Carolina A & T? They've got an incredible track program."

"Yeah, whatever. Anyway, MaryAnne goes to juco and then off to college, mom is by herself, and Yugo feels guilty about leaving them. But MaryAnne thrives at school and she's eventually considered a star sprinter on the team. There's talk she might even be good enough to go to the Olympic trials. Anyway, the two talk almost daily and do their best to stay in contact with mom, who hasn't been the same since dad left...or died. One year Thanksgiving is coming up, and they both agree to go home to Adeline to be with mom for the holidays. Yugo hasn't been home much since leaving at age eighteen. He knows he's been a shitty son, he's happy about seeing his mom, but he's most excited to see MaryAnne, who's his best friend. All those years growing up together, moving from base to base."

"Ok – go on. The shows gonna start soon the way you're dragging this out."

"I'm getting there, dude. You gotta know the background, so it makes sense. So Yugo drives down to Adeline all excited to see his family for the holidays, and MaryAnne and her best friend from high school, she also runs track at AT&T, is coming too. Yugo gets home and finds his mom isn't doing well. She's struggled with health issues since losing Mike, and she's been hiding it from Yugo. Truth is she's got breast cancer and the docs have given her only a few years to live. Different time not that long ago when people got cancer and just died, you know?"

"Yeah, it's amazing the progress treating cancer. My grandma died early from it."

"Yugo – actually it was Marion back then – Marion gets home and freaks out about his mom's condition. He knew she wasn't feeling well, but had no idea it was something as serious as cancer. Stunned he calls MaryAnne, who's on the drive home, and she admits she already knows about the cancer. That their mom didn't want to upset Marion so they decided not to say anything to him about it until they felt he was in a better place. They both worried Marion was lost, up to no good in Colorado. Yugo, I mean Marion, hears this and goes ballistic on MaryAnne. He can't believe she didn't tell him about something this important, and he lets her have it. So the next day is Thursday, Thanksgiving Day, and MaryAnne is getting in early afternoon to help cook the dinner. Only MaryAnne doesn't show. She's late."

"Yugo pissed her off, hurt her feelings, and she turned around? Or she went over to her friend's house instead?"

"That's what Marion thought so he called her cell and nothing. Figuring she's avoiding his calls he called her friend's place. They'd not seen them either. To get to the point, Walden, MaryAnne and her friend never made it. The police said not long after Marion and MaryAnne hung up, she swerved off the road on a curvy highway through the hills of Arkansas, flew several hundred feet down an embankment, and hit a massive tree, killing them both. MaryAnne was driving. The vehicle wasn't even found until the day *after* Thanksgiving. Yugo felt responsible. Pictured in his mind she started crying after he'd screamed at her. Distraught, with tears running down her face on mountainous roads, she lost control. No one really knows…"

"Holy shit, Cody. Losing a sister? Your twin and soulmate? Like that?"

"And he blamed himself...probably still does."

"Well, that seems like a hell of a good reason to go off the deep end. So drinking to get through that landed him in rehab?"

Cody takes another long drink and nods his head. "Word is Yugo took it hard, turned to the bottle. My Air Force contacts in Adeline say his father could be a big drinker. That sort of thing is genetic, you know. Yugo was trying to drink himself to death when someone finally stepped in and got him off to treatment. Haven't learned who."

"Man...poor Yugo. And his mom? Did she die soon after?"

"I assume so. Yugo made it out of rehab, but his life was a mess. Obviously, this was all before his bitcoin find. Eventually he made it back to Texas, maybe to take care of his mom, and then eventually settled here. Not sure how long she lived after he moved down. Pretty sure when he showed up in Austin his mom was gone too."

"I don't know what to say, Cody. Wow. So Yugo lost his dad, his sister, and his mom, all while he was so young...that's a lot of pain to get through."

"No shit, Walden. But let's not forget, and Dylan's the one who told me this, let's not forget those heartbreaking events Yugo went through are what molded him into the person he is today. They are tragic, but they're life. My guess is without them you're not spending every other week pouring your heart out to some dude named Yugo Free."

"Easy words to say, Cody, but shit...that sounds kinda heartless to me."

"Yeah, maybe so, but that's what I bet Yugo would say. You should ask him sometime about this if you can. That's where I got most of my info about this tragedy, from one of Yugo's old students, who said he shared all this with her."

I'm a little shaken after hearing this news. "Well, maybe I will if the time feels right...who knows."

Cody gets up and smiles down at me. He towers over the table, wearing a Dead & Company tie die t-shirt, his beard making him look like a big old bear. You can hear the sound check going on inside for the opening act. "No sad faces out there tonight, Walden. You hear me? This here's a celebration and we're gonna all get blown away by my baby Anastasia. Got that? Now go grab another beer and let's liven this place up!"

And that's what I did, and that's what we did. Anastasia (and her band) were *incredible.* Her stage presence was amazing – somewhere between Nora Jones and Erica Badu. She had the crowd in the palm of her hand, grooving and dancing – she's a beautiful, talented woman. Cody was smiling like I'd never seen him before. Pure joy was what he was feeling, swaying to the music, feeling so proud of this special person he'd somehow run into on this crazy planet of ours. And seeing Cody so happy made me even more grateful to be there with my girl Jessica, dancing together with her, laughing together, holding each other. Realizing how lucky I was to have this *amazing person* by my side. A person who loves me, listens to me, and is always there for me no matter what – warts and all.

Cody's cousin Dwayne and his wife Rosaline let loose and had a great time. You could tell they don't get out and party much. Let's just say it was an Uber kind of night for Dwayne. I hadn't spent much time with Cody's business partner, so it was good to hang out – a genuine dude but doesn't talk much. Jessica loves Rosaline. She's the talker in that couple and she had us cracking up all night. Bryan and Ally didn't stay long, which isn't like them. They're usually the life of every party, them and Cody, but I noticed they hardly danced at all. Things seemed to be a little strained, making me wonder if there was trouble in paradise, but surely not with Bryan. Then I remembered they've got two young kids at home to get back to – something I know nothing about. Maybe someday?

As we all get older, one thing is for sure – it gets harder to hang at these live music spots where the music doesn't get cranking until so late. I was ready to go home with Jessica after Anastasia's set, but we stayed until the headliner was almost done, around 1 a.m. And I will say this about Anastasia, her band, and their music. The genre cannot be defined other than to say it radiates light and lifts you up. If someone pressed me to classify it, I'd call it alternative indie psychedelic, with a dose of R&B and a little Red Dirt country. They even have this wild pedal steel guitarist who adds an awesome sound. I can't imagine any club not booking her band, "country and western" or not. When we left, we could see Cody and Anastasia in the back VIP area around the stage, slow dancing to the headliners, moving to the tunes, looking so in love. What a beautiful sight!

Oh, and this from Wikipedia on Cody's comment about a "one drop rule":

"The one-drop rule was a legal principle of racial classification that was prominent in the 20th-century United States. It asserted that any person with even one ancestor of black ancestry ("one drop" of "black blood") is considered black (Negro or colored in historical terms). It is an example of hypodescent, the automatic assignment of children of a mixed union between different socioeconomic or ethnic groups to the group with the lower status, regardless of proportion of ancestry in different groups.

"This concept became codified into the law of some U.S. states in the early 20th century. Before the rule was outlawed by the Supreme Court in the Loving v. Virginia decision of 1967, it was used to prevent interracial marriages, and in general to deny rights and equal opportunities and uphold white supremacy."

Looks like Cody got this one right. And it wasn't just a saying back then, it was an actual law in some states. And not overturned by the Supreme Court *until 1967*? Wow...

BJ III

Brett Jesak sits at the head of a massive, elegant dining table in the far south end of his office, looking down as noon traffic flows through Portland. From this vantage point he sees the Willamette River snaking through downtown and the Rose Island Bridge off in the distance. He initially purchased the massive dining table for his office so members of his senior executive staff could keep working while having dinner together; a brilliant means of getting more output from the team after hours. It also easily accommodates all ten members of Sahara's board of directors. The table is perfect for having outrageously expensive dinners brought in to pamper the board; a ploy to keep them on his side. It is a twenty-four-foot marble and brass icon to wealth, custom made in Tivoli, Italy, the cost of shipping alone more than most luxury cars.

But the reality is the board doesn't get together all that often, and Brett prefers eating his dinners, and now his lunches as well, alone. Brett has become more and more reclusive as his company and fortune continues to grow. He rarely, if ever, leaves his office for lunch anymore, preferring to work while he eats, rotating in executive after executive who provide him with business updates and briefs. He dines on exquisite, healthy, tailor-made meals made just for him from the best fine dining establishments Portland has to offer. Brett is working ridiculous hours even for him, usually more than sixty hours per week. He rarely sees Nichole on weekdays at all anymore, their time together now occurring only on some weekends or at special events they must attend together, usually affiliated somehow with Sahara.

Once Brett started eating dinners at work, he began arriving home later and later as the months went by. Sometimes, Brett never made it home at all, sleeping on one of the leather sofas spread along the interior inner walls of his office. Brett knows one of the reasons he stays later at the office is to avoid Nichole and the friction growing in their relationship. This week, it's hard to tell if Nichole is more upset about his insane work hours or that she learned Brett instructed staff to cut certain warehouse workers' hours to under thirty per week to legally avoid paying medical benefits.

Today Brett is waiting for lunch to be served, taking a brief reprise from his jam-packed, frustrating workday. He is flushed with irritation, impatience, and an intense, simmering, all-consuming anger.

His irritation comes from the sound of loud voices, frequent hammering, and a deafening power saw that's creating quite a distraction for the second day in a row. Several workers are installing a new Murphy bed in a side wall of his office. The idea for the bed, ironically, is Nichole's, who is becoming more and more worried about Brett's health and his overwhelming obsession with adding more wealth. Despite the growing friction in their relationship, Nichole still loves Brett and misses their time together, their intimacy and shared dreams. His happiness and health are of utmost importance to her. She fears Brett's lack of sleep is a big contributor to his irritability and headaches of late. A doctor friend and confidant suggested the bed might be a good way of improving his sleep, a known important contributor to mental and physical well-being.

As for Brett, he is frankly worried about the arrival of the Murphy bed. Thus far he's been successful holding off the ridiculous, unsolicited advances from the beautiful women his affluence now continually attracts. Knowing the marital strain he is under and the unremarkable routine their love life has become, Brett wonders if it's possible for him to stay true. Internally he knows that the immediacy, the privacy, and the seduction value this new bed offers will not be helpful to his cause. He is also increasingly aware that attention from the opposite sex, and the challenge to successfully seduce women he considers light years out of his league, sparks his adrenaline as much, or maybe more so, than closing a huge business deal.

Brett's impatience comes from his lunch, or lack thereof. His executive assistant knows the rotation of restaurants by day, that Mucca Osteria is for Tuesdays unless something unexpected comes up. The fine Italian restaurant is open only for dinner, but they make an exception for Brett, having one of their chefs and some of the crew go in early each Tuesday to make his lunch. The tips alone are worth it for Mucca Osteria, and the food quality, attention to detail, and service are always impeccable.

However, today we have a hiccup. Brett's longtime assistant, Miriam Dobbs, always calls the restaurant Monday evenings to confirm the lunch delivery for Tuesday. The last thing a high-end chef wants to do is go into a kitchen early to learn he has arrived for no reason, and this has happened twice. The Monday call was agreed upon to keep both Mucca Osteria happy and Brett's gourmet lunch coming. Unfortunately, Miriam came down ill late yesterday morning, and the call confirming lunch was never made, creating a panic once Miriam's fill-in got word of the situation, and all hands-on deck to get Brett's lunch.

But Brett's irritability and impatience are no match for his intense, all-consuming anger; for his simmering rage as he watches Sahara's stock price fall today tick by tick. It's dropped an astounding ten percent already, costing him billions of dollars with every little percentage point, and Brett sees no bottom in sight. And why? What is the logical explanation for this precipitous and unprecedented decline? According to staff, and he strongly questions the validity of this information, the teachings of some obscure guru nobody knows anything about called "Yugo" went viral on social media, catching the attention of the public, spreading like wildfire. This created a furor among the masses and, of course, caught the attention of Wall Street.

For reasons still unclear, Yugo asked people to boycott Sahara on Black Friday; to not shop with them for the holidays. Stock analysts, always researching every angle, quicky got wind of this viral spread. Assumptions were made about Sahara's all-important fourth quarter numbers not hitting estimates, and the stock went into a freefall.

There is no missed earnings report. No tragic accident at a Sahara facility with lawsuits threatened. No catastrophe somewhere in the world that might impact logistics or consumer demand. No logical reason exists. But the reality is, Brett is losing billions, yes that's billions with a "B", because some hippy, earth-hugging evangelist is spreading nonsense about materialism, and it happened to catch a wave on social media. What is the world coming to? Further angering Brett is the total lack of information on this idiot, Yugo. All they can find are blog posts, tweets, and social shares on the internet attributed to a picture of a large, obscure breed of dog his staff finally confirmed is a Portuguese Sheepdog.

As the construction work continues and Brett's stomach growls once more, he asks himself, "How in the hell can this happen now, when I'm so close? How can some pissant beatnik say something on Twitter and Instagram, and the next think you know I'm bleeding billions and billions of dollars?"

Frustrated to the boiling point, Brett turns angrily toward his desk, literally at the far end of his expansive office, and screams:

"Hey, Amanda!"

"Yes, Mr. Jesak. How may I help you?"

"Who is the richest man in the world?"

"That depends, Mr. Jesak, on how you define the term 'richest.' To some, it may be the person with the greatest power or influence. To others, it may be who has attained the highest level of spiritual enlightenment, the richest spiritual life. And to others, it may mean nothing more than who has acquired the most material wealth, as in the most currency."

At first Brett thinks instinctively, "Wow, the AI team has made remarkable advancements with the programming on this thing."

But quickly, the harsh reality of the moment rushes through him, and he shouts, "I'm talking about the wealthiest person in the world, you stupid bitch. The one with the most money!"

"I don't appreciate your tone of voice, sir, but thank you for the clarification. The wealthiest person in the world is Microsoft co-founder, well-known author, investor, and philanthropist Bill Gates."

With a searing headache, an empty stomach, and his blood pressure rising fast, Brett picks up the phone to find out where in the hell is his Tuesday lunch.

YUGO V

The river is my savior
She's running to the sea
And to reach her destination
Is to simply cease to be
And running till you're nothing
Sounds a lot like being free
So I'll lay myself inside her
And I'll let her carry me

"River" by Jason Isbell and the 400 Unit (from *Reunions*)

THESE LYRICS ARE JUST AMAZING. Like McMurtry, you could use Jason Isbell songs to illustrate just about every aspect of the human condition. He got his start with the Drive-By Truckers playing guitar, and get this, he got kicked out of that band for his drinking – *by the Drive-By Truckers.* They were as notorious for drinking and hard partying on the road as any band around back in the day. That's like getting kicked out of Bob Marley's band for smoking too much weed. How bad must it have been? Jason's been sober now a good long time, but you can tell from his songs it's not been easy – such a great artist.

My counseling sessions with Yugo are reaping fruit – I'm calmer, not so anxious, the small stuff doesn't get to me as much as it used to. Things like people being late, a bad day of sales at WP, traffic, idiot politicians. Jessica says she can tell a difference in me...sometimes. I think the thirty minutes a day of "spiritual exercise" is helping me create internal space – to feel less confined in my own shit if that makes any sense. Now when something happens, instead of reacting instantly, almost mechanically to the situation, there's a small layer of time in there where I have a chance to consciously think. I enjoy the twenty-minute meditations at the end of my meetings with Yugo so much at least half of my daily spiritual practice is making time to just sit in silence and "quiet my mind," as Yugo says. After Yugo compassionately helps me through the personal challenges of the last two weeks, he jumps right in:

YF: You ever hear of Howard Thurman, Walden?

WH: Howard Thurman? Nope, I don't think so. Doesn't ring a bell.

YF: Howard Thurman was an influential author, theologian, and civil rights leader whose message was about radical *nonviolence.* During a time of overt, unbridled discrimination and racism, his message was about compassion and love. Back in his day, he was thought of as one of the most important religious leaders in the country. He was the dude *before* Martin Luther King. The dude that influenced him, mentored him. But it's not surprising you haven't heard of him. Not many people have today. Back in the early 1940s, Howard said this in a famous commencement speech:

> "We must proclaim the truth that all life is one, and that we are all
> of us tied together. Therefore it is mandatory that we work for a
> society in which the least person can find refuge and refreshment."

WH: Beautiful.

YF: Albert Einstein, we were all taught about him, right? Everyone knows Einstein's one of the smartest dudes to ever cruise the planet. He wrote these words to a friend in a letter back in 1950: (*Yugo reaches down, pulls a slip of paper from his box and reads.*)

> "A human being is a part of the whole, called by us 'Universe,' a
> part limited in time and space. He experiences himself, his
> thoughts and feelings as something separated from the rest – a kind
> of optical *delusion* of his consciousness. This delusion is a kind of
> prison for us, restricting us to our personal desires and to affection
> for a few persons nearest to us. Our task must be to free ourselves

from this prison by widening our circle of compassion to *embrace all living creatures* and the whole of nature in its beauty."

WH: Wow, love that too. Compassion for all living creatures and nature too. What a radical concept in today's world, huh?

YF: (*Yugo hands me the slip of paper – the Thurman quote is on there too.*) So Walden, many decades ago, a world renown physicist, a scientist, the biggest thinker on the planet who you'd think would be concerned about theories and equations and pioneering new research – in his later years he's writing about love and compassion. That we are all a part of the whole.

WH: Pretty wild. Not what I'd expect from Einstein.

YF: And, he says human beings are living in delusion, that we think we're *separate* from the rest, and so we live our lives as though we are separate beings. There is this powerful illusion most humans believe that we are independent beings, that our existence is separate from the rest. But the reality is we're all a part of the whole, we are all *interconnected*. What both Einstein and Thurman are saying is human beings, on the macro level, are all one. And being that we are all interconnected, our actions affect not only ourselves, but they have consequences and ramifications for everyone else. When we hurt ourselves, we hurt the whole. When we hurt other people, we also hurt ourselves. It's like punching yourself in the face. Looking at other people is like looking in the mirror. *We are all one!*

WH: I see we're back in the spiritual realm this session. I hear the words you're saying, Yugo, and they sound really nice. But honestly, I'm not sure I get it. It's easy to say "all people are one." I've heard those kind of lines before. You got anything more than just 'famous smart people said it, so it has to be true'?

YF: (*Yugo puts his hands together, then pauses in thought.*) Ok, let's try this. Remember what I asked you early on? To get fully immersed in these elements, it helps if you have two leaps of faith. One, that there is a Universal Source, an Ultimate "Un-Created" out there far greater than us, and two, that human beings have a soul, a spirit. This sorta falls in line with that, cool?

WH: Alright.

YF: To get your head around this, a good place to start is to remember we were all created by, we all came from, the same original Source. Just like you got a big part of your momma and daddy in you, all of creation is built from the same stuff, the same DNA if you want to call it that. We all have the same building blocks of life as that *Mysterious Entity* that created us, because like our parents joined together to make us, that *Being* created all things, created *us*. What does that mean? It means we are all brothers and sisters, we are all family, interconnected. Our overarching societal health and evolution is dependent on how we treat *all people.* And Walden, the same holds true with all creatures – of the land, the air, the sea...even the plants and trees. Everything was created by the same hand, everything has the same maker, therefore we are all *related.*

WH: Ok, that helps...more than just hearing the words "we are all one."

YF: Here's another illustration. My parents made me go to church a lot growing up, at least twice a week, more when dad was home. Always Sunday school, then the Sunday night service, sometimes the Wednesday night thing. At church they'd throw the term "omnipresent" at me. That God was *always* present, always watching over me, like Santa Claus making a list. But they never talked much about me getting presents for being good. No, they always talked about him knowing all those times I'd been bad.

WH: Yeah, we kinda talked about that before. I didn't really get that kind of upbringing.

YF: *(Smiling.)* You can't believe how freeing it was to finally realize I was looking at this thing called omnipresence all wrong. Let's look at this through the lens of *Love* instead of the moral teachings of a small-town Sunday school teacher. Acknowledging God is omnipresent, *always here,* simply means the Universal Creator is all around us, is in all things, *always present.* The Great Spirit is omnipresent, is always here, because this Ultimate Being created all things so is *in all things.* This breakthrough was so comforting to me. It brought a certain amount of logic, but also peace and compassion. It's nothing like the image I had as a kid of an angry Father-like being looking down from his throne in heaven. Watching all my mistakes, judging me for my flaws, keeping track of all my shit, just waiting to knock me down and punish me. That's not a loving God!

WH: So it's like this. If God is in all things, he is in all of us too, therefore we are all children of God, therefore we are all interconnected.

YF: Yes! And to take it a step further. Because we are interconnected, we need to stay conscious of this fact, or maybe better words, we need to *get conscious* of this fact. We can't, as Einstein said so beautifully, live in delusion and think our thoughts and feelings are separated from the whole. And let's add here our actions too. Think of the implications. What this means is we should love *all people.* Not just Americans, not just conservatives or liberals, not just people who look like us – whites, blacks, browns, yellows, reds, multi-colors – not just people who think like us. No, we need to show compassion, love, and care for all people. Thurman said it so well, "...it is mandatory that we work for a society in which the least person can find refuge and refreshment." Makes you wonder how it's even possible, as far as humanity has supposedly evolved, that human beings today still go to war to kill one another simply because they're told to by our supposed leaders. There's still such a long way to go, Walden...

WH: Amen to that. Seems war and killing other innocent human beings should always be the absolute last resort, not a first or second option.

YF: Hallelujah! Now, let's take this down more to the personal level. What can we do personally to show more compassion, to help others? One thing we can all do is become *less self-absorbed.* To stop thinking so much about our own shit, and instead think about how we can help other people.

WH: I'm starting to see being too self-centered is one of my character flaws. When I practice trying to stay conscious of my thoughts, stop my negative thinking, and send positive vibes into the Universe, I notice I'm usually thinking about myself. Why'd this happen to me? How will this affect me? Why'd this person do that to me? How's this going to make me look? And I think the pressure to look good on social media makes our self-centeredness even worse. It's a breeding ground for self-absorption, narcissism.

YF: (*Nodding in agreement.*) You're no different from any of us. We all live under the illusion of the separate self. That life is all about *me.* Practicing more humility helps us get away from the feeling that the world revolves around me. There's an old saying in AA about being less self-centered, more conscious of others, while keeping a healthy love for yourself. It goes, "Humility is not about thinking *less* of yourself; it's about thinking of *yourself* less."

WH: Love it! Words to live by.

YF: Give back, Walden, because we are all one! I love the saying "Do something nice for others every day, and if you can, do it when no one's looking." Compassion and humility all in one sentence! The same is true, by the way, for doing something nice for Mother Earth every day.

WH: Yep, I know for me sometimes I don't mind doing good things to help other people. I kinda like it actually – makes me feel good. Like helping Frazier's friend's mom move the other day, or donating pet food to the SPCA. But man do I want people to notice it when I do. I want that pat on the back, that attention for being a good guy.

YF: (*Laughing.*) Yeah, don't we all. The difference is you're hearing shit now that means you should know better. Contemplate this. We are all like a flowing river, returning to the Source, but many of us are struggling against the current, fighting to have things our own way, the way we *think* they ought to be. We must let go of this struggle, release our ego, our false personalities formed since childhood, and return to our core Essence. Let the river take you, Walden, go with the flow until you become one again with the Source, one with *everything*. This is interconnection, and this is *freedom*. When we surrender and become one with the Divine Spirit of the Universe, then we are truly free, and the *power* we feel from letting go, from trusting and just be-ing, is unspeakable.

Yugo takes a quick break here to grab a glass of water and hit the restroom, so I start looking more closely around his office. All my visits we are always sitting together talking. I've never had the chance to really scope out what Yugo has lying around the place. I notice some pictures on the small desk over against the wall. I can't make them out from this distance, but one is a foldable two-picture frame with the images of two people. On the other side is a picture of a guy who looks in uniform. Being curious after hearing about Yugo's family from Cody, I go over to the desk to get a better look. In the foldable dual picture frame is a beautiful young woman, like a young Halle Barry but more jacked, with a gorgeous smile and sparkling eyes. She's in a nice dress – looks like a graduation kind of picture, or a photo from an event like a wedding or something. The picture on the other side is a dark Black woman, hard to tell her age, with short, cropped hair and an uncomfortable forced smile. She too is in a nice dress, but I get the impression she was neither comfortable nor happy to be wearing it.

The picture on the right side of the desk is of a military man in full battledress. He's incredibly white – like an even whiter Chris Simms, the sports announcer and Phil Simms's son if you know him. There is a difference though. This dude looks like a bad mother f'er. He has a look in his eye that he's serious business and you don't want to even think about messing with him. I glance down at the floor and the tidy stacks of books lying around, the bookshelves already full, when Yugo walks back in, startling me a little.

"Hey, Yugo, lots of books here, man. You must read all the time."

Yugo studies me, then surveys the floor. "Don't like to admit it, but a lot of these books on the floor? I've never read them. Many are gifts from students, friends. They all want me to read something and then tell them what I think."

"Really? You haven't read them? That surprises me."

"Oh, I've read tons of books, Walden, but you know what I eventually learned?"

"What's that."

"I learned at some point you gotta stop reading all the time about how to become more spiritual, and instead start actually *being* more spiritual."

We sit down to go over the assignment for the week and I do a little fishing.

WH: So those pictures I see on your desk. Is that your family? Girlfriend?

YF: (*Yugo turns and looks at his desk, then turns back smiling.*) Those? That's my momma and my dad. My dad was in the Air Force.

WH: Looks like a very decorated, serious dude.

YF: (*He grins.*) Right on both counts. And that girl next to my momma you called my girlfriend? That's my sister. I like having them back there smiling at me while I talk to people.

WH: (*I smile to myself, thinking maybe Cody's intel is mostly true. Then kick myself for asking about family members I've been told are now gone.*) Beautiful family, Yugo, beautiful.

YF: Yes they are, Walden. Thank you. Now before we get to our practice for today, I want to reinforce something, so it stays in your heart. I've alluded to this before, but it ties into the books you see around the office, the talks I'm giving, the opinions and ideas I'm sharing.

WH: Ok, shoot.

YF: While it's true we are all interconnected, it's also true we each have our own individual path to discover the Divine, Loving Energy at the Heart of the Universe. A path that runs through our own *personal experience*. Everyone's journey is personal, unique to our own history, our culture, our relationships. No one's journey is exactly the same. The steps and exercises we go through are guideposts. They're meant to point the way to find peace and contentment. But remember Walden, all of my students, including you, have to find your own best way to live and embody these ideas. Follow your heart and surrender. Ask the Universe for help, and see what happens. Spiritual growth is all about *your experience*, not what somebody dictates to you. If what we're doing is working, bringing you peace, contentment and clarity, cool – you're on the right path. If it's not, change it up a little, try something else. Your spiritual experience should be evolving, growing, never static or overly ritualized. Spirituality is *experiential.* Trust and then be free! Humanity's purpose is to grow, to evolve spiritually, to become more like our Maker. Simple as that. That's why we're here on this Earth.

The Practice

YF: You got a good base for this element from the practices you're doing already. Awareness of your thoughts and being spiritually fit are an important part of this. Now let's look at certain words, relationships, and our mechanical reactions to them. I want you to notice when you get a strong *feeling of otherness*, from either words you hear or relationships you are in.

WH: Come again?

YF: I want you to become more conscious of the times you get a feeling of *Us Versus Them*. Of I Am Right and They Are Wrong. Really drop into the feeling of *otherness*, of being separate, apart or different from something. Notice when you have an immediate reaction mentally or emotionally to something you feel is wrong. Some examples. You're a conservative and Stephen Colbert's on TV joking about the Republicans. You're a liberal and you click on the radio and Sean Hannity's talking about how liberals are destroying our country. You're concerned about mass shootings and gun violence in schools and the person you're having lunch with is a member of the NRA. You're a huge Bears fan and you see your new neighbor across the street hanging up a Packers flag.

WH: You're an Aggie, and you realize your new boss is a Longhorn. Yeah, ok. I get it.

YF: (*Laughing.*) Good! As divided as we are as a society right now, there's more examples than you can count. I hear of families who are torn apart, who don't even talk to each other anymore, over the silliest beliefs they feel certain are *true.*

WH: I hear you. No doubt people are in each other's face more these days. Pissed off all the time.

YF: Unfortunately, I agree. So, this is about awareness and then action,

Walden. First, recognize those times when you tighten up and feel that mechanical tightness that happens when you hear trigger words you might have like Trump, or Hillary, or climate change, or gun control, or immigration. You're in a relationship and someone says something you don't agree with, and boom. Just that recognition loosens the automatic emotional response your body has mechanically created for so long. Believe it or not, that *awareness alone* helps chip away at your crystallized reactions. Then once you've become aware, once you realize you're heading down that same reactive path, wake up and say to yourself, *"We are all One. We are all from the same Source. I do not know. Let it Be."* You'll notice this phrase is the last line on that paper I gave you with the Thurman and Einstein's quotes...so you'll remember.

WH: Ok?

YF: Alright, Walden, I know this might sound like wishy-washy bull-shit, but the reality is we are mechanical beings whose bodies and emotions just automatically respond to certain stimuli, and a huge one is this whole Us Versus Them mentality. The feeling that I know what is right, and they are full of shit. We have to get away from the automatic, unhealthy reactions we all have from the need to be *right*. This world is so divided. Family members not speaking, political parties not doing what's best for people but hoping for the worst so it hurts the *other guys*. It's a downhill slope, getting worse, and we all need to chill out and remember, *No one really knows*. Nobody is always right, and the bullshit the public is routinely fed that we call facts is usually manufactured half-truths.

It's time we all relax, admit we don't know everything, and stop getting so pissed off by other people who are just acting mechanically and "know not what they do." I promise you. Don't worry so much about being right and finding enemies. Become aware, then say the mantra, *"We are all one. We are all from the same Source. I do not know. Let it Be."* You will find peace. Period. That's what you're here for, right? Peace and contentment?

WH: Ok, got it. Everything else you told me to do seems to be working. My relationships are better, especially with Jessica and how I'm dealing with Mary. I'm worrying less, less angry. I'll give this a try. I can tell you three things right now that piss me off immediately without even thinking –Ted Cruz, Pitbull, and Sahara. I'll start there.

YF: *(Laughing again.)* Pitbull? Haven't heard that one before, but ok. And there's a second practice I want you to do that's at the heart of this element. It rekindles *compassion* and then keeps it alive. It's time to start consciously thinking about other people before yourself. Some small steps.

There's a last slice of pizza or only one beer left. Let the other guy have it. Your girlfriend Jessica wants Thai but you're craving Mexican. Do the Thai. Someone has their blinker on to come into your lane? Let 'em in.

Now the bigger things. You see a homeless family under the I-35 bridge? Go buy a family meal at KFC and give them a good dinner. You have a good quarter at Walden's Pets? Maybe donate some of those profits to charities that really help people. You have free time on the weekend? Volunteer at the food pantry or deliver for Meals on Wheels. And it doesn't just have to be for people. It should also be for our Earth. You go to the lake and see somebody left beer cans all over the place. Pick them up, recycle 'em. And I know this might sound like bullshit to you, Walden, but it's not. If you can, if it's possible, do some of this shit when no one else is looking.

This is the 5th element of Yugo's Way:

We are all one, all interconnected, from the same Divine Source. Have compassion and empathy for all beings, remembering, what we do unto others we are doing to ourselves.

WALDEN VIII

This friend of mine said:
'Close your eyes, and try a few of these'

"Your Bright Baby Blues" by Jackson Browne (from *The Pretender*)

SOME OF YOU might think I'm the p-word for waiting so long to write this part, or for having Frazier write about the *cluster-fuck* going on in my life before going to see Yugo, and I'm ok with that. You're probably right, and that's cool with me. Two lessons I learned from Yugo I try to always live by are 1) don't live in the past, especially reliving difficult events that spark the emotions, and 2), avoid negative thinking like it's poison to your body.

Both the experience I'm about to describe, and most of the events that led to my breakdown, fall into those two categories, so frankly I'd rather not rehash them. But it's a fact this story isn't complete without including what happened, and then the resulting collateral damage that sent me Yugo's way. Another reality causing my delay to get this down on paper? What Jessica and I experienced that night is very hard to clearly describe, hard to recreate in writing. I knew I needed more time to get comfortable writing so I could paint the most accurate picture possible of what happened – what ultimately convinced me to email Yugo back. Here goes...

My girlfriend Jessica and I went downtown on a Wednesday night to grab dinner – have some sushi and Chinese at this popular Asian fusion spot. As Frazier previously described in detail, I wasn't in a great place around this time, and Jessica thought it would be a good change of pace to get out and have a date night during the week. I'd already had a couple of drinks before picking Jessica up – I could tell she was a little pissed I'd started even before getting to her apartment. Even so, we had a nice conversation driving into town, but I noticed a few miles from the restaurant I was very low on gas. I mentioned this to Jessica, saying we'd need to fill up on the way home.

Dinner was fine, but one of my weaknesses is good sake. To me, you take away the sake and the wasabi from a sushi meal and you've stripped away the two best things (granted I'm no connoisseur). I'm on my third or fourth white ceramic decanter, obviously too much, when Jessica starts talking about my mom Mary and her dementia, which is, as you know, getting worse by the day. Father does a good job taking care of her now, but there's a growing worry that at some point Mary's memory will be totally gone and he won't be able to manage her on his own. That's the last thing I want to talk about tonight with everything else going on, and our nice evening starts going downhill – fueled I'm sure by too much rice wine. As we're finishing up the meal and I order one more round, Jessica puts her foot down and says if I drink anymore, she's grabbing a Lyft home. That's not what I want to hear, but, pissed off, I cancel the last sake, pay the bill, and sulk out into the parking lot.

We get in the car, obviously the tension is high, and the last thing going through my sake-soaked brain is that I need to get gas. Being this was a "date night," we preplanned for Jessica to stay at my place tonight – her bag is already in the back seat, her dog with a neighbor – so I start driving home. I live outside of town almost to the lake, so the road to my place is an extremely hilly winding road of ups and downs with the river on the left side of the road and cliffs and secluded neighborhoods on the right. A little more than halfway home, I look down and see again the light on the dash saying low gas. Our range is only six miles – shit! This thin, winding road has no service stations, stores, or businesses on it for miles. There's a Shell station up the road, but it's five or six miles at least, and the steep hills on this road are big time gas drainers. Knowing this could mean trouble, I confess to Jessica I forgot we were low on gas and it's somewhat "iffy" if we're gonna make it to a gas station.

This news is taken about as well as my order for another sake, and she starts going into a rant about how my drinking too much may cause us to get stranded on a dangerous road late at night. Let me stress here the extent of the hills on this road. At certain points, you go up a hill, not seeing any part of the road directly beyond the top of that hill, and once you hit the top of that hill, only then do you see any downhill view of the road in front of you. As Jessica begins to lay into me, we are reaching the pinnacle of one of the tallest hills. It's just after 10:00 p.m. and very dark – this isn't the type of road with any streetlights. What we're about to see as we crest the hill and look down into the valley below is truly beyond description.

At the bottom of the hill in the middle of the road, oddly turned sideways, is a large white delivery van, like a bread truck, totally engulfed in flames. The fire is roaring, completely out of control. Shockingly, stuck directly in the front radiator of the van is a motorcycle that must have somehow caught air, then slammed into the van as the van was turning onto the road from a neighborhood street. Even more shocking, the cycle is sticking *straight up in the air* – its back wheel stuck directly into the front radiator of the van. The bike must have been off the ground, in some kind of "wheelie" position in the air on impact. The cycle itself seems to be defying gravity. It's perfectly perpendicular to the road, like something was holding the bike up on its back wheel. The whole cycle, including its front wheel, is clearly visible jutting out from the van as the light from the flames silhouettes the burning motorcycle in the dark evening sky.

Upon seeing the unbelievable wreckage in front of us, Jessica immediately screams out and starts sobbing. She's always hated that I have a cycle, that I ride sometimes out in the Hill Country, and she's crying out intensely, "Oh my God! Oh my God! You can never ride that cycle again! You can never ride that cycle again!"

I'm in shock, almost frozen in time, trying to get my head around what's happening in front of me. We were driving full speed topping the hill, there was no traffic buildup, so this accident *just happened*, literally seconds before we got here. I slow down almost to a complete stop as we descend the hill, and I survey the scene as Jessica cries and the fire rages on. As we get right next to the burning van I'm thinking, what should I do? Should I pull over and try to help? I look ahead, up on the left side of the road, and see two cars already pulled over. Someone saw this right before we did, maybe even saw it happen, and they've stopped to help.

As I creep slowly past the burning van, the motorcycle also engulfed in flames, sticking straight up in the air, its back tire stuck in the grill, I see three guys bending down on the left side of the road about twenty feet from my car. To my horror, on the ground is a body in black leather-type motorcycle gear and a full-face racing helmet *covered in flames*. The guys around him are literally rolling his body along the ground as fast as they can while also pounding on him, doing all they can to extinguish the flames. My mind simply cannot process the sudden sight of a human being literally burning to death before my eyes. All I do is say, "Oh my God."

From the passenger side, Jessica, thank goodness, cannot see on the ground over to the left side of the road. She's turned away now, still crying, and fortunately avoids seeing the burning cyclist. In a complete fog, I start to pull over, but I'm also thinking, what can I really do to help with these three other guys already doing all they can? And, I'm embarrassed to add, I thought if I stop here, we'll run out of gas for sure and be stranded at this insane scene while the police, ambulances, and firetrucks shut down the road to take care of this tragic accident.

We are stopped now, just off the far-right lane on this thin, four lane road. Jessica is crying, and I'm fighting back tears not knowing what to do, suddenly very sober but also with no clue what to do next. The motorcycle rider continues to burn, the rolling totally ineffective. I think the cycle's gas tank must have exploded when it hit the van, covering the rider with gasoline, which ignited immediately on impact and now will not go out. I see cars on our side of the road in the rearview mirror now backing up. Some are slowly passing us by now, looking at the insane scene and then inching on past the wreckage and driving off. I look at Jessica as if to say, "Should I help?" But Jessica is in shock and disbelief at the unspeakable sights in front of us.

Completely shaken and confused, I too slowly drive off, picking up a little speed, getting back on the winding, hilly road, trying to understand what we just saw. Dazed, we drive in silence, Jessica no longer crying, staring blankly out the window. I immediately feel guilty and worthless for not as least trying to do something to help. As we get to the last hill on the way home, the steepest and longest hill on this road by far, I glance down and see the car's range estimate hit zero, thinking, what does it matter? Who cares about running out of gas when a human being is suffering what I'm certain is an excruciatingly painful death. But somehow the car keeps going with the gauge at zero and makes it the remaining mile or so to the Shell station, where I pull in, get out to fill up the car, and almost pass out from dizziness and lightheadedness. I do not feel well. My brain is on overload, unable to process such an unexpected tragedy.

We get home and I immediately go throw up, nauseous from the visual of a burning human being and that motorcycle, sticking up in the air like a cross, burning in the night. I doubt the wasabi, the sake, or the drinks I had before dinner helped my churning stomach, but I think my body was trying to purge those terrible images out of my mind. We talk about what we saw, wondered if the driver of the van or anyone else may have died. I then go to bed and I lay there, eyes wide open. The next morning, I felt like shit and didn't go into work that day. I finally got out of bed around 9:00 a.m. and went into the kitchen. Jessica was at the table with a cup of coffee, scrolling through Twitter and other news feeds, looking for information on last night's accident. Looks like she's not going in to work today either.

"You see any news about the wreck? I don't see any way that guy lived."

Jessica's twirling her hair anxiously, staring at her phone. "You're right, he didn't make it. He died at the scene. They're saying the driver of that van, a passenger with him and some guy who pulled over tried to help, but there was nothing they could do."

"Wow, the driver of the van and a passenger were lucid enough to get out and try to save him? I knew I should've stopped. Get out and at least do something. Instead I just froze and thought about the fucking gas."

"There's nothing you could have done, Walden. The impact that bike must have hit the van with? You said he was totally on fire."

"Man oh man was that awful. I've never seen anything like that before. I was thinking last night. Can you imagine the horrific images people see who are thrown into war? How do they manage through?"

"Many of them don't." Jessica pauses, then.

"I hate to say this, Walden, but it gets worse."

"Worse? What do you mean?"

"The motorcyclist had a passenger on his bike, his girlfriend. There were two people on that thing when it crashed."

"Oh shit...and she died too?"

Jessica nods. "They found her over a hundred feet from the van. She was thrown off on impact and flew far away from the flames. This article says she died from trauma. Probably why we didn't see her in the dark. She wasn't on fire."

"Holy shit!"

"But that's not all, Walden, there's more."

"More? How can there be more than that?"

"Sit down, Walden. Please, sit down."

I sit across from Jessica, study her face. Tears are forming, now streaking down her cheeks.

"The driver of that motorcycle? You're not going to believe who it was."

"What, you mean we know him? That guy burning on the side of the road is someone we know?"

"Well, you could say that. The guy who died Walden was Little Johnny."

"What? Little Johnny? You mean the guitarist? Our Little Johnny?'

"Yes, our Little Johnny. And the girlfriend on the back…"

"No, not Angelina. No, no! Not Angelina too!"

Jessica just shook her head yes, and we both burst into tears. Little Johnny Saxton was a young local guitar hero who'd taken the town by storm. This place is known for its guitar greats. It seems there's always another "next Stevie Ray Vaughan" people are raving about. But in the case of Little Johnny, the accolades were true – especially to me. He was one helluva guitarist, incredible live shows. And being he was young and unknown, just getting started, Jessica and me and Cody and all our friends got to see him play at tiny clubs and bars all over town, just waiting for him to be discovered and hit the big time, like Gary Clark Jr. or Stevie Ray.

And Angelina? Angelina? She was Johnny's girlfriend who was there at *every* show. A whirlwind of joy and energy in pigtails and a mini, twirling around in circles, smiling, dancing to every song, getting the crowd all into it – she was such a beautiful being. It was impossible to see Little Johnny play for the first time without having to ask somebody, *hey, who's that chick*? And the way he loved her, would look down from the stage and watch her as she twirled around in delight. He'd sometimes sing "Pride and Joy" to her, telling the crowd beforehand, "I'm borrowing this tune tonight from Stevie Ray to play for my girl Angelina."

My eyes are tearing up now just thinking about it. I could not understand why these two beautiful beings were so tragically taken out of this world – the senselessness, the randomness, the lack of fairness. I'm still not over it – the grief for the people who died *or* the accident itself. Every time I drive down that road, without fail, the memories come back. They've redone that part of the road with new barriers so it's impossible for a vehicle to take a left turn out of that neighborhood against traffic anymore, but it's too late.

Ok, so here comes the Cliff Notes again. While seeing a horrific accident shouldn't be enough to drive a man to the brink of insanity, I was already teetering on the edge, and so shortly after this I simply snapped. On top of the website kidnapping, the struggles at WP, Father's heart surgery and Mary losing her mind, my fucked up friend driving through a damn grocery store window, and the greatest cat in the world, Bob, friggin' dying, witnessing this tragedy was the final blow. I started drinking immediately after hearing Jessica's news – screwdrivers that morning to get me through was my rationale – and I didn't stop for over five full weeks.

A "friend" of mine who I'd partied with and seen several Little Johnny shows with came by a couple of days later after hearing I was basically at the scene when the accident happened. He of course brought booze and weed, which I don't even like to smoke anymore. But he also heard from Jessica I was depressed and couldn't sleep, was mentally unhinged and not going to work, so he brought me some benzos for anxiety – a full bottle of Xanax. Now if there's anyone on this Earth who should know not to mess with benzos and alcohol, it's me. I've seen firsthand how addictive they are, how hard they are to kick from watching T------'s terrible decline (my aforementioned friend who's been to rehab so many times, crashed through that plate glass window, spent months in jail).

Seeing the *absolute devastation* it's brought to her life should have been enough for me to say "no thanks" when pills were offered as a reasonable solution to make me feel better. Let's just say it wasn't. Five weeks of nonstop drinking, ten to twelve Xanax a day (yes, I had the bottle refilled), and rarely going into the office is what happened next. I effectively numbed myself from life and went into a startlingly fast descent into hell.

Trashed and going through benzo withdrawals – I ran through four bottles of pills in a month before finally realizing getting more was crazy – and feeling shame, guilt, and self-loathing from abandoning Jessica, Walden's Pets, Frazier, my friends, and my folks, I finally got my shit somewhat together and emailed Yugo about coming back to talk more about his services. Only Jessica knows the total extent of my downward spiral – not even Cody or Frazier – but there it is. They know now.

Oh they knew I was depressed, that the wreck and who died had hit me hard, that I was drinking too much. But I hid all the rest. Said I was working from home, etc. Jessica was my strength, my guardian angel. At first she left, saying my drinking was too much and she was done. But eventually she realized I might not be able to pull myself out of this self-created hell, that this time was different, that I really was in trouble. She came back, got me eating and taking care of myself again, helped me sober up and realize the futility of the road I was on. Without her love, who knows what happens? She saved me. Like the Jackson Browne song says, she took my hand and pulled me through. So, in summary, when I went back to see Yugo, let's just say I was one fucked up and wounded SOB, ready to listen and do almost anything to start feeling human again.

YUGO VI

But a lie's a lie, it destroys from the inside
Decays the teeth from behind that false smile

"Same Old Lie" by Jim James (from *Eternally Even*)

IT WAS IN THIS SESSION, during the counseling part, that I opened up completely with Yugo about what finally got me to surrender and ask for help – about the last straw that sent me on my downward spiral. I don't know what took me so long because as usual, Yugo helped me process things, see the situation in a new light, learn from it. I'd been upfront that I was having issues with alcohol and other things, but never got into these details until this day. As we talked, I asked him why such a tragic, sense-less thing could happen to these two young innocent souls and to everyone who loved them and would miss them. This was, I think, the first time Yugo talked to me specifically about his life experiences, his family. Maybe he knew that to help me through a question like this, he needed to show me he'd lived through similar pain – although his pain was far deeper than mine.

This was a watershed moment for me and our relationship. Although he didn't frequently talk about details of his life or family in our later meetings, he did interject things about his personal life at times from this point forward. Who knows why – maybe because I commented on his family pictures last meeting? This dialogue isn't part of the elements or practice for today, but after listening to my recordings, I think I should include it:

WH: So why does shit like this happen, Yugo? Why would God take such innocent, beautiful people at such a young age? I see so many horrible people living what looks like incredible lives. So how do you explain all the bad shit that happens to good people? And it's not just to them. It's pain for their families, their friends.

YF: That's one of life's big questions, and I hate to give you this answer, Walden, but I don't know. I cannot tell you why.

WH: *(You can tell a little agitated.)* That's it? You don't know? Come on, Yugo, you gotta have something. This is *the question* so many people struggle with when it comes to religion and God. How come random horrible disasters happen all the time to innocent people?

YF: I say I don't know, Walden, because *nobody knows*. Nobody knows the mind of the Ultimate Being, and anyone who says they do know is lying. No one really knows. Be certain of that.

WH: Well, surely you've thought about this question. You've got to have an opinion. What do you think?

YF: Maybe this helps a little. I've had tragedy in my life, as all people do. When I was younger, I lost my sister in a devastating, senseless accident...

WH: *(Kicking myself. I didn't mean to bring up pain for Yugo – I didn't mean for it to go here.)* Oh, I'm so sorry, Yugo. I'm very, very sorry. That must have been really hard.

YF: Yes it was, Walden, very hard. *(Long pause while he gathers his thoughts, hands coming together at his chin as if in prayer.)* I too asked those kinds of questions of myself and others for many years, and that's one reason I can tell you most certainly, *I do not know.* But you asked for an opinion, so I'll give you one that at least helps me with the pain. It's the best I can come up with after years of contemplation, but if you think it's nonsense, then let it go.

WH: Ok...

YF: Ok. First, human beings usually define *life* as our time here on Earth, our *physical existence* on this planet only. As we already talked, that's a tiny pimple on an elephant's ass of time when you consider all eternity. Second, life on this floating blue ball isn't always easy. It's painful, it's hard, it can be unfair, confusing, unforgiving. Third, who knows exactly what the afterlife will be, but most religions teach that if you live with love and compassion down here, it will be a whole lot better where you go in the next life, when you move on to that next plane. So there you have it. Those of us remaining may suffer terribly from the loss. Those who are taken early may be the lucky ones. They're moving up.

WH: Hmmm...interesting way to look at it. That was short. I was expecting a longer explanation.

YF: *(Shrugs his shoulders.)* I figure maybe it's like this. Life here on Earth is so short compared to all eternity, our whole physical existence here is like the blink of an eye. What's the big deal cutting out a tiny slice of time in this realm? Especially considering life down here can be such a struggle, while life on the next plane may be paradise if we do our part to live well and do our best. So, there you go. That's my theory on why good people die young. It ain't that bad a deal passing on early. In fact it might be a great deal, at least for them.

WH: Not what I expected, but ok. I can maybe see that.

YF: Humanity, these days, is scared shitless of dying. If we believe we are eternal beings, and we have faith in a loving Higher Power, scared shitless of dying is the wrong way to live. Now, I'm not discounting the pain that death causes to those left behind. Losing a loved one, especially unexpectedly and tragically, is terribly painful. Loss is hard. The loss of my sister was almost too much for me to bear. Trust me on that. *(Yugo pauses a few seconds, looks away, gathers himself.)* Missing the presence of your loved one is *pain*. And dealing with that takes time. Time seems to bring the only relief – even if that sounds trite, it's truth. That and maybe believing it was just the right time for them to evolve forward, to advance to where they are *supposed to be*.

WH: It is so hard on the family, on friends. I didn't even know Little Johnny or Angelina other than buying them some beers and talking a few times after shows. But the experience *affected* me so. The haunting images that won't go away. The burning body. To be so close to such violent death...

YF: Well, one other line of thought, or line of bullshit – your choice. I think it's true that without seeing that horrible accident, you may not have ever emailed me back to get together. True?

WH: Probably. Who knows?

YF: Right – who does know? As for me, I know this for sure. If my sister hadn't passed on the way she did, I wouldn't have responded the way I did. There's no way I would have crashed and burned when and how I did, falling apart, getting shipped off to rehab – which is what happened,

Walden. I fell deep into the bottom of a bottle and couldn't get out on my own. That started the beginning of my seeking. I wouldn't have met those exact people at that exact time, heard the same wisdom, connected with the same mentors, at least not then, without my dear sister's passing. It eventually changed my whole way of being.

WH: Kind of like something good coming out of a terrible tragedy?

YF: Maybe. It's something we can tell ourselves, right? But I don't like thinking my sister died so that I could get my shit together. It's dangerous to ever bring up the past and think you know why something really happened. Again, *we do not know why*. But I do know that difficult events outside our control happen all the time. And how we evolve as human beings depends on *how we respond* to those events. I responded to the death of my sister in the way I did, and you responded to Little Johnny's accident that night in the way you did. And here we are together today. Are they interconnected? Who knows exactly? But the Universe shows me all things are intertwined in some way, we just don't know how or why. It just *is*. Which is why we must stay conscious, be aware, and respond to events from our heart. And why we should live in awe and wonder each day, thanking our Higher Power for giving us the breath of life....

I still think about what Yugo said on this subject, as he'd say, "contemplating if it sounds true." I do know what he said helped me at the time, it made some sense. Who really knows? Now to Yugo's Way for the day. There's two elements this session, but since I thought it important to include that conversation with Yugo, I'll break them into separate chapters:

YF: So Walden, we started along this Way by understanding what it means to be eternal beings and by beginning to "work out" our spiritual bodies. Then we learned how important our thoughts are, how they are real and that they matter, not just to us but to our planet as a whole. Next, we covered the importance of being in harmony with Mother Earth, and how over-consumption is a big reason our planet needs our help. Now we begin work on living in a more spiritual way. So, let me ask you. What do you think it means to *live spiritually*?

WH: Live spiritually? Hmmm, I don't know. Pray more? Read spiritual books, the Bible, or whatever book your religion believes in. Go to church more?

YF: Well, those can all be positive. Have you ever tried any of them?

WH: I've been to church. A little as a kid, some with Mary in Wimberley, a few times with Jessica. Not really for me. I pray some, but I don't think I know what I'm doing. And reading the Bible? I tried reading Revelations once thinking it'd be cool. All it did was confuse the hell out of me – all that apocalyptic language.

YF: (*Smiling.*) To read something "spiritual" or hear something inspirational at church, then feel like we're *being* spiritual, that we're better somehow from this knowledge, is usually not true. Many of us read inspiring spiritual truths and then feel superior to other people, just because of what we read. That's vanity. That's pride. That's *not* spirituality. I know for me when I began seeking? I'd read something I thought was life changing and rather than leaning into the truth as it relates to evolving my being, rather than changing my thoughts or actions, I'd think, man does momma need to read this. Or one of my friends should check this out, or my girl needs to hear this so she'll change.

WH: (*Laughing.*) Ha! I do that all the time. Father and I don't always see the world the same way, so I'll read something I think is profound, and the first thing I do is think, Father really needs to read this.

YF: That's our egos talking – overriding our consciousness. Studying meaningful spiritual teaching is worthless if it doesn't change our actions, our thoughts, our intentions, our experience. We are not better people for simply reading a spiritual book. We're not more spiritual for hearing an inspiring sermon we think *others* need to hear. In fact, when we're exposed to teachings and don't act on those words, it's *worse* than never hearing them at all. We lose our excuse of ignorance. This is where the rubber meets the road, Walden. That's why most of the Way requires *action*, a change of being – not just reading words and feeling good about yourself. Sitting here with me, listening to my teachings, my spiritual path? Don't mean shit if it doesn't wake you up and change your actions, evolve your *be*-ing.

WH: .....

YF: Let me tell you a story. It's the best way I know to answer the question, *How do I live spiritually?* When I was in rehab, struggling for my life, a few weeks in and feeling no hope, I met with this wise spiritual counselor who saved my life. Still remember the dude's name – David Potter. I was in despair, living in darkness, anger and fear, all overshadowed by shame and guilt for my actions. Of course they go over the Steps of AA in there, and Step 2 is "Came to believe that a Power greater than myself could restore me to sanity." Then Step 3 says to turn my life over to "God as *I understood him.*" Well, after all the shit that'd happened to me in my life, I didn't have a Power greater than myself. I'd given up on God. I hated churches, hated religion. I looked at these Steps, just the second and third steps out of twelve mind you, and realized I was fucked. Because I needed to *get this program*. I knew in my heart if I didn't leave this place confident I could stay clean, I'd be back boozin' it up, on my ass in no time, staring death right in the face. So, I felt screwed from the start knowing I didn't have a Higher Power I could believe in, and I seriously doubted I'd ever find one.

WH: I hear people who've gone to AA using those words "Higher Power" all the time, like it's the big thing that makes it all work.

YF: Right. So knowing I don't have that much time left in rehab, and knowing if I go back out there drinking again I'm a dead man, I ask is there anybody I can talk to about this Higher Power and "God as I understood him" shit, cuz I ain't getting it. And they sent me to see David. He listens to me ramble about being lost, about having no faith in a God who'd let my sister die so young, who let my dad give me a kiss one morning, tell me he loves me, and I'd never see him again. A God who dropped me down in a judgmental, backwards West Texas town with only my momma for support and say, "Good luck."

YF: (*Yugo stops and takes a drink and I can't help thinking, did Yugo's dad just leave? Or maybe he did die? Hard to tell what he means by "never saw him again."*) So David looks at me and says, "Marion." That was my name back then. He says, "Marion, Steps 2 and 3 are simply about living a spiritual life and turning things over. Let's not overcomplicate this. Do you know what it means to live a spiritual life?" And I say I don't have a clue – that's why I'm here talking to you. And David says, "Being Spiritual is not about religion. It's not about church or 'morality' per se. It's not even about God if you can't get there. Spirituality is about *relationships*. Relationships you have with yourself, with other people and with your Higher Power, whatever you choose that power to be." And I told him that sounds good, but he didn't hear me. I already said I don't have a Higher Power and that's why I'm here. Then he says, "If your pissed at God right now for what's happened in your life, that 'power' can be as simple as your AA group, the group you meet with that keeps you sober. All you need is a *power greater than yourself.* For now, consider that group of guys in your building as your Higher Power. When you guys are together, they give you strength to stay sober that's more powerful than you have alone, right?" Well, that was true. That's what makes AA work. A bunch of drunks getting together to share their experiences, compassion, and hope. But I don't get any of that shit yet, you know?

WH: Yeah, I can see what you mean. Saying your Higher Power is your group? I don't know about that. Seems there should be something about *God* in there.

YF: That's what I'm thinking. So I say that sounds like bullshit to me, and he says, "Marion, I hear people all the time say they don't believe in God, that they don't have a Higher Power. They worship no one and nothing. But everyone, even atheists, have a higher power, something they worship, whether they acknowledge it or not. *We worship what we give our attention to.* Whatever we spend most of our time thinking about, that's what we worship. That is our *god*. Be it sex, or booze, or a relationship, or making money, or looking good to other people. Now, I know that doesn't sound like worshipping 'a god,' but it's true. What our mind spends it's time thinking about most, that's what we worship."

WH: Hmmm...I can relate to that. Sounds pretty wise. I think there's truth there that makes me worry about myself – knowing what I'm thinking about most of the time.

YF: No shit – it's humbling. So, being a raging, physically addicted alcoholic, I tell David, "Ok, you got me. What I worship is alcohol, and maybe sometimes drugs and sex, so if that's my higher power what the hell am I supposed to do?" And he says, "Change your thinking, Marion. Turn toward a different Higher Power and put your trust there. And to keep it simple, let's try two things. First, make the AA group you attend when you get out of here your Higher Power to start. You already agreed that's a power greater than yourself. And second, at night, I want you to pray for help to stay sober. Every night without fail. If you really want to get sober, you'll do this. Just pray out into the Universe, surrender, and ask for help. It doesn't matter if what you're praying to has a name. The Great Spirit knows when we are calling out, no matter the earthly name we use. Then, see what happens. See if you don't eventually come into a relationship with a Higher Power out there that helps you, guides you.

WH: So did it work? I assume you did that, right?

YF: (*Huge smile.*) I learned without a doubt a Higher Power, a power greater than myself, is there for me. Because somehow, I was given the strength I needed, the strength I didn't have on my own, to stay sober. It saved my life. And because later, I saw over and over this Power save other lives, change people consumed by the darkness of addiction and at death's door. I may not know this Power's proper name, but I do know without a doubt it's real, that it's out there waiting to help us if we ask.

WH: Ok, so I get what your Higher Power is, sort of, but when it comes to living spiritually, which I thought was the point of all this, you said it was about *relationships*? I don't get it.

YF: Thanks for bringing me back, Walden, sorry. For most people, I don't get into this Higher Power talk. They already have one. Jesus, Allah, Yahweh, the Buddhist tradition, Brahman, Vishnu, the Great Spirit. But you told me you're still working through your conception of "God." I can't tell you spirituality is about relationships, including a relationship with your Higher Power, if you don't have *something* there.

WH: I think I'll just go with praying out into the Universe like you did. Like I basically do now on those occasions when I do pray.

YF: *(Nodding.)* That works. Now, to the good stuff. David gets to the real point and he says, "So Marion, this is the answer to how to live spiritually, and it's simple. Living a spiritual life means being open and honest with yourself, open and honest with other people, and open and honest with your Higher Power. That is *all you need to do*." He says, "Do this, and you're living a spiritual life – period. No matter what anybody else says."

WH: That seems kinda simple-minded, doesn't it? I mean, I see spiritual people as religious people, those who are praying, meditating, studying about God, being charitable, helping others, going to church. Isn't that stuff way more important than just being honest?

YF: Here's what I learned, Walden. That stuff is all fine and can help a person lead a fruitful life. But without openness and honesty it means nothing. It all *starts here*. Like all good teaching, this is simple. But, when you try to live it, you realize it's not *easy*. Earnestly start here, and let everything else flow to you. Pretty soon I learned just *trying* to be honest in all relationships made me more spiritual, more real, than I'd ever been in my life. It taught me to use self-observation, to be conscious when I'm telling lies, to myself, to other people or to my AA group – who was my Higher Power at first. It was the beginning stages of self-awareness, which is the path to a greater consciousness of our internal being. Eventually, I felt connected with a Power greater than myself that was more than the group. I could feel the Great Spirit working through me. For some people that never happens, but for most it does.

WH: So you stopped using the group for your Higher Power and started using God?

YF: *(Smiling and nodding.)* Something like that, yes. Although I like saying the Divine Energy of the Universe. Walden, I promise you. If you'll earnestly practice this principle, you'll be more spiritual than most people on this planet, including preachers, rabbis, imams, and monks. But you have to actually work to do it. You can't just say it. What this means is being open and honest with *yourself*, with your internal talking. It's realizing when I'm telling myself bullshit that's not true at all. Once I gained some self-awareness, I realized I was lying to myself *all the time*. Next, it means being open and honest with the people we interact with in life, at least doing our best. This is what we think about first when we hear about being honest, right? Don't knowingly tell lies to other people. And it means being open and honest with your Higher Power when you pray, when you contemplate or meditate. And if your Higher Power is a "power greater than yourself" like using a group of people like when I started? Be open and honest with them.

WH: Ok, I'll do my best. I consider you a Higher Power, so I'll try to be open and honest with you first. Then be honest when I pray out into the universe, to the Great Mystery as you call it.

YF: That sounds good, Walden, but know this. I'm no Higher Power. Just be open and honest with me like you try to be honest with *all* people. And remember. This applies for business too, for romantic relationships, family relationships. And I'm not telling you to be brutally honest, like telling your girlfriend she looks fat in that outfit, or your Father he's a know-it-all pain in the ass. This element is not a license to hurt people. If you know the truth will be painful to share with another person, silence is the best way. As I said, this is easy to say, not easy to do.

WH: I'm sure it's not. I know I exaggerate, embellish stories all the time, kind of fudge things around when negotiating in business. There's no doubt I lie to myself all the time. Hell, look what got me here!

The Practice

YF: I want you to do two things. If you want, you can tie this into the first practice – working out your spiritual body at least thirty minutes each day. You may be expanding that time on your own, but if not, you might stretch your "spiritual time" out to forty minutes a day. First, when you wake up each morning, I want you to set an aim to be open and honest in *all* your relationships. Then, ask your Higher Power for strength, for higher consciousness, for awareness when you're missing the mark. Do this every day.

WH: Ok. I think I can do that.

YF: Then, at night before going to sleep, I want you to take a brief inventory of your day. Take a few short minutes and replay your actions from that day. Were there times when you were not honest with other people or with an event? Say the checkout guy at the store gives you an extra $10 by mistake. Did you pocket it? You tell Jessica you're going out for two beers and have eight. See what I mean?

WH: Yeah, simple, but not easy.

YF: You're getting this. Next, replay your thoughts, and see where you were lying to yourself. Maybe you were being honest to Jessica when you said two beers, but were lying to yourself instead, realizing in your subconscious there was no way you were only having two drinks. A very important part of this is taking your inventory in an *uncritical and non-judgmental way*. This is not to beat yourself up. *This is to evolve* – to get better. Be conscious when you weren't honest, acknowledge it, and use that example to get better. That awareness makes you stronger the next time.

WH: Ok, Yugo. Make a goal in the morning to be honest in all my rela-tionships and ask the universe for help. Then before going to bed, recap my day and see where I screwed up.

YF: That's it! The key, Walden, is be-ing conscious. Try to stay *awake*. Be aware of your words, your thoughts, your actions. Observe yourself and take notice when you're moving away from honesty. If you make this an aim every morning, to become conscious when you're not honest, you'll feel a rush of heat or a slight ping inside when you knowingly mislead someone. You'll become more aware when untruths are flying out of your mouth, and this will in turn help you think first before telling a lie. Now I'm not saying this turns you into George Washington – into someone who never tells a lie. We're all human. Perfect honesty is *impossible*. I lie every day, no matter how conscious I might try to be. But you must do your best, and when you do remember, you are *living spiritually,* even if you do nothing else.

This is the 6th element of Yugo's Way:

Living spiritually is simply being open and honest in all relation-ships. Be open and honest with yourself, with other people, and with your Higher Power, whatever you understand that to be.

YUGO VI.5

I'm amazed at the tv stations
I'm amazed what they want me to believe

"I'm Amazed" by My Morning Jacket (from *Evil Urges*)

WE TAKE a quick break while Yugo runs out to the front reception area to talk to somebody who'd knocked on his office door. I'm feeling a little overwhelmed. Knowing how I sometimes bend the truth, this last element is going to be a hard one. I'm sure I'll notice myself failing to be honest many times a day, but at least Yugo said to do everything in an uncritical, non-judgmental way – although I'm not great at that either. Yugo returns smiling, pulling his hair back, earring twirling, and we sit back down for the second element for today:

YF: Sorry about that. Appointment mix-up. Man, do I need to get an assistant! Ok, this next element is quick, but it's an important practice toward finding more inner peace, staying calm and remaining positive in this chaotic, stressed out world. In some ways it ties to the earlier element about interconnectedness. It helps calm the division many people are feeling.

WH: I can sure use that. Everyone seems so angry and confrontational these days.

YF: *(Nodding)* So true. This will reduce the feelings of separateness and fear that characterizes our country and most of the world today. This element is all about *protecting our spirit*. It's about avoiding the negativity and divisiveness that's eating away at our compassion, our hopefulness.

WH: So you're a miracle worker, huh? How do you expect to do that?

YF: Well I'm not saying this solves everything, but I know without a doubt it helps. It takes a lifestyle change that may be harder than you think, depending on your habits.

WH: Ok, so what's this change?

YF: The change is to stop our addictive consumption of "news" coming at us from so many different media sources. And by news, I'm not talking so much about the local news, but honestly, I recommend avoiding that too. I'm talking more about what's portrayed as news on talk shows, as news commentary, talking heads, "experts." That sort of thing. On television, podcasts, social media streaming, news talk radio, blogs. Any media pawning themselves off as "news experts" when in reality they're an entertainment business doing whatever it takes to get ratings or views (*most of the quotation marks are air quotes I remember from Yugo*).

WH: So you want me to avoid the news?

YF: Yes. I want you to take a break from all media professing to report or comment on the news. In reality, they're usually using addictive, manipulative practices to hook the audience and get you addicted to their content. The most successful hook is the "Us versus Them" trick. Look at what *they* are doing, trying to take away what's rightfully *ours*, and what are *we* gonna do about it? They purposely position stories so it's all about choosing sides. Creating enemies to fear, to hate, to be *against*. That's how they get you hooked. To get you emotionally invested because it's always "Us" against this evil other side.

WH: Oh, I get it. So you're talking about Fox News versus CNN and all the high horsing bullshit, right?

YF: (*Smiles and nods.*) Partially, yes but not just them. And on those rare occasions when these media outlets report on the "news" it's usually not news we all need to know about. It's depressing, horrific, tragic events with the primary purpose of grabbing our attention to get us to watch – to consume their product. It ultimately darkens our spirits. I should've asked you this first, but are you a big consumer of the news?

WH: Somewhat. I like to stay connected. I listen to talk radio sometimes driving. Use Twitter a lot to stay on top of what's going on. Sometimes I watch network news when something big happens or around election time, not that often. Depends on what's happening around the world. I probably listen to PBS the most...you know, KUT.

YF: PBS is generally not as bad. They're nonprofit so it's not so much about the money, but still skewed. Sounds like you've already noticed, but try this anyway. Watch CNN for an hour or two, then watch Fox News. Do this for two or three days and then ask yourself, which one is reporting the truth? Pretty sure you'll come to the conclusion it's neither. They have totally opposite spins on the exact same thing, which just happens to *always* match the agenda of whatever political side they're on. It's not "the news." It's manufactured storylines to get us attached, to get us *emotional* about the situation, to feel invested in the stories. It's choosing sides and placing blame no matter what's the truth or what's best for society. They manipulate the news to tell their audience what they believe they want to hear. It's not news, it's morbid entertainment for ratings and for dollars.

WH: I'll admit, I turn on ABC sometimes and hear their experts, then turn over to Fox and wonder if they're covering the same story. It's a totally different take – each one talking shit about the other side.

YF: Yes, that's right. Meaning it's not "news" but some networks or some podcasters spin on what they think their audience *wants to hear.* So, why fill your brain with bullshit and make yourself all fearful, pissed off, and anxious? TV news and talk radio are nothing more than purposely produced "entertainment" to get us hooked to keep us coming back for more. And why? What's the true motivator? To sell us more shit through the continuous stream of ads. It's only about money, Walden, like most everything else. Nothing about information or truth. All about the cash...

WH: I can see what you're saying for sure.

YF: And the most popular talk show hosts are the ones who get people to think that just by listening, they're the truly enlightened few who are "in the know." They're a special group of informed people getting the *real* truth, the real story. It becomes an addiction. People cannot *not* tune in. The goal is to get people believing what they learn makes them more informed, *better* than other people, because they have the real story about what's going on. This creates divisiveness, separateness, an "Us versus Them" mentality that breeds hatred and fear for the other side. These news outlets, podcasts, and streamers don't care that their half-truths divide humanity against one another. They encourage it. All they care about is viewers, followers, engagement, shares, ratings – all to *sell more ads.* It's a shady business, cleverly disguised as important news and information.

WH: Wow. Sounds like you really hate the news, Yugo.

YF: I don't hate the news, Walden. I'm just conscious of the negativity it breeds under the illusion it's some sort of "public service." It's not an altruistic search for truth – it's a typical money grab. Remember when I said there was one more element with negative aspects? This is the one – then we're done with the negativity, cool?

WH: Hey that's good by me. I'm all for staying positive. I wasn't expecting an element on the evils of the news media. What made you include this?

YF: It's all about avoiding negative thinking, Walden. One day I was watching Fox News and realized, every time I watched, my chest tightened up, my facial muscles constricted. I had a physical response in my body. But then, I realized turning over to CNN, or MSNBC, I felt the same tension. I got the same tightness in my body, the narrowing of the eyes, shaking my head in worry, fear, and hopelessness.

WH: Hmmm – interesting. So you came up with this element because of how you were physically feeling watching news on TV?

YF: Or streaming, or listening to the radio, paying attention to my emotions and internal being. There's one radio talk show host I'd click on. In five minutes I'd be ready to drive my car into a tree. And it's the same or worse scrolling for news on social media. Remember, these platforms don't let us use their apps for "free" for nothing. They do whatever it takes to get more views and user engagement to sell more ads. They already know how we think because of what we search. How we *lean* on certain issues. What we choose to click or consume. So when we search on certain topics, they bring back stories telling us what we *want to hear*. They show posts and trolls that all support how they already know we already feel. This assures me, the user, that hell yes I'm right! Look at all these experts confirming my opinion. It's "targeted news streaming" because the info they show you is personally focused on what you want to hear, not on truth. And it all reinforces this "Us versus Them" mentality.

WH: You don't have to tell me about that. Frazier's an expert on that shit. She shows me all the time how social media companies manipulate what's shown to you.

YF: Ah, Frazier. She's a force of nature by the way. Very complex that sister of yours. Quite an aura. How's the Yugo's Way thing going with her social media and blogging? I know she's got big plans.

WH: It's going good, Yugo, going good. We're just getting started, but Frazier's got some aggressive ideas we need to talk to you about to attract more eyeballs, gain more traction. She listened to the 4th element the other day and her wheels started turning.

YF: (*Rubbing his hands together grinning.*) Beautiful, Walden! Yes, let's set something up soon.

WH: I'll check with Sis and let you know. She's flexible.

YF: Perfect! Now, here's the idea I want to sink in before we get into the practice. It doesn't sound like you're a heavy news junky, but this *understanding* is crucial. No matter where you're getting your news, it's not the *whole truth*. It's not reality. The powers that be aren't ever gonna allow all the real facts to be out there to the masses. We're lying to ourselves if we think they are. I'm not saying there's not some truth out there, especially for smaller news stories, but for the really important shit that's going down? What the media is telling us ain't the full truth, my friend. Guaranteed. So if it's half-truths and manipulated bullshit, why consume it? It's simply another diversion from life. Entertainment for profit. Why let "the news" play with our emotions, make us fear and hate our fellow human beings, when it's *not real*? You should see how this element helps those who are addicted to the news when they pull themselves away. Almost immediately there's greater happiness, more peace, more hope, less conflict. And most importantly, our old nemesis, negative thinking, diminishes.

The Practice

YF: Ok, I want you to do two things, Walden, and if you feel you don't need this first step for verification, blow it off and move on to the second phase. And don't forget the practices on honesty we went over today too. That's at the very core of all this work.

WH: Ok...

YF: First, the next two or three times you sit down to consume news, however you do it – TV, streaming, social media, radio, even newspapers if you're still into that – notice the emotions you're feeling. Recognize if they are *negative emotions*, some of humanity's strongest. Is there anger, fear, anxiety, the want for revenge, sadness, grief? Media outlets know this about negative emotions. It's their holy grail. Once these emotions are triggered, they know that the mind, and yes even the body, craves them. We crave the adrenalin rush.

WH: I gotta admit, this last election really got me going. I spent lots of time worrying about all the insanity – too much time. Followed way more news coverage than usual. Lots of anxiety.

YF: (*Nodding.*) So see if you recognize these negative emotions coming up when consuming the news. If so, you have actual *experience* that validates what I'm saying is true for you. Then move on to step two. If instead you feel positive emotions – love, peace, happiness, hope, compassion, or even neutral emotions for that matter – figure I'm full of shit and this element isn't a big deal for you. Let your actual experience guide you, not just my words.

WH: I know you're right, Yugo, that I'll have negative thoughts right away, but I'll try it a couple times anyway. Just to validate.

YF: Good. This is all experiential! Ok, now the second thing to do is *stop*. Stop watching the news. Stop scrolling through social media news feeds looking for validation of your opinions, to pick fights or see what others are arguing about. Stop listening to news talk radio. Stop all of it until we meet again in two weeks. And this is the key. During these two weeks, *pay attention* to your internal being. Do you feel less stress? Are you calmer? Do you feel more love and compassion for others? Do you feel the urge to argue that you're right less often? Make note of how you feel. *Understand* if this practice makes a difference to your outlook on life. And one more thing. If you find this is really hard to do, you might learn that you're somewhat addicted to news programming.

WH: Ok, Yugo, I'll watch some Fox News, CNN, MSNBC, and see how I feel. Hit my Twitter news feeds and pay attention to my emotions. Maybe listen to somebody like Hannity. Pretty sure I don't even need to this because you're right. Then, I'll cut the cord, go cold turkey on the news, and see how I feel.

YF: (*Smiling.*) You say in three sentences what takes me five minutes.

WH: Hey that's alright, Yugo. I need that. It takes me a while to wrap my head around what you're saying. The more explanation the better. Just one question. What about sports?

YF: Sports?

WH: Yeah, you know, like sports talk radio or shows like *PTI* or something. I turn on sports talk in the car sometimes to decompress. Turn on Kornheiser and Wilbon. Is that cool?

YF: (*Big grin.*) Sports stuff is usually ok as long as you don't get too worked up over it. Just remember, it's only a game, right?

WH: Right – gotcha. Ok, that's good to hear.

YF: Don't fear, Walden. Total abstinence doesn't have to be permanent unless you prefer it. This step is about gaining *awareness* that the "news business" does damage to your psyche and creates a feeling of divisiveness. After you experience the freedom from being a slave to misinformation, it's ok to check into the news now and then, as long as it doesn't get habitual. But for me? I cut myself off and got used to not having all those negative feelings. Never went back. I check out sports, entertainment, the weather. Almost no news ever other than PBS if something big is happening. Got no good reason for it.

WH: Interesting. I don't think I'll miss it much either, but we'll see.

YF: Yes, we will see. For my students who don't consume lots of news, it's not hard to stop and the rewards may not be huge. But for those who are news junkies? The news is their go-to thing when they get home from work, get in the car, have downtime and feel that never-ending urge to scroll on their phone. For them, stopping completely is really hard. But the emotional rewards, the improved mental health, the freedom and a more loving attitude toward fellow humans is *significant*. Hardly anyone goes back to how it was once they are free!

This is the 7th element of Yugo's Way:

Stay awake when consuming the "news," and if you become attached or identified, stop. The news entertainment business breeds negativity, divisiveness, and darkens the spirit.

NOTE: I asked Yugo his political affiliation a couple of times and he'd always say he tries not to bring politics into counseling. But once, he did say this – the closest he came to giving an opinion:

"It's sad to see so many caught up in this whole Democrat versus Republican thing. Look at our nation and see what we've become. Families, friends, co-workers, our country split over two ineffective, archaic, self-serving parties. How can people be so passionate about something that's failed our country for so long? We're blowing up important relationships over *that*? Both have no vision or values and are controlled by special interests and lobbyists. They're driven by money and power, not what's best for the people or our planet.

"Think about this, Walden. It's been almost *170 years* since another party had a go at this – the Whigs way back in 1850. Isn't that long enough? We're trillions of dollars in debt and spend more on weapons and war than the next nine countries *combined*. They say there's no money to improve our struggling health care and education systems, but we spent over $500 billion for interest alone last year. Half a *trillion* of taxpayer money, our money, for interest on the debt? For nothing? And it doesn't matter who's in office, Republican or Democrat. They're both in bed with the military industrial complex, big oil, big tech, big finance, big pharma.

"But the thing is, we have the ability to change this, Walden. We live in a country where *We The People* can vote them all out. We have that power. So what are we waiting for? Another 170 years? Now I'm not saying it would be easy. It'd take miracles. But today with the incredible power of social media to reach people at such little cost? It's possible to build consensus, join together, and stand up for what really matters. If we want to get really passionate about something, Walden, how about we in the masses get passionate about something that makes a real difference? I say let's find a young, smart, compassionate, and caring candidate as the face of a *new* party and work for real change. A party for the people and for the planet that truly cares about the future of all humanity. Maybe call it something like the *Compassionist Party*. At the very least I bet we'd get their attention and spark some change!"

FRAZIER VI

BONJOUR! Walden is progressing nicely. Immersing myself again in Yugo's teachings, I realize he perfectly ordered the Way. It gracefully moves a person on the edge, like Walden was, back to safe ground. Yugo gradually reveals a mosaic. He thoughtfully reconnects you with your spirit. Your true internal self. He helps loosen the burdens of the "false world." Helps move the mind to understand what's really important. Gradually, you see a new picture. Coming up, you'll see how he takes that understanding and grows the spirit. Evolves our being. Infuses love, hope, and compassion for all things.

What a stunning response our social media campaigns created for that 4th element, huh? So many people embracing the idea of giving back on the holidays. Turning their backs on Sahara and overconsumption. Super chouette!

My eyes filled with tears reading about Walden's night and subsequent struggles; the night he and Jessica came upon the accident. I hung out with Angelina many times at the bars. Oh how I loved her and Little Johnny! I still can't believe what happened. So senseless. So much pain and heartache.

It's true Walden never shared the details of his descent with me. Yes, Jessica called me some during that time. Distraught and worried about Walden. Needing someone to talk to. But she never told me about the pills or how low he got. He was rarely coming into the office during that time.

We were all worried. I went over and checked on him at least twice. But Walden hid everything, said all was okay.

So let's move on to happier times and lighter topics! Reading Walden's prose, you see how much he loves music. It's awesome he's incorporating lyrics from musicians he loves. You get him and Cody together talking music? Forget about getting a word in. Anyway, I know if I don't praise some of the girls making music around here, it won't happen. Artists like Jackie Vinson and Kelsey Wilson. Tameca Jones and of course Anastasia. And yes, I know Walden's talked about Anastasia. But if she weren't Cody's girlfriend, that doesn't happen. I don't remember him mentioning her band's name. It's The White Beaches. So cool! The call out to her Antiguan roots. The double entendre (the band's half female, none white).

An artist I encourage everyone to check out is Sarah Jarosz. She grew up in Wimberley, the same town Walden and I moved to in Texas. In a word, she's amazing! A mandolin and banjo prodigy by her teens, Sarah was already making albums in high school. Jamming all over town in little cafés, stores, festivals. But this girl isn't just an incredible musician. She's an amazing singer and songwriter too. Already she's won four Grammys.

And you should see Sarah play live. Her beautiful voice, her aura, her eyes. The light she radiates onstage. You can't help smiling watching Sarah perform. So here's what you must do now. Even you guys out there. My favorite album is *World on the Ground*. Listen to "Johnny," "What Do I Do," "Maggie," "I'll be Gone." The whole album is a masterpiece. Follow the words and tell me it's not amazing songwriting. Hey don't wait. Put this book down and listen now!

It was Mary who first told us about Sarah Jarosz. After we moved to Wimberley, Mary got a job as a schoolteacher. All those years as one of the lead teachers at Nueva gave her the perfect qualifications. For twenty-five years, Mary taught fourth grade at Jacob's Well Elementary. Mary loved teaching fourth-graders. She said kids were still angels when they were nine or ten. That was the age she could do the most good.

Sarah's parents were both teachers around Wimberley too. Her mom and Mary would talk at area teachers meetings. They got to know each other that way. One day there was a music assembly at the school. Sarah came and played for the little kids and Mary was floored. Sarah was only in middle school then. Mary was convinced this teenaged dynamo in pigtails would one day make it big. So she took the whole family to see Sarah play when she was like fourteen. From there we grew up with her and her music. Mary even sang at some festivals Sarah performed in around town.

Now that I find we're in Wimberley, might as well go on. While Wimberley didn't have the awestriking beauty of Nueva Tierra, it was still a very beautiful place to live. Texas isn't known for its trees. But Wimberley is surrounded by spring-fed creeks and rivers that spawn huge, majestic cypress trees along their banks. Incredible! We lived a few miles northwest of town, out by the elementary school. And we swam in Cypress Creek almost every day. In fact, a section of the creek runs right through our property. The crystal-clear spring water comes from Jacob's Well. It's so cold and refreshing. The water temp is always around seventy, even when it's a blistering 102 outside.

Like many places in Texas, Wimberley's grown a bunch the last twenty years. Most locals, including Father and Mary, don't much care for that. When we were kids there were only 1,700 people in the whole town. There's lots more now. But moving there from our small, isolated commune, it seemed like a big city to me and Walden. What memories! Friday nights cruising the Dairy Queen after football games. Hanging out in the summer with friends at Blue Hole. Amazing pecan pie at Wimberley Pie Company. Tacos at the Shamrock. Hitting all the local art and music festivals. Wimberley was, and still is, a very artsy town.

When we got there, Father found some land cheap; about twenty acres. Back then land didn't cost much in an out of the way place like Wimberley. And, from founding Nueva, Father was an expert at getting land cheap and on credit. At the time, it seemed like we were way outside of town. Today it feels like our place is in the city limits. It's probably worth lots of money now. Mary knew she wanted to be a teacher, no matter where we ended up. Father wasn't so sure what he was going to do. How do you transition from founding a utopian society into a "real world" job?

Luckily for Father, Wimberley at that time was more like Nueva Tierra than the real world. Since he'd help build most of Nueva from the ground up, he had skills to do almost anything. And that's what he did. After making the old farmhouse on the land livable for us, he drilled a better well. Then he built a woodworking shed and metal shop. From there he built a small chicken coop, so we'd have fresh eggs. And of course he bought some goats. For mowing and for milking.

While Father did all that, we created a big garden. Mary, Walden, and I planted all kinds of vegetables. All kinds of fruit trees too. Peaches, pears, plums, figs, pomegranates. The growing season is much longer in Texas than Washington. There were already pecan trees on the land. But Father planted more after hearing what a pound of pecans could bring. Figured he'd augment our income quite nicely farming a few acres of pecan trees.

Once the garden got going we lived on the produce. And as the orchards flourished we had all kinds of fruit too. Mary and Father would sell what we didn't eat to local restaurants. Even the school district. We usually grew more than we could eat or sell. So we'd give away any unused food to friends and neighbors. There were always boxes of something at the end of our long drive. We had a sign that said, "Take what you need. Share the rest."

When Father was finished, our place looked like a mini-Nueva Tierra right in the middle of Central Texas (although Father always said the land wasn't near as fertile). Walden and I helped all we could. We didn't know anybody at first. So helping build our homestead together, build the garden, helped us stay busy. Made us feel we were part of creating our own little utopia while we gradually made new friends in town.

Father had business cards made. He took pictures of our new self-sufficient family enterprise. Then he went into town to start his new career; talk to everyone he could at the local coffee shops and bars. The card said:

Augustus Harrison
Farmland and Estate Engineer
Turn your Idle Land into a Self-Sufficient Enterprise.

On the back it said:

Woodworking, Welding, Fencing, Irrigation, Garden Creation.
If we can't build it or fix it, no one can.

He stapled his card to a flyer with pictures of our place. Then told people he could turn their plot of land into a little paradise like ours. Almost immediately Father had more work than he could handle. Lots of people lived in old rundown places. Or they had good land sitting there doing nothing. Soon Father was known around Wimberley as the guy who could take what you had and make it better. People heard Father's story about founding Nueva Tierra. About building a self-sufficient community from the ground up. That's all it took for him to gain instant credibility. His business grew until he had to throttle it down. To keep it from getting too big for him. Once he had ten people to help, he'd turn work away if it meant adding more employees. Unlike at Nueva, work didn't consume him down here. At least, not after he got things going.

Wimberley was awesome! The people were so friendly. They welcomed our family with open arms. In hindsight I realize how perfect moving to this area was. I can only imagine what our hippy, commune-dwelling little family looked like. Driving into town in our van, pulling our makeshift trailer holding all our possessions. In many Texas towns back then we'd have been ostracized. But Wimberley was full of musicians, artists, creatives of all kinds. It was, and still is to a lesser degree, an oasis for dreamers and nature lovers. Amazingly, we fit right in.

When school started it didn't take long to make lots of friends. Walden was well liked too, although he had only two or three close friends, as usual. It took him longer to fit in, to feel comfortable in our new surroundings. But Walden was more comfortable in Wimberley than Nueva once we got settled. Going to a new high school thousands of miles from home could have been traumatic for me. I was sixteen the year we moved. But the kids in Wimberley weren't like regular city kids. Many had parents with similar hearts as Father and Mary. Artists, teachers, writers, singers, craftsmen.

Walden and I had immediate street cred coming from a "commune" on the West Coast. Kids wanted to get to know us. I played soccer in school, sang in the choir, performed in plays. Back then, soccer wasn't a big thing for boys in Texas. Texas is a football state. But the only organized sports we had at Nueva was soccer. That and an old basketball hoop to shoot at. Since most of the "cool guys" played football, Walden gave it a try. He was actually pretty good after he learned the game. Especially since he had no experience and this was Texas. He played away from the middle, where you catch passes. I think he even made a touchdown or two. Even Father got to where he loved going to the local football games. It's the thing to do in Wimberley on Friday nights.

Writing Father's name on his business card reminds me. I should explain why we call our parents Mary and Father. I'm aware their names may sound like we're talking about a nun and a priest. Friends say all the time it's weird. Let me explain. To us it's what we grew up with. It's normal. At Nueva Tierra, the community didn't have formalities. Everyone called adults by their first names, including their parents. There were no "moms and dads" where we grew up. No "yes sir and no sir." My mom's name is Mary. So that's what we, and everyone else at Nueva, called her. Me and Walden never called her mom. It never occurred to us to do so.

There were two exceptions. Nueva Tierra's founders thought it important they be easily recognized in the community. For both the old residents and new members as they came in. They were our leaders. The drivers of the continual change required to evolve our society. A tradition was needed to instantly identify our founders as leaders in the community. Especially for the children, who were taught to respect Nueva's leadership. So, the whole community called all founders either "Father" or "Mother." Like with the name Mary, Father was the name everyone at Nueva called my dad. It's the name Walden and I have always known him by. Oh, and by the way. His friends down here call him Gus, or sometimes Augie. Father soon learned that Augustus was much too formal for smalltown Texas.

Now how did pumping up Sarah Jarosz get me here? Oh well. Now you know more about our move to Texas and our home in Wimberley. More about Mary and Father, what they did after we left Washington. As we both said, the move to Central Texas was good for all of us. Each one of us grew in our own way. Which brings me back to Yugo. The social media campaign was my gateway to talk to Yugo. To meet with him personally. Walden did a good job describing Yugo. But let me add this, from a woman's perspective. I unquestionably found him physically attractive. Primarily in a natural, animal magnetism sort of way (I know Walden's rolling his eyes). Outwardly he had this "wild child" look. His vibe grabs your attention and curiosity. Think a young Lenny Kravitz with lighter complexion. Lighter and longer hair too.

And inside? Inside all I can say is Yugo is a lighthouse. Beaming positive energy and love into our world. Just as Walden described. Present, compassionate, genuine, kind. This is not my personal story, so I won't go too deeply. But Yugo's wisdom touched my heart. He changed me internally. He helped me recognize and work through issues I let build up over many years. Thoughts and emotions that had hardened me. Had created a false illusion of who and what I really am. I will let Walden and his story unfold the rest of the Way for you. Just know my heart is wishful that Yugo's teachings, his essence, will change you too.

YUGO VII

"Sweet Resistance" by Civil Twilight (from *Holy Weather*)

A VERY COOL thing happened before I saw Yugo for our next visit. I got to the restaurant and headed towards Yugo's doorway leading upstairs when a waitress stopped me to say that Yugo was running late. He asked them to intercept me, tell me he's sorry, and to grab something to eat while I was waiting. Lunch was on him today. I hadn't eaten all day, so that was good by me. As the waitress walked me to a table, some guy stopped her and told her about a large party coming in later for some kind of gathering – to be sure and have a table set for twenty. As I sat down and she handed me the daily specials, I asked her if that was the manager she was talking to and she said it was. That he and his wife not only managed the place but were the owners. She pointed to a lady behind the counter, busy in the kitchen, saying that was his wife – she was actually her boss. After ordering, waiting for my food, the manager walked by and I caught his attention. He was wearing a black collared shirt and dress shoes, which I thought odd, but his beard and bushy brown hair gave off a casual vibe.

"Hey, I hear you're the owner of this place. Can I ask you a couple questions?"

"Sure," he said, and I pointed to the chair across from me so he'd sit down for more like a talk than a quick question.

"So, I meet with Yugo every couple of weeks, and wondered if you can help me?" I learned in persuasive sales classes you get more engagement when you ask people for help.

"Ok, whatcha need?"

"Well, Yugo's sort of a different kind of dude, you know. I mean, he doesn't charge for his services, his office is up above a restaurant in a very popular high rent area. I'm a business owner too so I wonder, you know, how does he do it? Rent around here has to be through the roof."

Now smiling and reaching out his hand, he says "I figured you'd grab me sooner or later. Many of Yugo's visitors do. Either me or my wife Julie who really runs this place. Name's Gordon by the way."

"Hey, Gordon. Nice to meet you. I'm Walden, Walden Harrison." We shake hands and he continues.

"I'll tell you what I tell all his students that ask. Yugo doesn't pay rent. He bought this building a few years back so we're *his* tenants."

"What? Really? You're saying Yugo *owns* this property?"

"Yep, and technically we don't pay rent either. Oh, we pay all the utilities. Water, gas, electric, all that stuff, but Yugo lets us run our business here rent free."

"You gotta be kidding me. Why?"

So here's what I learned. Yugo got out of rehab and continued searching. He went to monasteries, Vipassanas, spent time around Taos, Sedona, wandering in the Arizona desert talking to healers and authors, preachers, and philosophers. He immersed himself in spiritual seeking to strengthen his hold on sobriety. When Yugo moved back to Texas, he was broke, living in poverty like St. Francis. He eventually came to Austin where he'd heard there was a good recovery community. He sometimes slept in a halfway house near downtown, but was basically homeless. Yugo was deep in his search then, meditating, reading, praying, talking to others. Gordon and Julie would see Yugo meditating on downtown benches, talking with the homeless. It was Julie who first noticed instead of hanging out panhandling and drinking like many others on the streets, Yugo seemed to be counseling people, listening to their rambles, smiling and offering assistance and hope. Sometimes he'd walk around with a large black trash bag and a big smile, just picking up trash.

"Yugo hung around near the restaurant all the time, so Julie went out one day and offered him something to eat," Gordon said. "We had leftovers from our specials the night before, and she gave him a plate. They talked some. She was intrigued by what he said, by his kindness and what she called his gentle spirit. So we let him eat what we had left over for free when he was around and hungry, and man was he grateful. After he'd eat, he'd go back in the kitchen and help with the dishes, clean tables, take out the trash. Little chores like that, but we didn't ask him to do anything. Basically we saw he was helping others living on the street and was hungry, and Julie loved talking to him. So, we fed him."

"So his name was Yugo? Or did he go by Marion back then?"

Gordon gives me a nod for knowing Yugo's birth name. "Yeah, it was Yugo. So this goes on for several months, and one day Yugo comes in saying the 'Great Spirit' has smiled on him and he's thinking about getting his own place. He wouldn't be needing any more free lunches on us."

"Interesting." My head's churning thinking this good fortune was his bitcoin find, assuming that's really true.

"Yeah, right? Next thing you know, Yugo has this swanky condo overlooking downtown, he's got a nice car. He got some clothes and cleaned up. It was an amazing transformation, almost overnight. As you can see, we stayed in contact. He remembered our kindness. He loves Julie's veggie specials."

"Wow. So how'd all that lead to him owning this place?"

"One day Julie tells Yugo we got a letter from our landlord saying rent's going up over 50% because of rising property taxes, and there's no way we can make it work at this location with that kind of overhead. So, we start looking at our options to move out of downtown to a cheaper spot when our lease runs out. Well, Walden, believe it or not, before that lease was up Yugo'd bought the place. Said he needed an office and asked if we had room for him somewhere. Then said as long as he owned this building, we could be his tenants for free. All we had to do was feed him when he was around and hungry, and keep his favorite teas in stock. Talk about good karma doing a number on me and Jules."

"No kidding. That's crazy. The Great Spirit just smiled on him, huh? He must've come into a lotta money somehow to afford this spot. Any idea what happened?"

Gordon gives me a sideways glance and says, "You'll have to ask Yugo about that one. By the way, his students stop me or Julie all the time asking questions about him, and we always wonder. Why don't y'all just ask him yourself?"

"You know, I'm not sure. It's kinda weird. You feel like you're there on the clock having a session with a psychiatrist or something, so you're only supposed to talk about yourself. You know, asking your shrink personal questions seems out of bounds. At least for me."

Gordon shakes his head. "Yeah, I can see that. I guess we don't think about Yugo in that way."

My food comes and I start to thank Gordon for his time, but instead of leaving he looks at me and says, "There's more I like to tell his students who are curious, since Yugo'd never say anything. You know that nice condo he bought, and the nice car? He got rid of them and most all the other stuff he had in less than a year. Yugo said they made him soft, too comfortable. They just created stress and more things to worry about. Said they made him feel wrongly superior and disconnected from those less fortunate. His quote to me was they were 'rotting out his core,' whatever that means."

"Really? So I just assumed when you said he had a condo downtown that he'd hop on his bike to come to work every day – get some exercise and avoid parking."

"Yugo sold almost everything and moved out to a place called Community First Village. Ever heard of it?"

"Nope, I don't think so."

"It's an unbelievable place, Walden. Started by this visionary, Alan Graham, who also founded Mobile Loaves and Fishes to feed the home-less. He and his organization took unused land out on the east side of town and built a little community of tiny houses for the homeless. A place where they can live, find work, a chance to get back on their feet and regain their dignity."

"Wow. That does sound unbelievable. The homeless situation is so bad around here. I didn't know a place like that was out there."

"I don't know of any place like it in the world unless someone's tried to copy it by now. The homeless who move there have to pay a very small rent. They're required to find work to help regain their self-worth and confidence. But it's a micro-village all into itself. Some find work outside the community, but many start working again at enterprises right there in the village. There's a beauty salon, an auto repair shop, a woodworking area, a huge community garden where they grow food to eat and sell. They have an arts and crafts center for the creative artistic types. A market and gift shop selling the artwork and pieces they make."

"Now how cool is that? Can't believe I haven't heard of it. So Yugo lives there now? I don't get it." Yugo's story is getting crazier by the minute.

"Well, that's the best part, Walden. The founders of the community were smart enough to know it isn't wise to have a village housing hundreds of homeless people with no role models or mentors. Many people in that condition are recovering alcoholics, addicts. It's what got them on the street in the first place. Some need counseling and mental health support, which Community First has. But people fall off the wagon sometimes. Things happen where someone or something goes off the rails. They need role models living *in the community*. They need good civilians living in the village who are there when help is needed – a continual presence to keep things calm and cool, to talk and listen. Community First calls them *missionaries*."

"So Yugo is a missionary at Community First Village? That's where he lives?"

About that time, Yugo walks in the restaurant breathing hard, pushing along his bike. He sees us sitting at the table and steers our way.

"Hey, I see you met Gordon! Beautiful. He's an awesome dude, Walden. Sorry I'm so late. My bike had a flat on the way and I didn't have a tube. Long story but a kind soul peddling by stopped and had an extra in his bag. Give me a few minutes and come on up when you're done eating."

Yugo heads toward his door, and on the way, I see him say hello to a lady sitting with somebody in a booth. I'm positive it's that same lady I was ogling walking down the stairs back when I was just getting started with Yugo. As he walks past her table to go up to his office, she glances over and our eyes meet. She obviously saw us talking together, so must realize I'm a Yugo regular too. Just another lost soul looking for direction.

Gordon starts to get up and says, "Yep, so that's where Yugo lives. He and somewhere around 1,200 homeless people all in micro homes. Tiny places, something like 200 square feet. They all share community baths and kitchens, but hey, it's paradise to those who were living out on the streets. Go out there and visit sometime. They have tours on weekends for interested donors. It's one of our favorite charities."

"You say it's on the east side? How far away?"

"A few miles from the airport. Think the land used to be a dump or toxic waste area before they cleaned it up. No one wanted it."

"By the airport? So Yugo rides his bike from there? That's gotta be over fifteen miles each way."

"Yeah, it's insane. We keep telling him he needs to get a car – an EV or something. It's nuts riding a bike through downtown with all this traffic, plus think of the time he'd save. Maybe this flat tire will persuade him. Hey, good meeting you, Walden. You ever want to talk again, just let me know."

I'm thrilled how fortunate I was to come across the owner and think about all the coincidences that made it happen. Yugo's flat tire, the helpful waitress, plus Gordon being so cool and open. Between Cody's intel and Gordon's new revelations, I'm filling in the missing pieces of Yugo the enigma. Even more coincidental was the element Yugo went over that day – almost eerie really. Some days it seems to me like the universe is pulling everything together all in a logical fashion – and some days maybe not. Yugo apologizes again when I get upstairs, and because he's running late we cut short my personal counseling time. Honestly my life was running ok that day, so more than anything, I'm relieved I don't have to talk too much about myself:

YF: Before we start, how you doing staying away from the news? Any difference how you're feeling? How you're thinking?

WH: I have to admit, yeah, I do feel a difference. I didn't realize all the added stress I was putting on myself. All the fighting back and forth, the finger pointing, filling my head with all the depressing shit going on in the world. I do feel less angst, less angry.

YF: Good, good! And how about that "We Are One" mantra for when you're feeling a sense of "otherness"? How does that go again?

WH: *(Reciting like a school kid.)* "We are all one. We are all from the same Source. I do not know. Let it Be."

YF: *(Smiling.)* Perfect! That was a test you know. If you couldn't say it back right away I'd know you're bullshitting me about doing the work.

WH: Can't catch me, man. I told you, Yugo. I'm doing the practices.

YF: Beautiful. Ok, Walden, I'll tell you this next element upfront, so we get right to it. *Comfort is Overrated.* That's it. Comfort is Overrated.

WH: Ok?

YF: Contemplate this. It doesn't take long for most people to get complacent in life, to get lazy. Once we get through the challenges of childhood and adolescence, once we get a job, a salary coming in, and get settled, staying comfortable usually becomes the number one objective if we realize it or not. How about you? You feel some of that?

WH: Maybe. I've never really thought about it. I guess you could say now that I've built a business and have a few nice possessions I'm not as driven.

YF: That's a common path. Many of us live much of our lives, usually without knowing it, doing all we can to just stay in our comfort zones. To *not* push ourselves, to avoid change, to avoid being vulnerable.

WH: Yeah, I can see that. There's some of that in me.

YF: But here's the reality. When comfort becomes a goal and we're successful at it, we get stagnant. We stop truly *living*. There's no pushing the limits, no growth, no new experiences. Only when there's struggle, when we take chances, try new things and get out of our comfort zone do we become conscious not only of our strengths, but of our weaknesses too. And yes, even our failures. And Walden, we need these struggles and failures. They're important for our growth, for our evolution. Why? Because that's how we grow our faith! We learn through experience that we can rely on our Divine Creator to help get us through the struggles. To give us that spark, that energy to overcome our fears and break through our safe, let's call it *mechanical* existence.

WH: So take chances, push the limits, struggle, and then *fail*?

YF: Without struggle, without pushing outside our boundaries, we don't grow. And I mean this not only physically, but spiritually, mentally – expanding the mind. When we're not growing in all these realms, we're not evolving. And our faith is not growing. When we're comfortable, who needs a Higher Power?

WH: I think I get what you mean when you put it that way. Like the old saying about foxhole prayers…the only time you pray is when your ass is in trouble. When you're in deep shit and need help.

YF: Yes! Now, let's look at this from another angle. We crave comfort usually for two reasons. One, we're lazy and don't like change. We just want to chill and be comfortable. But there's another even stronger reason we seek comfort, and that reason is *fear*.

WH: Oh, I hear you there. Fear is the main reason I don't try new things – don't put myself out there. Always has been.

YF: *(Leaning in.)* Here's a saying that's true for many. "We are as afraid of *living* as we are to die." And we're more afraid of dying than ever before. Billions are spent on healthcare every year for people who have no quality of life, who's time to pass has come, but are hanging on from an overwhelming fear of death. And it's interesting it's so prevalent here, in a so called "Christian nation" where you'd think people would look forward to the afterlife.

WH: I agree our society is scared shitless of dying, and the medical field doesn't help. The way doctors don't seem to know when it's time to give up anymore. To let patients go when it's clearly time. I've seen that with my parents' friends, with Jessica's relatives. *(And I worry how it's going to be as Mary gets worse.)*

YF: *(Nodding.)* And because of that fear of dying, Walden, we're becoming *afraid* to live. Scared to push the boundaries. Scared to challenge ourselves and experience euphoria, the rush of adrenaline that comes when we accomplish something we never dreamed we could do! Charles Bowden, this writer dude who lived in New Mexico, said, "We live in a time when death is off the table, the thing unsaid. We wish to live forever and because of this desire, we *hardly live at all.*"

WH: I'm starting to get what you're saying. I can't remember the last time I did something that kicked my ass. Something that scared me or really pushed me. Outside my comfort zone as you say.

YF: And one more interesting angle. Society uses religion as a crutch to help us bear the fact that we're all going to die. To make us feel better about the ultimate fate of our physical bodies here on Earth. Religion is often used to give us hope that after death things will be much better in heaven. But Walden, using religion to resolve our fear of dying is completely *backwards*. We should use our religion, or better said use our spirituality and faith, to help us live life fully *now,* here on Earth. Trust! Instead, we avoid challenging, difficult experiences because of a subconscious fear of death. Gotta keep it comfortable, man, play it safe. But struggle and painful experiences should be embraced, sought out, savored...

WH: Hmmm. I think there's some truth here. Shake off the cobwebs and feel alive. Yugo, I'm getting a little worried about what you're gonna have me do in this Practice...

YF: *(Smiling and now walking around.)* Now, let's think about our attitudes toward life, and specifically, at all the *events* we experience in life. We must learn to have complete acceptance that the experiences we have, even those very *difficult* events we have in life, no matter how painful, how embarrassing, how challenging, are necessary for us. They're necessary for us to grow and reach our spiritual potential. We should even try to have gratitude for them, otherwise we find ourselves constantly complaining about all the shit that's happening to *me.*

WH: Be thankful for all the difficulties and challenges life brings?

YF: Yes. Embracing this more positive, accepting attitude toward life's events, no matter how hard, adds meaning and understanding to our lives, to our existence. It's the most effective way to get the most out of life. All the crazy shit that's been thrown at you this last year has made you who you are. Whether you know it or not, it's made you grow. It's gradually making an improved Walden.

WH: *(I know I've grown some, but still mechanically say.)* Well, I don't know about that...

YF: Be grateful for all of life's events, especially the hard ones. We should consciously welcome life's challenges, not shrink and worry about what's gonna happen to me. After all, when eternity is your timeframe, what happens to us physically or materially in this life doesn't matter all that much. Struggle, pain, and suffering bring about the most personal growth, the most spiritual growth. History shows us that. View them as opportunities to evolve your spirit! As hard as it's been making it through all the shit that's hit your plate, it finally brought you here, right? Those insane events molded you into the person you are today.

WH: Yeah, we talked about that. How all the stuff that's happened to you and the stuff that's happened to me somehow put us here together.

YF: *(Smiling.)* Maybe. Here's my attitude today. The Grand Energy of the Universe will never give us more difficult "events" than we can handle. Even if one is so intense that it sends us into the next plane and we pass on from this physical world, even if that happens, that's ok. If that happens, then it must be time for us to move on, to learn somewhere else. To evolve our Spirit in another *instance.* Or, possibly to find peace in our final resting place.

WH: *(A little uncomfortable.)* Now hold on a sec with all that, Yugo. I can't take it that far. I'll need a little time to ponder that. We've all heard that line before. That God never gives you more than you can handle. That's always sounded like bullshit to me.

YF: *(Nodding in agreement, and now sitting.)* Yeah, I hear you. I used to think that line was bullshit too, and not so long ago. My dad used it on me all the time growing up, and I tuned him out. Take what you want and leave the rest, Walden. If that makes no sense to you, that's cool. What it really comes down to is trust and faith in the Grand Creator, then letting go.

The Practice

YF: So there are three actions I want you to work on with this element, the first being what you'll think is easiest.

WH: Try me.

YF: I want you to do your best to put the *feeling of awe* back in your life. There's plenty of nature and beauty around here for inspiration, not to mention the sky, the clouds, the stars.

WH: Get the feeling of awe? Not sure I get it.

YF: We as a society have become numb to awe-inducing things. Or put a better way, we've stopped taking time to notice the beauty and splendor all around us. Things like sunsets, sunrises, a full moon, the stars at night, storm clouds rolling in, lightning strikes, birds gliding through the sky, truly *looking* at flowers, the pleasure of eating a good apple. Be present and feel the enormity of the universe around you, the *beauty* of our planet that we take for granted. I'd like you to consciously do this at least twice a week, hopefully more, and soon you'll notice you're naturally falling into awe more often without even thinking about it.

WH: Ok, I agree that sounds easy enough. I go out to the lake all the time. Sunsets out there are incredible. Hit Mt. Bonnell for an early morning sunrise. Stargaze. I'm cool with all that. I agree I don't slow down and take the time to be present and take those things in. I can make myself pay better attention.

YF: Good! And be *awake* when you're traveling. We're lucky to have lots of awe-producing places around here. Enchanted Rock, Hamilton's Pool, the spring-fed rivers and creeks in Comal and Hays County, the chain o' lakes. Soak 'em in! And don't go only to big cities for vacations. Take hiking trips, go camping far away from the crowds. Go to secluded beaches or the mountains. Nature reinvigorates us more than anything!

WH: Preaching to the choir there, Yugo. Most vacations I take are around nature. Skiing, rafting, hiking, hitting the beach. I don't relax much when I go to crowded touristy places.

YF: Beautiful! I should have known that – you growing up around Olympic National Park. Now the second action is more in line with what you're probably expecting. I want you to think about things you'd like to do but haven't because you're too scared to try. It's time to push yourself out of that comfort zone and live!

WH: Yep, you're right. That's what I was expecting.

YF: *(Smiling and rubbing his hands together.)* Let's think about this together. You ever wanted to be an actor, be in a play? Ever wanted to try singing in front of an audience? Maybe try painting for real? Not just tinkering around but getting all the right materials and truly painting something to show other people? How about making people laugh? Writing a book? Jumping out of an airplane? Run a marathon or do a mini-tri...

WH: *(Interrupting.)* Yeah, I see where you're going with this. Come up with stuff I've been too lazy to do or let my fears keep me from trying. Give them a go...

YF: Exactly! There's community theater troupes out there holding auditions all the time if you want to act. Open mic nights or hitting a karaoke bar is perfect if your voice is good but you're too scared to sing in public. Same with open mics at comedy clubs if you wanna tell jokes. Or go buy some paint and a canvas and let your inner Picasso fly. And speaking of flying, if you want to jump out of a plane, I know a guy...

WH: Ok, ok, I get it. Just how uncomfortable you want me to be? How many things you want me to try?

YF: Let's start with just one, Walden. Give it some thought until our next session, then let's decide. But don't just think of something you fear doing. It's best to find something you really want to do but haven't tried from fear, laziness, or both.

WH: *(Letting out a sigh of relief.)* Alright, one sounds reasonable. I was getting a little worried with all the shit you were ticking off.

YF: No need to worry. This is the fun part! And, just because I said only one now doesn't mean there won't be more.

WH: Yeah, I was afraid of that. Only one my ass...

YF: *(Laughing.)* Now I know you love music and outdoor festivals around town. Next time you're at a concert in the park, I want you to check out all the little kids, the younger the better, and watch how they dance. Smiling, bouncing up and down to the bass beat, flying their arms around, spinning in circles. They dance like no one's watching, letting the music move them. That's how we all should dance, Walden. But dancing like that changes once our personalities develop, once we start worrying that other people may be watching. And then, for some reason, it starts to *really matter* what people think. It becomes more important to us not to look stupid than immersing ourselves in the joy and the flow of music. That's when instead of being joyous and free, we humans are more worried about how we look.

WH: You're really hitting home, Yugo. I *hate* to dance cuz I'm too self-conscious...unless I'm drunk. And funny you say that about kids. Jessica loves watching the little kids bopping around. She points them out every time we're at an outdoor show. I know exactly what you're saying.

YF: Well maybe it's time you and Jessica danced with the little ones. Let loose! Now, here's the third exercise, and what many find the hardest part of this practice.

WH: Even harder than doing something that scares the shit out of me?

YF: I want you to start shedding some of the stuff you have that makes you too comfortable. Say you got four TVs in the house but only use one or two. Donate the ones you don't really need to a charity or a church. Have a closet full of clothes or shoes you hardly ever wear? Give them to the Salvation Army or Goodwill. Have a "toy" lying around like a motorcycle or a second car you rarely use? Sell them and donate the money to feed the homeless or help pay for college for the less fortunate.

WH: Start shedding, huh? I hear you with all the clothes and gadgets and stuff. There's no doubt I got way more stuff than I use anymore. I never throw anything away. Jessica's always on me to make multiple Goodwill runs. Not so sure about cars and TVs though.

YF: Trust me, Walden. There's freedom when you get the clutter out of your life, not to mention the positive vibes that flow out from sharing things with others. And there's other benefits too. Shedding has a beautiful symmetry with two other elements we're already practicing. First, it's a good reminder not to be seduced by materialism, to stop buying shit we don't really need. Shedding keeps overconsumption from coming back later. And second, shedding, letting others use items already manufactured that are only growing dust, is better for Mother Earth, better for our environment. It conserves resources and reduces our footprints on this amazing planet. We cool with all this?

Now I gotta admit, the third part of this practice, the part about shedding, I'd have probably ignored if my chance lunch encounter hadn't happened. It's one thing for a condescending preacher from a pulpit to say, "Live frugally, and give to help others." Yeah, right. But once I learned Yugo's path from Gordon, how he puts his philosophy into practice? Once I then compared my lifestyle to Yugo's? I mean, if the rumors are true, Yugo has enough money to live in a lakefront mansion on Lake Austin, drive a Bentley, and live a life of luxury with many millions left over. But in reality, from what I see with my own eyes, he owns a pair of khaki cargo shorts, some sandals, a few colored t-shirts, and a very nice bike. He lives in a 200 square foot tiny house as a missionary in a village helping the homeless – using a community bath and kitchen. Oh, and he seems to be the happiest, most peaceful person I've ever met, *by far.*

And me? I live in a 2,800 square foot house in the hills outside Austin. I still have that big ass SUV I should've got rid of months ago, a hot tub, a jet ski, a motorcycle in the garage that hasn't moved since Little Johnny... more clothes and shit than I'll ever need. And yet I'm the one going to Yugo for counseling to get my shit together.

And have all those "things" in my life brought me happiness? To be honest with you, yes, certainly for a little while. As Cody says, "You ever seen anybody frowning riding a jet ski?" But I think I'm beginning to fully realize that kind of happiness is only temporary. It doesn't last. Eventually all the superfluous stuff gets taken for granted. It doesn't take long until you start thinking about how much you really need that next new toy. Now I hope I'm not so obnoxious and full of shit to say having money doesn't make it *easier* to be happy – make it easier and more comfortable to live life. It's meaningless and total bullshit really for someone *with money* to say money doesn't matter when we all know it sure as hell does – at least to a point. Bouncing these thoughts around in my head as I walked out to my SUV after the session, I asked myself, how can I not at least give *all* these practices a try?

This is the 8th element of Yugo's Way:

Comfort is Overrated. Get out of your comfort zone, experience the feeling of awe, and truly live!

WALDEN IX

We burn these joints in effigy
Cry about what we used to be
Try to ignore the elephant somehow

"Elephant" by Jason Isbell (from *Southeastern*)

IT'S A BEAUTIFUL, mild, clear afternoon in Central Texas as I drive up to Bryan and Ally's house and survey the chaos that's overtaken their front and side yards. It's their son Bridger's tenth birthday, and they've decided this is one of those *big birthdays* where they throw out all the stops and spend a fortune on a big bash for everyone. Bridger's the oldest, but I see their daughter Estella, who's almost eight, has all her friends here too. There's a hive of little girls running around a soccer ball playing a game of "bunch ball" in the side yard. A huge inflatable bounce house that looks like a castle is prominent in the front yard, filled with kids jumping around like maniacs. Bridger and some of his friends are wearing those inflatable bubble bounce bumper balls that turn you into a human bumper car. Looks like they've got some kind of game going on that involves blasting every kid in sight – trying to knock each other over so they can't get back up.

Bryan's home is in an older neighborhood in the northwest hills, a prestigious part of town. Nothing too ostentatious, but it does have a huge yard and large pool in back – Bryan's done very well for himself. I haven't seen Bryan and Ally since our night out catching Anastasia and her band, so while I'm not too keen on hanging out with fourth graders eating cake and ice cream, I am looking forward to catching up with them and seeing our mutual friends. Plus, I know Bryan and Ally. Any party they put together will be as much fun for adults as it is for the kids. Open bar, great food, good conversation, good tunes.

Walking up to the house with a couple of obligatory bottles of wine in hand, I sidestep bouncing bubbles and running kids everywhere and head towards the back where I know the adults will be hanging out – drinking cocktails and eating appetizers by the pool. I see Ally, who looks stressed as any mom would be under the circumstances, give her a quick kiss on the cheek and hand her my Merlot. Bryan's out manning his massive grill engulfed in smoke, cooking up chicken fajitas, grilled veggies, dogs, and burgers for the kids. I give him a wave and he smiles, pointing to the bar for me to go grab a drink.

Surveying the scene, I see Cody's already here with a small crowd circling him that he's obviously entertaining with one of his stories. I grab a beer, walk over to the group, and he gives me a peace sign and smiles while he keeps on talking. From the glaze in his eyes I can tell Barringer's done his usual "pregame" before the party – he's perfectly lubed for the event, in true *storytelling form*. It's one of my favorites, a Cody classic about his college days, one I mentioned earlier that must be shared. Somebody at the party must have asked him where he went to college. He's a few minutes in, so let me give you some background.

Cody went to Austin High where he was one of those badass, party crazy kids you wonder how they made it through school alive, much less graduated – trust me, I've talked to some of his classmates. Barringer's a big man who played center on the football team, a three-year starter who twice earned first team All-District, and was third team All-State his senior year. As Cody says, he kicked the shit out of every nose tackle in Central Texas. While a really good athlete, Cody didn't have the measurables to get the big colleges excited – the bluebloods. He didn't have the fastest 40 time and certainly wasn't a workout hound, so he graded out a 2- to 3-star recruit – impressive and a Division 1 prospect, but not to a major school.

Cody didn't want to go through the pain and sacrifice playing college football unless it was for a D1 school, and he wanted to stay in Texas if possible, but the only D1 Texas school that offered him a scholarship was the University of Texas at El Paso – UTEP, the Miners. Without so much as taking a campus visit beforehand, Cody signed up, thrilled he could stay in Texas and go to college on a free ride. It wasn't until he packed his car and looked at the map that he realized while UTEP *was* in Texas, it was 580 miles away, a nine-hour drive from Austin and his mom's home cooking. So, Cody goes to UTEP to play big time college football, but coming home for the weekends to hang out with friends wasn't gonna be in the cards. Back then it was almost impossible for a freshman to start, but Cody was a damn good football player. Soon he was second team center, and was also the *starting* deep snapper for punts and field goals. This is where Cody was at telling his story, so I'll let him take it from here:

"Oh, El Paso was a cool enough place and all, good people, mountains all around and the Mexican food was truth, but talk about the middle of *nowhere*. I got out there after having hundreds of friends at Austin High and I was totally alone. Didn't know a soul but the assistant coach that recruited me on the phone, and he was a prick. I tried to make the best of it, met some cool dudes that partied, went over to Mexico a few times and went wild, but man I was *lonely*. I never dreamed I'd miss my momma like that, or hanging out with old friends.

"And the school part sucked. I had no idea what I wanted to do, so I was taking business courses and sucking like nobody's business. Getting just a C in any class was a pipedream. Not saying it wouldn't have helped if I'd gone to class more, but by October it's colder than hell out there in the mornings. It gets *cold as shit* in El Paso in the winter. Leaving my warm bed to walk to class sometimes wasn't an option. Coach got me a tutor and they got me to drop the classes I was failing. They put me in courses like Home EC, Film Appreciation, the History of Rock 'n' Roll. They called 'em basket weaving classes."

Everybody laughs, and about this time, Anastasia shows up with three other members of the White Beaches and gives Cody a hug. The band's been spending time in the recording studio, and they're taking an afternoon break. She looks striking as usual, and Cody smiles big and gives her a quick kiss.

"Hey, babe – almost done here. So anyway, I'm lonely, depressed, keep talking on the phone to friends going to UT or Texas State having the time of their lives at college – homesick as hell. And D1 football, man, is *hard*. The toll it takes on your body. I can handle myself pretty good, but shit man, I was hurting somewhere all the time. So my head's not right at this time, you know? So Thanksgiving's coming up, but instead of getting to go home for the holidays, we have a fucking home game on Saturday against Arizona State. Now UTEP ain't the football hotbed of America. The whole team knows we're gonna get the shit kicked out of us by ASU – they were favored by something like 38 points.

"I got up Saturday morning and the forecast for gametime was 26 degrees with a 75% chance of *freezing rain*, and I'm thinking, this a joke, right? So we play in this big old stadium called the Sun Bowl that's built into the side of a mountain, which is cool, but the trouble is no one in town gives a fuck about Miner football cuz we haven't had a winning record in something like fourteen years. So while the place holds 50,000 people, we go out for pregame and there's maybe 4000 fans in the whole damn stadium, 2000 of 'em from ASU."

About now Cody's drained his margarita and says, "Hey, Ana, can you grab me another 'rita real quick while I finish up?"

"Happily!" she says, grabbing his empty glass and rolling her eyes. "I've heard this sad ass story too many times." And she smiles and glides away to get another round.

Cody continues undeterred, "So we start going through pregame warm-ups and I'm not feeling this scene at all, freezing my ass off in this big empty stadium. It's time for the punter to do his practice kicks, and I'm what they call the deep snapper who snaps him the ball. So we go to midfield, and I grab the usual five balls to snap back so he can practice punting, and it starts *sleeting* like a bastard. There's tiny ice crystals bouncing off my helmet, but some of the fuckers are sticking and freezing, and I'm thinking, this must be the *freezing rain*. I bend over to snap, look at my arms covered in turf burns, two fingers taped together because one's jammed. I hear the punter say 'Hut' and I snap the ball back thinking, *Fuck this shit.*

"He punts the ball, and I grab another one and hear 'Hut' and I snap the ball back, thinking about my mom's homemade dressing, her crescent rolls, the pecan pie, and everything else I missed for Thanksgiving since I had to be here for this damn game, and I think, *What am I doing here?* The freezing rain's coming down in sheets now, I grab another ball, and without thinking anything really, nothing was planned, hear the word 'Hut.' I snap it, and I just took off running downfield, sprinting for the locker room that's up the tunnel at the other end of the field.

"After I'd made it about twenty yards, the special teams coach sees me running and he yells, 'Hey, Barringer, where the hell you going?' And I don't even look back. I just keep running, picking up speed as the sleet bounces off my face and helmet. Then I hear, 'Barringer, what the hell are you doing? Where are you going? Barringer, BARRINGER!!!!' And I just keep running, faster and faster, all the way downfield, straight through the end zone, up the stadium ramp, and into the dressing room, out of sight."

The group's dying laughing now as I'm off to the side, beer in hand, watching Cody do his magic. Someone says, "So you just ran off the field in the middle of warmups? What'd the coaches do? You get cut?"

And Cody grins and says, "What'd the coaches do? They didn't do shit cuz I didn't wait around to talk to any of 'em. I was peeling off my uniform, jogging up the ramp to the dressing room. Left everything lying on the ground as I went. Helmet, jersey, shoulder pads. I changed into my street clothes as fast as I could and boogied, man. Went straight to the dorm, grabbed my shit, and said *adios muchacho* to El Paso. And that, my friends, is how my illustrious D1 collegiate football career came to an end!"

The image of Cody running off the field in the sleet with the coach screaming his name in the background cracks me up. And he did all this without really knowing what the hell he was doing – just taking off running because his instincts were telling him to *flee*. Crazy MF'er.

The party was a hit as expected, kids and adults both having a great time, all ages jumping in the pool after we ate. As the party winds down and lots of people have left, Bryan sees me sitting in one of the pool loungers and comes over to talk, and I'm glad. We haven't seen each other much lately, we've both been so busy, and I love talking with Bryan. He's been such a huge help to me in so many ways – such an interesting guy, always thinking, a couple steps ahead of everybody else. If it wasn't for Bryan building our website, there'd be no WaldensPets.com, no doubt about that. We haven't been able to talk at all at the party with so much going on other than small talk. Bryan's been grilling, chasing kids, running all the birthday activities – being the perfect host.

"It's good to see you, Walden. Thank you for coming." I notice how Bryan's once jet black hair is a little salt and peppered now, and his eyes look tired.

"Sure, Bryan – wouldn't miss Bridger's big #10 for the world. You kidding me?"

Bryan smiles and looks away. "Hard to believe my little guy is ten years old. Seems like yesterday Ally and I were bringing him home, wondering how in the world the two of us could raise this tiny human." When he turns back, his eyes are tearing up a little.

"Hey, awesome party man. You and Ally sure know how to throw a bash. Where is Ally by the way? Haven't seen her since the swimming got crazy."

"Ally's wiped out. All the party prep and entertaining. Dealing with all these kids..."

"I can't imagine. How many kids were here, something like fifty?"

"Good guess. About forty-five. That's how many party favor bags we put together. Too many really. It wasn't my idea for Stella to have all her friends over too, but Ally insisted."

Bryan takes a swig from his longneck and looks away again, watching the kids who are still here jumping in and out of the pool over and over. He seems lost in his thoughts when he turns back, looks me in the eye, and says, "Can I share something with you, Walden?"

"Sure, dude, what's up?"

"Ally's got cancer." That's all he can get out. He chokes up and turns away, hiding his tears. I'm floored, the unexpected news hitting me like a brick.

"What? Ally? Your Ally? She's got cancer?"

Bryan tries to gather himself and after a pause says, "We've known about it for twenty-one days but haven't said a word to anyone. First making sure the diagnosis was true, then trying to understand the severity, the treatment options."

"Oh my God, Bryan. I'm so sorry...so very, very sorry. From what I hear cancer treatment is light years better than it used to be. Most of it's curable if you catch it in time, right?"

Bryan stares at me now, tears streaming down his face, "It's *pancreatic* cancer, Walden, but we did catch it early, although I fear not early enough."

"Pancreatic cancer? I don't know anything about that. What does that mean?"

"It means my dear Ally, our dear Ally, has a terrible form of cancer that's very hard to stop."

"So what stage is she in? You said you caught it early."

Bryan turns into his business persona and runs through all the painful information they've learned over the last three weeks, "Here's the data, Walden. There are three stages of pancreatic cancer. Localized, which means the cancer is in the pancreas and hasn't spread to other areas.

Regional, which means it's spread only to nearby structures or lymph nodes, and distant, which means it's all over the body. It's literally eating you up."

"So Ally is localized? Did you catch it before it spread?"

"Hold on Walden, let me finish. With pancreatic cancer, which by the way is one of the worst cancers you can contract, they give you a Five-Year Survival Rate. Basically what the statistics say your chances are for living five or more years."

"Ok."

"And the *localized* five-year survival rate is only 42%. Not even 50/50 to live five years. That's as good as it gets. The regional survival rate is only 14%, and the distant survival rate is 3%...virtually no chance."

"So Bryan, the cancer is still localized, right? Ally's a fighter and you guys can get the best medical teams out there. A 50/50 chance for Ally is one I'm betting on for sure."

"From what we know, yes, it's still localized, but the doctors haven't ruled out for certain it hasn't reached her lymph nodes. She told me tonight, before going to rest, that she was feeling tenderness. And even if it is 50/50, that's to survive *five years*."

"Oh Bryan...I don't know what to say. I know this is the wrong thing, but why did you have this party? Was it good to get her so tired? Under so much stress?"

Bryan starts to tear up again, his serious façade is gone. "Come on, Walden. You know Ally. You think there's any chance she would miss throwing a celebration like no other for Bridger knowing what she knows? It's his tenth birthday. We haven't told the kids yet...we don't know how to..."

"I can't imagine what you're going through, Bryan – can't fathom it. And keeping this all in, all to yourselves. Putting on this party. Just know I'm here for you, ok? Here for you, and for Ally, for the kids. Jessica can help with meals, taking the kids places. Frazier can help too. You know Cody will do anything."

I'm searching for more to say to help when Bryan puts on his strong face again. "Things are moving fast now, Walden. We just started chemo and so far she's doing ok. Most likely they will try to surgically remove the tumor. I'm talking to Johns Hopkins and the City of Hope about alternative treatments. Every option is being researched and considered. We *will* get through this. I keep telling Ally, 42% survival rate for five years is just an *average*. And an average from the past, not from using today's treatment options. I promise you, the way we attack this *Mother Fucker* will be anything but average. The way Ally fights is going to be anything but average!"

I shake my head yes, offer encouragement, and we sit together a while, drinking and staring off into space.

"I appreciate you being here for us, Walden. Now do me a favor. Not a word to anybody about this until I say it's ok. Got it? That's one reason I'm talking to you. I have to get this out or I'll explode, but I know you're one of the few who could keep this in confidence. Promise?"

"I promise. I'll do anything I can to help you, Bryan. Anything…"

After Bryan leaves to say his goodbyes to other partygoers, I sit by the pool, drinking, watching little Stella and Bridger play like little brothers and sisters do – teasing, pushing each other in the pool, throwing toys at each other, having a blast being kids. My eyes swell up thinking about their mom Ally, about how their young lives are about to change, how there's a very good chance their mom won't make it to their graduation – heck might not even see them start high school.

On the way home I break down crying, thinking about Ally, Bryan, their kids, and about my loved ones – how much I take for granted they're here for me day after day. Later, when Bryan eventually shared with me how he and Ally sat down and told the kids about their mom's illness, how the kids responded, we both started weeping. I mean, how in the world are children that young supposed to understand that something totally foreign and unexplainable has suddenly got hold of Mommy and may take her away from them forever. Why? How come it happened? Why can't they make it get better? Why can't they make it go away?

Hearing this news got me thinking about Mary and Father and how much longer *they've* got. Mary's dementia makes meaningful conversations almost impossible. You think you've had a good talk, but the next day you realize she has no memory of it. I've learned with her it's best to take it one conversation at a time. Just try and make the most of every conversation as if it may be your last, because in a way, since she forgets it took place anyway, it is your last.

With Father it's totally different. He's still sharp mentally, but it's amazing how fast old age has hit him physically. Knowing his heart condition and overall declining health, I thought it made sense to talk to him *heart to heart*. You never know what day could be *his* last. Now, I don't want to get all emotional here and go on about my dad, but growing up with a Father who's the founder of a community with a mission as intense as creating a utopian society wasn't the easiest. Like the mission he worked so hard towards, Father was an intense guy. We never had a cuddly, lovey-dovey father and son relationship. Father was direct and to the point, demanding in his own way (and incredibly liberal in others). I'm struggling here to explain this, but just understand we didn't talk much about feelings or emotions growing up. That was Mary's area.

So after Ally's cancer hit me like a brick, reminding me our time here on Earth is short, I decided to sit down with Father next time I was out in Wimberley and have a talk. We were in his old den drinking iced tea, resting after trimming back some trees, when I told him I was thankful he was such a good dad to me. For taking care of our family, for loving us, for loving Mary. For showing me what it's like to have a strong work ethic and for being a good role model in so many ways. Then, I told him I was sorry for not being a better son. For not talking to him more, for not sharing with him what was going on in my life, being more of a friend as we both got older – never truly letting him in.

Now, I gotta admit, I was surprised to see Father get a little teary-eyed on me (I did too...I cry all the time now for no apparent reason). Then he told me he was proud of the man I'd become, and he understood how it must have been hard for a young boy to be open with a Father who was so intense and driven. That he knew all along he was working too hard while living at Nueva Tierra, not spending enough time with me and Frazier, and that he was sorry for not being a more open and loving dad. It wasn't a long conversation, five minutes tops, but I'm glad we had it – maybe the best talk I've ever had with my dad. One I'll always remember.

When we were done Father said, "Walden, I need to talk to you about Mary. Now I know you and Frazier can tell her memory is bad, but I've been covering up for her for years so you two wouldn't worry about it. The fact is she can't remember anymore what day it is, what she had for breakfast, even who she talked to ten minutes ago on the phone."

"Yeah, Father, we know. Seems like it's gotten worse over the last six months."

"Well it's been coming on more like three years, but like I said, I've been covering for her the best I can. The reason I'm telling you this now is there's going to come a time when she doesn't even know who *we* are. Doesn't know where we live anymore, doesn't remember anything. And when that happens, if she makes it that long, it's going to be hell taking care of her."

"Yeah, we know. Frazier and I have been talking about that."

Then Father rubbed his chin and said, "Good, I figured you were. I'm doing everything I can to take care of her and be here for her now, but I'm not getting any younger. You never know when I'll be called home. The husband's usually the first to go, you know, which leaves Mary out here alone. Just giving you a heads-up, Walden. And I can tell you this for a fact...it won't be easy."

BJ IV

BRETT JESAK TAKES A LONG, slow sip of his morning coffee, rubs his temples, and tries to relieve the throbbing headache coming on with a vengeance. He looks over in disgust at the Murphy bed pulled down from the wall, disheveled, half the sheets spilling onto the floor. It looks like a pack of wild animals slept there last night. Having the Murphy bed installed, as he had feared, was like giving a cocaine addict the phone number to the best dealer in town. You knew it wouldn't be long before it was used, over and over again. Brett looks out the window as the sun is slowly rising, as Portland is waking up, wondering how much longer his undisciplined, risky behavior can continue.

Nurturing his coffee and firing up the desk monitors, Brett prepares for another business day; one where he will, once again, use his personal office bathroom to shower and look presentable. Brett remembers the first episode that started all this madness, all this very uncharacteristic behavior. His undoing was succumbing to that actress, the one named Rachel Davidson, who caught his imagination so intensely during that entertainment division lunch. He had run into her at a few "chance meetings," which he soon realized were clearly orchestrated by the actress, her advances becoming more overt and aggressive. With a stagnant love life at home, and his relationship with Nichole even more detached for a variety of reasons, he was totally helpless when Rachel called his office around 9:30 one evening, asking if she could come see him to ask a small favor.

Brett knows his self-discipline, strong will, and mental clarity are virtually unmatched in almost every arena, but also understands he can be completely overmatched when it comes to beautiful women throwing themselves at him. Life experiences, to this point, had not prepared him for such matters. A flood of guilt overcomes Brett as he remembers, ironically, that when he finally did submit to Rachel's advances, the Murphy bed, which he is beginning to despise, did not come into play. It began on one of the fine leather couches lining the walls, their tangled bodies eventually ending up on the floor. It became so intense that when finished, lying in each other's arms on the incredibly expensive Isfahan rug, panting, covered in sweat, he had carpet burns on both knees. How would he ever explain that to Nichole?

After that first episode, Brett realized he had to take action, and take it fast. He knew because the experience was so intense, the perfect combination of lust, adrenalin, and the fear of getting caught, there was no way he could keep from doing it again. But at the same time, he realized what he did was incredibly perilous, undoubtedly stupid. He was one of the richest, most well-known men in the world. It would be impossible to randomly have sexual relations with virtual strangers without a catastrophe of some kind happening soon; of this he was quite certain. These women are vultures, he thought, obviously doing this for his money, his power, possibly to get pregnant. Who knows what else? Brett was all too aware of his unremarkable history in the arena of love, so he had no doubt what spawned his sudden good fortune with beautiful women. Money buys looks, and looks buys money.

After his first dalliance with Rachel, Brett meticulously distanced himself from the sensual, physical aspect of his actions and analyzed the situation from a business and security standpoint. He then called in his most trusted attorney and had him draw up a Non-Disclosure Agreement, a "relationship contract" as it were. Should he find himself considering sex again with an unvetted partner, he had a document they must sign that stated they willfully participated, and they agreed to keep everything confidential, releasing all of their rights to speak publicly about any element of the relationship or sue for any reason. Every possible scenario was covered thoroughly by his attorney, who produced an ironclad safety net should an indiscretion ever happen again.

Brett then arranged for the actress he just violated, for Rachel Davidson, to get the leading role in an upcoming Sahara big budget movie production, a role far outside what she could ever legitimately expect to get. Then he tied this enticing role, and its impressive salary, to an ironclad NDA agreement concerning not only that first night together, but any other episodes that may or may not occur in the future. If she ever as much as implied there was any sort of relationship between the two, or that something improper had ever happened, her career was over. And then, Brett made a promise to himself to never again have what he considered to be "unprotected sex." That is, relations with any person who did not sign a document of silence and consent.

It did not take long for Nichole to become suspicious, eventually uncovering his indiscretions. Their physical relationship was so distant the rug burns were amazingly never discovered; Nichole hadn't seen Brett naked for quite some time. But Brett was never good at hiding things from Nichole. The feelings of guilt were taking their toll on his psyche. She could tell from the way he was acting something was wrong. He was either hiding some new policy he had enacted at work he knew she would despise, or he was having an affair.

After working at Sahara all those years, Nichole had several confidants still employed there at very high levels. Eventually one of her old friends confided to her about the rumors circulating around the executive suite. Nichole immediately confronted Brett, who confessed under pressure; in the realm of social relationships she always did have the upper hand. He swore it was the first time – it was not – and then he worked hard for a time to reestablish the original vibrant connection they had shared together for so long. After all, Nichole was the first, and still the only woman, Brett had ever loved.

It was his idea they go on a daytrip to the Fruit Loop, a favorite activity of their early years, when they would tour the orchards, gardens, and vineyards around the Columbia River Gorge and Mount Hood. It was something they did together often when they were younger, when it was a far simpler time. In the very early days of Sahara, when they were working outrageous hours and overwhelmed by stress, they would cut out early some Fridays, their tanks seemingly empty, then drive straight to the Fruit Loop before noon to avoid the weekend crowds, feeling like schoolkids playing hooky. After a day of orchard hopping – picking apples, blueberries, cherries, raspberries – they usually ended up at their favorite orchard and vineyard close to the base of Mount Hood. Sitting outside the winery on the hillside in Adirondack chairs, they marveled at the incredible views, so close you could see the detail in Mount Hood's snowcapped peaks, snow that would never leave even by the end of summer. They ate wood-fired pizzas, gourmet cheese, drank wine. It was the beloved cradle of many wonderful, lasting memories.

But this outing did nothing to repair their relationship, and in hindsight probably hurt more than it helped. Brett should have known the security detail that was needed to keep onlookers away only added stress; it changed the whole dynamic of their experience. All it did was illustrate how much everything had changed. There was no spontaneity, no feeling like they were working together to take on the world, no passion or unconditional love. Just a somber, tension-filled drive with a chauffeur that felt empty and contrived.

While Brett did not want to admit it, it was clear Nichole was angry and distancing herself from the situation to avoid getting hurt any further. His hopes of renewing their relationship were most likely going to fail. It was not long before Brett was at it again, and Nichole's trust was irreconcilably broken. Without trust in the relationship, and so little of the deep love they once shared remaining, the marriage was too fragile to be saved.

Now, this morning, Brett sits behind his massive Bocote desk staring at the Murphy bed, in disbelief things are so out of control; that the only woman he truly loves is lost forever. In addition, Brett's financial mind is scrambling, having a difficult time accepting the fact that the fortune he worked so hard to amass will certainly be diminished significantly, taken by Nichole and her attorneys in the divorce. He wonders if their separation was inevitable, that their marriage was destined to end even without the affairs. After all, they weren't getting along all that well before his indiscretions began; they spent virtually no time together. How many truly wealthy people stay married to the same person all their lives anyway? But deep in his heart, Brett knows it was his lack of discipline and willpower that did him in; that severed the relationship and ultimately forced Nichole to do what she was about to do.

As Brett had accurately intuited after crossing that line with Rachel, the adrenaline rush and excitement, the thrill of being with a woman who looked like the centerfold of a *Playboy* magazine, was just too much for him to circumvent. But what Brett did not expect, what came as a complete surprise, was once the sexual liaisons began, his business acumen, his drive to dominate the competition, his business intuition and new ideas flourished like never before. After Sahara recorded two straight record quarters, smashing analysts' estimates, Brett recognized the two had to be interconnected. The thrill and adrenaline rush of dangerous sexual encounters reinvigorated his business drive, sharpened his business skills, made him into an even greater marketing savant. Not only was he experiencing a sex life he could never, ever have dreamed of, he was making more money now than even he could possibly imagine.

On his desk is an article from *The Economist* detailing Brett's recent increase in fortune. The article explains the amazing value created from Sahara's latest results and soaring stock price, jettisoning Brett Jesak's net worth to unheard of levels. The article reads, "At the earnings rate calculation based on the change in net worth over the last quarter, as determined by Forbes, Mr. Jesak has earned an estimated $6.3 billion per month, more than $1.5 billion per week, and more than $210 million per day in the last three months." This recent massive accumulation of wealth should be soothing for Brett, the numbers virtually impossible to believe. But the overriding thoughts this morning that continue to percolate in his throbbing, aching head? Was it really worth it? Was the never-ending fixation on making money and all the meaningless sex worth destroying his marriage? Worth hurting and alienating the only person in the world who ever truly understood him; ever truly loved him?

As of this morning only Brett and Nichole know their marriage is disintegrating and unrepairable; they have purposely kept the marriage difficulties strictly to themselves for all kinds of reasons. But the reality Brett faces, because of actions completely of his own doing, is that whatever was built through their many years together, all of the wealth accumulated, all of the residences, the cars and the boats, all of it will be cut in half by a bunch of lecherous lawyers, concerned only with grabbing as much out of the estate as they possibly can. Brett is feeling emotional now, saddened and remorseful, as he considers all he has done to Nichole to extinguish their love. His life will change forever, he will never find another love like Nichole, and he has only himself to blame.

As he grabs a Kleenex, dabs his eyes, and blows his nose, Brett looks toward the massive credenza on the right of his elegant desk and says, "Hey Amanda, who is the richest man in the world?"

"Good morning, sir. Happy Tuesday! The richest man in the world, in terms of monetary wealth, is Brett Jesak, CEO and primary shareholder of the Sahara Corporation. According to the *Wall Street Journal*, Mr. Jesak was named the first centi-billionaire on the Forbes wealth index, and is now recognized as the richest man in modern history after his net worth rose to $147 billion."

"Thank you, Amanda. Thank you. Very thorough..."

Staring out the window now, looking at all the "normal" people driving to work on Portland's downtown thoroughfares, Brett wonders why Amanda's answer leaves him so hollow. Is it because all he has worked so hard for is simply an illusion? That once it was achieved it brought no true inner happiness? Or is it because Brett knows that the almost unfathomable wealth that Amanda just described, his wealth, will soon be divided by two?

YUGO VIII

Come on, children, you're acting like children
Every generation thinks it's the end of the world

"You Never Know" by Wilco (from *Wilco*)

YUGO WENT OVER two elements in today's session, so I think it's best to get right to them. A note here before we start. I love the more spiritual elements of Yugo's Way and these two are definitely in that realm – although I admit this first one was hard for me to follow in the beginning. Listening back on the recordings, you can really feel Yugo's passion around this 9th element. It was mostly new ideas for me to think about, so I just listened and soaked it all in. And man do I love the way he wrapped it all up – beautiful! But first, he kicked things off by backtracking to my last assignment:

YF: So Walden, you do any thinking about getting out of your comfort zone? Any ideas on what you wanna do first?

WH: Yeah, I'm thinking about doing a speech...

YF: A speech? Why a speech? You scared of talking in front of people?

WH: Always have been. I don't mind talking to smaller groups or holding meetings at work, but just the thought of getting in front of a *large* group of people scares the shit out of me.

YF: Hmmm. Ok, interesting. What kind of speech are we talking about here?

WH: Well, the Austin Chamber of Commerce asked me a couple of times to give a speech about Walden's Pets at one of their meetings – about how we work in the community. It's for one of those big functions they hold twice a year, like five hundred people – business leaders.

YF: Ok. Now that sounds challenging.

WH: Since speaking in front of a bunch of people is something I go out of my way to avoid, I've never even considered doing it before. Always told them I'm busy no matter what day it's scheduled for. That I can't do it.

YF: So now you're gonna do it? Is there something you have planned?

WH: Not planned. They haven't asked me again yet, but when they do, I'm thinking about saying yes. There's a thing called Conscious Capitalism that's catching on with some more forward-thinking businesses, and we've incorporated some of their ideas into our culture at Walden's Pets. I think it might do some good to encourage other businesses to try the same things.

YF: Awesome, Walden. That's beautiful! Overcoming a fear and helping others at the same time!

WH: Yeah, well don't hold me to it, Yugo. I might jump out of an airplane instead. Cody's been trying to get me to do that with him for years, but I'm a little scared of heights.

YF: *(Smiling.)* A little scared of heights? Sounds like a solid "maybe" on both counts. Why don't you see which opportunity the Universe throws at you first, then go for it from there.

As usual – sensible, sound advice from Yugo. Now on to the first element of the day:

YF: Today, Walden, I want to talk to you about evolution. Not so much evolution in the physical, material realm that we learn about in schools, the evolution of Darwin where animals adapt to nature and the strongest survive. This concerns a different realm altogether. What this element covers is the ongoing *spiritual evolution* of humanity.

WH: Spiritual evolution? Ok...

YF: Scientists say human beings haven't evolved *physically* all that much for thousands of years. There's been slight changes in average height and build, changes in the timing of puberty, in what's considered adolescence and adulthood, but overall the human physical machine hasn't changed much.

WH: I can see that, yeah.

YF: But we *have* evolved intellectually and *spiritually* over this time, although it's been a long, slow journey – and here's a big reason why. It wasn't that long ago that humans spent the vast majority of our waking hours in the pursuit of food – hunting, gathering, farming. It was a daily requirement for survival, a reality of human existence. And the further back in time you go, the higher that percentage goes up. Add on the time for gathering water, finding warmth, clothing, safety. So what does that mean? It means human beings have spent the vast majority of our time on this planet focused almost entirely on *survival*. For almost all of human history, basic survival has consumed most of our mindspace up until very, very recently. The point being, humanity hasn't had time for significant *spiritual* evolution.

WH: Interesting. Seems we're pretty lucky to be alive now when you think about the past.

YF: Yes, I agree. Now, let's fast forward to today, to a time when it takes less than five minutes to hit a drive-thru and grab lunch. When you can go to the grocery store and buy thousands of items immediately. Most people in this country don't spend more than a few minutes a day getting the food they need to survive. With the advances in technology, food production, science, medicine – much of it good, some of it not so good – people don't have to do very much to survive physically on Earth anymore compared to the 1800s and before. And because of this, our Earth, Walden, has entered into a *golden era* where the spiritual and psychological evolution of humanity can explode! Finally we actually have time on our hands to evolve mentally and spiritually – where it really matters.

WH: I get you to a point, Yugo, but what about work? I mean, most people spend eight hours a day working to put food on the table and a roof over their heads, right? There's not that fear of survival, but it takes up a lot of time.

YF: *(Nodding his head in agreement.)* Yes, you're right. It does take up a lot of time, but nowhere close to the mid-1800s and before. I'm not saying our society isn't busy and frazzled and feeling short on time. But I am saying we're in the best period in human history to have the time to evolve mentally and spiritually if we give it our *attention*. The purpose of this dialogue is to spark your thinking about evolution and bring you hope about the future. We look around at our world and don't see evolution happening, so we assume evolution occurred thousands of years ago and then stopped. My point is *everything is still evolving,* all the time. We just don't see it.

WH: Ok?

YF: Nothing stays the same. Nothing is static. So our ideas, beliefs, and understandings should be evolving as everything else evolves. Staying the same means we're not growing. And that's one possible reason why some religions are losing ground and have apathetic followers. They are static, unchanged for centuries, all created during a time when humanity's collective consciousness was at a much lower level.

WH: Yeah, I've read about the worldwide decline of Protestant and Catholic churches over the last forty years. Seems significant.

YF: Contemplate this. Most all of our major foundational religious books were compiled between two to four thousand years ago. The Torah in Judaism, the Tipitaka and the Sutras in Buddhism, the Vedas in Hinduism, the Old and New Testaments in Christianity, and the Qur'an in Islam. So does it make sense to you that the Creator of the Universe would inspire those spiritual teachers and prophets to write these amazing texts, then stop influencing humanity for the next few *thousand years*? Did the Supreme Being inspire and enlighten the Buddha, Moses, the Prophets, and Muhammad thousands of years ago and then take a leave of absence from our planet to some other locale in the universe? I don't think so.

Our Creator's influence and presence is and always has been here with us. The Great Spirit is here with us at this very moment, continually speaking, guiding, divinely inspiring new prophets and new teachers with ever evolving wisdom *if we will listen*. The miracles haven't stopped. The influences and inspiration haven't stopped. But we as consumers of major religion were led to believe our Creator stopped communicating with us after the writings of our canonical books. And so, we stopped listening. But our Universal Creator mirrors the Universe it created. Not static but ever evolving, ever expanding, always growing. We know this because everything created is always changing.

WH: Now that's intriguing. Doesn't make sense that God would actively inspire man's early religious teachings thousands of years ago and then just stop.

YF: *(Nodding.)* Right? So let's look at examples of the spiritual and "moral" evolution of humanity. If you want to see how times change, look at old Jewish and Christian teachings from the Torah and the Bible, from the book of Leviticus. Some speak of the infallibility or inerrancy of these books, and yes, they are filled with undeniable wisdom. But we have to remember, these words were shaped by the culture and values *of that time*.

Very few people strictly follow these teachings anymore because our collective consciousness has evolved.

For instance, in Old Testament times, it was written into law that women were to be stoned to death for committing adultery. Think about that today. Who'd be the moral authority to condemn a person for this transgression? How many people were wrongly executed back then? There's false accusations flying around all the time. If this were going on today, there'd be pissed off guys getting girls killed for nothing. Can you imagine? And by the way, the dudes got a pass on this one. No stoning for guys messing around. But Leviticus clearly says if a woman sleeps around, put her in a circle, find some rocks, and throw them at her till she's dead. It was the same way for people who spoke out against God – for "blasphemers." Speaking words considered blasphemy toward God was punished by stoning. It's in Chapter 24, around verse 13 if you want to read it yourself. But we don't do that anymore thank goodness. And why? Because we've *evolved* – spiritually and intellectually.

WH: Ok, I can see that. Pretty wild...never heard any of that stuff before.

YF: And there's many other moral decrees in there most everyone ignores today because times *change*. Detailed laws about menstruation and sex, about how to prepare certain foods. Eating shrimp and eating bacon were forbidden. Just think, Walden, shrimp brochette was doubly sinful back then. Public displays of animal sacrifice used to be required by many cultures and faiths. I bring all this up to illustrate how what's considered moral *evolves*. Human beings have a higher level of consciousness and are more aware today than when these laws, customs, and traditions were written. Many religiously devout pick and choose what they want to follow and ignore the other parts, and that's ok. We all pick and choose what we want to believe.

WH: I've never read Leviticus.... Maybe I will?

YF: It was an eye-opener for me, Walden. I read it and thought, hey, what about all these commandments? Why aren't I being told to do all this shit? Now I'm not discounting the wisdom and teachings in these beautifully written religious texts. I believe they were given to us by the Grand Creator to get us where we are today. They were written *for their times*, and still relevant today. But I am saying times change, moral compasses evolve, and the Bible illustrates that's true. This isn't meant to degrade certain religions. But some of the legalistic, moral teachings of these books, the "thou shalt nots" that people get all up in arms about, they were written for the times. Rather than focusing on legalism, we should focus on the core *spiritual messages* of love, compassion, empathy, humility, and forgiveness.

WH: I've wondered about all the rules of some churches. Some say dancing is wrong, but there were celebrations and dances in the Bible all the time, right? Some say drinking is wrong, but even I know Jesus turned water into wine and that was called a miracle. So what is it?

YF: It's confusing, right? The core spiritual teachings and foundation of these ancient religions are beautiful. It's just that some of the "words," the details around what's considered "moral," have become outdated over the last few thousand years. That's why the world needs new ways to express the same truths. Humanity has evolved *intellectually* too. Just think, a thousand years *after* the New Testament was written, many people still believed the world was flat. That if you got in a boat in the ocean and went too far, you'd fall off the Earth. Are we to base our society today strictly on books written more than a thousand years *before* we knew the world was round? Before we understood the sun didn't revolve around the Earth?

WH: I think I see what you're saying. We're focused on the teachings and morality of ancient books written during times when everything was different. So maybe we aren't evolving spiritually as fast as we could because intellectually we see religion as irrelevant, as stagnant.

YF: (*Nodding and smiling.*) Amen! And it's not just *religious* laws that are evolving. Look at our country and how our laws have changed. How what the public accepts as morally acceptable has changed. Women couldn't legally vote in this country *until 1920*! Just think. A hundred years ago, when my grandaddy was alive, women couldn't vote.

WH: That's wild. My knowledge of history is so bad. For some reason 1920 seemed like centuries ago in school. To think our grandads were living when women couldn't vote...hard to believe.

YF: And of course slavery was legal and institutionalized by our government until 1865 – not so long ago. Blacks couldn't own property. Lynchings were common. People were executed for stealing a *horse*. The examples go on and on, clearly showing how our collective consciousness is evolving *for the better*.

WH: Yeah, I can see your point. You hear old folks say all the time how much better things used to be in the "good old days," but I guess where you stand depends on where you sit, right? I don't think things were better back then for many groups of people – they were much worse.

YF: Right, well said! Now, let's think about *social* morality – about accepted practices in society. Have things evolved over the years? The Romans threw Christians to the lions for slaughter in front of thousands of cheering spectators, *for entertainment.* Until the late 1700s, mainly in Europe but in this country too, people were literally burned alive in front of the entire town if they were considered "witches" by religious leaders. And the community was ok with that. They'd go to watch. Not so long ago, two people who had a major disagreement would settle it in a gunfight, a duel to the death in the middle of the street. *(Yugo's standing now, pacing.)* And consider, just *sixty* years ago, a person like me couldn't drink out of the same water fountain as you, *by law.* Couldn't think of eating a meal in the same restaurant, couldn't dream of going to the same school. It was against the *law.* And the vast majority of our society, people who considered themselves morally upstanding citizens, were all cool with that. You getting this? How intellectually, spiritually, and morally we're evolving, even though for most of our existence, humanity has focused primarily on physical survival?

WH: Yep, I'm getting it loud and clear. The implication being, now that we have more time to spend on our spiritual thinking, on working out our spiritual bodies as you say, our evolution should start happening much faster.

YF: Yes! You got it. Ok, now to switch gears. Once we get a little older, most people think that our generation is the last generation that has our shit together. That overall, society was ok when we were growing up, but everything's going to hell now, right before our eyes. And what does every generation think about its youth? They're complacent, they lack discipline and drive, they don't have a clue. We worry that everything we cherish is changing, that the world is coming to an end! This is what *every generation* thinks, and it's simply not true!

WH: Haha! That's *exactly* what Father thinks, and I hate to say this but I'm having some of those thoughts lately too. That the world may be coming to an end soon.

YF: *(Smiling, sitting, pulling out a slip of paper.)* Ok, Walden, I want you to listen to this dialogue about the state of affairs from a novel I just read:

> "I give the present dispensation ten years," he said after cataloging the horrors of the modern world. "After that, the most appalling and sanguinary bust-up that's ever been." And he prophesized class wars, wars between the continents, the final catastrophic crumbling of our already dreadfully unsteady society.

"Not a pleasant look-out for our children," I said. "We've at least had our thirty years or so. They'll only grow up to see the Last Judgment."

"We oughtn't to have brought them into the world," he answered.

WH: Hmmm. That's dead on with what you were talking about – how people feel things are getting worse and it could be the end of days.

YF: Yes, but Walden, those words are from a novel published in 1928. It's from *Point Counter Point* by Aldous Huxley. Almost one hundred years ago, the same dialogue many are having today was taking place then. As it was with the generations before them, and all generations after. Every generation *thinks* it's the end of the world. But we're not even close to the end. The potential to evolve the human spirit is unimaginable. With all the incredible advancements possible in this technological age? Now that we have the time to evolve spiritually?

WH: I'm not so sure about all that, Yugo. I mean, look around at where things are going...

YF: There's so much more to come, Walden. We've learned more about our place in the cosmos, more about the universe with the Hubble and now the James Webb telescopes, but most of the universe is completely *unknown* to us. Quantum physics has us wondering what's even real. Some physicists say the universe is made up of something called "vibrating superstrings" with *multiple dimensions* all coexisting together. We're looking at space travel, even time travel. Who knows what's in store! Totally new laws will be discovered around *space* and *time*. That's one thing I'm pretty sure about, Walden. Humanity doesn't have a clue yet about the true *nature of time*. New forms of energy are on the horizon. Maybe one day we won't even need words to communicate. Our thoughts will be enough. Who knows what's ahead, but one thing is pretty certain. Our generation is far from being at the end of human evolution. How egotistical we are to think after all these thousands of years it ends with us...

WH: Now you got my head spinning, Yugo. I've tried to read up some on quantum physics and it makes my head hurt.

YF: (*Laughing.*) Yeah, well me too! There is one huge watch out here, though. And I'm sad to say it does make me sound like every other generation. I believe we're nowhere close to finished evolving if, and only if, we take better care of our planet, of Mother Earth *now*. And there's no time to waste. If not, things may look a whole lot different. We may *devolve* back to a time when survival is all that matters again – the search for food, water, and shelter. Not the end for all, but really hard times.

WH: So Yugo, I follow your line of thinking and like the ideas, but is there a big takeaway I need to get out of all this?

YF: (*Smiling.*) I get it. This element is different from the others. It's not so much about something you can *do*, it's more about thinking about life and humanity's destiny in a *new way*. It's about using true spirituality, using love and hope, to evolve our understandings and beliefs as our knowledge of the world and the principles around it expand. Remember, the wisdom of the Divine Energy of the Universe is still being shared with humanity all the time in many ways. Just because it's new doesn't mean it's not truth for our times. There are many modern-day spiritual and intellectual visionaries out there doing their part, leading the way for humanity's continued spiritual and intellectual evolution.

WH: Yeah, like who?

YF: We never know who or what it may be. For me, I met a woman outside Taos who let me stay at her place for weeks when I *really* needed help, a woman named Juanita Goldsans. She was more divinely inspired than any human I've ever known. It felt like angels put her before me to absorb her spirit, like a sponge. She had a sign in front of her old adobe home that said "Lawyer, Philosopher, Rooms," so I knocked on the door and she let me in. I listened, learned, and stayed for a while. She had a reading room, a library, the books she turned me on to, the amazing food, the peace and contentment she shared. It was incredible how the local children, the animals, they would all hang around Juanita's place. She taught me about humility and showed me *unconditional love.*

WH: Wow, that does sound incredible.

YF: Another visionary I met in the Arizona desert had a profound influence on me, a man named Paquala. He was native Yavapai, meaning "People of the Sun." Ironic since I was out of water and dying in the blistering heat, very unprepared for summer hiking in far south Arizona. He miraculously appeared with water, wisdom, and other Yavapai remedies. I was miles from anywhere when he found me, feel certain I wouldn't have made it out of there without his help. After sharing with me his water, his provisions, we hiked together for many days in the desert, and his spiritual knowledge and wisdom filled my soul. He told me in the Native American languages still spoken today, they have no word for "religion." They don't consider their beliefs as a religion. There's no list of written rules or fixed dogma. There's only the understanding that a person is to seek their *own personal path* and to live in harmony with nature, the world, and other people.

WH: Hmmm – beautiful. I like that. I feel I'm getting that same kind of spiritual boost from you, but are there any modern influencers like authors I can read? Any books you recommend?

YF: There are, Walden, and I will, but let's not clutter your mind at this stage of the journey. Just know, most authors on the slips of paper I give you are a good place to start. And here's another example of new wisdom, more tangible than two shaman-like angels I met in the desert. Look at AA and the wisdom of the 12-Steps. Just read the steps, you don't have to read the whole book, and you'll know there's no way Bill W and Dr. Bob, two of the biggest drunks who ever lived, could ever put that shit together without the influence and inspiration of a *Higher Power*. No doubt they were *divinely* inspired!

WH: I've read the steps before, Yugo, trying to get a friend sober. Seemed very wise to me how it was all put together. Ok, so what's the practice for this element?

YF: There is no formal practice, Walden. Just remember this. Humanity has been evolving spiritually on this planet, very slowly, since the beginning of our time here. Early in our development we were given wisdom, commandments, laws, books that were needed for us to get along. But those writings are thousands of years old, written at a time when human consciousness was at a far lower level than it is today. Written at a time when slavery wasn't questioned, when women were to be seen and not heard, when war and slaughter were accepted as a way of life. Humanity, more slowly I'm sure than our Creator likes, is raising our level of *be*-ing, raising our level of consciousness. And now, it is our calling to *evolve as spiritual beings* further toward compassion and love.

WH: But I don't even know what that means, Yugo. Evolve as spiritual beings. How?

YF: *(Big smile.)* By doing the practices we are learning. By working out our spirits every day. By avoiding negative thinking, by sending positive thoughts into the know-osphere, by being honest in our relationships, living in harmony with nature and having compassion for our fellow man because we are all one. By *waking up*, Walden, and staying conscious of our *internal* being. Consciousness, moving away from mechanical thinking to higher awareness, is *Light*.

WH: Ok. I think I see what you're saying…I think I'm getting it.

YF: Hopefully humanity is nearing a time when our "collective consciousness" recognizes that war is no longer an option. That sending our young people off to war to kill other young people, simply because the "powers that be" demand it, is no longer accepted. Hopefully we're nearing a time when the amazing abundance in the world is shared with the poorest among us. When we feed the hungry and comfort the sick. When we realize the suffering of any human being means we *all suffer*. I believe the time is coming when humanity *rises up* against the negativity surrounding us all! But to evolve our planet toward love, we must *do it together*, not alone. We cannot do something of this magnitude, raising the consciousness of humanity, alone. This evolution must be done together, and by practicing these elements, you're doing your part to be the difference maker you were put on this planet to be.

WH: Beautifully said, Yugo. Maybe your teachings and inspiration will help me be a part of this evolution – help me make a difference.

YF: (*Eyes sparkling.*) Everything is evolving, even today, including human spirituality and morality. We have so much more time on our hands today to contemplate, to grow our consciousness, to evolve internally, spiritually. The time is now for people to join together, to pray for the continued evolution of humanity toward consciously chosen love!

This is the 9th element of Yugo's Way:

We are living in a new era of the spiritual evolution of humanity. Actively participate in the evolution of our planet toward consciously chosen love.

YUGO VIII.5

AFTER A QUICK BREAK stretching our legs and grabbing something to drink, we sit back down and jump right into the second element of the day. While a little relieved there's no practice tied to today's first element, I know Yugo, and understand clearly he wouldn't have this element in if it wasn't very important. I'm thinking I'll need to ask more about what he means by *not doing this alone* when he jumps into the next topic:

YF: Ok, Walden, when we first started, I asked you to work out your spiritual body at least thirty minutes a day, right?

WH: Right, and I've gotten used to that. It's now a part of my day as much as my exercise routine.

YF: (*Rubbing his hands together.*) Beautiful! If you'll remember, I gave you that practice with very little direction. Just general suggestions on how you might spend those thirty minutes. Now that you're used to the time commitment, let's define one piece of the practice that should *always* be part of your daily spiritual workout. Let's talk about meditation.

WH: Great! I love the time we sit after our sessions. At first I didn't, but I do now. Not sure what I'm doing, but it relaxes me, calms me down.

YF: That's good! So first let's talk about spiritual practices. Now I'm not saying it's like this for everyone, but in general, over many years, humanity has moved away from the simplicity and transforming power of silence and contemplation, and turned toward organized religion. To churches and rituals more focused on moralism, relieving our fear of dying, and religious dogma than on our inner peace and personal growth. This can create a spiritual life that's stagnant, soulless, *non-experiential.* Of course there's many exceptions, but overall we've moved away from taking responsibility for our own spiritual path and either moved it to the church or checked out altogether. As we already talked, there's many who pay no attention to their spiritual life. So Walden, it's time we all take charge of our own spiritual evolution, not pawn it off on organized religion or simply ignore it. And the best way to do this is to tap back into the transforming power of *silence.*

WH: So silence as in meditation, right?

YF: Right. So let's talk a little bit about prayer. Many people believe praying means asking God, or your Higher Power, for what you want, what you need for happiness, for help with the problems of life. That's ok, but we need to stop always asking and start *listening* to what the Grand

Creator wants to say to us. Prayer shouldn't always be a one-way mono-logue to God. It's most important to listen in silence to what our Higher Power is saying to us. Then it becomes a dialogue!

WH: I hear you. The rare times I do pray, I'm usually pleading with God to get me out of some mess I've created. Praying for direction or some kinda miracle to help me get my shit together.

YF: *(Smiling and nodding.)* As we all do, Walden. And then there's praying for spiritual bliss. People have been praying for enlightenment, searching for enlightenment, since the beginning of spiritual seeking. But are we praying with the right questions? The question shouldn't be, "How do I attain enlightenment?" or, "What do I need to do to awaken?" The question we should be asking is, "What am I doing now that makes me *unenlightened*?" Instead of wondering what we're missing inside, what we need to gain to finally become enlightened, we need to realize we are *already there*. We are already naturally *awake*!

But "life" obscures our natural state of awareness, our consciousness. Why does this happen to virtually everybody? Because our enlightened spirit, our Essence, has been covered up since early childhood by the constantly growing crust of life. By expectations and worries and fears and insecurities and customs and bad knowledge from parents and teachers and friends and TV and movies. In Zen they say enlightenment, or awak-ening, does not come from moving forward. It comes from falling back. From returning back to our true *Essence*, our true nature. And that's what meditation, sitting in silence, helps us do. It peels away the layers of crust that's grown over our core Essence. It brings out in the open those crip-pling lies we tell ourselves, lies that keep us from waking up. It helps us expose and surrender our false, mechanical selves and return to our core Essence.

WH: Well that sounds good and all, Yugo, but sometimes when you start talking like that my eyes glaze over and I don't follow what I need to do to make things better. What can I do to stop making myself "unenlight-ened"? Just meditation?

YF: Well, you probably won't like the answer, but on top of meditation, which increases your *self-awareness*, we should all stop doing the things we've become conditioned to do when life gets hard.

WH: Like what? Stop doing what?

YF: Like grabbing a drink whenever you're feeling a little uncomfort-able. Like zoning out your emotions by watching sports on TV or playing video games. Like picking up a double Whataburger with cheese and a large fry after an argument with Jessica. That's a start. Try to become aware when you feel uncomfortable and instinctively want to go straight to something to numb your feelings. Then, stop it. Don't do it. Just sit there with your emotions. Feel them. Welcome them. *Accept* them.

WH: You're right, I am starting to be sorry I asked...

YF: No but it's good you did! Sometimes I may say words that sound ok, but if you don't really know what I mean it doesn't do shit. What I'm saying is instead of coping with life the way the world teaches us all to cope, surrender to your feelings, accept them and *feel* them. You'll find that when you do, that false energy, the emotions and the lies we tell ourselves that get us all worked up, often fall away. But remember, I said accept and *surrender*. Don't sit there in silence while your mind is replaying whatever upsets you, or making up bullshit that might happen in the future to worry about. That mind play is what we want to stop. And the best way to stop it is through *self-awareness*. Listening through meditation.

WH: Ok, so when we sit together after our sessions, you tell me to quiet my mind and "just be." But first, I don't really know what that means, and second my mind never stops thinking. It's hardly ever quiet. Are you gonna teach me how to meditate? Is there a book I can read?

YF: There are thousands of books on mediation, some really good, but from my experience, most say in 250 pages what can be said in less than twenty. Meditation is a simple practice that I believe can be learned with a few simple principles. The Great Silence calms the soul and nourishes the spirit. Just sitting alone in the silence, being *present*, that is enough. Just slow down, sit in silence, and "be." Let the Universe talk to you. Listen, and this new relationship with *be-ing* will evolve over time.

WH: Ahh, come on, Yugo. That's the same thing you told me the first time we sat down together. Surely there's more to it than that.

YF: (*Smiling and now walking around the room.*) I hear you, Walden. Ok, here's some pointers. Before meditating, I always take a minute to set my *intention*, to become conscious internally of my purpose. This may change as your practice evolves, but to start, I recommend this intention: *May I quiet my mind, open my heart, and become one with the Grand Energy of the Universe.* As you meditate more, as your practice becomes your own, make your intention whatever you need, but to begin with this is a good one. Then, the idea is to do nothing at all. To simply sit in the presence of your Higher Power and to feel the energy, the spark, the awareness and Essence inside your body. To be *present*.

WH: That's it?

YF: Well, saying you're to do nothing isn't completely accurate. When I say "do nothing" that's implying not to think at all. But everyone finds out pretty fast that's impossible. The mind is relentless and will bring thoughts into your consciousness, whether you want them or not. The key idea or technique here is to not obsess too much about stopping the mind, but to simply *ignore* it. To not become *attached* to your thoughts. Easier said than done, I know. You'll often have thoughts coming through and you'll follow them. You know, like your mom called asking you to drive all the way out to Wimberley again, and how much time it's gonna take, and how can you juggle your schedule, and why isn't she more grateful for what you do for her, and how will you take care of her when your dad's gone. Next thing you know, you're five minutes in the meditation and you've been riding this thought train the whole time. Do your best to be *aware* when thoughts pop into your head, and then *separate* from them. Don't become identified or attached to them, but acknowledge them and let them go. Let them be, accept they are there, but don't listen to them, don't follow them. It's almost like dividing yourself in two, observing with your spirit when your mind jumps on that thought train. The sooner you can ignore a thought, the better chance you have of not taking it for a ride.

WH: Ok, that helps.... And how did you know Mary's whirling around in my head?

YF: (*Grinning and sitting back down in his chair.*) Just a wild guess after today's counseling session. Ok, some more pointers. It's important to be relaxed when meditating, to be in a comfortable chair or a relaxed position. And a good way to get in a relaxed state is by being aware of the small muscles in your face. If *they* are not relaxed, then be assured *you* are not relaxed. Become aware if your eyes are tight, if your jaw or your mouth is tight, if your lips are pursed or tight, if your forehead is creased or tightened. If they are, breathe in and out very slowly and concentrate on relaxing all of the muscles in your face. Then, simply concentrating on your breath is an easy way to relax and quiet the mind.

WH: Hmmm, ok, that sounds easy enough.

YF: Another suggestion to calm yourself is a short mantra that goes with your breath. Inhale slowly and think "breathing in calms my body," then slowly exhale and think "breathing out quiets my mind." Inhale and "breathing in calms my body," exhale and "breathing out quiets my mind." This brings a calmness and presence to the breath early and can be repeated several times at the beginning of your sit. And if later you catch your mind taking off in the silence, return to the mantra to quiet yourself again – to reset.

WH: Ok...

YF: Some suggest you choose a "sacred word" to use when you notice your mind is jumping on a thought train. Pick a word, it can be anything, and when you notice you're attached to a thought, repeat that word to yourself to break the thought train and return to silence. The word I use is *Listen*, which reminds me to be quiet. Some like to use a religious or spiritual word, but one thing to avoid is choosing a word that has an emotional pull to it. Repeating a word that brings up emotions can actually increase your thinking. Using a sacred word to reset is how I stay focused. I know it works.

WH: I'll have to think about that one. For some reason the word *Silence* comes to mind.

YF: Yeah, that's a good one! Another technique if you're really having trouble quieting the mind is to become conscious of your breath, then visualize you are breathing in and out through your chest. Inhale and exhale and envision it's your chest actually doing the breathing, not your face. This gets you out of your head in the beginning. It takes your focus away from that big brain that's always churning. You don't want to think about breathing through your chest the whole time obviously, because then you're thinking. But it's a nice way to calm the body and mind to begin. And, when you're sitting in silence with the Great Spirit, notice when your awareness is primarily in your head, especially in your forehead. That's usually a sign you haven't stepped away from your chattering mind yet, that you haven't truly *dropped in*.

WH: Hmmm – seems a little out there but I'll give it a try if my head won't settle down.

YF: And one last curve to throw at you that's not all that simple. Every so often, like once out of every ten meditations, I want you to contemplate the question, "What am I?" or "Who am I?" Really focus on your physical body, your *Instinctual Body*, and try to feel the energy, the life that is *flowing in you*. What is it inside you that's beating your heart, pumping blood through your body, keeping you alive? What is it that inhales oxygen from the air, moves it into your blood, then exhales out carbon dioxide, the simple breathing that *keeps you alive*? What does that? Is it *you*? How does a cut on your arm heal itself over a few days? How do you digest food and turn it into energy? How do you do that? Do most humans have a clue how any of this just happens *automatically*? We all think we're so smart, that we know everything, that we are our minds, our thoughts, our big brains. But in reality, we have no clue how we even keep ourselves *alive*. This aliveness comes from our core *Essence*, Walden. It's who we are, and it is *not* overlayered or crusted over with life's events. It's pure, it's from our Divine Creator. *It is life* and it is universal, in all of us! It's the Divine operating system we're all given that makes us one, interconnected. And it's something most everyone is not conscious enough of, aware of.

WH: Now you're kinda blowing my mind...

YF: *(Big smile, nodding his head.)* Our mind, our *Intellectual Body*, is cluttered with all kinds of nonsense. Stories, lies, wrong ideas, trivial knowledge. Yet most of us believe, *This is Me*. And our emotions, the *Emotional Body*, are filled with all kinds of emotions that hit us when events happen, overriding our Intellectual Body. Emotions take over our minds and they overwhelm us. Sometimes these emotions are so powerful they affect our *Physical Body*, can make us sick. We must remember, our minds and our emotions *are not me*. So, What am I? Who am I? Well that's something for you to contemplate in silence. And when you do, be present and aware of your core *Instinctual Body*, the spark in your being that literally *keeps you alive*. That's a miracle we take for granted every minute of every day.

WH: Instinctual Body. Intellectual, emotional, and physical bodies. That's a lot to think about – trying to figure out what I am, Yugo.

YF: Yes it is. We are complex beings. Yet still, underneath all that, what is the true Essence within that experiences life, that *lives*? Ultimately are we simply consciousness? *Pure awareness*? About every tenth sit I want you to ask yourself, "What am I?" or "Who am I?" Sit in silence, listen, and see what comes back.

The Practice

YF: The practice for this element is simple, Walden. Spend twenty minutes of your spiritual workout each day in meditation, in silent prayer. You said earlier you already increased your spiritual workout to more than thirty minutes a day. Twenty minutes of that time in meditation shouldn't be a problem, right?

WH: I don't see a problem with that. Sounds cool to me. I may have to cut back some on my walks in nature, but I can figure that out. I do love my time outside.

YF: (*Smiling.*) While I recommend a true sit-down meditation as the general practice, there is such a thing as *walking meditation*. Just do what we talked about while walking in nature. Set your intention, clear your mind, and embrace the silence while walking. That's fine too.

WH: Awesome! Good to know.

YF: But like all of this work, you must do it to bring results. Make the time for this soul exercise like you make time to exercise your physical body. Start with twenty minutes a day, then let it grow naturally. For me, I try and have two sits a day to center myself and feel the Divine Presence in my being. One in the morning to welcome the day, and one in the evening, to give thanks. But it's important not to make this too demanding a journey to avoid burnout. Once a day for twenty minutes is good, then see where it takes you.

WH: I burnout easily so I'm taking this slow. Maybe someday I'll get to two...

YF: Very wise, my friend. Slow is good. Oh and Walden, remember. Always look at your meditation time in an *uncritical*, non-judgmental way. Don't try and grade yourself or judge how well you did quieting the mind. Every meditation has its place and purpose. They are *all good*, no matter if you're sitting in perfect silence, at one with the Great Spirit, or if your mind is uncontrollable, rambling away. You are not trying to "gain" anything when meditating. Not holiness, not enlightenment. You are trying to *subtract*, to reduce the ego and your false self. Ok? You think you got enough to get going?

WH: Got it. Yeah, I have enough to get started, but you said there's good books out there on meditation. Any you recommend?

YF: (*Yugo reaches down, grabs a slip of paper from his box, and walks me over to the pillows for our sit, his hand on my shoulder.*) I thought you might ask that. Here, take this. Should give you all you need and none of these are too long.

This is what the paper said:

"There is no need to run, strive, search or struggle. Just be. Just being in the moment in this place is the deepest practice of meditation. Most people cannot believe that just walking as if you have nowhere to go is enough."

Thich Nhat Hanh

Books on Meditation
True Meditation – Adyashanti
Open Mind, Open Heart – Thomas Keating (Christian approach)
The Miracle of Mindfulness – Thich Nhat Hanh (Buddhist approach)

Intention: May I quiet my mind, open my heart, and become one with the Grand Energy of the Universe.

Mantra: Breathing in calms my body, breathing out quiets my mind.

This is the 10th element of Yugo's Way:

Take time each day to meditate. Immerse yourself in the Great Silence, listen, and be.

WALDEN X

Why didn't I see
The forest on fire behind the trees?

"The Forest" by José González (from *Vestiges & Claws*)

THE RESPONSE we got at Walden's Pets from Frazier's social media posts on meditation was incredible. She did such a good job taking Yugo's wisdom and condensing it down, making it brief so people would read it. We heard from people all over who began meditating and saw results in their attitudes, in how it lowered stress and gave them more peace of mind. Some said when they started, they couldn't sit five minutes alone in silence without *going crazy*. But this practice showed them they were too distracted, too caught up in the trivial bullshit we all think is so important. Frazier had people send in video testimonials on TikTok – it seems thousands started meditating, finding time to sit in silence and just be. Frazier showed Yugo some of the videos and said his face just lit up.

Then she came to me and said we should talk to him about becoming his "marketing agency." I told her with all she was doing, we already kinda were except instead of making Yugo money we were spreading his message – that's all he wanted. Plus we were getting the added benefit of engaging people in our brand, which I know brought more loyal, like-minded shoppers to WP. Other than the materialism element about not shopping at Sahara, this one on meditation got us the most engagement and positive feedback. Who knew *Silence* could be so compelling?

This feels like a good place to let you know how practicing Yugo's Way was going for me so far – if it was actually making a difference I could notice. As Yugo says, the best way to understand the quality of your spiritual health is to honestly look at your own personal experience – bottom line, is it working for you or not? You know I was a mess when I went in to see Yugo, so the room for improvement in my emotional and spiritual health was off the charts. There's no doubt the counseling sessions, the "psychiatric part" we did before going over the elements, helped me significantly – especially at first. Having a calm, wise influence like Yugo to pour my heart out to was *so needed*.

I'm not good at expressing my feelings, and I've never had anyone I felt comfortable to talk to about *everything*. There's Cody to a certain degree, but there are things I tell Yugo that I'd never tell Cody. And also one thing that attracted me to Yugo – he told me upfront we wouldn't have to do this for years and years, going over the same old shit. The purpose of Yugo's Way was to give me tools, a new way of thinking and being, so I could get through life *without* having to go to someone like Yugo every couple of weeks just to keep my act together.

But Yugo tells me this is a long journey, so we need to keep doing the work – to read over all the elements from time to time to keep them alive, keep them fresh, and do an assessment on progress or sticking points. Around now the practices were coming more naturally to me. Instead of feeling like homework I had to do, they were becoming more a part of my normal thinking and behavior. I began to notice I was living more at peace, more accepting of the curves life threw at me – "wearing life like a loose garment" like one of Yugo's AA sayings. Some of the elements I'm doing ok in my opinion – working out my spiritual body, taking better care of Mother Earth, reducing consumption, not obsessing on the news. Other elements I have room for improvement, like catching negative thoughts quickly and sending them away – I still suck at that one. Or being open and honest in *all* my relationships all the time. The good news, I'm conscious I still need to work and I'm not lying to myself that I have everything figured out.

I think Yugo's guidance is helping me treat other people better – and I'm not just saying that. I've heard it from Jessica, Frazier, people in the office. Even Cody sees a difference, but he says not as big as the change he saw in Dylan. It wasn't that long ago that if I ever had some free time without work or family commitments, I was damn sure going to be drinking. It's not always like that now, although sometimes it is. But sometimes now, I'll go to the lake to sit and meditate, or I'll go walk in the woods and just listen. Sometimes I don't even mind driving all the way out to Father and Mary's to help them with whatever. That used to bring feelings of self-pity before – worried I was wasting my valuable time.

Now, I don't want to mislead you. I'm still a self-centered prick. I just catch myself being that way sooner, or sometimes stop myself once self-observation shows me I'm going down a negative path. But *please believe me* when I tell you this. There's no way I'd be spending all this time writing a book if I didn't know Yugo's Way could change people – and maybe help change our world.

Which brings me to this part that I'm doing because, as Yugo says, it gets me out of my comfort zone (and I realize I've been stalling to get to it). My goal is that this story helps others who are struggling with similar life experiences, most I assume more traumatic than mine. My whole life, the one thing I *never* expected to talk to anybody about, was Felicia. But Yugo drew it out of me slowly, as he worked with me on my insecurities, my guilts and fears. This *drawing out* brought healing. Talking about it to another person made it seem smaller, lessened its hold on me. It helped me process what happened and yes, let most of it go. So here goes:

Earlier I briefly mentioned Felicia Featherstone and her family at Nueva Tierra – they were "on the other side of the fence" as Father would say. She was much older than me, seven years, and sort of a friend of Frazier's. They weren't real close but did hang out together sometimes, even though Felicia was several years older than Sis too. It was summer break from school, I was eleven but turning twelve that summer. One of Felicia's brothers came up to me one afternoon and said Felicia told him to tell me she had something cool to show me at Miller Falls – that she knew I'd really like it.

Well, I'd never spent any time with Felicia, didn't really know her at all, so this surprised me and got me curious. She was one of the best-looking girls at Nueva and she knew it – she didn't mind teasing guys with her looks either. I had zero experience with girls, but was getting to that age when moms who were breastfeeding or women going topless around the compound during festivals started catching my attention. Just the thought of me going out to Miller Falls, which was a couple miles hike at least, and being alone with a girl as pretty and older as Felicia scared the shit out of me – made me nervous as hell just thinking about it. So, being a kid I just said ok to her brother and then didn't go.

A few days later her brother found me shooting baskets and asked why I didn't go out there. He said I'd hurt Felicia's feelings, and she was upset she'd gone all the way out there to meet me – that it was rude I didn't have the decency to even show up. He said she told him to say she'd forgive me if I'd go see what was out there today. That she knew it was something I'd think was really cool, and it was the least I could do after I treated her so wrong. So, scared about what I was ever going to say to an older girl, shaking a little really and feeling guilty for not going out there last time, I hiked out to Miller Falls, which as I said, was way out in the woods away from everything.

Miller's was a place the older kids would go sometimes to swim and party – everyone from Nueva had been out there at some point. It was a beautiful falls coming down through the forest about twenty feet high that poured into a small pool that was good for swimming. The water was cold as hell though, so you couldn't stay in long, and because it was so far out people didn't go out there all that much. Even though the beauty was amazing, there were plenty of other places closer to home just as nice – point being it was very secluded.

As I got close to Miller Falls I heard someone humming, so I stopped in the forest behind a tree before getting to the pool, to look and see who's there. I see Felicia standing there by the pool in a skimpy yellow bikini, all by herself, and it looks like she just got out of the water. She's very dark, I think her dad was part Native American, and has straight black hair tied in long braids, and like I said, she was cute and a flirt so seeing her in that bikini sorta stopped me in my tracks. I got a little bit closer, but being super nervous about what this was all about I ducked behind a big tree to calm my nerves and see if I could tell what she was doing. Felicia kind of glanced over my way for a second and my heart stopped. I feared she'd seen me sort of spying on her, but she quickly looked away, sat down on a towel she had spread out, and grabbed some tanning oil to put on after her swim (in hindsight, she'd obviously seen/heard me and knew I was there).

Felicia starts slowly rubbing that oil all over her body and my privates start getting all excited, just like I'd noticed they were sometimes doing looking at some of the women at Nueva. I really couldn't believe what I was seeing when Felicia then took off her top and started slowly rubbing oil all over her body, almost like it was a show, her tan lines making things look even more incredible. Well this was too much for almost twelve-year-old little me to see, so I started moving to turn around and run home when Felicia all the sudden calls out and says, "Walden? Hey, Walden? Is that you?"

I stopped in my tracks knowing I was busted, and then she says, "I thought I heard somebody over there. You spying on me?" The tanning oil all over her body was glistening in the sun. I was mesmerized – hardly believing what I was seeing. "You come on over here, Walden. I want to show you something."

So, scared out of my wits and again literally shaking, I came out from behind the trees and walked over to the pool. When I get close, Felicia looks at me with a smirk and says, "I think you were spying on me sunbathing, Walden Harrison. You think I oughta tell your Father about that?" She then looks down at her breasts, which are amazing, smiles up at me, and starts slowly massaging them.

Stunned and scared I say, "I wasn't spying on you. I heard somebody humming and stopped to see if it was you. You're the one who wanted me to come out here."

Looking me in the eyes and still rubbing herself, then looking down at my shorts, Felicia says, "Yeah right. If that's true how come your thing down there is so excited?"

Embarrassed, I looked down and saw with horror that I'm standing at full attention, and you can see it clearly through my basketball shorts. Stammering now and unable to reply, Felicia then says, "Hey, let me see that thing." And she quickly pulls down my shorts and now I'm standing straight at attention, waving in the summer breeze, harder than a rock. Next thing you know Felicia puts me in her mouth and I'm shocked and have no idea what's going on. Adrenalin is flying through my body, I'm lightheaded as can be, and I just stand there speechless as she molests me.

Suddenly she stops and she pulls down her bikini bottoms, turns around on her towel, gets on her knees, and spreads her rear right at me. Then she says, "Ok, Walden, I want you to put that thing right here."

Shocked and in disbelief I say, "What? What are you saying?"

And she says, "I want you to put your thing right here." And she points to her bottom and starts slowly rubbing it with oil. "This is the best place cuz you can't get me into any trouble putting it here."

As I stand there stammering, she reaches back behind my legs and pulls me towards her, then grabs me and puts me inside her, rocking back and forth, back and forth. "That's it, Walden. I seen how strong your

Father is. I knew you'd be good at this. Go faster, go harder, come on, don't just stand there."

So I start going faster and harder, not knowing exactly what or why I'm doing it, but feeling like I've never felt before. And Felicia starts moaning and rubbing herself frantically between her legs, faster and faster, and I just keep going along with it, obviously aroused but not sure what I'm doing or why. After what seems like several minutes of this I start feeling really tingly down there, like I've never felt before, and things seem to be swelling up, getting bigger and bigger like I really have to pee, only way better than that.

Honestly, I'm starting to feel just about as good as I've ever felt when she tosses her pigtails back at me and says, "Pull on these, Walden Harrison. Ride me like a pony, Walden, ride me like a pony." And so I do, and keep getting more tingly, and feeling better and better, and her hands moving crazily now between her legs when all the sudden it feels like I literally explode down there about the same time she seems to be doing the same thing. Something starts coming out of me like I've never seen before and it feels unbelievably good, indescribably good, and then finally it's over.

Looking down I'm both shocked and curious at what I see, trying to understand exactly what's happened here, and then Felicia says to me, "Oh my God, Walden, look at what you did! I can't believe you just did that to me!"

"Did what?" I say, immediately feeling guilty and defensive, and she says, "You know what you did. You just raped me, and you even made a big mess that's gonna get you in a lot of trouble. I'm gonna to tell your Father and Mary what you done to me."

And now I'm shaking again and still unsure what just happened – I don't even know what rape means for sure and I want to cry. And then I say, "I didn't mean to do anything to you. You're the one that had me come out here and started all this."

And she says, "You're the one that got all excited and put that thing of yours inside me. I swear, Walden Harrison, if you don't be quiet about this and do everything I tell you to from now on, I'm telling your parents what you did to me and you're gonna be in so much trouble." So that's the story of my predator at Nueva Tierra – and I lived in fear, guilt, shame, and confusion for years.

Not even twelve, Father hadn't talked to me about the birds and the bees yet, and I was too young then for any of my friends to talk about sex other than sneaking looks at boobies. I'd been assaulted by Felicia, and she'd convinced me I was in the wrong and would be in big trouble if anyone ever found out. Who knows why I finished at such a young age, but I think it was Felicia and her looks, her age, and her crazy actions that finally made it happen.

So, it wasn't Jacob's mom or the First Baptist Church of Forks that got me all bottled up inside and changed me that year (although I admit, going there right after this happened, hearing about sinful ways leading to *hell*, didn't help). It was Felicia and her unwanted and unexpected advances, and then her mind games that closed me up (which is what made me want to go to Jacob's VBS in the first place – to get away from Felicia at Nueva).

And while I'd like to say here that this was the only time it happened, she tricked me, cornered me, and seduced me and made this same thing happen two more times, until I finally made a pact with myself to never let it happen again – to avoid her at all costs. I could no longer bear the fear of getting caught, and the guilt and the shame of it. But at the same time I never could understand why, even though it made me feel so bad after, that I could not stop this insane urge that popped into my head every so often to do it again.

I never told *anyone* about this until Yugo. I'd hear other guys around Nueva talk big about Felicia, hear them brag about how they'd had their way with her, and I'm sure some of them did. But never did I hear anybody close to my age say anything like that, and so I never said a word – to *anybody*. In many ways it was so very confusing. Growing up, I'd hear guys say if you ever got seduced by an older woman like a teacher or a friend's hot mom or something, you were the luckiest kid in the world. But it didn't really feel that way to me. There was way too much fear and bad feelings afterwards for me to feel like I was lucky. It seems people, especially men, have a different reaction when it's a boy who's taken advantage of by an older woman. How would you feel about this story if the eleven-year-old child here were a little girl and the abuser a nineteen-year-old guy?

In some ways I can see why there's a different reaction. I mean, it's not like Felicia had to hold me down and force me to be with her. It's not like my life was shattered and it was the most disgusting and horrible thing that's ever happened to me. I mean heck, I let her coerce me into doing it again twice – that's one reason for all the shame and the guilt. I sometimes considered myself fortunate it was Felicia that did this to me and not some creepy priest or pedophile teacher. But the reality of all this is I was constantly scared that Felicia was going to tell, or Mary and Father were somehow going to find out, or even that Felicia might someday tell Frazier, and how embarrassing that would be.

All I know is, to a boy as young as I was who had no idea what was really happening, who had never even ejaculated before, the trauma and negative emotions created from these events were real and lasting. I suppose all this messed up my thinking a little about sex for a time, and Felicia *never* let me forget. Talking to my parents was not an option – everything that happened was all my fault. That's the biggest reason all those years ago, as we were driving our van out of Nueva Tierra heading to Texas, I was so relieved and yes, *happy*. No longer would I have to constantly keep running from my predator. Maybe now, I could stop worrying that what happened between me and Felicia would one day all be found out.

Finally, after so many years, Yugo helped me realize I was only a child who was sexually exploited by a much older person who manipulated me. That I did nothing wrong. He said this scar needed to be brought out into the light, treated with love and openness and allowed to heal. Researchers say over 50% of sexual abuse victims never even report it, so Yugo said real statistics are impossible to know for sure. But current research estimates 20% of girls and just over 5% of boys have been sexually abused *as children*. That's just so hard for me to get my head around. *One out of every five girls* has been sexually abused *as a child*, and that number is almost certainly higher.

He also said statistics show over *40% of all women* say they've been a victim of some form of sexual assault – so almost half. Just unbelievable numbers that show the soul sickness that's festering in our society. Just as alarming, statistics clearly show people who have been sexually abused, especially boys, are far more likely themselves to become abusers. And now, with the stories coming out about the sexual abuse of children at the hands of religious institutions, most recently the shocking stories about the abuse by Catholic priests in Baltimore? They say it's been going on *for at least eighty years*. The sad truth is there are so many stories like this out there now, almost like mass shootings, that we've all become numb. So now is not the time for me to worry about what might be uncomfortable.

Yugo says the most helpful thing a person can do to start healing from trauma like this is to *talk to somebody* about it. To let it out with someone you trust and realize completely that it's not your fault. That you did nothing wrong. I know the tough part is knowing for sure who you can trust. Yugo says, start with a trusted family member if you can, be it your parents or if not them a sibling or relative you feel very comfortable with. If that's not an option, like with me, try confiding in a counselor at school or maybe someone from your church if you have one. And if that comes up empty, and you don't have the money for a therapist, try at least talking to a trusted friend.

The key is to get this out in the open no matter when it happened – bring the unspeakable memories that cannot be said into the light. And for anyone looking for support options, there's Sexual Assault Survivors Anonymous (SASA) or Survivors of Incest Anonymous (SIA). You can find them and other help groups online to see what's available for you. I have no experience with these groups, but they are 12-Step based and it's a way to talk with other people who've had similar experiences. Yugo told me they're out there, that they can be a good way to start the healing.

I'm sorry if I offended anyone with this story. I never planned on sharing this with anybody, especially in something like a book, but I started writing and it wouldn't stop coming out. If this helps just one person suffering alone with the trauma and memories of sexual abuse to seek help, to reach out to others for healing, it's worth it to me. As Yugo says, the events that happened to me made me who I am today. Accept them, learn from them, and help others because of them if you can. Statistics say this affects so many people, so I figure writing about this is the right thing to do. And if the editors don't like it, then they can take it out. After all, *Comfort is Overrated*.

FRAZIER VII

Wow. I said I was curious about Walden's comment about Felicia. But I wasn't expecting that. Reading the last chapter sent shock waves through my whole body. Made the hair on the back of my neck stand up. Hearing what Walden went through, all alone, makes my heart hurt. And it makes me angry with myself. I knew something was different about him that year. Walden was never outgoing. But that summer he really went into a shell. He changed. Not knowing any better, I just assumed it was Jacob's mom and their church.

So here's why I'm so shaken up. First of course is Walden's story. Honestly, I can't believe he told it. But what also made my hair stand up? What happened to Walden is almost identical to what happened to me! Reading it was like going back in time. When I was fourteen, Felicia invited me to meet her out at Miller's Falls. When I got there, she was doing many of the same things. Then, she seduced me. She was the first person I'd ever been totally intimate with. I'd kissed a few boys. Let them do some harmless petting. That was all. But Felicia took full advantage of me.

I wasn't sure what to think when it was over. How I should feel. She told me she was doing me a favor. "Showing me the ropes." Teaching me how to be a real woman. She said I should thank her for sharing her knowledge. For giving me worldly experience I would need later in life. Now, I see clearly, she abused me too. Like Walden, Felicia and I were together again more than once. And, when I was with my first boy? She was there too. Felicia sort of arranged it. And now, thinking back on some of the romantic relationships in my life? How they turned out? What she did probably affected them in some way.

I made fun earlier of Walden's "relationship roundup." His implying I was promiscuous. But I was actually very relieved he was so brief about me. Since Walden just opened his soul up to you, it's time I open up too. History shows that I *am* promiscuous. Any reasonable person would agree. I was married once in my mid-twenties to a wonderful man. A man who loved me, and who I loved too. But that marriage collapsed fast. Not as fast as Walden's, but in about a year and a half. I was caught having an affair with a girlfriend. It was too much for him to forgive, and I understand.

I started to say I was married twice, but that's not true. I was almost married a second time in my very early thirties. To a lawyer who swept me off my feet. We dated two years and decided to commit to each other. But again, I was caught cheating. This time literally days before our wedding. Again, I was with another girlfriend. He was devastated. My family was embarrassed and hurt. I felt shame, guilt, and confusion.

I always thought my open attitude towards sex was who I was. It's how I was made. But now, I wonder? How much did my experiences with Felicia at such a young age influence who I am? I never thought of myself as a *victim* of Felicia's. That was one of her talents. Having her way with you. Then making you think it was your idea; that it felt good. We were just two girls having fun, right?

Walden's story, and my vivid, suddenly awakened memories consumed me for days. Was Felicia a sexual predator, wanting to hurt people and feel power? Or was she just a sex addict? A nympho looking for her next adventure? Was she abused by her dad or someone else at Nueva? Was she just acting out what she was forced to do herself? Who knows?

Thinking back, I'm reminded of talks with Felicia. She bragged about "doing it" with some of the other kids of founding Fathers and Mothers. She made a point to brag to me which ones she'd "gone all the way with." Now that I know Walden's story, was she trying to corrupt the founders' kids? Was she trying to stain, to put her mark, on the kids of the respected, almost worshipped founders of our community? Who knows?

So, to open up with you more. The world's told me most of my life I'm physically attractive. That I'm "pretty." So, I'm always smiling, always happy, always positive. Doing my best to look good. It's important to me that it looks like I have my act together. Important for my profession too. But my life, sometimes, feels like I'm acting in a play. An actress playing her part. Playing my role. And underneath, on the inside? At times there's unsettling insecurity. Anxiety, sometimes depression. You see, I know what I'm really like on the inside. The selfishness and the petty jealousies I have. Being judgmental of others. The promiscuousness. The inability to always be truly there for someone else. To surrender all my love. And my commitment.

I've heard everyone has their own demons to conquer. No matter who it is. No matter how happy they may look. Everyone is fighting something inside. And I think that's true. I talked with Yugo about it one of those times we were alone. But never did I share with him anything that made me look really bad. My vanity and need to always look good always won out. On the surface, I might seem accomplished and outgoing. But on the inside, I can feel inferior, confused, shameful. Not to mention I know I'm self-centered. My life is too much about me. After all, that's what being an influencer is all about. Posting about me.

Writing the social media campaigns for Yugo's Way got me curious. Then watching Walden change for the better got me interested. And so, eventually, I began doing the practices too. They are helping. They are making me a better person. Once I finish upgrading me, maybe I'll get married that second time. But only when I know I can trust myself. When I stop lying so much to myself. The first thing I did after reading Walden's last chapter was go to him. To tell him right away, I'm sorry. Sorry for not being there when he needed me most. For knowing something was wrong and just assuming I knew why. For never asking why he seemed so different. And, of course, Walden said, "No big deal, Sis…"

YUGO IX

"If I should ever die, God forbid, let this be my epitaph:

The Only Proof He Needed
For The Existence of God
Was Music"

Kurt Vonnegut – *A Man Without a Country*

MY NEXT COUNSELING session was an emotional one. Bryan and the kids were really struggling with the reality of Ally's cancer. The emotional roller coaster, the doctor's visits and resulting schedule, was brutal. Ally and Bryan were searching for alternative treatments, new test trials – she was already on rounds of chemo. With the type of aggressive cancer she has, timing was critical to hit it hard and fast. I was trying my best to help with Bryan's kids while also juggling my parents' welfare needs way out in Wimberley, running Walden's Pets, and hoping to have some time left over for Jessica and our relationship – Jessica was a *huge help* with all this too. Thank God I had Yugo and the practices to help me through this time. Without them, I'm pretty sure I'd have been drinking every night to numb my brain, drown the stress, help me fall asleep.

When today's counseling part of our session was over, Yugo told me he's enjoying his time with Frazier finetuning the social media messages before they go out. He keeps saying she has a light and energy that's *pure*. In lots of ways I agree she does, in others, not so much – maybe that's because she's my sister.

I'm still trying to get my head around the fact that Frazier went through the same sort of experiences I had with Felicia. I assume like with me it messed her up a little too, and so we're now talking about it together some. One thing I know for certain with this new knowledge. I need to have more understanding and compassion about her relationship woes. Yugo said he loves talking with Frazier about our time growing up in Washington at Nueva Tierra – that he's fascinated with Father's vision of building a utopian society. When I walked into his office today, I noticed a copy of *Walden Two* lying on the floor next to Yugo's chair by his little wooden box, so I asked him about it as we started the elements:

WH: Hey, I see you got my namesake down there – *Walden Two*. You reading it?

YF: (*Smiling.*) Almost done. Frazier got me interested. It's fascinating! Your Father must be an unbelievable dude, Walden. Trying to build a society like the *Walden Two* in that book? Talk about pursuing your dreams. Was he really like that Frazier character?

WH: Hard for me to say since I was his kid, but yeah, I can see people thinking he was like that. Very focused and driven – strong willed. But remember, there was more than just Father. There were five of them who all had the vision together. What they were able to build at Nueva Tierra was amazing. It's crazy it lasted as long as it did.

YF: Well, I'd recommend this book to anyone. A great commentary on human nature and our potential, not to mention all the trappings of "society" we all just *accept*. You don't talk a lot about Washington, so I enjoy hearing Frazier's take on what your life was like – what your Father built. I've been thinking, it'd be cool to meet your dad sometime. Sounds like he's one of a kind.

WH: That's an accurate description. The self-sustaining farm he built in Wimberley's pretty amazing too. Maybe you can go out there with me sometime.

YF: Yes, maybe so! I told Frazier thanks for recommending the book to me, but next time you see her, thank her again. She's great you know. The way she's spreading the message of the elements to so many people – and in such creative ways!

WH: (*Kinda wondering if Yugo's getting the hots for my sister.*) Yeah, I know....

YF: Ok. Knowing what you really like to do, this next element's a freebie. I'll be preaching to the choir on this one.

WH: Awesome! I've already got enough practices to work on with everything else going on in my life.

YF: Yes, but because this first one is so familiar to you, we'll go over two elements today. The second one probably won't go down as smoothly as the first. We'll see.

WH: So hit me. What's this freebie element of yours?

YF: *(Big smile.)* I doubt you're expecting this one, but it's *music*.

WH: Music? How do you mean?

YF: Music is an essential influence for us on our spiritual journeys. It brings joy, happiness, nourishes our spiritual and emotional bodies. I know you love *live* music, right?

WH: Hell yeah I love live music.

YF: Think about how you feel in the presence of really great live music. The driving beat of the bass shaking your core, the beauty of acoustic guitar and piano, harmonizing vocals that make your eyes water. The ecstasy of the musicians when they know they're creating magic together.

WH: And don't forget the pedal steel. I love bands that use that now to add nuance and a vibe to the sound. Love me some pedal steel...

YF: *(Smiling and nodding his head.)* I knew you'd love this one, Walden. Music actually ties into a previous practice, the one about consciously bringing *awe* back into our lives. Really good music creates awe and wonder. And check this out. Science is now learning that music opens up the passageways between the right and the left brain to bring balance, internal harmony. Not to mention how it opens the heart.

WH: You *are* preaching to the choir, Yugo. Music's a big part of my life. It sustains me.

YF: Good! It's amazing how many people I talk to who've lost touch with music. People who say music used to be important to them, when they were kids, in their teens, going to concerts in college. But now that they're older and working, raising a family, they don't have time for music anymore. Instead they say the TV's always on, or radio stations today suck, or now they listen to talk radio, sports talk, or podcasts.

WH: You know it's funny, Yugo. Music is a big part of my life now. I listen to music all the time, check out live shows all over town, go to festivals. But there was a time after I got out of school I stopped paying attention to music too. Not sure why. I was too busy working I guess, and my friends weren't around as much to go see live shows. Maybe that's what most people do as we get older?

YF: All these reasons are understandable, they're a reality of life, which means we must *make the time*. Music feeds the soul. Music gets your heart pumping and your brainwaves flowing. Music sparks your emotions. It brings back old memories and creates new ones.

WH: I had no idea you were so into music, Yugo. You never said anything about it before.

YF: I grew up in a house that loved music, was usually full of music, and that love stayed with me. Different types of music too. When I started my spiritual journey, I realized how important music was to my emotional health, to staying balanced, to experiencing joy and awe. Life's experiences taught me that my spirit *needs* music.

WH: How cool is that! So what kind of music was it? What'd your folks listen to?

YF: (*Looking out the window in thought.*) My dad was gone a lot, traveling all the time. When he was gone, momma got to play the music she loved, music from her African roots. So that's what I grew up listening to when dad was away. She loved African Juju and Yoruba music. People like Fela Kuti, King Sunny Ade, and Sir Shina Peters were her favorites. And African desert blues like Ali Farka Touré. She liked reggae too when she was in the mood. She'd jam to some Peter Tosh, Bunny Wailer, Jimmy Cliff when she was feeling it. Bob Marley too of course. And she'd put on Marvin Gaye or Anita Baker or Bill Withers – good R&B. She wasn't big on contemporary music, pop music, but she always did love Prince...

WH: Can't say I know much about African music, but I have heard of King Sunny Ade. He was popular around here for a while – good vibe, lots of percussion. And who doesn't like reggae?

YF: Yeah, true. But when dad would come home it was all his music then. Mainly '70s and '80s rock, some '90s grunge, and "No Depression" type alternative. I liked some of that cuz it's raw and dark. So I'm a Black dude who grew up listening to rock and grunge. Crazy, huh? I liked Mom's taste in music more, but some of dad's stuff was cool. Dad would always say there were three kinds of music he *hated* that could never be played in the house. One was country and two was western. He thought that was funny.

WH: And three? What was the third?

YF: He'd say, "And don't you even think about bringing any of that rap shit around my house."

WH: (*Laughing.*) Yep, sounds about right for most dads back then.

YF: Yeah, for most *white* dads. Dad was a hard ass when it came to our language. He was always on me and my sister to "*talk white*" as he'd say. Formal, military type talk – yes sir and no sir. And if we ever used street language or slang in the house he'd shut that down hard. He thought rap and hip-hop music was the gateway drug for us to start talking shit, you know?

WH: Hmmm, interesting.

YF: Well ok, so you don't need this part of my usual talk, but I'll give you a condensed version of it anyway, so at least you get your money's worth.

WH: Yeah, from that zero dollars an hour you keep gouging me for?

YF: (*Now he's laughing.*) So when I talk to students who no longer listen to music, I ease them back in with suggestions. I try to get a general understanding of the kinds of music they like, but these songs are universal and work for most everybody. I say, next time you're feeling down, just listen to the song "Believe" by Lenny Kravitz. Or sit back and listen to the tune "Glory" by David Crosby. Or "Let It Be" by The Beatles, or "What's Going On" by Marvin Gaye. It's impossible to listen to these songs and not feel uplifted – feel peaceful and hopeful.

WH: Great songs, awesome picks for turning people back on to music! Nothing gets my juices flowing more than good emotional music from the heart. Not sure I know that Crosby tune though. I'll have to check it out.

YF: It's mystical. There's a band from my momma's South Africa that's played around Austin before, Civil Twilight, who has beautiful, emotional songs.

WH: Crazy you say that Yugo! I saw Civil Twilight play a free show in the Waterloo Records parking lot during *South by*, and it was incredible – loved them ever since. I didn't know they were from South Africa. There's a local guy out in the hills of Dripping Springs, Israel Nash. Incredibly peaceful stuff, man. He calls it *hippy spiritual*. Listen to the albums *Rain Plans* or *Lifted*. Once a year, he opens up his land and music studio out in the hills for people to come and listen to bands all day. They have a little main stage, they play in his recording studio, they even had a teepee one year with bands playing inside. It's called "From the Hills with Love" and Jessica and I go every year.

YF: Now that sounds awesome! I'll give him a listen – love the local musicians. There's a Nigerian artist I'm into that momma would have liked named Mdou Moctar. I know you like good guitarists the way you talked about Little Johnny, so think you'd dig it. Check out the album *Afrique Victime* and listen to "Chismiten." Mesmerizing guitar. And then "Ya Habibti" for a good taste of acoustic. When I hear it I picture momma swirling around the house.

WH: Cool – I'll check it out. I love all kinds of music. Cody gives me shit, but I even listen to classical stuff every now and then. Johann Sebastian Bach is the man. I especially like his piano concertos. Sounds like me and you should get together and listen to some tunes some time, Yugo. I'm always looking for new music.

YF: *(Huge smile.)* Ahhh, J. S. Bach. I enjoy Bach when in the right frame of mind. Talk about a way of transporting yourself. You know what else is great about music? It's entertainment, yes, but it also takes you *out of yourself*, transforms your being unlike some other forms of entertainment that can feed your ego. Ever noticed when watching a football game how you're convinced the shit you're doing is determining the outcome? Where you're sitting, what you're wearing, whether or not to get up and go grab a beer?

WH: Ha! That's so true. You should see all the superstitious shit my friend Cody does watching a UT game. It's crazy. And I feel it sometimes too, like the game's going good so I'm not moving.

YF: I had a girlfriend once who was convinced if she didn't drink sangria during Broncos football games they were gonna lose. Almost everyone feels this otherworldly power to alter games – it's normal. But think about those inner thoughts that on the surface seem harmless. Are they? Somehow we think we're so important that what we are doing actually determines the outcome of a big game played hundreds of miles away. Not to mention what we're seeing on TV is slightly delayed. It's *already happened* seconds before.

WH: Yeah, it is pretty ludicrous, huh? Never thought about that time delay thing...hmmm.

YF: Think how strong our egos are. How powerful our minds are to make us believe we have an effect on the outcome of a game when we're simply a lump sitting on a couch numbing our brains with sports, booze, and food. But Walden, if we're paying attention to our random inner thoughts trying to wake up, this can be a great time to grow our spirit! Stop believing this shit your mind is telling you and do the *opposite*. Go get a beer when you want one. Sit in a different chair when a critical part of the game comes up. Get up and go take a piss when you have to go. It's not gonna change the game! Let that false feeling of self-importance go. Let that part of your ego vanish into thin air.

WH: Now you're cracking me up, Yugo. And this has relevance to music how?

YF: Oh right, sorry, got off track. Well, my point is music, unlike some other forms of modern entertainment, doesn't get you pissed off or nervous or hateful toward another team, another fan base, or another person. Music nourishes the soul, *especially* live music. You know the power of music when you can't remember the name of your neighbor, but you can sing every word to a song playing on the radio you haven't heard since middle school.

Then Yugo bends down and pulls out a slip of paper from his box and says, "And don't just take my word for it. Look at what these world-renowned minds wrote about music. Read it, not out loud but to yourself."

Meaningful Quotes on Music:

"God has given us music so that above all it can lead us upwards. Music unites all qualities: it can exalt us, divert us, cheer us up, or break the hardest of hearts with the softest of its melancholy tones. But its principal task is to lead our thoughts to higher things, to elevate, even to make us tremble.... Song elevates our being and leads us to the good and the true."

Friedrich Nietzsche – *A Philosophical Biography*

"After silence that which comes nearest to expressing the inexpressible is music.... When the inexpressible had to be expressed, Shakespeare laid down his pen and called for music."

Aldous Huxley – *Music at Night and Other Essays*

"Music stands quite apart from all the other arts.... Yet it is such a great and exceedingly fine art, its effect on man's innermost nature is so powerful, and it is so completely and profoundly understood by him in his innermost being as an entirely *universal language,* whose distinctness surpasses even that of the world of perception itself.... We must attribute to music a far more serious and profound significance that refers to the innermost being of the world and of our own self."

Arthur Schopenhauer – *The World as Will and Representation*

And, I should point out, the Vonnegut quote at the beginning of this chapter was on this paper too.

The Practice

YF: So here comes your freebie, Walden. Pretty sure you're already doing all this and more.

WH: *(Now I'm smiling!)* Ok Yugo – what you got?

YF: Well, first I tell students if they're not already listening to music, not taking the time to *enjoy* music, they should start. The first step is to listen to music consciously at least three times a week if not more. Listening to a station on the car radio is ok, but isn't the best for this exercise because it's so random and there's so many distractions. If you're streaming something you choose to listen to that's different.

WH: Such a freebie.

YF: Then I tell them, if you don't have a streaming service, get one. Spotify, Apple Music, Tidal, use YouTube Music, whatever works best for them. These services don't pay artists nearly enough, and hopefully that changes soon, but for now, it's the easiest way to access almost anything you wanna hear.

WH: Check on that one. I use Apple and I listen every day, usually working out, but other times too.

YF: Good! And that's a good way to find time. If you work out during the week, listen to music while you're doing it. Obviously, swimming or doing yoga classes isn't gonna work, but it's great for running, biking, weights...

WH: Yep – I take the headphones with me doing all three.

YF: Perfect segue. It's also good to listen occasionally like it's a meditation. Just sit down with some good headphones, clear your head of chattering thoughts, and let the sounds overwhelm you. You know the power of music when you get chills hearing a song, or when a song brings back memories that are dear to you. Let it transport you from the day's worries and cares.

WH: Agree!

YF: And the second practice. Go see live music of some kind *at least* once every two months. This can create those feelings of *awe* we so badly need to rekindle. We're blessed in Austin with tons of places with live music every night. But some small towns may not have many places for live music. If that's the case we must make the extra effort to go enjoy live music, to experience music as it's created! Maybe go to a nearby town if you have nothing close. Find a country and western bar and go two-stepping. That counts. Maybe catch a local symphony if there's one in a nearby city. Look around for concerts or festivals coming to places nearby. If you haven't been to a live concert in a long time, *go*. Most people have no trouble finding live music if they want to.

WH: That's it? Man, am I getting off easy!

YF: Not quite. I also ask you to be open, curious, and receptive to all of the arts. I've seen all kinds of art have profound impacts on people – actually raise their level of consciousness. I know people who've been changed by watching a movie that spoke to them, by reading a novel, by seeing a play that somehow gave them exactly what they needed that night. By a poem. Our Higher Power uses art to reach souls *who are searching*, who are listening for revelations and inspiration. The arts are mystical cosmic forces, gifts for humanity that can make us whole.

WH: Will do. I've been changed by books, or seeing a great movie like *Arrival*...loved that movie. I agree, the arts are important.

YF: We must all support our artists! We're living in the infancy of AI and the unchartered ways technology could begin "producing art." The digitalization of everything. It's getting harder and harder for artists to survive, so we must support them financially if we can. Musicians and other artists are having a hard time everywhere simply making a living. Show up to their live performances, buy their works, recommend great art of all kinds to others so it doesn't vanish from our society. Without art humanity suffers, we regress, we are not completely *alive*. Without art, we are not whole. The spiritual evolution of humanity needs art like trees need sunlight.

This is the 11th element of Yugo's Way:

We must make time for music. Music creates joy, awe, and peace while nourishing the soul.

YUGO IX.5

So I'll meet you at the bottom, if there really is one
They always told me 'When you hit it, you'll know it'
But I've been falling so long, it's like gravity's gone
And I'm just floating

"Gravity's Gone" by Drive-By Truckers (*A Blessing and a Curse*)

BEING I was already *tuned in* to this session, pun intended, Yugo moved on to the next element right away:

YF: So Walden, this next element – I got the impression you were worried I was gonna throw this one at you early on.

WH: Oh really, why's that?

YF: Remember when we first talked and I warned you about my language? I said something about AA, and you made it clear you wanted *nothing* to do with that.

WH: Oh shit, Yugo. You're not gonna lecture me about my drinking, are you?

YF: *(Laughing.)* No, I'm not gonna lecture you about your drinking. But this element is the closest one I have on what the world would call "morality" around our behaviors. And I will be offering some *advice* about alcohol.

WH: I guess I figured something like this was coming...

YF: You'll not find any elements in Yugo's Way that dictate morality. Living a healthy, loving, balanced life are hopefully outcomes of practicing the Way – natural results that come from living more spiritually. We are meant to live on this planet as well-balanced beings in harmony with our Earth, and part of that means being spiritually fit, but also physically fit, emotionally fit, intellectually fit. And to do that means we're trying lots of different things, experiencing life, trial and error. *Living life*! There are behaviors considered by some as "unhealthy" that people take to extremes. Things like drinking too much, taking drugs too much, gambling too much, having promiscuous sex too much, smoking, purging, hording. Look at all the different 12-Step programs out there and you'll see.

Humanity has many behaviors we take to unhealthy levels because of obsession, because of addiction.

WH: Uh-huh. I'm pretty familiar with some of those.

YF: But there's plenty of what's considered "healthy" behaviors we can be obsessed with too. I had a friend growing up whose dad took up running to relieve stress after work and lose weight. What started as two miles a day three days a week turned into five miles every day, then eight, then sometimes twelve. He'd come home from work, put on his running shoes, and run for hours, coming back only to eat dinner and go to bed. He spent no time with the family, and his knees eventually gave out from all the pounding on his body. Ended up skinny as a light pole – very unhealthy looking. We'd be driving around town and see him out running, *miles away* from home, and just start laughing.

WH: That is going to the extreme. I know guys like that in the gym. Start working out to get fit, then get obsessed working on their body.

YF: *(Nodding.)* And there's plenty more examples of usually "healthy" activities becoming a problem. Working too much, golfing too much, eating too much, shopping too much, even praying or meditating too much. The point here, Walden, is that we must learn to take everything in life *in moderation*, no matter what it is. No matter how it's labeled by society. One thing humanity has proven over and over is we can overdo *everything*. And so, we must be careful to live our lives in moderation.

WH: Hmmm. Ok, makes sense to me. Seems pretty basic.

YF: Yes, and that's the beauty of it. The simplicity. Rather than go over all the enjoyments and vices of life and say don't do this and don't do that, the Way simply says *everything in moderation*. Instead of hard rules like don't eat red meat, or don't drink, or smoke weed, or gamble, or use caffeine, simply live your life in moderation. Who's the "moral authority" to determine what's "good or bad" anyway? Some people say gambling is evil, some say drinking alcohol is evil, some say eating animals is evil, some say marijuana is evil, some say liberals are evil, some say conservatives are evil. See what I mean?

WH: Yeah, I see.

YF: Now let me be clear. I'm not talking about behaviors that are harmful to other people. If you're doing something that's hurting others, stop it. If you're breaking laws that cause harm or bodily injury to others that'll get you thrown in jail, stop it. There's no room for moderation there. That's where this element stops. It's not truly *everything* in moderation if you get my drift. Common sense comes into play here. And when I say everything in moderation, I'm not saying you can never let loose and overdo it. Outliers happen. People have to decompress, let off steam, party with friends and relax, and that's cool. I'm just saying don't take any of your activities and behaviors to the point where they *take control* over you – where they become an obsession or an addiction. And don't hurt other people. Cool?

WH: Cool.

YF: So I told you before, part of what made me who I am, part of what got me here today, was a crushing addiction to alcohol. An addiction that almost killed me but that I'm thankful for today. I won't bore you with the details of my story, but since I know you like to toss back a few, and since I am an expert in this area, let's talk a little bit about booze.

WH: Ok, but like I already said, I'm not an alcoholic, and I'm not going to AA…

YF: I know, I know. Just consider this as *educational*, ok? So, alcohol and nicotine are two of the most addictive drugs on the planet, some say the two *most* addictive, and ironically, these two drugs are legal in this country. Some researchers put heroin and cocaine above alcohol and nicotine, others do not, but you get the picture. These two drugs are incredibly addictive, they kill people every day and they're *legal*. Now I'm not advocating any type of drug use, but I am saying from experience, and from the experience of many friends and people I know, marijuana is far less harmful for the person, and far less harmful for society, than alcohol. And it's not even close. If the roles were reversed and weed had been legal for a century and alcohol was illegal? The people wanting to legalize booze wouldn't have a chance. It tears apart your body, it ravages the mind, it crushes the spirit, and it *kills*. The drunk driving carnage all over our streets is undeniable. How many times do you hear of somebody smoking weed and going on a rampage, beating the shit out of their wife and kids? How often do you hear somebody got high and went on a crime spree, crashing cars or killing people? People smoke marijuana and want to chill on the couch, maybe eat some Doritos. Now again, I'm not saying anyone should smoke weed – I'm just saying it's much less *harmful* than alcohol. If there's a choice between the two, that's a better choice – *in moderation*.

WH: Interesting. Yeah, there's no doubt alcohol ruins lives more the marijuana. *(Thinking about the hell my friend T------ is going through.)*

YF: Just look at Willie Nelson, man. He says weed saved his life. He was drinking whiskey like it was water, chain smoking cigarettes, getting in fights, crashing trucks, brutalizing relationships, killing his body. Then one day he figured it out. Every time bad shit happened to him, he was drunk. He was wasted on booze, out of his mind. So he decided, hey, I'm only using Mary Jane from now on. No more whiskey, no more cigs.

WH: I read a story about Willie saying marijuana saved him. Think maybe in *Texas Monthly*...

YF: Willie Nelson may be the greatest advertisement for marijuana of all time. The dude's ninety and still putting out albums, still playing live shows all over the country. Most eighty-year-olds I know can't drive, much less play guitar, sing, and put on a concert in front of 15,000 people.

WH: I hear you, Yugo. It's just that for me, I smoked too much weed when I was younger. I don't like how it makes me feel anymore so I don't do it very often. I know it's better than alcohol, no hangovers, not as bad for you.

YF: Alcohol was my drug of choice, but I did other things too. I don't smoke weed anymore at all since getting sober. Not an option for me. It just makes me thirsty, makes me want a drink and get more fucked up. And I've grown to love the *mental clarity* from abstaining. The joy of continuous sobriety!

WH: I've stopped drinking before for a couple weeks, just to see if I could do it. Have to admit, I did like feeling better, more clear headed.

YF: *(Smiling and nodding.)* So this is another very important part of this element, ok? It's one thing to say, everything in moderation, but for some of us in certain situations, moderation isn't even a *possibility*. For me and alcohol, moderation will *never* work. For others and say gambling, moderation won't work. For others and cocaine? Moderation won't ever happen if the money is there. We have to learn what our weaknesses are, those things we cannot control, and for those, unfortunately, we must *abstain*.

WH: *(Yugo pauses and I tense up, thinking a lecture on my drinking is on the way.)*

YF: So Walden, you told me you went down a bad path for a while, and drinking was a big part of that bad path. Now I'm not implying at all you have a drinking problem. That's nobody's business but yours. But it sounds like, at times, you're a heavy drinker. Usually I don't talk so much about alcohol in this element, but since alcohol is such a deceptively dangerous drug that could lead you down a dark road at some point, I'm gonna share some hard learned *experience*. That cool?

WH: Ok. I figured this was coming, but I'm listening...

YF: *(Clasping his hands, looking at the ceiling, then flowing.)* Ok first, one thing that makes alcohol more harmful than marijuana is that it's *physically addicting.* People build up a tolerance over time, so they have to drink more to get the same feeling they like to get from booze. This higher tolerance makes people drink more and more until eventually, the body develops a *dependence* on alcohol. The body starts to believe it *needs* alcohol just to feel ok. Once that happens, a person can become physically addicted to where the body tells them they *have to drink* or else. They have to take a drink to feel normal. They eventually feel they have to drink just to stay alive. Once this happens, Walden, you're fucked.

WH: Yeah, I've seen that firsthand. It's some ugly shit....

YF: And that's why people who are physically addicted to alcohol keep drinking, even though their lives have gone to shit. Even when their loved ones are begging them to please stop. Even though they're losing every-thing. They have to keep drinking because, dammit, without it they're going to die. It's incredibly fucked up.

WH: Yes, I know...

YF: Second, I'm sure you've heard the term *hitting bottom.* That someone with a drinking problem won't ever get sober until they've hit bottom. Well, I hate to say it but it's true, which sucks. But something you don't hear is that everyone's bottom *can be different.* Some people get a DUI and quit drinking, years before they're physically addicted. Some people get fired from a job or get drunk and do something really embar-rassing, and they quit drinking. That's the "bottom" for them. They had a high bottom, but it was enough. Others, like me, go on and on until almost killing themselves. They have horribly low bottoms, filled with pain and despair. And there are others who *never* hit their bottom. They die before they ever get there. Their bottom is the grave.

WH: Yeah, some dark shit, man. I know people who've died from booze, and have a friend that should be dead. I don't think she'll ever hit her bottom...

YF: Ok, so listen because this is *real* and it can save your life. There's two behaviors that if you're doing them, you're on a fast track to physical addiction, to a life of pain and misery. I know this from my own experi-ence and from watching many others fall. By the time we reach a low bottom, *physically addicted,* we're pretty much all the same. It's a long hard road out and many don't make it.

WH: Anything that helps me avoid the pain I've seen my friend suffer through is welcome. What you got.

YF: Number One, if you're hiding your drinking from other people, that's not *normal*. It's a sign you've got a problem. And by hiding, I mean drinking in the car on the drive home from work so nobody else can see. Drinking alone at home before going out so you've got a good head start buzz on everybody else. Hiding alcohol around your place, or in the car, so you know you've always got a pick-me-up if you need one. And this one's a biggie. If you're buying those damn little airline bottles and hiding them all over the place so you can grab a quick hit when you need it? In the garage, the closet, under the seat of your car, maybe your briefcase. Once that happens, know you're on a death spiral, and it ain't gonna get any better on its own. The longer you wait to get help, the harder it will be. The *lower* your bottom will be.

WH: Ok, I think I'm all clear on number one other than drinking a little before going out. That's just a little pregame. Everybody does that, right? I mean, I got nobody at home to worry about so why would I hide anything there?

YF: How about when Jessica stays over? How about when you're at her place? How about when you're visiting family? Are you sneaking drinks then? Maybe taking a quick hit off a bottle when no one's looking? Are you stopping off at a bar on the way for a couple of quick shots? Think about it. Would a normal drinker ever think to hide what they're drinking, or sneak a few to keep others from knowing how much they're drinking? No. So here's the deal. If you're hiding it from others, you must know, at least subconsciously, that what you're doing is not good. If others saw it, they might say something, right? So just watch out. This behavior is an *early* warning sign. It helps keep your bottom high. Cool?

WH: I'll watch out. It's cool. I know you're right...

YF: And one other thing about *hiding*. This tends to be true with other addictions too. If you're hiding what you're eating, hiding snacks, hiding pills, hiding your shopping, your gambling. It's a sign that what you're doing is *not* in moderation. *Wake up* and address it. Ok?

WH: Got it.

YF: Ok, and Number Two. If you ever notice an urge in the morning to take a drink just to feel better? To help you get by so you can make it through the hangover that morning? That, Walden, is your body telling you upfront you're developing a dependance. This starts for most people on the weekends. You know, wake up Saturday morning feeling like shit from Friday night, open a beer to settle things down. Doesn't seem like a big deal at first, but that's a sure sign your body is building up a physical addiction to alcohol and it's pulling you, almost forcing you to grab a quick drink just to feel *normal*. But normal people don't do that. Normal people wake up with a hangover, feel like shit, and swear they're never gonna drink again. They'll go days or weeks without drinking to get the booze out of their system. Walden, be *consciously aware* of these warning signs, because if they go unchecked, you will eventually be fucked. Now I'm not saying anyone who does these two things is an alcoholic. Some people are doing them today and getting along ok. But what I am saying is it's not *normal* drinking, and that if you keep doing it, it's highly likely you'll eventually get physically addicted and lose the ability to even choose if you want to drink or not. You will *have to* drink. And, you'll have a low bottom, flirting with death. It's a form of very slow insidious suicide. The whole point of this, Walden, is to stress, if your drinking gets to where it's causing problems in your life, you can *choose your bottom*. Keep it high!

WH: I hear you, Yugo. I know you speak from experience and from working with people on the street. I'm sure you've seen it all. I have to admit, some weekend mornings I do pop a beer to get my head right....

YF: You know, I'm pretty sure my dad was a functional alcoholic. It didn't seem to affect his job in the Air Force, but momma later confided in me it was a problem for her and for his career. That they both hid it from us kids. Alcoholism is hereditary, it's genetic, but that doesn't mean everybody who has the alcoholic "gene" becomes an alcoholic. Some people never drink enough to cross that line from when one day you're drinking for fun and enjoyment, and the next you're drinking because your body's screaming you *have to have it now*. I crossed that line into physical addiction and it was pure hell. But I wouldn't have learned the lessons I have on this planet without that experience – finally surrendering and humbly asking for help.

WH: There's alcoholism in my family too. Not my parents, but they each have brothers who've struggled. Seems many families do.

YF: So true. Alcoholics aren't responsible we got the gene that can cause alcoholism. We didn't do anything to get this "predisposition gene." It's not our fault. But alcoholics do have the responsibility to go get help. To accept defeat and surrender if drinking starts interfering with life. Being consumed by the deadly disease of alcoholism and not getting help is like someone with cancer not going to a doctor for treatment. It's insanity, but it happens all the time. Hundreds die from alcohol related illnesses *every day*, and a big reason why is the stigma society puts on alcoholics. Making it a moral issue and not a disease, an illness. A person doesn't hesitate to tell his boss he's going to the doctor when he's hurt or sick. But tell a problem drinker he needs to ask his boss for time off to go to rehab? Some would rather die than go through that fear and humiliation. No doubt it's better now for people to come out, but many still die every day.

WH: I hear your warnings, Yugo, and I know you're sharing this with me to keep me from making the same mistakes you did. I'll watch out. I'll be honest with myself.

YF: I know you will! Alcoholism is a spiritual illness, a soul sickness because remember, to live a spiritual life means to be open and honest in *all* our relationships. Practicing alcoholics, we lie to ourself every day about what we're doing. We deny the problem, refuse to confront it. And we lie to others about what we've been drinking, where we've been, what we're hiding. And we're lying to our God if we have one – *hiding* is maybe a better word. Problem drinking and honesty don't go together, so beware.

WH: I hear you...

YF: *(Smiling.)* Ok then. I wish someone would've told me the warning signs when I was younger, but I would've probably told them they were full of shit. So Walden, that's all I got on social morality, on what to do or not do. *Everything in moderation*, my friend.

The Practice

YF: Ok, since the Music practices are a freebie, I want you to work on keeping all the other practices fresh. Things like remembering our thoughts are real energy so stop sending negative thoughts into the know-osphere. Like taking care of Mother Earth, being conscious of overcon-sumption and materialism. Like remembering we are all one, intercon-nected, so treat everyone with love and compassion, because what we do to others, we're doing to ourselves. Sound good?

WH: Sounds great! I'm already doing those practices...nothing new so far.

YF: Beautiful! And the second thing I want you to do before our next session is take time when you can be alone. I want you to contemplate, become *conscious of*, any behaviors you're doing that are *not* in modera-tion. Are you working too much? Are you worrying too much? Are you eating certain foods too much? Is there anything in your life you're obsessing over? Overdoing, overindulging? Is your drinking in modera-tion? You get the idea. Take the time to assess if you're doing something that's not in moderation that needs cutting back.

WH: Sounds cool to me. It's probably good to do an assessment like that – to see if I'm overdoing anything. I've never really thought about it before.

YF: Yes, and like all the practices, it's a good idea to keep the reflection going. To make it a way of life. If you do come across a behavior that's not in moderation, that you're overdoing, you've already taken the first step, which is *awareness* it's an issue. Then you need to find *acceptance*, and do your best to cut down – to get your behavior back in moderation. If you find you can't do that, then let's talk about it and we'll look at the options for help. Talking about it with someone to get it out in the open takes away its grip – it's always a good place to start. Often awareness, acceptance, and honest effort is all you need if you catch things early. Ok, before we do today's meditation, here's a quick story that might help you see behaviors you wouldn't expect could be outside moderation.

WH: Ok.

YF: You know my dad was a military man. For the most part he was disciplined, he was intense, he worked out, took care of his body, watched what he ate. He did what you'd expect a special forces pilot in the Air Force would do, right?

WH: Right.

YF: Well, dad *loved* sweets, but he did his best to stay away from sugar unless it was a special occasion. And that usually worked ok except for one thing. For donuts. There was this little shop outside the base called Jack N' Jill Donuts that he loved so much he went and asked for their schedule when they made them, cuz dad wanted to get them when they were hot. He figured out what time to leave work so when he got there, a hot batch was coming down the line and he'd buy a dozen hot glazed. He'd come home with three of them already gone, glaze all over his face. He'd throw me and MaryAnne a bag of donut holes to keep us quiet, and we'd sit there and watch him devour a dozen donuts in seconds. One after the other, no milk or nothin'. Did it all the time when he was in town. And that, Walden, is a good example of *not* practicing moderation.

This is the 12th element of Yugo's Way:

Remember, everything in moderation. And if that's not an option, we must abstain.

WALDEN XI

I should call my parents when I think of them
Should tell my friends when I love them

"Old Friends" by Pinegrove (from *Cardinal*)

I'M RIDING in Cody's black extended cab GMC Sierra pickup and we're heading north outside Austin towards Temple to jump out of an airplane. I know it's crazy, but Cody saw a two-for-one coupon for this place and called me to go out there with him. As part of the *Comfort is Overrated* session, Yugo told me to do the first thing the Universe presented to me – speak at an Austin Chamber of Commerce meeting or skydive. Truthfully, I'm glad Barringer called. I'm so scared of speaking in public that jumping out of an airplane sounds way less stressful overall. I can get this over with fast with one quick jump rather than worrying about doing a speech for weeks, and I can drink beer and spend time with Cody too. With both our crazy schedules, we haven't seen each other in a while so we need to catch up. Yugo always talks about the importance of relationships, but I know I don't reach out to friends enough – just to stay in touch or be there for them.

On the way out I start decompressing to Cody about what's going on with my parents – about how strange it is being their caretaker now that they've somehow gotten old and in bad health overnight. For some reason, taking care of aging parents is not something I ever thought about having to do. I tell Cody that Father's heart is giving out. He's had another mini-stroke and his heart is in what the doctors call "A-fib," which stands for atrial fibrillation, an irregular and chaotic heartbeat. He has an "ablation" procedure scheduled for next week to try and get his heart back into a normal rhythm. The doc said they go in with some kind of heat ray and make tiny cuts to try and block the bad electrical signals going off in his heart, which is causing the irregular heartbeat. Sounds pretty wild, but that's what they told us. I'll be driving out to Wimberley the day before and bringing Father and Mary back to my place to stay so we're closer to the hospital for the procedure the next morning – it's first thing, 7:00 a.m. I'll be taking them, then waiting with Mary. Being with Mary, sitting with her in the waiting room, will be one long, challenging day.

Mary's early onset Alzheimer's is full blown now. Sometimes I go visit and when I'm still in the car driving home Mary's already calling, asking when I'm coming out to see them. She has no memory I was just there – and it's even worse for Frazier. She goes out there sometimes on the week-ends and stays overnight, and then Mary will call me Monday morning asking if I've talked to Frazier lately – that she hasn't seen her in weeks and she rarely calls. It's terrible. Sometimes I get eight to ten calls in a day from Mary asking the same questions, over and over. I can't imagine how Father deals with it every day. And Father's condition is making Mary's memory and mental health worse. She's constantly stressed and full of worry, *fretful* as Father calls her. Mary used to be the most carefree, easy-going person I've ever known, but this disease has turned her into a chronic worry machine. She's become an entirely different person as this disease progresses, and it's hard to watch. Father is sharp as ever mentally, but he's dying physically and I fear doesn't have much longer. Mary is healthy as a horse physically – she never goes to the doctor for anything other than routine checkups. But mentally, her mind is dying faster than Father's body. The *real* Mary is just barely there anymore.

I share my family woes with Cody, then we switch over to talking about Bryan and Ally and all they're going through with her cancer treat-ments, the kids, Bryan trying to act like things are ok and keep working. Cody says he feels really bad he hasn't talked to Bryan like he should, using the excuses of work and that he's really busy to avoid making those very difficult calls. I'm about to admit I do the same thing sometimes, that I need to call Bryan more to see if I can help but don't know what to say, when Cody breaks in suddenly with a bombshell.

"Anastasia and I are breaking up."

"What? You and Anastasia? Breaking up? You're kidding me. It looked like things were going so great."

"Yeah, well they were until her career took off like a rocket. I knew she and the band were great, but hell, I didn't see them getting so big so fast."

"What do you mean so big so fast? They get a new record contract or something?"

Cody's maneuvering down I-35, a ridiculously busy interstate that's constantly packed with cars, changing in and out of lanes effortlessly, but I look at his face and I can see the pain.

"They're about to kick off a six month North American concert tour. You know that band Khruangbin out of Houston? Anastasia's tight with that hot looking bass player and they've asked her and the White Beaches to open up for them on the road. Leon Bridges is gonna make some of the shows too."

"Khruangbin? Yeah, they've really hit it big-time. I saw them at a festival not long ago. That guitar player's great...so cool. They're super popular."

"Yeah, well they're stealing my angel, and I'm not good dealing with this kind of shit."

"Stealing your angel? Just because she's going out on the road for a few months doesn't mean it's over, Cody. You can stay in touch, maybe go hit some of her shows. You should be happy for her!"

Cody swerves into the left lane at the last second, narrowly missing an eighteen-wheeler in front of us that's only going seventy. On 35 if you're not traveling seventy-five or eighty, cars fly by you like you're standing still. It's three and four lanes across with almost bumper to bumper traffic – like driving in NASCAR really.

He glances over at me and says, "I *am* happy for her, but she broke up with me, Walden. It's over. Oh, she let me down gently, saying it's not right for me to have to sit home and wait for her all that time while she's on the road having fun. But she made it very clear. We're through."

Cody's gripping the steering wheel, knuckles white, face flushed. He's really fallen for her, and he's torn up. I can't remember the last time someone broke up with Cody, so this is somewhat new territory for him.

"But I gotta hand it to her, Walden. Anastasia was a beast. You shoulda seen her. It was like I was watching myself break up with an old girlfriend, she was so masterful. The way she broke the news to me made it sound like she was doing *me* a big favor. Like she was being a kind and thoughtful person letting me go free. And I just sat there with my head spinning."

"Shit, Cody, I'm sorry, man. I know she means a lot to you. I've never seen you so into somebody before."

Then Cody puts on a bright face and says, "Well fuck her then – that's what I say. I wish her and the band the best and all, but life goes on, you know? Dwayne and I were thinking about doing this expansion thing with the business around Dallas again, and with her setting me free, I figure we might as well go for it. God knows I'll have the time now."

So Cody and I go on lamenting back and forth about the shit we're dealing with, while also getting more and more nervous as we get closer to this skydiving place. Truth is I'm scared as hell, wondering if I've got the cojones to actually pull this thing off. We finally get there after driving several miles of backroads, and see this tiny, beat-up old runway that's literally in a wheat field. We're truly in the middle of nowhere and Cody says to me, "You can't go soft on me now and back out of this shit. Remember, you asshole, *comfort is overrated*, baby!" So off we go, two middle-aged men scared to death, paying good money to jump out of an airplane.

The jump was mind blowing – *indescribable*. Now I'm not saying I wasn't scared shitless, I was, and I'm also not saying I'd do it again – although I might do it again, I'm not sure. Being it was the first time for either one of us to do this, we had to do what's called a tandem jump. That's when an experienced jumper goes with you – is tethered to you – so you know in case you pass out from the fall or something bad happens, there's someone there to pull the cord and make sure you make it down ok. But still, sitting in that plane flying up, waiting, thinking about what you're about to do. Then having them open those doors, you standing there looking down at the ground and then actually jumping out – it was scary as shit.

The first few seconds are pure *madness*. All of your senses are going, "What the fuck am I doing?" and the speed and wind and rush of every-thing is overwhelming. But sooner than you think, and I think a big part of this is because someone's jumping with you, you get your shit together, and rather than chaos and unmanageable speed from falling, your body kind of adjusts and then it's just *wild*. It was funny because Cody was more scared of taking the plunge than I was – he was pissing in his boots all the way up.

We get back to the truck, crack a couple of beers that Cody brought along for celebration, and Cody says, "Holy shit, did you see that diving instructor? Did you see her? *Un-believable*! And I got her number too. If it wasn't for her, I swear to God, there's not a chance in hell I would've jumped out of that plane."

So here's what happened. We get in the plane flying up, a beat up old Cessna they've obviously been flying for years, and right away Cody notices there's this amazingly hot girl going up with us. He's scared to death, but he can't stop staring at her either. He's telling me over and over he doesn't think he can do it, that he's not jumping, that he's flying back down with the pilot. And so I tell him – You can't do *that*. Not with this incredible babe going up with us who's gonna see you chicken out. And he just sits there, freaking out, literally shaking. But then, when we get up close to jumping altitude, this beautiful girl jumps up and straps on a parachute – it's obvious now she's one of the instructors. And let me say, I agree with Cody – this girl was unbelievable. Too young probably for Cody in my book, but every bit a 9.5. So once she gets up and straps on the chute, she turns to the group and says, "Ok, so who's first? Who's going with me?" And Cody almost pulls a hamstring he jumps up so fast, all of his fears temporarily suspended. It was hilarious.

"Hell no you wouldn't have jumped," I say as we're hopping back in his truck. "You whined all the way up there. But you shoulda seen how fast you shot out of your seat with the thought of that girl strapped to your back!" Now I'm laughing. "Even better was that look in your eyes when the door opened and you looked down. That look of pure terror on your face, even with that hot instructor..."

"I was scared to death, Walden – maybe the most scared I've ever been in my life. Let me tell you something I shoulda told you before we did this. I didn't cuz I knew if I did, you wouldn't come out here with me."

"Yeah? What's that?"

"You know Dwayne? He and one of his buddies came out to this exact same damn place years ago to do a jump for the first time. They're driving on the backroads heading out to the airfield and his friend looks up and sees a plane up in the sky doing a jump. About five guys jump out, and Dwayne says they must have been experienced since none of them looked tandem, and each one is falling and one parachute pops open, then another, then another. But they notice, there's one dude who's falling and his chute's not opening. He's just falling down to the ground faster than shit and nothing's happening. And they can kinda tell from the way his arms are jerking and his legs are flailing there's something wrong with the chute – it's not opening. And Dwayne says once they realized what was happening, they stopped the car and just watched as this dude falls all the way to the ground until.....splat!" Cody starts the truck and glances over the top of his sunglasses at me.

"What? Dwayne really saw that shit and you didn't tell me?"

"Sure did. Said after he hit they just looked at each other, turned the car around, and got the fuck out of there. Dwayne says when they got close to the interstate, an ambulance went flying by, rushing out there to pick that poor son of a bitch up."

"Well, surely the guy died, right?"

"No, they say he didn't. Dwayne's buddy was curious and called out there later to ask if the guy made it and they said he'd broken all kinds of bones, but he was still alive."

Now I'm shaking my head. "That's the craziest story I ever heard. I'm not sure I believe that shit."

And Cody looks over at me as he's driving out of the parking lot, takes a big draw off his beer, and says, "Believe it. Why else you think I was so damn scared?"

So we're driving home now, going through Belton, and Cody's still talking about that skydiving instructor:

"I don't know if I've ever seen a woman prettier than that, Walden. That girl was hotter than a Walmart parking lot in July."

"Yeah, well speaking of Walmart, there's one coming up off the highway. Pull over at the next exit so I can get us some snacks and some more beer – my time to buy."

And Cody says, "I don't like shopping at Walmart anymore. Let's hit a convenience store."

"You don't like shopping at Walmart? Why not? I thought you shopped there all the time."

"Well, I used to after you told me to stop buying anything at Sahara, but now that Walmart's owned by the Chinese, I just don't feel right shopping there."

"Owned by the Chinese? What the hell are you talking about? Aren't they still owned by the Walton family? I haven't heard anything about them selling out to the Chinese."

"Oh, they're still partially owned by the Waltons, but those Walton kids sold out a big chunk of it under the radar. Wasn't publicized hardly at all but it's a fact, Walden."

"A fact?" I'm looking at Cody in disbelief. "Says who? That's too big a story for me to miss, Cody."

"Dwayne has a cousin who works for Walmart at that big distribution center outside New Braunfels. She says they had a meeting and told everybody about it. All the employees there know, and they were all told to keep it hush, hush. But the family's been selling off pieces for years...the Chinese are now big owners of the company."

"Really? Doesn't seem possible, but ok, Cody. If Dwayne's got a relative that works for them, maybe it's true."

Perplexed by this news, when I get home I go straight to Google and type in "is Walmart owned" and the first prefill suggestion that shows up in the search box is "by China." The third suggestion says, "by the Chinese." I think, *WTF*? Can this be true? How can something this big happen without me hearing about it in the business news? So I start researching and find a *USA Today* article that says, "Fact Check: No, Walmart was not sold to Chinese Investment Group."

Apparently, a rumor started on Facebook that this happened, that clandestine, shady figures were trying to keep it quiet, and then the false news spread all over. But according to *USA Today*, and other sources I checked including "Walmart ownership" on Wikipedia, the rumors of Walmart's sale to Chinese investors were verified as untrue. It's become so hard to know what's truth anymore. I can see how Cody would buy into this, especially if Dwayne said he'd heard about it from a Walmart employee. What a weird world we're living in.

I start to turn off my laptop when my cell rings, and it's Mary. I pick up the phone to answer and immediately feel a little guilty. It's almost 8:30 and I've forgotten to call and check on her and Father all day...

YUGO X

Just find this song, close your eyes, and listen...

"Sandusky" by Uncle Tupelo (from *March 16-20, 1992*)

MY COUNSELING SESSION with Yugo this day was very impactful. Through our back-and-forth discussion, he helped me see that internally I'm thinking all wrong about all the shit going around in my world lately. Rather than feeling sorry for myself for the added stress, the time commitments, the extra work created by helping my parents, from doing my best to support Bryan, Ally, the kids, etc., I should stay awake to the fact that what they're all going through is *WAY* worse than any of the inconveniences happening to me. I should do what I can to help, and I should be grateful I have family and friends who need me and trust me.

Ally, Bryan, Bridger, and Estella are doing their best to live through the nightmare of serious cancer – a cancer with little hope for survival. I can't even imagine how that must feel. Father is literally dying, and he knows it. Mary is losing her mind, and she knows it (although not as much anymore...even that's going). But how difficult must that be? All I'm doing is making myself available to take care of some of the things that come up that need to be done – and hopefully showing compassion. As Yugo told me, "What's happening to you really isn't all that important. Do what you were put on this Earth to do."

The element we covered today was also impactful, and the timing was perfect:

YF: All of the elements are important – they all tie together. But this one today is *especially* big for bringing an inner calm, peace of mind, and for living life to its fullest.

WH: Well alrighty. I could sure use more of all those things.

YF: (*Smiling.*) Ok, Walden, contemplate this. Our minds are constantly spinning, constantly thinking, and frequently these thoughts are replaying events that happened to us in the past. What happened five minutes ago or maybe what happened many years ago is going round and round in our heads. We're living in the past. But we're also frequently worrying about what's going to happen next, what *might* happen later. We're projecting out into the future. This means humanity, the majority of the time, is not living in life's sweet spot, that truly alive spot that's living in the *present*, enjoying now, experiencing now. Truth is, no matter where we are or what we're doing, it's *always Now.* But internally, we don't usually live in the present. Our minds are living in the past or worrying about the future. You think that's true for you?

WH: You keep asking me stuff I've not really thought about, but yeah, I'm sure I spend more time than I should worrying about the future and thinking about the past.

YF: We all do. It's a reality for all of us. But the thing is, when we're reliving the past or making up the future, we're *out of synch* with life. We're only partially there, intellectually and spiritually. So we're living life most of the time not fully conscious of all the *dimensions* of life. We're not fully experiencing life because we're not totally present, in the Now.

WH: Hmmm.....ok?

YF: And by the way, those thoughts of the future we make up in our minds? Those things we worry about that might happen? They virtually never do. Those scenarios we all create in our head rarely happen. They're simply "movies" our brain cranks out that create unnecessary worry and ultimately keep our spirits grounded.

WH: Mary's become such a worrier lately. It's a never-ending stream of fretting over this or that. Her mind's consumed with worry now, and I know my mind gets that way too. Worrying about the business, worrying about my relationship with Jessica, about Ally and Bryan...

YF: Understandable. We're all usually unconscious of our stream of thinking, which most of the time is living in the past or making up the future. So the purpose of this element, Walden, is to get us to *wake up!*

Instead of living in a self-created dream world built on a faulty memory and a fictional future, wake up and become more aware of our continuous thoughts. Recognize when we're not living in the present and return to the Now.

WH: That's a saying I've been told before. I should "live in the present." Sounds good and all, but I don't really know what they mean other than "stop bothering me about the same old shit you won't let go of."

YF: *(Laughing.)* Well that can be a part of it, but there's far more to it. Know this, Walden. Our memories are *faulty*. We are not just replaying the past in our head all day. We're *recreating* the past, so it fits better into the internal image we have of ourselves. *We* determine what was important, what was said, what was not said. Our memories of the past are often inaccurate because we filter them. They are *not* truth. So, when our minds spend most of the time recreating the past or making up stories about what might happen in the future, we are living in an illusion. A make-believe existence that's not *real experience*.

WH: Interesting. I know my memory isn't always right, or at least it's different than other people's...notice that more and more as I get older.

YF: Yes, as we get older our memories can *shift* – they're pliable. And in these times, Walden, not only are we constantly replaying events or worrying about what might happen next. We as a society are also *asleep*, not present, because of continuous meaningless distractions. Things we're honestly addicted to that keep us occupied, entertained, anything we can find to keep us from truly experiencing life. From simply *be*-ing in the present moment.

WH: Yeah, I know we're all distracted. How can you not be with one of these things in your hand all the time (*I pick up my cell from the chair arm and wave it*).

YF: Agreed! Just look around when you're at a concert, a football game, the airport, a restaurant. People aren't present. At most, we're only half there, one foot in the life experience and the other foot in the digital realm. Glued to phones, glued to social media, games, news feeds, glued to streaming endlessly on our personal entertainment devices. The lack of *presence* in our society has never been greater. Next time you go see live music, look around. Notice how many people aren't really there, even when what's going on around you is amazing! We're all tied to technology, shooting videos, taking pictures, posting, messaging. We're not really *experiencing* the music. It's a sad reality of today's human condition.

WH: Oh, I don't have to do that, Yugo. A huge pet peeve of mine is going to a show and seeing everybody staring at their phones, not watching the magic happening onstage.

YF: (*Nodding his head.*) I bring this up because this element isn't just about being aware when you're living in the past or worrying about the future anymore. We need to also recognize when we're distracted too, not present – not wholly there.

WH: Got it.

YF: And this is really part of the practice, but I'll say it here anyway. I want you to pay special attention to your relationships, to conversations you have with other people. Are you really *listening* to what they're saying, or are you thinking about what you're going to say next? I used to be so shitty remembering people's names. Then finally I realized when I met someone and we shook hands, I wasn't even listening to their name. I was too busy thinking about what I was gonna say next. It wasn't that I sucked at remembering names. It was that I never *heard* the name in the first place.

WH: Ha! Well that one hits home. I'm the world's worst at remembering names, and you're right. Instead of just saying I suck at it, maybe I ought to start trying, huh?

YF: (*Big grin.*) Well, I can speak from experience that actually hearing the name first does help! Tell you what I do. Now I try to listen intently and replay the name in my head two or three times, then think of a mnemonic device right then to help me remember it. Something that rhymes with the name or associates with them somehow. I'm pretty good with names now, but it took awareness.

WH: I'll have to give that a try.

YF: So, why is this element such a big deal? Why is life better when we live in the present? Because living in the past stirs up negative emotions and pain that can actually alter the path of our lives. So many people are living in the past, replaying the times they were wronged, replaying resentments, regrets, jealousies, suspicions. Often this means reliving past hurts over and over, experiences that caused real pain and suffering. But we mustn't let the past *define* who we are, Walden. Let the past shape you, let it educate you, *accept it* for what it was, but don't let it determine the person you're ultimately going to be. We must move forward and let the past go. Living in the past is one of the greatest causes of negative thinking there is. It's holding humanity back from evolving into our ultimate potential.

WH: Interesting. There's a lot there…

YF: Yes, and there's more. It's a big deal because living in the future creates unnecessary worries. Rather than being present, truly experiencing the joys of life, we're making up events or stories in our minds, stories that rarely come true, but that create huge amounts of unnecessary worry, anxiety, and fear. Again, all *negative* emotions. And it's a big deal because living in the Now, truly present, brings so much more definition, clarity, and *aliveness* into living. It's like trading up from an old analogue TV and living life in high definition! When we're not truly present we don't experience *all of life*. Our senses are dulled and life is muted. When our minds are churning with thoughts about the past or future, it's like going to a movie but checking our emails while we're there. We don't really hear. We don't really see. We miss lots of the movie. That's how many of us are going through life.

WH: I like that analogy...

YF: Not everyone relates to this, but here's an example of clarity from living in the present. Do you have any fond *reoccurring*, random memories that just pop into your head out of the blue for no reason?

WH: *(Silence while I'm thinking.)* Hmmmm, you know, yeah, I do. One I have is of me and Father planting our orchard out in Wimberley. Me digging holes in the soil with my hands. Planting the first fruit trees. I can picture the sky, how blue and clear it was, and Father showing me the best way to place the seedlings...

YF: Good! Most people have them. I have one with my sister when I was about nine. A San Diego Chargers game was on TV, they were wearing their powder blues. And momma's in the kitchen frying up some koeksisters, these sticky donut things we loved she grew up with in South Africa. Braided fried dough that made the whole house smell so good and she'd drench them in syrup and sprinkle on cinnamon. And while she's frying, me and MaryAnne go outside and throw the football around. I feel all warm inside when this pops into my head out of nowhere. Those old, good, clear memories we sometimes have for no reason? I think they're moments in our lives when we were *totally present*. For some reason, that day I was totally locked in, living in the Now, so the memory is clear and lasting. Just think, Walden. So much more of life can be like *that*, filled with clarity and joy – when we stay present.

WH: *(Still reminiscing.)* Hmmmm. You know, I have other good memories too that come back at the oddest times. Almost like déjà vu. Hiking in the Hoh Rain Forest with Frazier one day in a light rain, looking for hidden waterfalls, and we find this little spring just full of tadpoles. And catching this random pass in a Wimberley football game for a first down. It was a good catch on the sideline, but I had way more meaningful catches. But for some reason I clearly remember every detail about this one. The down marker guy staring down at me on the ground, Coach Mac waving his arm signaling first down on the sideline, the Navarro player, number 21, reaching down to help me up…

YF: Crazy, huh? We should live like every moment matters because every moment does. That's why it's so important to stay present and *wake up.* To not fall into that mechanical way of being where we're simply going through the motions. Much of the detail, the subtlety, the influences of life simply pass us by. I spent years of my life drunk, stoned, numb to the point where a life-changing opportunity could have punched me in the face and I wouldn't have noticed. I wouldn't have had a clue the Universe was presenting me a path. We never know how many amazing opportunities we miss that are right in front of us, but we're not present enough to even notice.

WH: Now that's a trip. What great opportunities passed me by because I was unconscious or too distracted to notice?

YF: *(Nodding.)* Being present, paying attention, means so much. We never know what moments in life will matter the most. That's another reason to do your best to stay conscious. You could bump into somebody on your way out of this restaurant today that changes your life forever. Maybe buys your business, maybe gets you to run for public office, maybe motivates you to write a book to help our planet. Who knows? You could decide to hire a person tomorrow who changes the entire direction of your company, maybe the direction of your life. This conversation, if you truly listen, absorb, and remember, could change the rest of your life by waking you up!

WH: Wait, Yugo. Run for office? Are you nuts?

YF: *(Big smile and now walking around.)* When we're using the majority of our brainpower dwelling on the past or imagining the future, we're wasting so much mental capacity on nonsense. So many of our waking moments are lost and become meaningless churn when we could use our intellectual powers for such *higher* purposes! The spiritual teacher Eckhart Tolle enlightened me on this truth about living in the Now. He estimates that 98% of human thought is repetitive and pointless. Now I don't know about 98%, but I bet it's at least 90 when you truly become conscious of your thoughts and pay attention. When you wake up and really listen to all the shit flying around in your head all day. Songs swirling around, replaying events that pissed you off, worrying about something happening that will never take place. How humbling is that? Realizing that *90% of my mental output is pointless*? When we realize and accept how worthless, how wasteful, and how self-absorbed our thinking is, surely we can be open to trying something different. Open to the possibilities of waking up! And that change begins with *self-awareness*. With observing our thoughts and emotions and becoming aware when we're not living in the present.

WH: Well I can't put a percentage on how much of my thinking is worthless, but I've got songs running around in my head all damn day. So if that counts as trash, plus replaying the past and worrying about the shit coming up...it's gotta be really high. Wow. Think how much more productive I could be....

YF: Now, I don't want to shortchange you, and what we've already covered gives you enough understanding to become more present, but when it comes to this element, there's nothing better at laying it all out than Eckhart Tolle's book *The Power of Now*. And by the way, Tolle is one of those contemporary spiritual visionaries you asked for that's evolving our planet for the better. Nothing I can say is better than the wisdom and passion he shares in that book. Have you read it?

WH: No I haven't, but I assume it might be part of an upcoming practice...

YF: (*Laughing as he picks up a copy of the book on a bookshelf, walks over, and hands it to me.*) You know me too well, Walden. Hey, at least you don't have to go out and buy one. But, before we go over the practice today, here's something else I want you to read and to save. Reading this book properly will take time, so I want you to read this now to get a feel for the importance of living in *Presence*.

Yugo bends down, opens his box, and pulls out a slip of paper. And this is what it says:

> "When we get lost in our stories, we lose touch with our actual experience. Leaning into the future, or rehashing the past, we leave the living experience of the immediate moment. Our trance deepens as we move through the day driven by "I have to do more to be okay" or "I am incomplete; I need more to be happy." These "mantras" reinforce the trance-belief that our life should be different from what it is."
>
> Tara Brach – *Radical Acceptance*

"Always say 'yes' to the present moment. What could be more
futile, more insane, than to create inner resistance to what already
is? What could be more insane than to oppose life itself, which is
now and always now? Surrender to what is. Say 'yes' to life – and
see how life suddenly starts working for you rather than against
you."

Eckhart Tolle – *The Power of Now*

The Practice

YF: As you correctly guessed, the first thing I want you to do is read Tolle's
book *The Power of Now*. It's not a long book, but it's a deep book, so please
take your time. Read a few pages and then ponder them. Our journey
through all the elements is almost over. Don't feel like you have to finish
this by the time we're done with our sessions together, ok?

WH: Ok. I'm almost done with a good book I'm reading now. I'll finish
that and then start on this. Looking forward to it after all your high praise.

YF: Beautiful! And the second thing I want you to do is to consciously
work on being aware of all your thoughts, on *Waking Up*.

WH: Be conscious of my thoughts? But aren't I already doing that
during the practice about remembering my thoughts are real?

YF: Well yes, sorta. But not exactly. The intention of that practice is to
make you aware of any *negative* thoughts you're having, and to stop
spewing them out into our environment. Stop polluting our know-osphere.
This practice is about becoming aware of *all your thoughts*. Of putting a
regulator on your mind. Recognizing those times when your mind starts
replaying a past experience, or making shit up, worrying about what might
happen later.

WH: Ok, I see…seems a little difficult.

YF: It is, especially at first. We all suck at this, so don't stress over how
well you're doing. If you catch yourself living in the past or worrying about
the future just two or three times a day, that's good progress! It will grow
from there. Do your best to raise your consciousness about your "*thought
life*," including when your mind is playing the same song over and over
like you say happens a lot. See if you can make it stop. Now *that's* not easy.
This'll sound weird, but what works for me is singing Bob Marley's

"Buffalo Soldier" in my head. For some reason, doing that overrides what-ever's going around in my head, and soon that goes away too. Probably just me, but if it works for you, tell me.

WH: That is crazy, but I'll try it and let you know. I know that tune... some heavy shit, huh?

YF: (*Folding his hands together and nodding.*) That it is, Walden, that it is. Another suggestion is to listen to instrumental music to clear your head since it's usually songs with lyrics that stick. Some Miles Davis or Bach, maybe try this dude Seckou Keita from Senegal, the album *22 Strings*. He plays a magical instrument called the kora. Beautiful. Or the Austin band Explosions in the Sky. Love their *Big Bend* album. And remember too, this isn't just about not reliving the past or projecting the future. It's about being conscious when you're *distracted* and shouldn't be. When you should be present but you're letting some outside influence, like your phone, take you away from the present moment. Cool?

WH: Sounds cool, especially this African kora player, but hey. How am I supposed to stop thinking about the past or the future? It sounds good and all, but this is new to me. How am I supposed to get back to living in the present moment?

YF: Ahhh, Walden, I'm glad you asked. One thing you'll experience when you become *aware* you're not in the present, when you *observe* the thoughts racing around in your mind. They often stop on their own. Once you bring them into your consciousness, bring them into the light and accept that you're having them, they often fall away...for a time anyway.

WH: Hmmm....ok.

YF: But when that doesn't happen, or when they come back, here's a few suggestions. First, stop what you are doing and just breathe. Concentrate on your breath. Inhale and exhale slowly. Feel the air flowing through your nose and mouth. Feel the rising and falling of your chest. Feel the air coming in and out of your lungs. Because a miraculous thing happens when you focus on your breath. Your thoughts stop. Immerse yourself in the breath, breathe, and your thoughts will vanish away.

WH: So your saying just stopping everything and focusing on my breath will stop my thoughts?

YF: (*Nodding.*) Try it. It works. Another way to come back to the Present is to feel your feet on the floor. Concentrate on the feeling in your feet, grounded on a solid surface. This makes you conscious of your body and takes you out of your mind. Then, you can cross your hands across your chest, and feel your lungs breathing in and out. Try and feel your heart beating. Become totally aware of your breathing, of your heartbeat, of your *being*.

WH: So what if I'm driving? I can probably do the breathing exercise, but maybe not.

YF: If you're in a place where these two methods aren't possible, or when simply observing your thoughts, being aware of them, doesn't make them go away, try this. Scream to yourself internally, yell at yourself inside, "***HEY, WAKE UP!***"

WH: *(Laughing.)* Or maybe, "Wake up, you unconscious bastard!"

YF: *(Laughing too.)* Hey, whatever works, man. And one last thing with this practice, Walden. Please pay special attention to staying present in all your *relationships*. The truth is the health of any relationship relies on us bringing our total presence to the other person or people. When you're with your parents, or with friends or fellow employees at work, *listen*. When Jessica is talking to you, *really listen*. Be present, be there and really hear what's being said so you can truly participate in the relationship. Try to notice when you shake your head yes and say "Uh-huh" but you're only half hearing what was said. We cool?

WH: Got it, Yugo.

This is the 13th element of Yugo's Way:

Wake up and live in the Present, for it is always Now. Be aware when your mind is replaying the past or making up the future so you can return to the Present and live Now.

FRAZIER VIII

"Maggie" by Sarah Jarosz (from *World on the Ground*)

THE GREAT SPIRIT compelled me to include Sarah's lyrics. It's an homage to Walden; to his idea of using lyrics in the book. And I am, actually, driving across a desert. The Chihuahuan desert lands of New Mexico. I'm on my way to stay with Juanita Goldsans outside Taos. I have some time to kill before she's expecting me. So, I'm meandering my way across the rugged backcountry of New Mexico. It's beautiful, so isolated. And it's been an emotional journey.

It's likely I'm trying to escape too. I'm in a life situation that's creating painful and unnecessary drama. I'm sure my actions aren't helping matters. I'm hoping Juanita can help me chill; to see things more clearly. Yugo gave me her card some time ago, after one of our talks. He said at times it may be better to confide in another woman. That I should reach out to Juanita if I ever want a feminine influence on spiritual guidance. He raved about Juanita, what she did for him. Said she was an angel who rescued him, restored him, healed him.

I've stopped at a New Mexican food dive in the middle of nowhere. It's a few miles outside of Socorro and I can't believe it's open. Ordered cheese enchiladas with red sauce and a chile relleno covered in spicy green chili sauce. Yummm! I planned to have a margarita or two and catch up on Walden's latest writings here. Then write my final contribution if the spirit leads. In the end, my writing didn't get finished until later. But the stop was well worth it. It's amazing to see Walden so close to finishing the book. He doesn't need my help anymore.

I must first tell you more about Yugo. About what he did for me. I didn't do formal counseling like Walden. But working with Yugo on the social media campaigns was amazing. Once I got to meet him, I knew I wanted what he had. Of course, I also knew I have issues. The greatest thing he taught me was the power of self-observation. And, just as important, how little of that I was doing. He taught me how to divide myself in two. To be an observer watching myself, like from above. To become conscious of my thoughts and emotions before they turn into wild actions. He made me see I was asleep much of the time. Unconscious of my internal thinking. That I often live life mechanically, doing the same behaviors over and over without questioning. Not fully alive; more on autopilot. I also learned how to recognize my negative thinking. How to avoid it like poison to the soul.

Yugo helped me see I can be too preoccupied with me. With my *self* (geez...now Walden's got me using italics too). Often, I'm too self-centered. Concerned mostly about what happens to me. Sometimes I'm too self-conscious. Worried about how I look to other people. Lots of times I'm driven by self-gratification. What feels good to me. He told me the same phrase he told Walden, "Don't think less of myself, think of myself *less*." Yugo gave me a note I keep in the top right corner of my bathroom mirror. That way I see it every morning I'm home. It wakes me up when I'm fixated on myself, or thinking snarky thoughts about others. It says:

The elimination of selfishness is the key to happiness and can only be accomplished with our Higher Power's help. We start out with a spark of the Divine Spirit but a large amount of selfishness. As we grow and come in contact with other people, we can take one of two paths. We can become more and more selfish and practically extinguish the Divine Spark within us, or we can become more unselfish and develop our spirituality until it becomes the most important thing in our lives.

Twenty-Four Hours a Day – March 4th

That's so perfect for me! He also helped me see I'm not always honest. With myself or with other people. Through self-observation I see I can lie about the tiniest things for no reason. Yugo says that becomes habitual. It can settle in your being and you don't even know it. He says self-awareness is the key. I like to think I'm doing my best. But life has a way of tossing me around, stealing my focus.

I wondered if Walden would mention Ally's cancer in the book. I'm glad he did. It wasn't necessarily a part of his work with Yugo. But Bryan and Ally are a big part of Walden's life. My heart goes out to them. They're so strong and brave. Watching Walden selflessly help their family proved to me Yugo's path works. He picked their kids up from school, took them to practices. Bought them groceries, took them meals. He'd stay with Bryan and Ally during treatments at the hospital. The old Walden I knew wouldn't do all that. He would have been too busy working at Walden's Pets. Plus, everything he's done for Mary and Father? And honestly for me too? It's so different from "pre-Yugo" Walden.

So, I finished off my first margarita, enjoying my late lunch in an actual restaurant. It's an old family-run adobe diner. Tattered booths. Homemade biscochitos and pralines for sale at the counter. The owner's kids busing tables. And the food? Muy fabulosa! The green chiles soooo hot, the chile relleno fried nice and crispy. Just how I like them. You can't find Southwestern food like this in Texas; local red and green chilis! It's almost two o'clock and the place is emptying out, but I had one more chapter of the book to edit. So I ordered another drink to enjoy with some chips while reading.

I'm lost in Yugo's element about living in the Present when the bells on the front door jingle. I look up, and a rugged local cowboy/rancher walks into the café. His sunbaked skin is brown and tan, like dark leather. His hair is long and jet black, tumbling out the back of his dusty, sweat-stained cowboy hat. His slightly torn work jeans are deeply faded to a light blue. They fit him like a glove. He makes his way past my booth as I'm sipping the straw on my drink. His deep, dark brown eyes make eye contact. Then he nods at me and tips his hat. I quickly smile back as he passes by, thinking, this is a real-life *Vaquero*. This guy's the real deal. And he looks like a dream.

After reading another page, almost done with my second margarita, my curiosity is raging. So, I get up to go to the bathroom. Oh, I needed to go, a little. But the main reason I got up was to take another look. And, to see if I could catch his eye. Sure enough, walking by his table I can feel his eyes. He's noticed. So I casually pass by, moving just so for effect. On my way back to the table, he stares me up and down. He's not even trying to hide it now. And my heart races. He's hooked!

I sit down in my booth, take another sip of my drink. Now my mind races. Why don't I just go grab this hot cowboy? Take him into the back cab of that big rancher truck of his and *ravage* him. I've got two days before I'm expected at Juanita's. Maybe I could spend some time at this vaquero's hacienda. See what a real New Mexican cattle ranch looks like. But then, thank God, *ping!*

I wake up from this steamy daydream and realize. What in the world am I thinking? What's wrong with me? Wake up! I don't know this guy from Adam. Get control of your thoughts, Frazier. Slow everything down. Get your check, pay your bill, and leave! And that, my friends, is the Power of Yugo's Way. Oh, I know it may sound trivial. But the old Frazier might have been making this man's day in the back of that truck. And who knows what would have happened then. Very doubtful anything good. And considering the drama I'm running away from? The relationship I need to talk with Juanita about? It's things like this that can get a girl into trouble. *Wake up*, girl!

Ok, so back to the book. I'm so proud of Walden for seeing this through. Well, almost through. He's not quite finished. You have no idea how many times he said he's quitting. But I kept saying, you're getting so close. Finish what you started! Writing this was so hard for Walden. It doesn't come easy for him. But we both know Walden's work, like our social media campaigns, will spread Yugo's Way. That it will help people. Bring more compassion and understanding into this nutty world. And hopefully, it will change the way many of us treat Mother Earth before it's too late. But now comes the really hard part. Getting it published. I haven't mentioned that to Walden yet, but I'm sure he's thought about it. May the Divine Energy of the Universe intercede and make it happen!

Thank you, dear readers, for putting up with my interruptions. Helping Walden write this book was cathartic for me. It further opened my eyes. Helped me learn more about myself. Helped me learn more about Walden. Reinforced Yugo's Way in my daily practices. And now, I'm off to Juanita's for rejuvenation and for healing. And some legal advice for one of my businesses. Can't believe she's supposed to be a great lawyer too. *Pura vida et au revoir!*

YUGO XI

Light of the world, shine on me
Love is the answer

"Love Is the Answer" by Utopia (from *Oops! Wrong Planet*)

TODAY'S my next to the last meeting with Yugo, the day we're going over the final element of Yugo's Way. He asked me to plan for at least thirty minutes extra for today's session, saying it will go longer than usual, so obviously I'm anxious to hear what he has to say. Rather than a long intro it's best to get right to the dialogue, but a quick note on these lyrics. This is one of Mary's all-time favorite songs, one she used to sing with the community musicians and singers in the hills of Nueva Tierra. It's been covered by others, but Todd Rundgren wrote it while with Utopia – it's perfect.

YF: Today we arrive at the last element, the most important one of all in my mind, and to begin, I'll summarize it in just a few words. *It's all about Love.* So there you go. Simple and straightforward, so it seems. But it raises a question we should all have inside, and that question is, What exactly *is* love? If it really is all about love, we better understand what love is, right? So what do you think love is, Walden?

WH: Hmmm.... it's hard for me to put into words, Yugo. It's caring, it's taking care of someone, being there for them. Putting their needs ahead of yours. Something like that? But there's romantic love too, having deep feelings for someone. You know, being *in love*. And there's really, really liking something a lot, like loving music…

YF: *(Smiling.)* L-O-V-E. Talk about a vague and misunderstood word. So what exactly *is* Love? We've talked about other words, their meanings, that they're only guideposts. And love is a *really* hard one to define. Some interesting aspects about the word love. In the English language there's only one word for love but many, many different meanings, different usages, so it's true that when I say, "It's all about Love" it loses some of its juice in English. Because sometimes we say things like I love this song, or I love this ice cream, or I love this weather. And then we use the exact same word to say I love my daughter, or I love my wife, or I love my God. Obviously, the verb used in the last three examples holds a very different internal meaning than when we say I love ice cream, or I love this shirt.

WH: Yeah, hmmmm, that's really true. The word love means so many different things depending on how it's used.

YF: *(Yugo stands up, is walking around the room.)* Right. But in Spanish there's two different words for love, which is a little better. *Amar* for really strong passionate love like I love my wife, and *Querer* for more common types of love, like loving that pizza. "Love lite" it's sometimes called. In Hebrew or Greek, there are many different words for love so there's more clarity. There's a distinct word from the ancient Greek in biblical times for God's divine love. This word is *Agape*, and it refers to an unconditional gracious love, a compassionate and kind love that seeks the best for who's loved, no matter what. *Philia* is more of a friendship kind of love, *Eros* a romantic love, *Storge* is more of an empathetic or affectionate kind of love, like between parents and their children, just to name a few.

WH: Interesting. Yeah, I've heard some of those terms before. Eros love, agape love.

YF: And check this out, Walden. In Sanskrit, the ancient language of Southeast Asia, there's over *ninety* different words for love. Astounding! Some of these words mean friendship, others are more of an affectionate kind of love, some words mean a sexual, erotic kind of love. So Walden, do you see the limitations we have with words that I talked about when we first met? Words are guideposts, but their meanings are dependent on the culture and the language. And love is a very hard one to nail down, especially in English with the very different situations when the word is used.

WH: I get it. Saying I love sleeping in on Saturdays or I love drinking beer isn't close to the same thing as I love Jessica, but I'm using the same word.

YF: (*Now smiling and looking down at me.*) Exactly. So when it comes to Love, I say keep it simple. I look to Jesus and the Bible for this one because it's summed up so beautifully there. Jesus was once asked what's "the most important thing," and he said, "It is to Love your God." And then he added that the second most important thing is to "Love your neighbor as you would love yourself." Well again, that begs the question, what exactly *is* love? And for that, the Bible gives us the best description of the kind of love this element refers to – this "Love that it's all about."

(*Yugo's standing by his chair, reaches down, pulls a slip of paper from his box.*)

YF: You'll want to hold on to this one. It's from the Christian Bible and it clearly explains what love is. I'll read it to you slowly, so the words sink in.

> Love is patient, love is kind. It does not envy, it does not boast, it is
> not proud. It does not dishonor others, it is not self-seeking, it is not
> easily angered, it keeps no record of wrongs. Love does not delight
> in evil but rejoices with the truth. It always protects, always trusts,
> always hopes, always perseveres. Love never fails.

> I Corinthians 13: 4–8

WH: Now that's a solid guidepost. Words for the whole world to live by. I've heard that before, Yugo, but I've never really *heard* it, you know? Never really *listened*.

YF: Beautiful! And another good way to uncritically observe yourself, to see if you're living in Love, is to have an awareness of what love is *not*. Here, you read this, the one at the bottom.

WH: (*Now Yugo hands me the slip of paper, and I read the bottom paragraph:*)

> Love isn't resentful, angry or judgmental of other people. It's not
> selfish, greedy, self-centered or uncaring of those in need. Love isn't
> condescending, vain or consumed by self-pity. It doesn't gossip,
> isn't suspicious, jealous, fearful or anxious. Not dishonest, hateful
> or unkind. For whenever our being says yes to any of these
> thoughts, emotions or actions, we are not living in Love. We're not

advancing the evolution of humanity toward consciously chosen
Love.

--YF

WH: So good! Now that's about as clear as you can get. Thank you, Yugo.

YF: *(Pulling his hair back and sitting down.)* Yes, these are reliable guideposts for living life the way we should. They help us observe when we are missing the mark, to recognize when we need to move away from mechanical, unconscious living and wake up to our Essence, which is pure Love. And I'm sure you know that's not easy, especially in today's world.

WH: I'll be sure and keep this one, Yugo. Pretty sure I've kept all the notes you've given me except that first one about Randy describing eternity. Think Cody kept that one.

YF: *(Reaching over and patting my leg.)* Walden Harrison, you're a good student. One who has put in the work. The beauty of this element is its simplicity and universal truth. But there are two more quick sideroads I'd like to take you down.

WH: Sure, hit me. I feel like we're just getting started.

YF: Living for love means more than being compassionate, selfless, serving other people, the planet, all creatures. It also means standing *against* the corrupt and oppressive powers and systems that rule the world – in a non-violent way, of course. That too must be done, through what we give our time and attention to, who we support, how we use our resources, how we use our influence, supporting worthy causes. And it means working in tandem with the Divine Energy of the Universe and other like-minded people to create a new way of life that's very different than the norms and supposed wisdom that others accept unquestioningly today.

WH: Wow, Yugo. Hearing what you just said sounds kinda like what Father was trying to build so many years ago at Nueva Tierra – in his own way. Building a new way of life, different from the norms of an unquestioning society, using our resources wisely...

YF: You know, Walden, it does. So very cool! From what you and Frazier said about the village you grew up in, about the experiment your father designed and created, sounds like you're right. Such a grand experiment you were raised in! Something so few have experienced.

WH: Yeah, I think Frazier and I were pretty lucky...

YF: Yes, there's no doubt you were. And one last sideroad tied to this, but so relevant in our society today. I need to stress this because I talked about standing up against corruption and oppression. That standing up has to be done *in Love*. Contemplate this. Deciding who and what we're against gives us a fast and easy picture of who we think we are. That's why many people fall into a kind of wrong thinking. So often we define ourselves and our image of who we are by what we're *against*. By what we hate, by what we think is wrong. Why? Because that's easy to do. And that's the wrong way to view the world. Instead, we should be defining ourselves by truly contemplating what we *believe in*. By gaining clarity and passion about what we love. That's not so easy...

WH: Yeah I see what you mean. I rarely see people rallying around what they love and respect. People usually get all excited about crushing what they hate. About how the other side is screwing them and how we have to stop them now before it's too late. There's no love there. It's the opposite of love...it's hate.

YF: *(Nodding in agreement.)* When Jesus said to love your neighbors as much as you love yourself, it's interesting there were no qualifiers on *which* neighbors to love. It's *all* neighbors, period. It's clear direction to love *all* people, not just those like yourself. A call to live a more *selfless* life than a selfish life, which in turn is living in Love.

The Practice

YF: You probably noticed the practices are more intense and time consuming in the beginning because we're going through, what for most people, is a new way of thinking. A new way of living and being. The practices seem less demanding as we go along, but in reality, they're more difficult to actually do. The same holds true with this last element.

WH: Sounds good. The practices aren't really *work* for me anymore. For the most part they've just become a way of life for me. A way to keep my shit together, stay on track.

YF: That's the hope, Walden. That is the hope. Not everyone gets there. Like I said, you've done very well. Ok, all I'd like you to do with this element is to raise your consciousness of love.

WH: Raise my consciousness of love?

YF: Yes, to raise your consciousness of those times when you're living outside of love. Use the words from Saint Paul on what love is, and my words on what love is not, and *observe yourself*. Become aware when your thoughts, your emotions, or your actions are not loving.

WH: Well, ok, but I may be doing that all day long. That's a pretty long list of things to do and not do.

YF: *(Smiling.)* Yes it is, Walden, it's extensive. There's no way you're gonna catch and stop even 10% of the times you fall away from *being in love*, especially at first, but the important thing is to use self-observation to become more aware when this is happening, so you can truly change your core being – over time. This is a lifelong exercise. I want you to do your best to catch yourself when not acting in a loving way throughout the day, and then at night, before bed, when you're doing your daily reflection on being open and honest, ask yourself. Where did I miss the mark? Where was I not acting or thinking in a loving way?

WH: Hmmm, ok. The element is beautiful in its simplicity, but the practice sounds impossible.

YF: At first it'll be hard, but you'll find if you work it, over time you'll become more conscious of yourself, more aware, *more present*, and more loving. After all, that's the goal, to evolve toward consciously chosen love! And please always remember this. It's absolutely 100% necessary that you do all of this self-reflection, all of this self-observation in an *uncritical, non-judgmental way*. This is not to put a guilt trip on anyone. It's not to illustrate that you're flawed. You're a beautiful reflection of the Divine Light. This is simply to raise your consciousness, raise your awareness. And it's a way of staying more in the present, in the Now. If you catch yourself only a few times a day to start, then do a quick reflection on your day at bedtime, that my friend is A+ work! Just see where this takes you. It's a good, long path to peace and to freedom.

WH: You got it, Yugo. All this time together you've given me a solid foundation to fall back on when the shit hits the fan. I'm sure this last element is important.

YF: *(Huge smile.)* It's the keystone. I can't believe we're already almost done, Walden. How wild time flies. I hand out another note to my students during this session on love. I'm always tempted to give this one out at the beginning, when I ask you to start "working out" your spiritual body every day. Some people have no clue how to begin something like that. They want direction and this prayer feels like the perfect thing to give students to help them get going. But I've learned it's way too early to do that then. Most people's *beings* in the beginning aren't ready to truly appreciate the wisdom and direction of this prayer. And everyone needs to learn for themselves, without too much outside influence, what spiritual practices work best for them.

(*Yugo bends down, grabs another slip of paper, and smiles.*)

YF: Today's a big day for little notes, huh? This one's called the "Prayer of St. Francis." It's attributed to St. Francis of Assisi, but scholars have never confirmed he's the author. It wasn't a part of his known letters or writings, but over the years he's the one recognized for it. It sure *sounds* like St Francis. There's various translations, but I've retranslated it slightly to read better for the 21st century. After your meditation time, or after your evening reflection, or maybe as part of your spiritual workout, I want you to read this prayer. That's also part of this element's practice, Walden. And eventually, maybe this prayer finds its way into your memory. It's a roadmap for living a selfless life, for embodying this last element, for *Being Love*. I'd like you to read it out loud, if you don't mind.

WH: (*Yugo hands it over and this is what I read – and still recite to this day after meditation:*)

PRAYER OF ST. FRANCIS – *(YF Translation)*

Light of the Universe,
Make me a channel of your peace,
That where there is hatred, may I bring love
Where there is wrong, may I bring the spirit of forgiveness
Where there is conflict, may I bring harmony
Where there is error, may I bring truth
Where there is doubt, may I bring faith
Where there is despair, may I bring hope
Where there is darkness, may I bring light
And where there is sadness, may I bring joy.

Great Spirit, may I seek to comfort others than to be comforted
To understand than to be understood
To love than to be loved.
For it is by forgetting about yourself that one finds.
It is by forgiving that I am forgiven.
It is by dying that I awaken to my true Eternal Essence.

WH: That's beautiful, Yugo. And so powerful. Beauty and power!
(*Yugo gets up from his chair, reaches down for my hand like a bro shake*

and pulls me up, looking me in the eyes. And then he says something that surprises me.)

YF: Let's skip our sit today, Walden, since it's our final formal teaching day. Will you join me downstairs in the café for some tea and we can continue our talk?

WH: Heck yeah, that sounds great, Yugo. Let's do it!

And so, Yugo leads me downstairs and finds a waitress to get us a table, and I'm pumped I'll have a chance to talk to him for the first time in a "non-doctor-patient" kind of setting – where it's more comfortable to just talk. I must say here that since we went down to the restaurant, I didn't record our conversation at first, but once Yugo got going, I asked him if he minded me turning it on. The recording was sketchy in spots, that restaurant's always hopping and the background noise was terrible, but I got much of it – although some is from memory.

The waitress comes back to see what we'd like and Yugo says, "This is on me, Walden. It's past lunch so I'm just having some tea and a snack. Cool with you?" And I say sure, that I already had lunch and I'm not all that hungry, and he turns to the waitress and says, "Robyn, bring us my favorite black tea with oat milk and a little agave on the side. And we'll have a toasted whole grain English muffin, with almond butter, a little honey, and some cinnamon." And Robyn smiles and says sure thing Yugo, and we start talking.

Yugo says he's loved getting to know me and hopes our sessions have helped. He asks me if I'm feeling better from our time together, functioning well day to day, enough to where I'm ok going forward after our formal meetings are done next session. I tell him his counseling was a miracle for me, that it came at a time when I was spinning, lost, and couldn't find my bearings. I say I don't know what's been more impactful, his advice on living life and dealing with all the crazy shit that comes up every day, or the elements and practices he taught me afterwards. Then Yugo tells me most people, after getting used to having a sounding board and a routine schedule, find they miss the sessions. There's a void and that can become an issue. He says unfortunately, the way he does his teaching, not charging and all, he has a wait list of people wanting to meet with him, so he can't continue counseling students indefinitely. He has to move on to help other people who are searching and willing to work, but there are ways to stay connected. He hears honking outside in the street and gets distracted, looking out the window at the mass of people clogging the sidewalks, cars bumper to bumper on South Congress.

"You enjoy living in Austin, Walden?"

"I love living in Austin. There's so much to do, great food, great music."

Yugo's still looking out the window thinking and says, "Yeah, Austin's great, but it's gotten so big and crowded. It just feels different to me lately. It's strange, but I feel something inside pulling me away from Austin, to maybe go somewhere else that's not so busy, so cluttered."

And I say, "Yeah, there's no doubt it's not the same. Too many people, that's for sure..."

About this time Robyn shows up with her tray of tea and an English muffin, and what follows was so memorable to me, yet so mundane, it'll be hard to describe the experience well. I'm just glad I was *present* that day. Yugo looks down at the food, briefly closes his eyes, and when they open, they're gleaming. He takes the saucer from under his teacup and places one half of the English muffin on it, then very slowly spreads almond butter on top, swirls a little honey on it, and carefully sprinkles on some cinnamon. He smiles at me and slides it over saying, here, take this and see if you like it, I think they're awesome! And then he asks if I'd like a little sweetener in my tea, and I say I've never even had black tea with oat milk before. Does it need any? And he says he likes it that way, just a touch of agave. It makes it perfect. Yugo takes the tiny container and tips in a small amount, then moves the tea bag up and down, slowly mixing the agave in. Steam is rising from the cup, you can tell it's nice and hot, and he slides my teacup over and says, take this too, it goes perfectly with English muffins – and then adds he treats himself to this at least once a week.

Then Yugo prepares his muffin and tea, and I know this sounds stupid, but he reveres them. He looks at them with gratitude and wonder, slowly lifts the tea to his mouth, and sips. And the smile that comes over his face is indescribable. It's as if he's in heaven, experiencing the greatest extravagance ever. And I watch him as he silently eats his muffin and sips his tea, and I try mine and agree. The tea is awesome with oat milk and agave. I know I'll be drinking this all the time now for sure. And I try the muffin and holy crap the English muffins at Omelettry Lane are incredible, and toasted with the almond butter, honey, and a hint of cinnamon. It *is* perfect. Yugo's so focused and engaged I feel there's no room for discussion, and so we just sit there for a moment, sipping tea and eating our muffins – it doesn't feel right to talk. But when we're almost done eating our muffins, Yugo reaches into his t-shirt pocket, his shirt is plain white today, and he pulls out a slip of paper and hands it to me, saying something like he's sorry for interrupting my tea, but to read this when I'm finished because it's important. And here is what it says:

> Tea is an act complete in its simplicity.
> When I drink tea, there is only me and the tea.
> The rest of the world dissolves.
> There are no worries about the future.
> No dwelling on past mistakes...
> ...This is the act of life, in one pure moment, and in this act the truth of the world suddenly becomes revealed: all the complexity, pain, drama of life is a pretense, invented in our minds for no good purpose.
> There is only the tea, and me, converging.

Thich Nhat Hanh

And Yugo smiles at me and says, "Even when we're doing something as common as drinking tea, we can remember to stay present, to *be in the moment*, to quiet the mind and experience how great it is to be alive." And about this time, thank goodness, I realize I should probably be recording this if it's ok by him, it seems like a continuation of our lesson, and he says sure, to turn it on.

YF: So to pick up where we were before tea, about a void you might feel once our sessions are over. A few people quit coming to see me entirely after we've gone through the Way, but many drop by sometimes when they're around the area. If you do, just give me notice to make sure I'm here and I'm free. I have a feeling you're more the type who's relieved to be done talking about yourself, so I may not see that much of you.

WH: Oh I might surprise you, Yugo. I know I'll miss our time together, so count on hearing from me after we're technically done. And hey, remember, you said you might want to drive out and meet Father sometime. I'm up for that!

YF: (*Smiling.*) I'd love that, Walden, very cool. And while I can't see old students nearly as much as I'd like, there's an even *better* alternative for you. Some of my past students pulled together what they call a "support group" around here that's evolved over time. They get together to help each other, to talk about their paths, to share and grow with like-minded people. Life is all about relationships, and when you're done with me, I can introduce you to future relationships that will help you grow, have accountability, and decompress. Remember, we all have our own personal struggles to work through in life. They never go away. This group lets people unload all the shit that's happening with them, get support and advice, and build lasting friendships.

WH: Yeah, ok, Yugo. I might do that.

YF: Now come on, Walden, don't bullshit me. I can tell from your reply you have little intention of getting together with these people. *Please* consider it or you may see our months working together slowly fade away. Our last meeting is mostly a time for you to ask me *any* questions you have from our time together, but it's also to discuss a game plan for the future so you don't lose your spiritual momentum. We'll talk more about this group thing and how I can get you connected in two weeks. Ok?

And while I immediately start thinking of all the questions I'm going to ask Yugo at our next meeting, he reaches in his pants pocket and pulls out this little wooden box. It looks like a miniature version of that cool varnished box he's been pulling slips of paper out of all this time. He hands it to me smiling and says to open it, and when I do I see inside a shining silver necklace. A beautiful necklace with a pendant that's the exact same loop that's dangling from Yugo's earring. Surprised and touched, I pull it from the box and look at it, watching the loop twirling, glimmering in the light. For some reason I almost feel like crying.

WH: Wow, Yugo, you kidding? Is this for me?

YF: (*Huge smile.*) It's for you Walden, and please know this. I don't give this necklace to all of my students. This is for the ones I feel will continue living the elements and practices far after we're done meeting. Consider it an early graduation present.

WH: It's incredible. I love the design. I've been too self-conscious to ask, but what is it? I figure since you wear it all the time it's got to be more than just a loop or a ring or something – have some kind of special meaning.

YF: (*Now turning his earring pendant and smiling more.*) It's a möbius strip. Its creation comes from mathematics, but the form and design are truly *magical*. It's meaningful to me for three reasons. First, the design of a möbius strip shows that two sides, let's call them the inside and the outside, can join together and become one side. This symbolizes unity, non-duality, and oneness. The concept that we're all one, all inter-connected.

WH: Hey yeah, I see how the two sides become one...

YF: And second, a möbius strip has a never-ending path along its surface, and that symbolizes infinity and endlessness. Eternity you could say. Eternal interconnectedness!

WH: *(Twirling the loop and studying it.)* Interesting – I love it! And what's the third reason?

YF: *(Yugo pauses, his eyes go a little teary, and he looks at me and says.)* An angel in the neighborhood where I live, a woman named Maya, has lived through more hardships than you or I could ever imagine. When I first met her, she was a tortured soul, barely hanging on to life. And I've watched as her inner strength, her faith and reliance on her God has transformed her being. She's become an incredible artisan. She makes these möbius necklaces and earrings and sells them at a little shop where I live. While the möbius is magical, the ones Maya creates are *mystical*, blessed. They're from a Higher Power.

WH: *(Overwhelmed by his kindness, shocked by his gift.)* Incredible. Thank you so much, Yugo. I'll wear this and cherish it always.

YF: *(And while I'm placing the necklace back in the box, Yugo adds.)* And know this. That box is special too. You can't just find something like that anywhere. There's an old dude named Donny who lives down the street from me that makes those boxes. All sizes. Tiny ones like that, medium like the one in my office, and big ass boxes you can put toys in. He sells them at the same shop. When you feel that necklace during the day, Walden. Feel that pendant dangling against your chest, your heart. It's my hope you'll be reminded that you're a spiritual being loved by our Higher Power, that your thoughts are real, and to wake up and live for love!

WH: I don't know what to say, Yugo. It's so unexpected. Thank you…

The audio from here is shaky because of the noise, but we mainly talked about personal things, family things. Stuff from my counseling. Towards the end, I can't stop myself from asking Yugo a question, which I'll include:

WH: Hey, Yugo, I know these sessions aren't meant to be religious, even though some of them seem like they are.

YF: Yeah, I guess that's true depending on how you look at them.

WH: Well, one thing I was hoping we'd get more into talking about is the afterlife, about what you think happens after we die.

YF: Now that's the million-dollar question, isn't it, Walden? It's the real reason humanity has had all these different religions since our time began on this planet. We've always needed reassurance that *surely* everything doesn't just stop when we die.

WH: You know, I'd get together with a friend of mine in college, and we'd get high and talk about what we thought were life's great questions. We'd talk about death and he'd say, "What's it gonna be like when you die? I think it's gonna be exactly like how things were before you were born."

YF: Pretty thought-provoking answer for a stoned college kid.

WH: Yeah, it sounds intriguing, but then I'd start thinking about it and go round and round in circles. It's not easy to get your head around when you're high. So what do you think, Yugo?

YF: Well, Walden, I admit over the years I've done my share of contemplation on that question, and through all that deep thinking there's only one thing I can say with any certainty.

WH: Yeah? And what's that?

YF: (*Eyes twinkling.*) That whatever I think's gonna go down after we die is *not* what's going to happen.

WH: Oh come on, humor me, Yugo. You must have something? A wild guess even?

YF: Ok, you asked, so here's your "wild guess." But consume this with a hundred grains of salt. I think maybe we all came down from the stars as stardust, dropped from the Universe, created by God. Who knows why, but Earth is where our Higher Power or the angels determined our souls should be. The place that would teach us the most. This indescribably beautiful planet, but let's face it, also this incubator of Pain. First life throws experiences at us to mold us, to shape our nature, to learn about ourselves. This creates our "personality" as we grow up – our survival skills. And we develop our mechanical way of being, our habits, our thoughts and beliefs, through culture, parents, teachers, friends. But eventually, when we're ready, life's *events* are meant to help us evolve our spirit to a *higher level* of consciousness that's above our worldly personality. Above our ego and false self, as our awareness grows and we transform our be-ing back to compassion and love. Each one of us is on this planet to *evolve our being* back to our core Essence, to an acceptable reflection of our Divine Creator. Back to Love, to the *pure spirit* we were born with when we splashed into this world.

WH: (*Not sure I'm getting this.*) So we're born, shit happens, life shapes us and makes us who we are, then we're supposed to use events to help us evolve back to how we started in the first place?

YF: Hey, you're the one who asked, but yeah, back to our Essence, pure awareness, *presence.* Life's events are our tests, Walden...every day. And when we die? If we still have a lot of work to do, we're put back by the angels into another instance, another dimension maybe to give it another go around. To evolve our spirits further, to hopefully live more consciously this time. To let go of the lie of separation and embrace our *interconnectedness* with all creation. In love with all people, in love with our planet and all creatures. And, when we've developed as far as our human spirit needs to go, into a purer form of awareness deemed by the powers that be as acceptable, then I think we get to move on to the next plane. To be angels ourselves if we want that, to rest, to play, to live as *higher* be-ings.

WH: Wow...ok. So you're talking something like reincarnation then...if we don't evolve as far as we should?

YF: Well sorta, only my guess is we're not coming back as a butterfly or a pigeon or a tiger. We're given another shot at our humanity, as our *spiritual selves* in another instance. To get better, to evolve so we can move on from here. And let me throw in that we should *never* wait for the afterlife to experience heaven. As Jesus said, *the kingdom of heaven is within you.* Heaven can be, and should be, experienced right here on Earth, *now.* Don't waste your time on this planet waiting to get to heaven. Live life to its fullest here, now, because the kingdom of heaven is here, *within you.*

WH: Hmmm...that's a little bit deeper than my old college buddy...

YF: (*Smiling.*) But remember this more than that potential line of bullshit I just gave you. As the Buddhist tradition says, "Those who say they know *do not* know, and those who say they do not know, *know.*" My "on the record" answer is – I don't know. Don't think I haven't realized my afterlife scenario fits in rather nicely with the meaning and purpose of the Way. It's an idea that's still evolving for me.

WH: Yeah, this one's quite a rabbit hole, but at least you've given me more to think about.

YF: That's good! We all must come to our own understandings, our own beliefs, through our own experience. What I choose for my *basic understanding* is that we're spiritual beings created by a Higher Power, and that our core nature, our core energy, is Spirit that's eternal and does not die. For many people that's all we need. That's enough. To believe that when we die, something else happens. That the movie isn't over.

WH: I think that's enough for me, Yugo. I mean, why stress over it if there's no guaranteed way to figure out the details, right?

YF: Right! Hey, I am intrigued by that idea of your college toking buddy though. I wonder, knowing our human conditioning that needs an assurance we'll live forever, would his scenario be ok with most people or not? I'm thinking maybe not. Just remember this, Walden, as St.

Augustine of Hippo said about our Grand Creator, "*If you understand it, then it's not God.*" Zen Buddhist philosophy says over and over we must remind ourselves that we do not know. They call this shoshin, or "beginner's mind." And I agree. No one really knows. I don't know, Joel Osteen doesn't know, your Father doesn't know, the preacher at the First Baptist Church of Forks doesn't know, the Pope doesn't know, the Dalai Lama doesn't know. *No one knows.* So trust the core Spirit inside you to guide and direct you along the way.

This is the 14th element of Yugo's Way:

In the end, Love is all that *really* matters. It's the Divine and Grand Energy of the Universe.

BJ V

Brett Jesak stares off in the distance as light from the slowly setting sun casts mesmerizing images off the glaciers on Mount Hood's peak. Sweat pours down his face as he pumps faster and faster on his recently installed top of the line Peloton bike, a new addition to the office aimed at keeping his body fit, reducing stress, and giving him the cardio workout his doctors say he so sorely needs. It's week three since the arrival of this new bike, and Brett now looks forward to his late afternoon exercise; to breaking an intense sweat and working out the frustrations built up from a workday the average businessman could never even fathom.

The divorce with Nichole is final now, and although he misses her dearly at some point during most days, Brett is doing his best to move on. In part to counteract the emotional void from Nichole's leaving, Brett is having a yacht built, a yacht he envisions as a bachelor's paradise. But a void this substantial requires a big boat, and this one will be over four hundred feet long, the world's largest sailing yacht. Construction has not gone well, weekly meetings on the progress are extremely frustrating, and revised final cost estimates are now running in the half a billion-dollar range. Quite expensive for one man's boat. The added stress and rising costs, docking and maintenance fees alone are over $50 million a year, have Brett wondering if he made a big mistake, but it is too late to turn back now.

The office liaisons with various women, while reduced in number, still happen on occasion. But Brett has evolved somewhat to enjoy the personal interaction of relationships almost as much as the physical side. Impromptu meetups with virtual strangers are now fewer than actual dates with women he finds interesting. Dates that often end up, eventually, at his new place. Once Brett gave into his desires and encouraged the advances of gorgeous women, women far outside of his league looks-wise, he did what he had always done in new areas of interest important to him. He researched and studied all he could find on sexual expertise and the art of lovemaking; threw himself completely into this new area of study. Over time, Brett became far more accomplished in the sensual arts. Especially compared to the naïve young man who was so shocked a girl as wonderful as Nichole would ever agree to have sex with him. Brett took pride in his advancement, always doing his best to ensure the pleasure of all his partners.

As Brett pedals up the last imaginary hill on his Peloton, heart rate flying and perspiration covering his workout clothes, thoughts of yacht cost overruns replaying in his head, Miriam Dobbs, his trusted executive assistant of so many years, appears in his office holding an Express envelope.

"Mr. Jesak, I am so sorry to bother you, sir."

"What is it, Miriam? Can't you see I'm in the middle of killing myself on this damn thing?"

"I'm sorry, sir, and yes I figured you'd still be riding. But I'm about to leave for the day and I found something interesting in the mail you might want to take a look at."

"Something interesting in the mail? What is it?"

Miriam cautiously approaches, clutching the envelope. "Well, Mr. Jesak, you get more mail than you'll ever know from people all over the world asking for all kinds of things. We have a low-level assistant who opens it, just to make sure we're not throwing away something that's important you might want to see."

Almost to the plateau of Arizona's Mount Lemmon and breathing hard, Brett snaps back, "I'm aware of that, Miriam. Get to the point."

"This came Express Mail today addressed to you, and I noticed the forwarding address was from a Yugo Free. I remember that name vividly because I forgot to order your lunch from Mucca Osteria one day I was out. When I came back, I heard that name over and over in your office. Such an odd name. Anyway, since he seemed so important, I wanted to make sure you saw it before someone threw it out."

"An express package from Yugo Free? What in the hell could that be about? Okay, Miriam, just throw it on my desk and I'll check it out later."

Miriam places the envelope on Brett's desk, says good night, and leaves him to his exercise. The mountain climb finally conquered, he is now in the cooling down stage. A lot has transpired since the Yugo's Way viral activity that rocked Sahara's stock price so dramatically and cost Brett billions of dollars, on paper anyway. But the name Yugo Free is still fresh on his mind. Brett, dubious of its origins and nervous about its content, wonders why someone claiming to be Yugo Free would send him a package. After toweling off, getting water, and changing his shirt, Brett sits at his desk and considers if he should open the envelope or not. As he clears out late day emails and reviews his jampacked schedule for the next day, something is pulling him to the Express envelope. He can't get it out of his mind.

Brett thinks, *Why would I let some pissant like this get a direct letter through to someone as important as me? Who the hell does this guy think he is?* He picks up the envelope addressed in what looks like green Sharpie marker, the penmanship similar to what you'd see from a sixteen-year-old girl. Precise but bold letters with flow and grace, lots of loops. After pretending the letter's presence is uneventful for several minutes, Brett finally relents, pulls on the tag, and opens the envelope, finding a simple one-page letter inside. Putting on his reading glasses and leaning back in his insanely expensive fine leather office chair, Brett reads:

Hey Brett, first my apologies for the stock hit. I was floored how people latched on to those social media posts and everything went so viral...you never know when the wind will be blowing in the right direction. We didn't plan on singling out Sahara at first, but as large as you guys are it was the best example that came to mind to get people to notice. I had no idea all that would happen, but it seems the whole stock thing turned out okay for you, so I hope there's no lasting hard feelings. I'm sure I created a lot of negative emotions in you for a while, and I'm very sorry for that.

I'm writing you now because some Force out there keeps telling me to, and I try to listen when the Universe talks. You're the richest and in my opinion maybe the luckiest man in the world right about now. I'm not just talking "money rich." I'm talking rich from the unheard-of power, influence and resources you've built over the

years. And I'm talking "lucky" because it seems to me you could be
The One. The one uniquely blessed and positioned to use your
power and resources to become the most famous and well-remem-
bered human being who's ever lived. Now sit back and contemplate
that for a moment. You could be the most impactful human being
ever!

I say you're lucky because instead of being remembered in human
history as just another name who had really, really lots of money
for a short period of time on planet Earth, you could be remembered as The Spark that ignited a shift in our culture from me-first
materialism and a disregard for Mother Earth to a kinder, more
loving society where we preserve and cherish our resources, where
the least among us are treated with kindness and charity. You can
be the torch bearer that encourages humanity to wake up and
evolve in love. To become the species our creator intends us to be.

I assume you're skeptical, thinking some kook who cost you a
bundle is throwing wild ideas at you. But let me ask you this, Brett.
Are you happy right now? Are you fulfilled? Will the next ten
billion that comes in make a difference? If the answer is yes, stop
reading this now and toss it in the can. But if after all your incredible material accomplishments the answer is no, please contemplate this. Just think if your legacy, a legacy that all mankind will
know and remember for centuries, is that you gave up everything
to make more money than anyone else ever on Earth, but then you
evolved and used that money and influence to save the world when
it needed it most. You're best positioned to become the person
whose voice, high profile, and money can start reversing the
damage we've done to this world and save our planet for future
generations!

The time is now, Brett, to regain and restore your Spirit. To evolve
your consciousness to higher levels and soar like the angels! And I
promise you this. When you see all the people you're helping, when
you see the positive changes all around you, you'll feel a lasting joy
that you've never felt from closing a big business deal. I'm certain
of that. You know you can do it. You can figure out most anything!
If I can help you in any way, my email is below, and my services are

free. Maybe we can set up a time to talk about ideas? And I bet your friend Amanda can help too. After all, what really matters in this world is Love and Compassion, and you're uniquely blessed to spread the Light more than anybody.

How cool is that, huh? Peace, Yugo

YUGO XII

It's only love, it's only pain
It's only fear that runs through my veins
It's all the things you can't explain
That make us human

"Human" by Civil Twilight (from *Civil Twilight*)

IT'S A BEAUTIFUL, sunny spring day without a single cloud in the sky – strikingly blue and brilliant. Yugo said I could ask any questions I might have during our last session, so I've mentally pulled together a list. I want to be prepared. Some are personal questions – he did say I could ask *anything* – and some are questions about the elements. Also, this week I've been dealing with a vendor at Walden's Pets who's threatening to take away our volume rebate for flimsy reasons, and I'm struggling to stay calm about it. I know Yugo can help me relax and let this go – help me realize it's not a big deal in the grand scheme. My plan was to leave the office a little early today in case Yugo could see me early so I have as much time as possible for our last official visit. Unfortunately, my asshole vendor, excuse the French, calls right before I can grab my keys to head out, so my plan of arriving early is shot down. The call does nothing but intensify my anger and frustration. We're talking a high five-figure rebate that's owed us here, and I'm beginning to wonder if I need to get our lawyers involved.

I can't believe how fast this time with Yugo has gone by – that my counseling sessions are almost over and I won't be able to go to my twice monthly visits anymore. It's crazy what started out as something I dreaded going to quickly turned into a break in my schedule I now look forward to. I know I'll miss Yugo, the advice and his teachings, but also just the opportunity I've had to spend quality time with someone so unique, so present.

As I've done now for many weeks, rather than check in with a waitress when I enter the restaurant, I head straight for Yugo's office doorway to go upstairs and get started. But today I see the door to Yugo's office is closed, then check the knob and it's locked. This is odd so I turn and look around the restaurant to ask a waitress why the door is locked – to see what's up with Yugo. Even when Yugo's with other patients upstairs, he's never closed or locked the door going up before. His waiting room is there to hang out in if he's running late. I'm thinking he must have a really tough session going on, that my hopes of getting some extra time today probably won't happen, when I look over on the wall to the left of the door and notice that the little paper sign saying "Yugo Free" with an arrow pointing up is gone. As I survey the room, I notice that attractive lady I'd checked out coming down Yugo's stairs many weeks ago sitting at a table with a few other people. We make brief eye contact, and as I move on, looking for someone who works here to ask if they know where Yugo is, she gets up and walks over to me standing in front of Yugo's locked door.

"Hey...uh, hi. Are you here to see Yugo?"

"Oh, hi. Yeah, I've got a two o'clock, but looks like he's out for the day or something. Hey, I've seen you leaving Yugo's office before. You're working with him too, right?"

"Yes, yes I am. Ummm, you got a quick second to sit down?" she asks, now looking around for a place we can sit.

"Well, sure. Looks like Yugo's gonna be late or maybe not show, so I have some time. Actually I'm kind of excited to talk with someone else who's been working with Yugo."

She smiles, sees a couple of empty spots at the bar top, and motions me over as she's walking to grab the open barstools. Right before we sit, she extends her hand.

"We haven't formally met yet but I've seen you a few times coming and going from Yugo's office. I'm Magdalene, Magdalene Summers – my friends all call me Maggie."

"Well hello, Maggie. My name's Walden. It's nice to finally meet you. I've seen you around here a couple times too. Isn't Yugo great?"

"Walden, you haven't heard, have you?"

"Haven't heard? Haven't heard what?"

"Walden. Yugo's gone."

"Gone. Gone where? He didn't tell me he was going anywhere."

"Gone in a bigger way than not being here. In a tragic way. Walden, Yugo passed away."

"Passed away? What? When? What are you talking about?"

"I understand the shock. We're all trying to process this, to figure out what happened and try to understand why. It's such a monumental, heartbreaking loss. It just makes no sense..."

And Maggie starts to cry, and I grab a napkin and hand it to her, reeling, my heart pounding.

"Well that's just crazy. It's *fucking insane*. So what happened? How could this be true? Yugo was doing great the last time I saw him. The usual happy, joyful Yugo. How can Yugo Free be dead?"

Maggie dabs at her eyes and sniffles, and I'm sorry for my language. Then she says, "Did you know he lived out at Community First Village?"

"Yeah, the manager here Gordon told me."

"Well, he rode his bike here every day when he had sessions. He was biking home at the end of the day, riding through that road construction that's been going on for years – you know how 71 going to the airport's been torn up forever? He was biking home on the access road, probably smiling that huge Yugo smile of his, waving at passing cars, and he was hit by a truck."

"Hit by a truck? Are you kidding me? Yugo's riding home on his bike and gets hit by an F-150 and that's it? He's gone forever?" I'm out of my mind now, borderline hysterical.

"Not a pickup, Walden. He was struck by one of those big construction trucks coming out of a work zone. It was late in the day, low visibility, sun going down. He was riding along those temporary concrete barriers, you know that divide the lanes, and maybe didn't see there was an opening to let vehicles in and out. It's just so heartbreaking, so tragic. None of us can understand..."

And now Maggie is full out crying.

"But how can this happen? I haven't seen anything on the news..." And then I remember, I don't really pay much attention to the news anymore.

And through her tears Maggie says, "We heard one of the local stations mentioned it briefly, that a man riding a bike was killed while riding through a construction zone. But people die in traffic accidents around here all the time. This is Austin. They don't report on that kind of thing very often. Yugo was just another low-income housing resident caught in an accident. After all, not many people knew who Yugo was, *what* Yugo was."

I sit there dumbfounded, my mind swirling like a tornado. How can this be? Yugo is pure Light, he is Love, he's caring and generous. He turned my life around – maybe saved my life considering where I was going with alcohol and pills. While I'm staring out into the café's kitchen in a total fog, Maggie gathers herself and grabs hold of my hand.

"Walden, I'm so glad I ran into you today. You needed to hear this from me, not from some stranger who works here that hasn't spent time with Yugo. You see those people over at the table I'm sitting at?"

I look over and see everyone at that table is watching us, some with tears streaming down their faces. And I can tell they understand what's going on – that I'm here for my session with Yugo and just learning the news for the first time.

"Those are Yugo's people. They are like you and me. They got help from Yugo, he saved them from themselves and showed them a new Way. And many learned of his passing just like you did. They came for a meeting and saw the door was locked, and someone here told them right out of the blue. One moment you're looking forward to a blissful time with Yugo, and the next you're rocked to your core, questioning everything..."

I tried to smile their way, gave a faint little wave and looked back at Maggie, tears welling up in my eyes now as I remembered my last time in the café with Yugo. Our tea together, his kindness, his unconditional love for me. His beautiful smile that I can see so clearly now. I can *feel* the möbius on my chest.

"They're all patients of Yugo too? He's been working with all of them?"

"Yes, Walden, he's been helping all of them. He's been helping all of us. And for free. Yugo was doing all this good work for free."

Then she looks me in the eyes and breathes in deeply to regain her strength.

"You know what, Walden? You know what all of us have come to believe?"

"What's that?"

"Yugo wouldn't want any of us sitting around here crying about his passing. He's probably zipping around the stars, free from this planet, free from all its pain and suffering. Free to be closer to the Great Spirit. I don't know about you, but Yugo let it slip to me how he was feeling some kind of divine inspiration to move on to somewhere else. He told me one time he looked at death as simply a new life, a new adventure."

"Well, Yugo told me he was curious to see what happens when we die. Something about moving on to the next *plane.* Maybe he's smiling somewhere. I guess now, *he knows.* But holy shit, this shouldn't happen until he's helped thousands more people – when he's more like eighty-five."

"You're right. And I'd be lying if I said I really had any kind of feeling Yugo would be taken from us so early. I'm probably making that part up in my head just to make myself feel important. Like he was somehow keeping me in the know..."

And I just sit there in stunned silence until Maggie finally adds, "But knowing Yugo's thoughts about death, I think he would say don't mourn for me. One of the guys at the table over there said Yugo's now living out one of his favorite AA sayings. He's happy, joyous, and *free.*"

"Yeah, well maybe that's true, but that's not helping me too much right now, and I don't think it's doing a great job helping you either," and now I'm the one that's beginning to cry. "Because Yugo was my anchor, Maggie. He was the one thing I could always turn to for support. The one I could always trust to help me make some sense of this world – to help me feel better. I'm so not ready for this..."

And now Maggie's holding my shoulder and patting my hand, trying to comfort me, "That's true for all of us, Walden. We all needed Yugo's compassion and love. But we've all agreed after mourning, crying, and feeling sad for our loss that Yugo would want us to look at this tragedy as another event to learn from. Think how lucky, how blessed we are to have met and spent time with this miracle of a man. To hear his teachings and message of love. Think how few people got to hear his wisdom. But we all have! We are the lucky few who were chosen by the Universe to spend intimate time with Yugo Free. That's a powerful thing to remember. Yugo wouldn't want any of us to cry for him, even though as you can see, I still do. He would want us to be telling others what he taught us. To think positive thoughts."

And then I said, "Thank you, Maggie. Thanks for coming over and telling me what happened. I'm sure it was really hard to do. You know, Yugo would sometimes say 'shit happens,' but I wasn't ready for this kind of shit. It's going to take me some time to process through this, I know. I do appreciate you telling me what happened, but I gotta get through this alone right now."

And I get up to leave and Maggie gently grabs my arm and pulls me around slowly, tilting her head slightly, looking me in the eyes. "Walden, that makes perfect sense. It's taken all of us time to process this. To try and make some sense of it all. And that's not possible, by the way. I haven't been able to make *any* sense of it. But one thing I'd like for you to think about. When you are feeling better, or if you get lonely and need to talk with others about how to hold on, those who can make it come here for group meetings on Saturday mornings at 10:00 a.m. up in Yugo's waiting room. It's free group therapy once our official time with Yugo is over, and it's a way for us to talk about the troubles we're all living through. We share, we listen, and we get advice and compassion from friends who are working the Way. Yugo created it. It's been going on for some time now. He knew people would need ongoing help and relationships. He called it Way-A. Get it? Instead of AA?"

And I smile. Way-A *is* pretty good, and so Yugo. And I say ok, that I'll think about it, that Yugo was supposed to talk to me today about some kind of ongoing meetings with old patients and this must be it. And Maggie says, "We talked to Gordon, and he says the Saturday morning meetings will always go on here as long as people want them. In the meantime, we're certain there's a few other students who haven't heard the news yet. They deserve to hear the right way, so we're all taking turns to catch anyone coming in to meet with Yugo. Sometimes a bunch of us show up, as you can see. Yugo had no phone numbers, contact lists, or records, and of course no assistant. There's no other way to contact people to let them know."

I shake my head and agree, knowing at some point it'll be really nice to share stories with other people about this incredible man, and to dig more deeply into the teachings and ideas of Yugo Free. I know without Yugo around, I'll eventually need an outlet to unload all the struggles that keep coming up in my life. As I get up to leave, Gordon and Julie, who saw us talking from the kitchen, come over and hug me – strange since I hardly even know them. All of us are crying now, and honestly, I can't remember what else was said. And so, with tear filled eyes and a shaken heart, I stumble out of Omelettry Lane, onto the crowded sidewalk, cars honking, slowly passing by, squinting into the sunny, beautiful, incredibly clear blue skies.

WALDEN XII

IT'S ABOUT four or five weeks later and I'm driving over to meet Cody at Zilker to catch up and chill out. We've texted and talked on the phone, but haven't seen each other since jumping out of that airplane about two months ago – seems like a year ago. After learning the news about Yugo that day in the café, I called Cody right away and filled him in. He's an emotional dude and took it really hard, even though he's never met Yugo personally. I explained how it happened and we talked about the sense-lessness of it all, the tragedy of losing such an inspirational teacher at such a young age. I'm happy Cody called me this morning saying that it's Thursday so let's go hang out this afternoon. He said he has some *big news* to share with me if I can break free, and I'm thrilled just to get out of the office. I can't tell you how much I needed some down time just hanging out with a friend, so I told him I'm all in and I'll bring the beer.

Although I'm devastated he's gone, Yugo's elements and practices are helping me get through his passing, reminding me to stay awake and present with my inner thoughts and emotions. By remembering to stay conscious, in the present moment, and not get buried by negative emotions, the Way is keeping me far from going off the deep end. However, it didn't take long for me to realize I couldn't be my best going at life alone, so I took Maggie up on her invitation. By the time I'm driving to see Cody, I've already been to three of those Saturday morning meetings with fellow Yugo students. I don't like sharing in front of all those people, it's not comfortable for me yet, but the meetings are good – I like them, and I know I'll keep going. We all agree we can't let Yugo's life and wisdom be forgotten, so we're also talking about ways to spread Yugo's teachings to others.

A different person leads the meeting each week, talking about one of Yugo's elements, a practice, or one of his handout notes and what it means to them. Then we all take turns adding comments or talking about issues we're dealing with that we need to get off our chest – mostly the latter honestly. It feels strange being up in Yugo's office without him around. We all sit on those extra meditation pillows I'd see lying around Yugo's waiting room every time I went to a session – always wondered what they were for. After about forty-five minutes of talking and sharing, we all get in a circle and sit in silence. I think there's power in that – surrendering to our Higher Power together, in relationship, in silent prayer. They told me Yugo used to drop in on the Saturday morning meetings about once a month to say hello, listen, and sit for the meditation. It was his way of encouraging people to keep getting together – to keep working, to keep evolving their own spiritual paths together.

After Yugo's death, I felt extremely fortunate to have made it through all the elements before he left this world – so incredibly lucky. But talking to other students after our meetings, I realized there was more that he'd shared with them, and more he would have shared with me later had I periodically kept going to see him – which I know I would have done. Sitting there listening to others, I learned Yugo taught the same spirituality and path with everyone, but he changed it up some based on the student. Some had slips of paper I didn't have. I think he shared more music and nature references with me because he knew I loved music and the outdoors so much. It sounds like he spoke more about poetry, writing, and the other arts, and used more references from different religions with other students – things I don't know much about. After thinking about it, I told Maggie I bet that's why Yugo didn't have any tangible guides or hand-books for the Way. The core foundational elements were the same, but the more peripheral examples and practices he'd add to make you really *understand* seemed to be a little customized based on the student.

Maggie laughed and said maybe, or maybe it was just because Yugo was a "slip of paper kind of guy." What he gave to each person may have just depended on what he was feeling that day. But then she added,

"Maybe Yugo didn't write a book or create manuals that were permanent because the Way was always *evolving*, always growing, just like we're supposed to, just like Yugo did." I liked that – I think she's right.

Frazier actually went with me to the last meeting and she loved it – of course she made new friends right away. Speaking of Frazier, I'm reminded again that without her I probably wouldn't have started this book and definitely wouldn't have finished it. Just like with Walden's Pets, if it wasn't for her pushing, for her help, for her telling me not to quit, I doubt anything lasting would have happened. For me, Frazier, and most of the other students who get together now, I wouldn't call it our religion – it's not that at all. But Yugo's Way has become what you could call our own personal improvement program, our self-help guide for life. When we're struggling, when we need guidance, we just think: So what would Yugo say about this? What would Yugo do? And, we have the group for support when we need to talk things out – to hear other opinions.

I can tell you this for a fact because I've *experienced* it. I learned Yugo's Way does work – it brings more peace, contentment, more compassion for others and for our planet. It brings more purpose to my life when I remember that all of my thoughts *matter*. I can be one of those *agents for change* who spreads positive thoughts and love into the know-osphere. But it only works if you take action – if you work it. If you read these words and feel encouraged, maybe even enlightened for a brief moment, then do none of the work? Like Yugo says, it means nothing without changing your way of thinking, without changing your way of *be-ing*.

Because my curiosity was killing me, I had lunch with Gordon the café owner, and asked him what would happen with Omelettry Lane now that Yugo had passed away. He said the lawyers were still looking everything over, but Yugo had a detailed will. Some lawyer who was the executor had reached out to Gordon, and while everything still needed to go through probate court, as it was written, Gordon and Julie were left the restaurant property with stipulations. They had to keep feeding others in need like they'd done for Yugo, donate a portion of profits to charity as they were already doing, and keep holding Saturday morning meetings for free as long as there remains an interest (with the understanding it could become more meetings a week if the need arises). Yugo had no immediate family – his mom, his dad, his sister and all his grandparents were gone – so Gordon believed most of Yugo's earthly possessions were going to charity. But there was some sort of sizeable investment of his dad's with a group of investors that the lawyer said was complex and could take time to sort out.

And now I'm thinking, *sizeable investment*? From Yugo's dad? Could my intel be off on how Yugo suddenly came into money?

I arrive at Zilker Park, grab my rolling cooler from the back, and start walking over to meet Cody at our usual meeting place across the street towards the back – closer to the river. I'm thinking about Jessica and how important she's been helping me through Yugo's death, not to mention all the other craziness that's happened recently. Things are going well with us – we're even talking about her moving into my place, although nothing's 100% yet.

We got two new puppies together from the shelter, they're staying at her place now, but I know that will probably speed up our cohabitation. One of the perks of donating surplus pet supplies and food to the Austin SPCA is they give me a call sometimes when nice looking dogs come in. These are adorable pups, a brother and sister from the same litter – an Irish Setter, maybe poodle, and who knows what else mix. They have curly soft mahogany fur and don't shed – I love them already. We named them Little Ann and Old Dan after the two dogs from my favorite book as a kid, *Where the Red Fern Grows*. Mary would read that book after lunch to every class she ever taught, including my class at Nueva Tierra and every class in Wimberley ever since. It still makes me cry like a baby.

On beautiful days like today it's hard to feel down, but since Yugo's accident I've been somewhat of a yoyo mentally. Some days are good overall, but then something will remind me of Yugo, Father or Mary will have another setback, or there's another mass shooting at a school or a church – seems like they happen all the time now. The *insanity* going on around us all can be so much. Somedays it's harder than others to make any sense of the shit that happens for no apparent reason. Why, oh why is everybody so pissed off and angry with each other? If we'd all do what Yugo said and look away from the news media, the social media, the endless streams spreading hate and fear and anxiety and just talk to one another as fellow human beings, I know things would get better. *Love would win out.* Humanity would evolve spiritually and then maybe the world would make a little more sense.

I'm walking across the park, remembering I need to think more positively, when I see Cody's dog Max flying around, catching frisbees like a pro and hanging out with a group of very cute coeds who are in awe of him. Looks like he's already making the rounds. This immediately makes me smile and brings me out of my temporary mind funk – I can't wait to hang with Cody. I see him off in the distance sitting at our usual table, and as I get closer, I notice he's at it again, studiously peeling another tangelo, as focused as a brain surgeon removing a tumor. Cody has two Negra Modelo tall boys on the table, one I'm sure is already a dead soldier, maybe both. It's nice to see he's already in full "Thursday is Friday" mode. When he sees me walking up, I'm shocked that he sets down his beloved tangelo, gets up, and comes over to give me a big bear hug.

"Hey, Walden, so cool you could make it. It's so good to see you, man." And we hug and I say it's great to see him and why don't we get together more often – which I really mean. We used to see each other at least a couple times a month, but life keeps getting in the way. Cody's beard is in full bloom, and he's wearing a light blue Goose t-shirt, his new favorite band that he keeps telling me I *have to go see live.*

"How you doin', man? I haven't seen you since that insane Yugo news. You said everything was alright on the phone. You really doing ok?" And Cody goes back to trying to peel the tangelo in one continuous strip – he's already almost done.

"I'm doing ok. Hanging in there all things considered. Hey, what's with the Modelos? I told you I was bringing the beer."

"Had to get started, Walden...had to get started. There's so little time."

"Well, I've got a twelve pack of ice cold Tecates and limes in here, so at least you'll be staying in Mexico."

"Muy bueno, mi amigo. Muy bueno. So Frazier tells me you guys went to some kind of meeting at Yugo's old place. She said it was incredible. It's helping you? You like it?"

I grab a beer, point to see if Cody wants one, and he shakes his head yes.

"Yeah, I like it. It's far from replacing Yugo, but it's the next best thing. God knows I need to talk to other people more. Everyone there's really chill, very thoughtful and loving. It's amazing Yugo thought to start such a thing – his own support group. He called it Way-A by the way."

Cody successfully finishes the peel, dangles it in the air at me, and smiles as I garnish his beer with a lime slice and slide it over.

"That's what Frazier told me, that she was going to Way-A and I said, what the fuck? And she said no, not AA, *Way-A*, and we laughed. By the way, you think I could go to those meetings sometimes? I wasn't technically a Yugo patient, but I followed all of Frazier's posts and talked to you and Dylan about it all the time. I bet I know more about Yugo's Way than anyone else on the planet who's not a student. And remember, dude, I'm the one who told you about him!"

"Heck yeah you can come. There's a good number of us originals meeting up there now, but we're trying to spread the word to as many people as possible. The more the merrier and we could see each other more often."

I crack my beer, squeeze in some lime, and take a huge gulp. Is there anything better on a sunny day than ice cold Tecate and lime?

"And don't you worry that I'll ever forget it was you who introduced me to Yugo. I'm eternally grateful. You know, at first I thought his card was a little hokey when you gave it to me, but Yugo truly was my Philosopher, my Guidepost, and my Light. He summed up his services perfectly in just three words. But enough about that. You said on the phone you had some big news. What's up, dude?"

Cody slams the rest of his Modelo tall boy, then grabs the fresh Tecate, takes a long draw, and gives me a huge grin. "You ain't gonna believe this, Walden, but guess what?"

"Guess what? I don't know Cody, you tell me."

"I can't believe it, but Anastasia and me are getting back together!"

"Really? I thought she was out on the road for months opening for Khruangbin?"

"There's a two week break in the tour after Atlanta so the band all came back to Austin yesterday. She came by the house and told me she really misses me and knows now after being apart she wants us to be together." Now Cody's eyes are getting a little watery.

"Hey, that's awesome, Cody! That's great news! I knew you were really missing her."

"She told me she was sorry about the breakup, but she only did it because she thought I'd want it that way with her on the road all the time. That I'd feel tied down and get all antsy if my steady girl was gone for so long."

"Well, you told me she was a master breaking up with you. Sounds like what she told you was true. That she was only thinking about what was best for you when she broke up."

And now Cody's grinning and nodding his head in agreement. "Yeah, I think that's true. I think you're right. But there's more."

"More? What else you got?"

"We're talking about me becoming The White Beaches' tour manager and booking agent. Going out on the road with them, making sure the contracts are all good and fair, taking care of Anastasia and the band.

Sounds incredible, don't it?" Cody looks excited, but also seems to be needing a little inspiration.

"Well hell yeah it sounds incredible. Cody Barringer and tour manager go together like Cinco de Mayo and tequila! With your business smarts, negotiation skills, and world class bullshitting, you'll be the perfect tour manager – as long as you don't stay too fucked up on the road."

"Oh, don't you worry about that, Walden. I've always known when I gotta take care of business. That always comes first!" And he takes another long pull on his beer.

"So what about your business with Dwayne? What about the home security business?"

"Well that's one of the things I gotta figure out first. With this news, I'm thinking me and Dwayne shouldn't do this Dallas expansion. What the hell do we need those headaches for? In fact, I'm talking to him now about selling our business to those people in Dallas. Let them deal with that shit, and let me hit the road with Anastasia!"

And so, Cody and I spent the rest of the afternoon at Zilker – talking, reminiscing, drinking beer. We talked about Bryan and Ally and how they're temporarily moving to Southern California to be near the City of Hope, a world-class cancer research hospital doing all kinds of alternative cutting-edge treatments. Ally is hanging in there, but there's miles to go before any hope of remission, and Bryan says the new clinical trials in California are totally new with no known recovery rates. Their lives are upside down and our hearts ache for them.

We talked about Jessica and how we're thinking about moving in together (Cody says it's about damn time). We talked about music and Goose, about Anastasia, and Father and Mary and Cody's family and Dylan. It's a wonderful day – there's not much better than sitting with a friend outside just talking, being with each other.

Eventually we circled back to Yugo, the insanity and suddenness of what happened, why something so tragic could happen to someone so good. While I'm showing Cody the necklace Yugo gave me – he's mesmerized by the möbius and wants to know where he can get one – Max shows up exhausted, plops down his well-worn frisbee, and lays on the ground panting. (Full disclosure: Cody never really did use the Barringer 3500 with Max at the park. It's great for most dogs, but Max is way too high a flyer for that disc.)

Cody fills up a bowl with water for Max from a big red thermos and says, "This world's one screwed up place, Walden. What a crazy story, and for it to happen that way? Holy shit. Can anyone explain why something like that happens to a ray of light like Yugo? And you got pieces of shit running all over the place still taking up space…"

"Yeah, it's crazy alright. I've quit trying to make any sense of it. That's what Yugo used to tell me. Stop trying to figure out why and just accept that it's the way things are. Accept it, know it's there to help you grow, learn from it, and go on."

"Yeah, well easier said than done, my friend. Easier said than done."

"No shit, but that's what I'm gonna keep trying to do, Cody. Acceptance and surrender. And honesty and love. I didn't get to have my last session with Yugo, but other people said he used that meeting to say honesty in all relationships is the one element in the Way that's absolutely required or the other stuff won't work like it should. You can't do any of the elements anywhere close to perfect, but that's the most important one to waking up and evolving. That and remembering *Love is the answer*."

Cody tips his beer at me and says, "Here, here, Walden. I love it when you talk Yugo."

I tell Cody thanks for calling me to get together, it's been awesome talking, much needed, and congrats again on Anastasia and maybe on his new career as a tour manager. And then I say, "All I know is, a lot of crazy shit's been happening around here lately, and hopefully we're coming into a lull so we can all catch our breath a little. Yugo gave us the tools to get through whatever life brings, but I could sure use a little less *crazy*."

Draining my beer I stand up to leave, tossing the empties in my cooler, and Cody says, "Hey, speaking of crazy, you remember what I told you about China buying up the world, even owning Walmart now?"

And I say, "Yeah, I remember. You were wrong again by the way. I fact-checked it myself online. Forgot to tell you."

Closing the cooler lid and turning to walk away, Cody keeps on going, as if he didn't even hear me. "Yeah, well you hear what's happening over in China now? Some crazy ass virus sprouting up in someplace called Phootan? Supposedly hatched from some sort of bat stew or bat blood or something and it's contagious as hell, spreading like wildfire. Even killing people from what I hear. Hasn't hit the US mainstream media yet, but a dude I know told me about it today. You heard it here from me first, Walden."

And I just keep walking, shaking my head smiling, thinking to myself, *I love Cody. Here he goes again.* So I yell back, "Deadly virus in Phootan?

From bats? Killing people? What the hell are you talking about, Cody? I've never even *heard* of Phootan before. Is that even a place?"

And Cody goes on, "Who the hell knows what could happen with something like this, Walden, but they say it's so contagious it could even make it over here. I'm serious, dude, this is some real wicked shit that's brewing over there. Could be something bigger than that Bubonic Plague. You better check this out."

And I say, "Oh I will, Cody. I promise you, I will."

EPILOGUE

I LISTENED to many hours of recordings writing this book, focusing mainly on Yugo's Way and the elements. But I also went through some of my old counseling sessions too (nowhere near all – my whining got old fast). It's crazy hearing some of the things I was so stressed out about – trivial stuff I made out to be life-and-death situations I can barely remember now. Hindsight shows most of my worries were a waste of energy. Yugo said that's a good reason to keep a journal. You can go back months or years later and see that the things you worry about usually turn out to be nothing. Besides, like he said, what happens to us here on Earth doesn't really matter all that much. Life's events happen, some good and some bad, and there's very little we can do about most of it. What really matters is how we *respond* to those events. How we learn from them, accept them – how we can help others from our common experience.

As you'd suspect from Cody's directionally correct news that day at the park, I've had some free time on my hands, partially responsible for the writing of this book. Maybe that's *one* good thing to come out of all this craziness. I must say I seriously doubt I could have managed through this time without Yugo's Way to ground me. And thank God after everything was shut down for a while, Way-A and Maggie put together Saturday morning Zoom meetings so we all had a way to stay connected – had an outlet to share our fears, frustrations, and pain. We're finally back to meeting in person again and man does that feel good. I now see clearly through experience what Yugo told me – that my meeting group truly is a *"power greater than myself."*

I meticulously went through all my saved "notes" from Yugo, making sure I didn't miss any of them, and I found one he gave me at some point outside of our element discussions. There's no recorded dialogue that I could find mentioning it. But I remember he gave this to me early on, must have been after one of our meditation sits when I wasn't recording – maybe after the elements on working out our spiritual body or preserving Mother Earth. Since I had no context from the Yugo's Way recordings where it goes, and since I want to be certain I share all the notes he gave me, I'll just put it here...

A Prayer for Mother Earth

Divine Light of the Universe,

I pray for the continued evolution of humanity toward consciously chosen Love. May you raise our level of consciousness and show us the interconnectedness of all things so the divisiveness, the anger, and the violence so prevalent in our world is greatly diminished.

Help us enhance the *know-osphere* by using the power of self-awareness and self-observation to recognize our negative thinking. May we be conscious of these negative thoughts or emotions quickly, not become attached to them, and return to positive thinking, sending life-enriching energy out into the Universe.

Help us take better care of our *atmosphere* by greatly reducing our reliance on fossil fuels. May we cut back our carbon emissions where we can and embrace cleaner, renewable forms of energy like solar, wind, and water power. May you bless the scientist, the entrepreneurs, the inventors, and companies who are exploring technological solutions and alternative forms of energy, and may we embrace them to protect our Earth for future generations.

Help us take better care of our *waters*, the sustainer of life on our planet. May we stop the mindless pollution, especially of single use plastics, flowing into creeks, rivers, and eventually our oceans. May we work so all beings have access to clean and safe drinking water, and may we stop the dramatic overfishing of our oceans, wreaking havoc and upsetting the balance of our seas. May we understand what's harming our coral reefs, and take measures now to restore them as beautiful sanctuaries for marine life.

And help us take better care of our *lands*, to conserve and better manage our forests and wilderness areas. May we stop the senseless cutting down of old growth forests and jungle lands, the very lungs of our Earth. May we awaken to the realization we are *all* here to be good stewards of this planet. To take care of Mother Earth, of all her creatures, and of all beings as was intended by You since the beginning. Thank you for our Essence, for your splendor, and for your grace.

—YF

THE FOURTEEN ELEMENTS OF YUGO'S WAY

1. We are primarily Spiritual Beings who live on for all eternity. Take time each day to work out your spiritual body, strengthening your eternal, internal Being.
2. Our thoughts transmit real energy into the know-osphere, impacting ourselves, other people, and our planet. Be aware of thoughts and emotions, stay positive, and counteract the negativity influencing our world.
3. Mother Earth is all-giving, but she needs our help now. We must restore her by taking responsibility for what we buy, what we drive, what we eat, what we throw away, what we support. Changing our way of be-ing does make a difference.
4. Consume less and consciously make choices in harmony with nature. Don't be seduced by the false promises of materialism or the allure of instant gratification.
5. We are all one, all interconnected, from the same Divine Source. Have compassion and empathy for all beings, remembering, what we do unto others we are doing to ourselves.
6. Living spiritually is simply being open and honest in all relationships. Be open and honest with yourself, with other people, and with your Higher Power, whatever you understand that to be.

7. Stay awake when consuming the "news," and if you become attached or identified, stop. The news entertainment business breeds negativity, divisiveness, and darkens the spirit.

8. Comfort is Overrated. Get out of your comfort zone, experience the feeling of awe, and truly live!

9. We are living in a new era of the spiritual evolution of humanity. Actively participate in the evolution of our planet toward consciously chosen love.

10. Take time each day to meditate. Immerse yourself in the Great Silence, listen, and be.

11. We must make time for music. Music creates joy, awe, and peace while nourishing the soul.

12. Remember, everything in moderation. And if that's not an option, we must abstain.

13. Wake up and live in the Present, for it is always Now. Be aware when your mind is replaying the past or making up the future so you can return to the Present and live Now.

14. In the end, Love is all that *really* matters. It's the Divine and Grand Energy of the Universe.

As a new independent author, it will take you spreading the word and great reviews for this book to get noticed. If you enjoyed Yugo's Way and think others will benefit from reading, please tell your friends and family and write a positive review!

Enough humans are operating at a higher level of consciousness that the time is ripe for an explosion of love, compassion and peace—for *all* people and our planet. If you're looking for a way to overcome anxiety, meaninglessness, and fear, an outlet to share your experience, strength and hope—something like group therapy that's basically free—go to YugosWay.com. We're thinking about how to help people have informal "Way-A type" meetings if anyone is interested. If we hear from enough like-minded people looking to evolve spiritually, who knows what may blossom. As was once said, *where two or more are gathered, the Great Spirit works miracles*. Peace!

ACKNOWLEDGMENTS

Thanks to those early readers who told me it had a long way to go, to Chuck and Peter who helped me keep going, and to Bree for her insight, tenacity, and wisdom (and for making the book better). Thanks to Gary for your advice and friendship, to Ernie and Kat for your kindness and willingness to help, and to my editor, Dave, for all his help. Thank you to one of my first Yugos, David P., who if it wasn't for his wisdom and honesty, I most likely wouldn't be around to write this book. Thanks to everyone in the rooms, for sharing your experience, strength, and hope. And of course, none of this happens without my Guardian Angel and my Higher Power.

I've been blessed by the wisdom of so many inspired teachers and writers who helped quiet my chattering mind and finally listen, and who influenced so much of the writing in this book. In so many instances, it's their wisdom Yugo is trying to share—I'm merely a consolidator and a conduit. I'm indebted to Eckhart Tolle, Thomas Keating, Pema Chodron, Thich Nhat Hanh, Richard Rohr, Adyashanti, Howard Thurman, Ilia Delio, Kahlil Gibran, Maurice Nicoll, Aldous Huxley, Octavia Butler, B. F. Skinner and yes, Kurt Vonnegut, who's the best ever at making you laugh and think at the same time. I encourage you to read them all.

Finally, so much gratitude, thanks, and love go to my wife Carrie. For her patience, encouragement, support, and wisdom, for reading my early work, and for putting up with me for all these many years. Here's to loving and taking care of our amazing planet. To compassion and mercy, empathy, and victory over the lie of separation. To consciously choosing love, and *be*-ing more like Yugo to further evolve this crazy, beautiful world of ours.

And...to music!

– *GTP*

ABOUT THE AUTHOR

It's no secret that life can be wilder and more interesting than fiction—just look around. Many of the events in this book actually happened (although the names and certain details were changed to enhance the story and protect everyone involved). So it could be said that "Life" is the author of this book. Other parts come from imagination and inspiration, usually sparked by influences. Eckhart Tolle said in *A New Earth*, "All creativity comes out of inner spaciousness. Once the creation has happened and something has come into form, you have to be vigilant so that the notion of 'me' or 'mine' does not arise." Wise stuff. Actual events wrote this book. Influences, inspirations, Life wrote this book. And since we are *all* interconnected, it is also right to say that *WE* wrote this book together. After all, *We are all One!*